Counterfeit Cowboy

Sharon Ervin

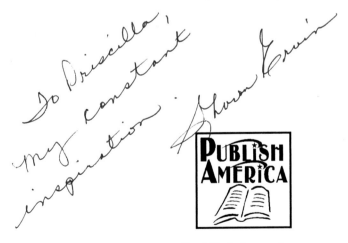

To Priscilla, my constant inspiration.
Sharon Ervin

PublishAmerica
Baltimore

First printing

ISBN: 1-4137-4955-0

PUBLISHED BY PUBLISHAMERICA, LLLP

www.publishamerica.com

Baltimore

Printed in the United States of America

To Bill,
who knows when and how to push all the right buttons.

Acknowledgments

Jackie Bielowicz and my RWI critique sisters,
who knew where this one should begin.

Myra Manning with Shakespeare & Company Bookstores,
for gentle persuasion.

Sponsors of the First North American Fiction Contest,
for rewarding its potential.

Jennifer Enderlin,
who took time to offer advice and encouragement.

Willem Meiners,
who indulges my dreams.

Ronda Talley and Teresa Atkerson,
friends in deed and copy readers extraordinaire.

Chapter One

Chelly Bennett sifted among people hurrying through the concourse on the ground floor of the Sheppard Building. The day after Christmas, everyone seemed to be in a hypnotic stupor. Without bothering to check the directory, she walked briskly to the first open elevator and pressed "11," just as a large hand reached around her.

"What floor do you want?" she asked without a glance at the person attached to the hand, obviously a man.

"You got it."

As more people entered the elevator, Chelly turned slightly and ventured a casual look at the man's long, somber face. His eyes were hidden behind dark glasses, which he retained, despite the elevator's dim lighting. He was tall, towering several inches above her 5-foot-7, and ruggedly handsome.

Looking down his nose at her, his lips formed a broad line, which curved up at the ends in a token smile. He didn't seem quite detached enough to be a native. He had dark hair that curled a little at his ears and neckline. And he smelled good.

Chelly dismissed the interest she felt. Probably nerves. Being in the city. The job prospect. Or maybe it was rebound. Rejected by one man, it seemed reasonable that she might seek approval from other men. For a long time, she had practiced ignoring men, given Eric's edicts. Now she might be vulnerable. She would have to keep a handle on any renegade emotions. To be smart, she probably should avoid men altogether, at least for a while. She definitely would never let herself trust another one. That would be her mantra. Never, never trust another man. She thought of her dad. Okay. Never trust a man under forty.

Still she pondered. If she were looking for a man, this one would be choice. He exuded the confidence of the mature alpha male, absent all the posturing.

7

Of the handful of passengers sharing the elevator, two exited on the third floor. Self consciously Chelly kept her gaze averted, particularly avoiding eye contact with the tall man. Was his suit an Armani? Either that or a really nice knock off.

She looked up and focused on the lights monitoring the elevator's climb. Hairs bristled on the back of her neck. She had the eerie feeling the tall fellow was watching her. He was definitely the kind of man who gave the term "power suit" its reputation. She looked back at the floor. Seeking a distraction, her eyes drifted to his feet. Cowboy boots?

The worn, scruffy footwear rudely nullified the man's G.Q. look. Maybe he was a wealthy eccentric. More likely, this cowboy was from out of town, like her, and didn't know any better. Head still bowed, she bit her lips and smiled to herself.

After the other passengers exited at the next stop, the tall man eased over in the car, putting himself directly behind her. Chelly stared at the stainless steel doors that barred her escape and shimmered his warped reflection with her own. Was she imagining it, or was he appraising her?

He had followed the girl in the drab brown suit through the revolving door of the Sheppard Building, marveling at her gosh awful taste and frumpy hairdo thinking it must be a costume. He hadn't been to Tennyson in a couple of months. Was this a new rage? Lord, he hoped not. What kind of style would camouflage feminine curves like hers in a tweed awning? Would any thinking woman purchase clothes like that on purpose? And the clunky shoes? Well, he admitted grudgingly, they certainly completed the ensemble.

He was oddly mesmerized, however, as he watched her flow across the marble floor of the concourse, directly to an open elevator. She moved gracefully, with an admirable economy of motion, surprising for a woman as tall as she was.

When she turned to study the selection board inside the elevator, he saw her face, classic features, attractive—acceptable nose, full mouth, and large, dark, almond eyes behind those ridiculous glasses.

She pressed "11." His floor. Good.

He avoided eye contact. Women were too damned aggressive these days, if a man appeared even mildly interested. He was surprised when she asked what floor he wanted without looking at him. Unusual.

She had a deep voice, a tone lower than he expected. He liked that. As he verified she had selected his stop, he moved with most of the other occupants further back in the elevator, betting with himself about whether or not she would look at him. He was surprised to be interested, yet he continued watching her.

Ah-ha. There. She glanced at him.

But instead of the come-on he was used to, she quickly averted her eyes. What was this? A reticent female in downtown Tennyson? Well, what do you know?

Keeping her head down, a few moments later she sneaked a look at his boots. He saw her swallow the smile. He glanced at his aged footwear and his mouth twitched. This woman was... interesting. She certainly piqued his curiosity.

Perhaps she was self conscious about her poor eyesight and that kept her from flirting with him. Were those bifocals? He looked more closely but didn't see any lines.

After everyone else abandoned the elevator, he moved over behind her, giving him the angle to peer through her glasses.

What the hell? There was no correction in the right lens. He shifted and leaned a little to check the other one. No correction there either, not even magnification. The frames looked too cheap to have come from a professional.

Now why would such a sweet thing sabotage her own good looks? What was her game: the ridiculous wardrobe, hair bound up, phony horn-rimmed specs? Also, where was the cough-inducing fragrance? This female smelled of soap and shampoo, maybe a subtle cologne. Curious. Very curious.

The woman minced forward, as if moving as far away from him as possible in the confines of the elevator car. He stifled a wry smile and eased back a step to get a better angle, see her from tip to toe. If she stood straight, she'd be tall, maybe five-eight. Striking.

Despite the oversized clothing, she had too much bust to be willowy. Of course, that wasn't necessarily a bad thing. His taste ran to well-endowed women. He bit back another smile.

Her ankles above the clunky shoes were shapely and he could visualize legs that stretched up and up, a long, long way.

Why was she going to DMD? A new client maybe. She wasn't wearing a wedding ring, but she had a tan line where a ring had been. Maybe she wanted a divorce. Not his job, but he could find out who she was, where she was going, maybe meet her.

When they reached the eleventh floor and the doors opened, he loitered as she scurried off the elevator. She was careful to move aside, out of his way, but he was suddenly in no hurry.

Now what? She seemed to be having second thoughts.

Chelly was sweating by the time the monitor reached "11." The muted bell bonged and the heavy elevator doors yawned wide. She glanced back. The man nodded, indicating she should go ahead. She stepped out quickly, moving forward and to one side, clearing the way. She drew a deep breath and hesitated as she surveyed the layout.

The Diet, Manning, Diet lobby was done in mahogany/burgundy posh and was reverently silent. Standing in the terrazzo entry, stalling, Chelly inhaled again, enjoying what seemed almost a religious experience.

Thinking how goofy she must look, standing there staring at the place like a country bumpkin, she bit her lips to squelch a giggle, laughing at herself. She glanced from side to side to make sure no one else witnessed her provincial behavior.

No. The woman behind the receptionist's desk was busy. She looked like a model, straight, sleek, with just the right blend of nature and make-up. The threadlike headset appeared to be something of a halo as she pressed keys and her dulcet tones hummed into the button-sized microphone poised in front of her broad, luscious mouth.

Chelly had dressed with the intention of appearing unglamourous, but she obviously had carried the look too far for this dazzling place with its ostentatious atmosphere.

Suddenly she felt intimidated. She should have known a glitzy place like DMD would project a certain image. The palatial ambiance and the drop-dead-gorgeous greeter signaled tough requirements ahead.

Unnerved, deciding in a flash that, dressed as she was, she was not DMD material, Chelly eased back two steps before she turned around and was startled to find herself face-to-face with the Armani. The man wearing it glowered down his nose at her and raised his hands in what she supposed was a defensive move to keep her from running him down.

Undisturbed by their sudden proximity, the tall man's gaze appeared to be on her, although she couldn't really tell, since his eyes were still hidden behind the shades. He regarded her curiously, a half smile on his face. "Problem?"

"No." She knew she must look like an idiot.

As his huge hands settled on her shoulders, steadying her, she bit the inside of her lower lip, mentally groping for some reasonable explanation. When none came to mind, she shrugged out of his grasp and pivoted. It would be easier to confront the angel behind the desk than this stunning man who seemed to be taking some kind of personal interest in her.

The glamorous receptionist gave Chelly a cool look, but her expression warmed as her eyes found the man at Chelly's back.

Ignoring the receptionist's "Hello," he assumed a forbidding look as he strode forward without a word.

The worn cowboy boots thudded softly as long strides carried him over the terrazzo entry, across the deep plush carpeting to skirt the receptionist's desk and down the hallway marked by brass lettering on the mahogany wall.

Chelly read the first in the line of names and titles listed. "D.R. Manning." The old man. The headhunter himself worked in an office right down that corridor. That realization revived Chelly's courage. Straightening, she moved forward. "I'm here about the clerk's job." Her gaze followed as the receptionist glanced at the lingering shadow, evidence of someone lurking in that hallway, just out of sight.

The receptionist's expression became plastic as she reached into a side drawer, withdrew a clipboard and an application, and thrust them into Chelly's hands. "Fill this out. Completely." She tapped a button. "Diet, Manning, Diet and Harned. One moment, please."

Chelly glanced back at the hallway. The shadowy figure was gone.

She settled into one of the leather chairs in the reception area, fished in her purse for a pen, secured the application on the clipboard, then bent to the task. If the guy in the beat-up cowboy boots could get into the place unchallenged, it might mean there were real people in the back doing real work. And she could be one of them. After all, how many applicants would they have for this job who could boast three semesters of law school? She hesitated, not knowing if she should play that trump card, yet. She filled out the application without noting her graduate work.

When Chelly entered the office of Tom Bixler, Personnel Coordinator, she realized it would take another kind of trump to win him.

Fortyish, overweight, balding, Bixler was the kind of man who addressed himself to a woman's chest. He focused on Chelly's breasts as interviewer and aspirant shook hands and he motioned her into a chair.

He spoke directly to the area of her anatomy beneath the bow tied at her throat. "Ms. Bennett, we are an old-line law firm. We've been in business since nineteen forty-five." He sounded as if he were an attorney but his vanity wall showed an associate's degree from a downtown business college. "We've had a dozen people apply for this job. What do you have to offer that would convince me to hire you instead of one of them?" He continued studying her chest.

Chelly rolled her shoulders forward a little and realized that, dressed as she was, she had little hope of being hired by this man. He was probably giving her a full interview to avoid a discrimination claim later.

Before she could speak, the intercom buzzed. Bixler picked up the phone and listened to what sounded like a growl as it resonated into the room. He suddenly raised his eyes all the way to Chelly's face and regarded her skeptically. He nodded, opened his desk drawer and thumbed a small red star.

"Yes, sir, I'll be glad to." She could hear the dial tone before Bixler said, "Good talking to you, sir," and hung up. He licked the star and pressed it to the upper left corner of her application. His facial expression soured. "Go down the hall to your right. Ask for Anne Beed."

Chelly stood. "Do you mean I'm hired?"

His sneer reflected his annoyance. "No, I do not mean you're hired. You get to take the typing test is all."

Anne Beed was black, businesslike, a dapper dresser and beamed at Chelly as if they were acquainted. "You've got friends in high places." She regarded Chelly up and down, apparently puzzling.

"I don't know who that would be." Chelly fidgeted beneath Beed's scrutiny. "I don't know anyone here. I hardly know anyone in the city, except a couple of high school classmates. No one I've seen in a while."

The woman shrugged. "Well, someone important has anointed you and we does what pleases the big boys." She grinned broadly and winked. Her pointed use of the vernacular made Chelly relax a little for the first time since she'd entered the building.

"Mr. Bixler said I have to pass a typing test."

"Yeah, well, you look like a quick study to me. You'll probably figure out that what Bixler thinks and what is are seldom the same thing. Now, me, I'm a regular DMD guru and I'm predicting you're as good as hired, honey. Now slip out of that oversized clown's coat and let's finish up this fool application so's you can polish off the typing test and we can go to lunch.

"You'll start at ten bucks an hour, time-an-a-half for everything over forty hours. We'll issue a permit for the parking garage next door. Free parking's one of the perks. I'll give you a packet with all the insurance and retirement stuff. You'll have to take a physical. It's a doctor here in the building. A formality. I'll set it up."

Chelly stared. "I don't understand. Obviously, there's been a mistake."

Anne raised her eyebrows and cocked her head slightly. "You honestly don't know who's backing you?"

"I swear. I don't know a soul here."

"How'd you get here in the first place?"

"An ad in the classifieds."

Anne grimaced. "Well, then, we'd better get you on payroll before Bixler finds out you're a mistake. I have a feeling you're going to be something special around here, Miz Bennett."

Chelly trotted to keep up with her new mentor. "So what if I can't type?"

"With the backing you've got, it won't matter."

Puzzling, Chelly decided to wait to ask any more questions.

Half an hour after she finished the typing test—68-words-a-minute with one mistake—Anne invited her to lunch in the food plaza on the ground floor.

"We have a terrace with glass all around. On sunny days like this it's comfortable, even in the dead of winter. The fresh air will inspire you."

Chelly stretched and looked around for her suit coat. "Thanks. I wish I could, but I've gotta' go find a place to lay my weary bones."

Anne's eyes widened. "You don't have an apartment?"

"I just got to town at this morning."

"This morning?"

"Right."

"But if one of them's sponsoring you… ?"

Chelly froze and her eyes darted to Anne's face. "One of who?"

Anne suddenly looked annoyed. "If you want to play it that way, it's okay but, Chelly, you can trust me. I know a lot about privileged communication."

Chelly smiled uncertainly. "Anne, I promise, I have no influence. No connections. The newspaper ad got me in the door and Bixler sent me to you for the typing test."

"Yeah, yeah, yeah." Anne's tone sounded sarcastic but the look on her face indicated she was struggling not to believe Chelly's protests. She paused for several seconds studying her new charge. "Your application is sportin' a red star. Someone with clout said, 'Hire her.' That usually means you have a nod from one of the principals. My guess would be Leonard. You're his type. But then, of course, all busty females under forty are Leonard's type. Do you know Leonard Diet?"

Chelly raised and lowered her shoulders as she shook her head. "No."

"Diet?" Anne prodded again. "Leonard Diet. Fiftyish, rotund, redheaded, lecherous. Heir apparent to the throne at the foot of the board room table?"

Chelly shook her head again. "Bixler goofed. He's confused me with someone else."

"Yep, he's a confused kind of guy, all right. He's had a dozen applicants but you're the first one he's sent for a typing test. I imagine having one of the big boys interfere chapped his butt." She gave a bawdy laugh.

"Maybe the right applicant got lost or changed her mind," Chelly said. "It looks like I turned up in the right place at the right time."

"Well, I have to admit, honey, usually the applicants who come with a red star do not punch out 68 words a minute on a strange machine. You're a first and I'm leaving the red star right where it's at."

Chelly retrieved her suit coat from the rack by the door. "I hope I have the same luck finding an apartment. Have you got any of those red stars to spare?"

Anne nudged Chelly toward the door. "No problem, babe, with your connections, you'll probably wind up in a penthouse within walking distance. Where're you looking?"

"I have an interview with a woman who lives at the Epperly Apartments. Are you familiar with them?"

"I know where they're at. Must be respectable because they definitely don't look pricey."

"You know my range. Not pricey is good."

Anne sobered. "Bennett, in spite of what you say, with your looks and smarts, I expect you'll stay clerical around here about long enough to learn your way to the ladies room. You'll get some attention." The supervisor cocked one eyebrow. "Of course, you'll do better if you give up the martyr's sackcloth and ashes and unveil a little of that shape you're trying so hard to hide. Want some advice?"

Chelly nodded.

"Let your hair down and spring for some contact lenses."

Chelly smiled but didn't respond.

Anne's eyes narrowed. "Are you part of a religious cult or something?"

Laughing lightly, Chelly said, "No."

Anne wasn't to be deterred. "Someone around here has plans for you."

"It's a fluke. Someone made a mistake." Chelly jammed her hands into her jacket sleeves, pulled it around her, buttoned every button up the front and walked toward the door.

"Funny," Anne mumbled, her face serious, "You don't act like a gal who's sleeping her way to the top. I hope you get irreplaceable around here before people find out it was a glitch that got you in. I think I'm going to like you, Chelly Bennett. I think I'm going to like you a lot."

Chelly flashed Anne her best Mona Lisa smile and left without another word.

Chapter Two

Exactly one and seven-tenths miles from the Sheppard Building stood the dated, sandstone Epperly Apartments. Chelly liked the Epperly at first glance, charmed by the expansive elms that stood sentry at either side of the entrance. Closer scrutiny indicated the trees' roots were responsible for the buckled sidewalk along the front of the building.

She stepped into the foyer, located the mailbox with Kitchens/McClannahan on the label and buzzed.

"Whozit?"

"Midgean Kitchens? It's me, Chelly Bennett."

The buzzer startled her, making her move quickly to yank the inside door open.

"Here!" a voice called over the bannister. "We're on four. All the way to the top."

Chelly smiled. Just as Anne Beed had predicted: The penthouse.

She began the climb as Midge called encouragement. "The stairs give us a huge advantage. No need for big, expensive exercise machines. We have our own stair-stepper. It's our at-home workout program, guaranteed to keep us fit."

Chelly laughed lightly. The steps were steep. She considered herself to be in pretty good shape but she was breathless, upright, but unable to speak by the time she achieved the landing of the third floor. She looked up again into dark eyes and a fun-loving grin.

"Come on, you sissy. One more flight. Make those long legs earn their keep."

Chelly sucked lungs full of air, hiked up her skirt and took the last flight two stairs at a time.

In the hallway of the fourth floor, she doubled over, hands on her knees, and gasped, twisting her head to look up at the other young woman.

Midgean, probably in her mid to late twenties to Chelly's twenty-five, was round but petite, with dark hair and eyes. Height-wise, Chelly dwarfed her.

She looked Chelly over and grimaced. "I guess we won't be borrowing each other's clothes."

Chelly grinned and straightened, still panting. "Guess not... " was all she could manage.

"Did you get the job?"

Chelly bobbed her head up and down, still sucking air. Midge obviously was not sympathetic. "It's better to take the altitude slow at first."

Still breathless, Chelly followed Midge to the living room of the tiny apartment.

"It's $250-a-month each and utilities." Before Chelly could comment, Midge held up a hand and continued. "People line up when one of these puppies comes available. This one's been passed from one roommate to another for years. I think you're required to name an heir to it in your last will and testament."

Chelly granted the expected polite chuckle that seemed to please her companion.

Midge guided her through both modest bedrooms. There was an aged maple twin bed, bedside table, and highboy chest in the drab little room that might be Chelly's.

"What do you think?" Midge asked. "Your first impression. Feel free to be totally honest."

Chelly smiled. "It seems friendly."

"You've got the good attitude, girl. We have forties-vintage faucets in the kitchen and bathroom. Genuine antiques, but they do the job. The hot water tank's a small, economy number. The bright side is, we don't have one of those water guzzling dishwashers, which leaves more hot water for rinsing the shampoo out of your hair before the temperature nose dives."

Chelly allowed another appreciative laugh. Midge responded to the encouragement.

"My old roommate and I didn't have a lot of rules. Mostly we tried to be tolerant. You and I can make some up as we go, if you want. One handy signal Paula and I had that I might recommend was Aunt Mazie."

"Is that your aunt?"

Midge flashed a mischievous grin and raised and lowered her eyebrows. "I haven't got an Aunt Mazie. It's code for 'I need privacy.' It's for special events. Later there'll probably be somewhere you can sleep over if I should ever get courage and opportunity coordinated for an all-nighter."

Watching Chelly's face, Midge hastened to add, "Not to worry. There won't be a parade of guys. Usually when I get hooked on someone, he wants to be platonic. What I'm saying is, if the day ever comes when one of us finds Mr. Right, the lucky girl just says, 'Your Aunt Mazie called.' See? It's a signal." Her eyes narrowed as she looked at Chelly. "You already have a guy, right?" She pointed to Chelly's ring finger. "I see where the ring goes. What's the story on that?"

"He fell in love with someone else." The words sounded callous, but they didn't hurt as much as she'd expected. "I'm off of men."

Midge allowed a tinkling little laugh. "I am so sure. You can't tell me a dolly like you hasn't got a spare stashed some place."

"No." Chelly sobered. "There are more important things in a woman's life than men."

Midge sobered. "Yeah? Name one."

"Career, school, family, friends."

Midge looked comically skeptical, holding silent. It was Chelly's turn to blurt a reluctant laugh. Midge's trilling giggle chimed along. "I was wondering if you really believed that." Midge flashed a broad, toothy grin. "We're gonna get along fine. Just fine. Come on, I'll help you lug your stuff up."

Chelly cringed at the thought of facing the stairs again. "I'm afraid it's going to take more than one trip, even with both of us carrying."

"Yeah? Well, it's a bonding thing. If two women can move one's junk up four flights together, their friendship's sealed."

Discussing the cost of utilities, the pair clattered down the bare wooden stairs together.

Patiently, during Chelly's first week on the job, Anne assigned her simple tasks, helped her get familiar with the filing system, the machines and the personalities. When they passed the rotund Leonard Diet coming off the elevator, he did a double-take, stopped and scanned Chelly up and down. Anne introduced them. Leonard grinned broadly, surprising Chelly with his obvious interest. This partner was at least forty-five or fifty years old, had three chins, was round, soft and wore his carrot red hair in a crewcut.

"If you have questions, Ms. Bennett, come see me."

"Thank you, Mr. Diet."

When he had sauntered down Corridor South, he glanced back over his shoulder to wink at Chelly who responded with an uncertain smile.

Anne groaned. "What does he think I am, chopped liver?"

The women laughed but Chelly knew the encounter convinced Anne that the younger Diet had not sponsored her for the clerk's job.

Chelly learned the daily drill quickly. She avoided contact with the young male lawyers who gave her occasional, curious notice, in spite of her consistently drab clothing, and she watched for the cowboy, more out of curiosity, she assured herself, than actual interest. When she hadn't happened across him by Thursday afternoon, Chelly launched a search under the guise of learning which lawyers inhabited which offices.

There were four main hallways radiating from the lobby where the luscious Monica Lynch reigned over the reception desk and directed phone calls. Each corridor led to the office of one of the principals in the firm and was referred to by the boss who toiled at its end. "West" was also known as "Harned;" "South" was "Leonard;" "East," "Manning," and "North," the firm's retired founder, "Old Man Diet." Each corridor was lined with offices—secretarial work centers, staff attorneys, and storage and supply rooms.

Chelly was assigned an out-of-the-way, closet-sized space near the end of "North" or "Old Man Diet."

With a twinge of guilt for her curiosity about the cowboy—residual loyalty to Eric's controlling decrees, she supposed—during breaks Chelly traversed the corridors, peering tentatively into each of the cubicles. When a module was occupied and that tenant glanced up, Chelly smiled, mumbled, "Wrong office," and hurried on. No one seemed surprised about a new clerk lost in the sprawling facility.

By Friday, Chelly's curiosity about the cowboy, his presence there on Monday, his absence thereafter, had become a challenge. Her search had nothing to do with any personal interest. Still, she didn't examine her actual motive too closely. Where was he?

She argued herself in circles. Maybe he didn't belong there and wouldn't be back. But he had walked right by Monica's desk. The receptionist enjoyed wielding her authority. She would not have allowed a stranger to stroll Corridor East unless he were authorized.

Also the much-sought-after Monica had spared the cowboy one of her rare come-hither smiles.

Okay, Monica knew the guy. Chelly could ask her who he was. But each time Chelly got up her nerve, she was rebuffed by the receptionist's cool indifference. In spite of her job title, Monica was not the least bit receptive. Her glare hardly reflected the attitude of a woman who would provide information freely—certainly not to someone she obviously considered an underling.

Besides, it was the week between Christmas and New Year's. A lot of people were absent. Chelly made a mental note to check the unoccupied offices again after the holidays.

She had other conversations with herself about the cowboy. Were thoughts about him a defense mechanism, a diversion to keep her from thinking about Eric? Did she really care who he was? Life was less complicated without a man in it. Still, her image of the cowboy, with memory enhancement, made him just about the sexiest male she'd ever seen. She hoped he'd reappear after the holidays, if for no other reason than reassurance that he was only flesh and blood, and, of course, so she could take another gawk.

Also during that first week, she realized she was having an inordinate number of chance meetings with Leonard Diet who was more affable and more talkative with each encounter. He seemed too old to be flirting with her. Whatever could the chubby old rascal be thinking?

Chapter Three

By Sunday, New Year's Day, Chelly had regained much of her old confidence. She and Midge had stayed home on the biggest party night of the year, toasted each other with sparkling grape juice and ordered a pizza—a supreme.

Her family called about noon to wish her happy new year, each of them on a separate telephone.

"Mom," Chelly was the first to broach the subject they all were obviously avoiding, "I'm sorry about what happened. I know how crazy you are about Eric."

Before her mother could respond, Chelly continued. "And, Dad, I know how you love it when Eric fills out the golf foursome on Sundays. I know he's always been sort of the son you never had. I'm sorry that now he'll never be part of your family."

"Baby," he interrupted and Chelly yielded, "golf reveals a lot about a person." His voice dropped to a confidential tone. "Eric shaves his score, sweetheart. He cheats."

She heard her mother's gasp before her dad hurried on. "He does it almost every hole, and he doesn't even have to, playing with us." He drew a new breath. "A man that'll cheat playing a game, sugar, probably will cheat in business… and in his personal commitments, too."

The pall of silence was broken by fifteen-year-old Angela's snickering. "I never could tell you this before, Chelly, but Eric's dull. He's been right next door practically all my life and I can tell you the man has no humor, Chel. No soul."

"Come on, Angela, you always thought Eric was cute." In spite of her words, she felt a special warmth toward her sister. "You're just ragging on him for my sake, and I appreciate it, really I do."

"Cute, yes. Interesting?" Angela gave an huge, audible yawn. "Give me a good algebra book and Eric pales by comparison. And you know how I feel about algebra."

Chelly snorted a little laugh. Her mother snickered before her dad and Angela began laughing, too.

"Thanks, everybody," Chelly said finally. "I really do think things are going to work out."

Three voices chimed agreement, spirits obviously buoyed as they said their good-byes.

As she hung up the phone, Chelly stretched, feeling strangely content. She was getting comfortable with her new life, taking hold at the office under the prudent supervision of Anne Beed; at home, enjoying the tutelage and wacky philosophizing of Midge Kitchens, and being generally ignored by the male population which, Chelly assured herself, was exactly what she wanted.

And forgiveness fostered a reemerging warmth for Eric. The Chastains lived next door. She and Eric had played together in the sand box before preschool. Eric had always been exactly who he was. Motivated to please his father, he had never been the man Chelly imagined. It wasn't his fault that he wasn't who she wished he was.

"You know, I don't think you were actually in love at all." Midge's comment broke the early afternoon's comfortable silence. She sat cross-legged opposite Chelly in the living room floor where they were drinking coffee and sharing a package of powdered sugar donuts and the Sunday newspaper.

Chelly flipped down a corner of the newspaper to look at her roommate's face. It was sometimes hard for her to tell when Midge was kidding and Chelly felt a little annoyed by the flippant observation. "I most certainly was."

Her apartment mate had brought the subject up before and each time Chelly's memory of her last talk with Eric stung less, the humiliating scene on Christmas night when he confessed he was in love… with somebody else.

Midge waggled her head. "How do you know?"

Chelly was surprised that what she felt this time was not so much regret as a dull ache at her temple. She closed the newspaper to one hand and massaged the tender spot on her head with the other.

"Well, because… " She licked her lips. "I guess, well, true love sort of defies definition."

Midge's skeptical look became disbelief and she shook her head. "I think you talked yourself into thinking you were in love. Your parents wanted it.

You were the right age. He was willing. Why not? He was, wasn't he?"

"Willing?"

"No, dopey, in love?"

"Obviously not or he wouldn't have gone to bed with the first skirt that spread her legs." Chelly cringed, remembering Eric's winsome account. "Sorry. That was crude."

"So you were and he wasn't, is that what you're saying?" Midge pruned her mouth. "I don't think so."

"Why do we keep discussing this?"

"First, because I've been studying the situation and I've decided you haven't hurt long enough or hard enough to have been in love at all. The prick just pricked your pride."

Midge had struck a nerve. When Chelly thought about the breakup, she was less heartbroken than embarrassed. Apparently everyone in Blackjack knew about Eric's new girlfriend before she did. Still, that night he had touched on a couple of her most sensitive suspicions about herself. "Eric knew me pretty well. He said some things."

"What kind of things?"

She recalled the scene. Taking the offensive, Eric had glared at her and set his jaw. He'd looked like his dad right then—accusing, belligerent, daring her to try to defend herself. "He said I overanalyzed everything; that I wasn't the kind of woman who can fall in love. I was too cerebral. Not passionate enough or affectionate or... like that."

"He said all that?"

Chelly scowled. She wasn't being fair. "Not in those words, but what he did say... well, what I gave you was the gist of it." She paused again but Midge waited. "Then he popped his knuckles. It's a habit of his that always irritates me. I think he was showing me my opinion of him didn't matter any more. Then he added what he considered the final and worst insult of all. He said I thought too much."

"Whew." Being sarcastic, Midge blew raspberries. "So?"

"Apparently falling in love doesn't require premeditation. It seems to be more of an emotional collapse than a rationale. Bright women—not that I'm bragging about my marvelous brain, understand—but maybe I'm too academic to fall in love."

Midge chortled and stuck her tongue out. "You definitely were not in love if you can seriously consider that bunch of crap he unloaded on you and find yourself guilty. He was just trying to justify himself by making you look wrong too. Can't you see that?" Midge scrambled to her feet, dusted the backside of her sweat pants and paced to the window. "No, ma'am, you definitely were not in love. Not only that, I don't think he was either. In my opinion, you do not yet know the meaning of the word."

"Okay, Ms. Expert, define it for me."

Midge lifted her eyes toward the ceiling, as if seeking divine guidance, folded her hands together in front of her chest and assumed an angelic pose. "At first, you feel like you have the flu."

Chelly laughed, but Midge flashed her a warning look. "The symptoms are similar, believe me. I speak from experience. I've been in love eight times." She hesitated. "Maybe nine." She shook her head, apparently shaking off a worrisome thought, and continued.

"A person recovering from love-gone-wrong goes through agonizing mental gymnastics, genuine physical pain. She doesn't eat, can't sleep, can barely function." She turned a wizen look on Chelly and dropped her voice to a rote recitation.

"You, on the other hand, loaded your bags, canceled your life, moved to the city, and treated yourself to a high-cal hot chocolate. There was no gnashing of teeth. Tossing off the old, rewarding oneself, and beginning anew is not the way your normal jiltee gets over it."

"Okay, so I did it differently than you would have. Maybe that's the way cerebral people do things."

Midge's angelic pose withered. "Meaning, a mental giant like yourself doesn't feel passion passionately?"

Chelly began gathering strewn newspapers and folding them. "Midge, I don't know why we're dredging through all this. I thought I was in love. I got dumped. It was humiliating. Maybe the humiliation is the source of my pain. I don't know."

But Midge was like a bulldog with a sock. She wouldn't turn it loose. "Let me ask you this." Midge lowered her voice to a suggestive pitch. "Did Eric turn you on physically?"

"Well... no." Chelly conjured a mental picture of Eric as she pushed the newly stacked papers off to one side and stretched her legs. She, too, was wearing sweats. It felt good to wallow on the floor. Tall and slender, blond and fair, Eric had finely-chiseled features and high coloring. He actually was more pretty than handsome. "But I'm not the kind of person who allows a physical attraction or hormones to dictate her behavior. My brain has total control of the physical plant."

"What?" Midge stepped from the window back to the middle of the room, staring in disbelief.

"Besides, Eric and I... weren't physical people."

"Chelly, love means not being able to keep your hands off each other. Were you at all involved?"

"He was. Sometimes. "

"Woman, we're talking here about coupling. S-E-X. It takes two."

Chelly exhaled noisily, shook her head and avoided looking directly into Midge's accusing glare. "Our relationship wasn't like that."

"You didn't have sex?"

"No. Well, not exactly."

"Why not?"

Chelly felt the blush. She didn't want to be disloyal to Eric, but she didn't like thinking their problems were all her fault.

"Eric and I petted some, but things didn't work exactly like they're supposed to."

"What things?"

"This is embarrassing."

"Just say it."

Chelly wrung her hands and focused her eyes on the floor. "He would... go off."

"He would leave?"

"No. He would... fire. Before it was time."

Midge suddenly looked enlightened. "Oh. He ejaculated prematurely?"

"I guess. I don't know. He said it was my fault. But it always happened while we were still fully clothed."

"What happened when he was finished?"

"He'd cuss and grab the front of his pants and go home."

"And what did you do?"

Chelly shrugged. "I got mad. You know. Well, I was interested. Certainly curious. It was frustrating. He said it was my fault, but I didn't know how to keep it from happening."

"So you've never... ?"

"No. I've never."

"And you are how old?"

"Twenty-five."

"I cannot believe this." Midge walked in a tight circle before she noticed the woeful look on Chelly's face. "No, no, girlfriend, don't go there. It definitely was not your fault. You needed a man. I mean a real man, not some immature sissy wuss." Midge paced to the kitchen, wheeled and returned to stand facing the window, her back to Chelly. Then she pivoted slowly.

"Let's back up here. I need answers to a few pertinent but very basic questions." Midge's face was kindly, her manner, calm. "You do like guys, right?"

Chelly chuckled. "Definitely."

"Okay. Have you ever seen a male who turned you on, just looking at him?"

"Well sure." Chelly felt a warm flush creep up from her shirt collar and she tried not to giggle. "Hasn't everyone?"

Midge maintained a businesslike demeanor. "Was he more tall and thin or short and muscular?"

Chelly shrugged but she immediately got a mental picture of the cowboy on the elevator at DMD. It had been the one big disappointment of the week—not seeing him again.

Midge eyed her shrewdly. "Come on. I can see you're thinking of someone. What does he look like?"

"I don't know him." Chelly's blush deepened.

"But you're thinking of him right now, aren't you?" Midge lowered her voice. "It's okay, Chelly. He won't know we're talking about him. You can whisper, if it makes you feel better."

Chelly laughed lightly, stalling, then her voice dropped. "He's tall, probably six-three."

"Fat or thin?"

"His shoulders are broad, his hips are narrow. He has muscular thighs." She was warming to the game. "And calves big enough to break the line of expensive trousers." Chelly didn't realize she'd noticed so much about the cowboy.

Midge prodded. "Dark or fair?"

"Tanned, at least his hands and face are. And… "

"What?"

"He has big hands."

"How about his hair?"

"Dark brown."

"And his eyes?"

Chelly's mouth dropped open. She couldn't remember. How could she not have noticed the color of his eyes? Oh, yes, the sunglasses. "He was wearing shades."

"What color should his eyes be?"

"Dark brown with black flecks."

"And his face? How about his features? Is he pretty?"

Chelly clamped her lips closed over the grin and shook her head. "No. He's got a big nose, a square jaw, high forehead, a long, rugged face. He looks like he could take a punch. Like he probably has."

Midge looked perplexed. "Chelly, this guy doesn't sound like your type at all."

Chelly blurted a laugh. "You asked what kind of man appeals to me and I told you."

Midge fixed her with a penetrating stare. "Okay, now the biggie. Have you just described Eric Chastain?"

Chelly's laugh erupted into the room. She locked her arms around her knees thinking of Eric's fine features, his thin, fragile body. She rocked back against the couch, and guffawed toward the ceiling.

Midge arched her eyebrows and spoke to an imaginary person. "Apparently not."

Chelly's laughter continued. It felt good to let go.

"Chelly. Chelly! Come on, we're not through yet."

Her laughter ebbed, but the intermittent giggles continued as Chelly turned her attention again to Midge.

"Now, how does this man of your dreams make you feel?"

Chelly lifted herself to the edge of the couch, crossed her legs, propped her chin in her hand above the elbow braced on her knee and squinted. "Sweaty. Queasy."

Midge arched her brows. "Yep, I'm afraid he's what you need, all right. But, let me tell you one thing. If and when you snag this guy, you'd best hang on, girl, because you'll be in for a wild ride. We have now established that your suspected broken heart wasn't. What you thought was a break was more of a scrape. It didn't even leave much of a bruise. Now, take my advice. Re-engage that powerful brain you're so proud of and rethink this no dating policy. I've got a couple of ideas."

Chelly's smile faded. "I don't want to date."

"Even this guy? What do we call him?"

"I don't know his name."

"He wears cowboy boots?"

"Yes."

"Okay. What I'm saying is, you need to practice dating city guys, hone your skills, be prepared for when the cowboy comes calling."

"No, no, Midge. I'm not going out. Not for a long, long time. Not with anyone."

Midge looked skeptical. "Not even with the cowboy?"

"I don't know him, not his name, or where he works, or anything about him."

Midge arched her eyebrows. "As a future lawyer, you need to know something. Your answers throughout this entire interview have been non responsive. You may have the high-dollar education, sister, but I picked that little nugget up off TV." Midge smiled knowingly, her expression smug. "I can't wait for your cowboy to turn up again. I have a feeling he will, maybe sooner than you think."

Chapter Four

"Anne, thanks for coming. How's it going?" Wayne Harned liked Anne Beed and valued her opinions. Walking around his desk to shake her hand, he motioned her into a chair and closed the door.

Inside her, warning bells jangled. Wayne Harned was a named partner at DMD, mid forties, a strong family man, a good guy, in Anne's opinion. "Things are good at my end. What's going on with you?"

He smiled. "Straight to the point. That's one of the things I like best about you. How's the new girl working out? Bennett."

She gave him a curious smile and nodded. "She's fine. You're not usually interested in the clerical help."

"Well, this one's... different. I had Bixler hire her on someone's recommendation. The someone wants periodic evaluations of her job performance."

"Why?"

Harned shrugged. "He wants to know how she's doing."

"She's only been here a week. She's a good typist, has picked up glitches in a couple of pleadings. She can do legal research. She's alert about time running on cases, has some legal expertise." Beed hesitated. "She's damn good. Meticulous. Thorough." She paused a moment. "Personally, I like her a lot."

"Good. That's good to hear. I want you to update me once a week or so. And send her to me when she has questions about pleadings or procedures. I'd like to get acquainted with her."

Anne afforded him a skeptical look. "Okay."

He met her gaze. "Don't mention my interest."

"No, I won't."

Harned settled back in his chair, his attention drawn to papers on his desk. Obviously, Anne was dismissed. As she rose to leave, she was more curious than ever about her badly dressed protégé.

On Tuesday of her second week in the city, as Chelly's ambition and self esteem began to blossom, she made a brazen tactical maneuver.

Clerks and secretaries alike disappeared when the perpetually absent D.R. Manning faxed; panicked when he e-mailed items addressed to them by name. Curious, Chelly interrogated Anne about the main man's extended absence.

The supervisor rolled her eyes and lowered her voice. "Count your blessings."

"But no one seems to know or care where he is from one day to the next."

Her supervisor grew solemn. "Oh we care, and get this straight, no matter what else you're doing, Manning's orders take priority. If you're near a monitor when he makes contact, do whatever he says as quick as you can, and be sure it's done right. He spells phonetically, like a lot of old timers, but he's got no tolerance. He expects you to interpret his meaning and do a job. He can be brutal."

"Maybe his arteries are hardening."

Anne arched an eyebrow. "I doubt it."

"Why do we indulge him?"

Anne chuckled. "That's not exactly the way it is, honey. Manning's the best damn corporate raider in the business. It's he that indulges us. He calls the office here The Shop and everyone working here, Shopkeepers. The way he says it, it's no compliment.

"It's Manning pulling down the big bucks that support the shop in the manner to which we have become accustomed. We are actually only a storefront for him. As long we run smoothly here, he keeps his nose to the grindstone there. Keeping that man long distance guarantees the cash flow and makes for happy campers at home. Believe me."

Chelly couldn't read Anne's face. "Do you genuinely not like him, or are you just hamming it up?"

Anne flashed Chelly a dour look. "When you look up the word 'tyrant,' you'll see Manning's picture right there in your Merriam Webster."

Chelly coughed a little laugh. When Anne remained somber, her mirth subsided. "I'll check that out. I'd like to see what he looks like."

"You'll know him when you see him."

"How?"

Anne arched one eyebrow significantly. "By the way we genuflect when he comes through the door. You'd better learn to curtsy nice. He's like the Mad Hatter. After he passes, the walls whisper, 'Off with their heads. Off with their heads.'"

Chelly smiled uncertainly, prompting a giggle from her supervisor. She'd heard stories of Manning's legendary temper. "Is everyone afraid of him then?"

"Physically, no. But don't ever argue with him. He's got this rapier tongue that can cut you off at the knees."

"Is he married? Does he have a family?"

Anne snorted a laugh. "You're kidding, right? The man's got an evil attitude about women. 'Use 'em and lose 'em' is his motto."

Anne's phone rang and she picked it up, but before she opened the line, she added, "Manning and ladies? You definitely don't want to go there." Anne pressed a button to attend the caller.

Chelly went to the storage room during her morning break to find the windowless chamber unlocked, as usual.

Dozens of file boxes were stacked floor to ceiling. She peered at labels yellowed with age and dusted off two or three, trying to decipher the system. The labels provided the client name, style of the case, and the names of the opposing attorneys.

She unstacked boxes down to one that showed Manning as the in-house attorney. She pulled it free, tossed the lid aside and flipped through the tabs on the file folders.

The binders bore the usual titles, Correspondence, Motions, Plaintiffs' Depositions, etc., until she thumbed to one marked, Theory.

She slipped that file out of the box and opened it to find jumbled notes, loose, handwritten on lined pages torn from legal pads. The bold scrawl was barely legible, the spelling atrocious, but the work, in outline form, reflected organizational genius.

On the first line was the name of the client; the second, the subject of the takeover and the kind of acquisition—friendly or hostile—this one was marked Hostile.

There followed a list of facts—the corporation's earnings the last ten years, ownership, type business, all the nuts and bolts operational information, including the executives' names, addresses, family profiles, hobbies, and job evaluations.

Pages four and five outlined a step-by-step acquisition plan, neat, concise and ruthless in its inevitability. There were margin notes, a single word followed by a page number. On the pages indicated, Chelly found lists of possible solutions to anticipated problems.

This theory file contained Manning's entire mental process, efficiently drawn. In this one manila folder he had compiled what he obviously considered the most sensitive information of the entire project. If opposing counsel somehow got hold of this one file folder, they might be able to defend against him. Here was the dragon's underbelly—the master's vulnerable spot. The data was easy to follow, like a recipe provided a novice chef.

Chelly smiled. Manning's adversaries would pay handsomely to get a glimpse of his theory file, if they knew this kind of intelligence existed, conveniently located in one place.

Of course, the matter fanned in front of her was ancient history. But what about the theory file on a current case, one being prepared at this moment?

An enemy in the office could deal Manning a lot of grief.

Peculiarly, Chelly felt a surge of loyalty to a man she'd never met—one who was only e-mail on a computer screen. It seemed a curious impulse. A person might not like the man, but any lawyer would appreciate his genius.

Chelly spent her lunch break in the dank storage room. From a corporate-merger standpoint, she thought Manning very nearly invincible. When the subject of the takeover opposed him, he became ruthless. This treasure trove was Chelly's opportunity to learn from the master, to pick his brain.

The more she studied his methods, the more determined she became until her thoughts hardened to grim resolve. She'd been docile, submissive too long. She would learn combat tactics from a field general. Then she would march to war, take guff from no one, least of all bullies like Harmon Chastain. Maybe she could even encourage backbone in Eric, help him stand up to his dad and be the man she knew he could be—if she could convince him he needed to change.

She would get close to Manning. Be a foot soldier in his army. And like her leader, she'd take no prisoners.

"Does Mr. Manning ever call?" Chelly asked Anne late that afternoon.

"You're sure asking a lot of questions about him."

"Just curious. Does he call?"

"No. His only mode of communication is his laptop, e-mail or fax. He's got an aversion to using telephones when he's in, what he terms, 'enemy territory.' Why?"

Chelly didn't answer, only smiled.

Later, using the aged computer in her capsule-size office, Chelly happened onto a memo from Manning, which was to be hard-copied for a file.

He was in the process of finalizing a friendly merger that would benefit all parties involved, but there was a glitch. Chelly read carefully:

All of a suden, the Antenium people refuse to let the logo—that phony cote of arms—be part of the sale. Dam idiots never had a genuin cote of arms. The great granddaddy who started the busniss was a bookeeper who slugged his way in. He desined the insignia to make his new busniss look like it had substansial backing. The desine's got absolutely no senemenal or historical sygnificance. They're holding onto it for some dam sentamental reason but they're determened. They insist the sale price NOT include their presious logo.

Fischer wants the trademark to help hold the company's currint custumers.

I've wiped their buts through this hole deal. I'm sic and tired of the hole mob.

Bottom line: This deal is going, with or without cooperashun. I've been nice. Its head-nocking time.

A memo, of course, did not anticipate a response. Chelly knew he intended it only to be printed and put in the file. She wondered if she should correct the spelling first, but she had an idea. It might help. The elusive inspiration worried her for an hour before she made a decision.

Just after five o'clock, when the offices emptied and the cleaning team arrived, unlocking doors to facilitate their work, Chelly lugged her computer into the reception room of Manning's private suite and closed the outer door.

A box containing details of the Antenium sale was one of several under the conference table. She slid it out, hoisted it onto the table and began browsing.

There it was, his nemesis, the Antenium emblem. As she remembered, it was an ink drawing, actually only an etching, in black and white.

Chelly eyed the logo, considering. Would a field general appreciate advice from a lowly foot soldier, or might that kind of audacity get a person fired?

His temper was famous, but it seemed to her the stories of his tantrums had a common theme. They were usually triggered by incompetence in the shop.

She sat at the table and jotted notes on a legal pad, stewed, rereading, refining her suggestion, trying to make it more palatable. Finally, she honed the message to one paragraph and squared her shoulders. Then she dropped to her knees to sort electrical cords and cables under the table and hook up her machine.

"*Manning,*" she typed, when she was online, "*the Antenium logo is black and white. The new company could adopt a similar design but in vivid colors instead of the drab coat of arms Antenium has used all these years. It would freshen the company's image, retain its familiarity and appease the family, all at the same time.*"

She could say more but decided against it. She hit "send" before she lost her nerve.

Twenty minutes dragged by without a response. Chelly paced, entertaining her options as second thoughts assailed her. She hadn't identified herself. Probably no one would suspect her of this mischief. But if her meddling set him off, she couldn't let someone else take the blame.

Damn and drat!

Her hands and feet got cold and she checked the screen often, unwilling to leave for the day until she got some kind of response.

Finally, a message. "*What's your name? What do you do there, sweep out? Manning.*"

Was he angry? It sounded like he was.

She typed, "*Chelly Bennett. I can sweep, if you like, but my designation is file clerk.*"

"*Who gave you the idea for updating the logo?*"

"*I read your memo and looked in the Antenium file. I didn't think my idea was a deal maker or anything. I was just trying to help. Sorry.*"

His next communication was concise. *"You are wrong, Bennett."* She gasped It was over. She had to force herself to read his next words. *"Your idea WAS a deal maker."* She exhaled, startled. *"We were locked in our positions. We couldn't see an out. I thank you for your help. We all do."*

Chelly's laugh was tremulous, on again, off again, as she hugged herself and twirled round and round the room. She closed down the machine, grabbed her purse and jacket and leaped, tossing a triumphant fist in the air as she darted to the elevators, whooping as she raced through the deserted corridors.

At the other end of the line, Manning leaned back in his chair and watched the DMD security monitor relaying Chelly's exuberance.

He smiled at first, then a rumble rose from his chest and out, a rolling laugh. Nodding approval, he continued laughing as monitors along the hall showed her executing a circling waltzing sidestep down the corridor and onto the elevator.

Among many delivery items in his satchel the next morning, the courier had an envelope for Chelly Bennett.

Anne Beed, who had a message of her own for her newest employee, took the missive from the messenger. She fingered the flap on the envelope, which wasn't sealed, and opened it.

Enclosed were two tickets to a touring Broadway musical making a weekend appearance in Tennyson, and a gift certificate for two at the Trenton Hotel brunch buffet.

The accompanying note read: *Bennett: Apprechiate the help. Manning.*

Anne went to Chelly's small office, fingering the tickets, dumbfounded, her initial suspicions about Chelly renewed. "What's this?" She tossed the envelope onto Chelly's desk.

Chelly examined the contents, grinned broadly, then cast a dubious look at her mentor. "I didn't expect... He already thanked me. Does he always do stuff like this?"

"Not that I ever heard of. What kind of help?"

"A suggestion."

Anne's sardonic expression lifted to a puzzled smile. "There's more. I, too, have a message. You've been promoted."

Chelly stood, astounded. "Bixler promoted me? He hates me."

Anne's derisive laugh confirmed her thought. "Bixler? Promote you? No, no, honey. This is practically over Tom Bixler's dead body. Manning's ordered you assigned to him exclusively. You're his new executive secretary and, get this, you're off hourly wage and on salary. Your income just doubled."

Chelly dropped back into her chair. "Can he do that?"

"Manning? Are you kidding? He can do anything he damn well pleases. Your instincts are good, honey." She nodded puzzled approval. "Bixler's having apoplexy as we speak, but he's acting like it's his idea. No one crosses Manning. You've referred to him as our commanding general. I guess you can think of this as a battlefield promotion."

A slow smile eased across Anne's face as she continued. "You know, I actually predicted this. I said you'd move up around here." Then she frowned, worrying her lower lip. "But even I didn't foresee this. Keeping Manning happy is one thing, inspiring rewards is another. You're giving the man new dimensions."

When Beed reported the news about Manning's promoting Chelly Bennett, Partner Wayne Harned seemed interested but not particularly surprised.

Chelly put her hair up but wore a fitted dress, and left the horn-rimmed glasses at home when she and Midge went for Sunday brunch at the Trenton and to the matinee performance of "Les Miserables."

In the lobby during intermission, she noticed a tall man, stunning in a stylish, three-button suit, studying her from across the way. When their eyes met, his mouth bowed in an easy smile. She dropped her gaze and turned her back to him. Seconds later, however, she realized she recognized him.

The cowboy.

She wheeled and shot a glance to where he had been, but he was gone.

She scanned the lobby, maneuvering through the crowd, from one end of the massive hall to the other, but he had vanished.

"Who are we scouting?" Midge asked, trailing Chelly. When her friend didn't answer, Midge caught her arm. "Is it Eric and his lady? I'd like to have a look at him. No? You are blushing, girlfriend. What's going on?" She surveyed the hall. "Oh. I get it. You saw your cowboy, didn't you? Was he with a date? Was he alone? Did he see you?"

Chelly only shook her head, scanning the crowd, looking for but unable to find the tall man. She couldn't concentrate on the second half of the performance, fidgeting, searching faces in the darkened theater. But she did not see him again. Her one consolation was that he had apparently recognized her, too. And he had smiled.

What would she have done if she had located him? Would she have approached him? Spoken to him? She honestly doubted she would have dared to do either one.

If he was interested, why didn't he approach her?

He was probably there with his wife, stupid. She groaned. Married men should be required to wear wedding rings. There ought to be a law.

Via e-mail that week, Manning prodded Chelly's initiative, assigned her two active files to review, alerted her to potential trouble spots, and said he was open to suggestions. Anne made sure necessary exhibits were delivered to Chelly's office.

Suddenly staff people treated her differently. The receptionist, the luscious Monica Lynch, began calling her by name. Monica's acknowledgment alone indicated an elevation in status.

"And Bixler is grumbling hellos to me in the hall," she told Midge. "He even looks me in the eye occasionally."

Yarnell Tuggle, a mousy young woman from the secretarial pool, confirmed Chelly's new standing by volunteering her assistance.

And Leonard Diet asked her for a date.

"Astonishing," Chelly told Midge at the apartment that night. "Mr. Diet grabbed my arm in the hallway about four-thirty, whirled me around and asked if I could join him for dinner."

"Congratulations. Did he call you by name?"

Chelly spewed a low giggle. "No, as a matter of fact, he didn't." She sobered. "I don't think he knows my name."

"So, what did you say?"

"Nothing. His beeper went off and he flew down the hall. I don't think he gets beeped much. Anyway, he disappeared. I seem to have that effect on men." She chuckled and Midge laughed too.

Although Chelly's salary and her standing with her coworkers improved with the new title, the size of her office did not as she remained closeted in the same eight-by-ten, windowless space.

When Manning's workload began overwhelming the tiny office, she asked Anne about larger accommodations. Anne spoke to Tom Bixler then reported.

"Bixler will give you more space, Chelly, but you have to ask him for it yourself." Anne grimaced. "I'm afraid he's going to require groveling."

Reluctant to open what she feared might be a Pandora's Box, Chelly made do with her glorified broom closet.

Finally, Manning tersely ordered the change. *Don't wate for the copyer in the supply room,* he e-mailed after a delay in receiving papers he needed. *Use my office. Get a key. Funkshun.*

Annoyed by the tone of the message and carrying a hard copy with her, Chelly went to ask Bixler for keys to Manning's suite. She asked politely at first.

"Can't do it, honey." There was an audible sneer in the man's voice. "Manning wouldn't like it."

"He's the one who told me to use *his* space and *his* machines, so I can get *his* work out faster."

"I'll have to have that in writing, sweet cheeks. *His* writing, not yours."

Chelly placed the hard copy of the message on Bixler's desk with all the feigned humility she could muster.

Bixler blustered as he read it. "Function?" He smirked. "The man sure put you in your place." She didn't answer. "You should have shown me this in the first place. I'm surprised he contacted you instead of me." He reached into a desk drawer and produced the requested keys. "Want these?" He dangled them in front of her face as his eyes settled firmly on her breasts. Chelly remained as she was, unmoving and silent. "What'll you give me for them?"

She bit her lips together and stuck out her chin, struggling not to blurt words she might live to regret.

Bixler seemed to guess. "Don't get smart. Remember, I'm the guy who hired you and I'm the guy who can damn well un-hire you."

That might be true, she supposed, and her face must have reflected her concern because Bixler allowed a smug grin, still focusing the salacious leer intently at her chest.

She nodded, indicating she understood. The nod seemed to satisfy him for the moment. He tossed the keys on the floor, at her feet.

"Oh, dear, excuse me, sweet cheeks." He stood, ogling as she stooped to retrieve the keys.

Stinging from the humiliating exchange with Bixler, Chelly's mood lightened as she unlocked Manning's inner sanctum with her own key. She had sneaked into the reception room several times after hours but had never ventured beyond into his private quarters.

His lair was posh, with lavish views that scanned the city below in three directions. Just after five o'clock, she stood there, absorbing the sight of people scurrying like ants along the frozen streets eleven stories below.

Eventually, she tore herself from the breathtaking view to drift around the chamber. She admired the original oil paintings enhanced by portrait lighting. She touched the heavy mahogany and leather furnishings that shimmered with the sheen applied daily, even though no one was there to appreciate it. It gave meaning to the age-old question, if a tree falls in the forest and no one hears it, does it make a noise? But that was the past, which was past. Now she was here, authorized to enjoy every silent, immaculate corner.

When she strolled into the bathroom, her eyes popped. It was huge, done in very masculine maroons and browns. It even had a shower with multiple gold spigots, which could spray the occupant's body at various heights all at the same time, and a linen closet complete with terry cloth robes in cellophane wrappers.

Trying to settle down, to think, to force herself to function in this Taj Mahal, Chelly examined Manning's sprawling workspace equipped with the newest office machines. His computer, hardware and software both, were updated regularly, despite their scant use.

Chelly sighed. If there were a corporate division of heaven, the offices probably looked like this.

She settled onto the edge of his executive's chair and flipped the computer's power switch. There was e-mail, from Manning. "Bennett, let me no when you get there."

"I'm here," she typed.

There was a delay. "What do you think of my digs?"

"Scrumptious. B.J. and Doreen Rose, the janitors, will be happy to reclaim my old office for their buckets and mops." She was feeling a little heady in the new, lofty atmosphere and continued tapping the keys. "Would you please ask Bixler to gold-leaf my name on the door here? We can move your nameplate to my broom closet, since you're never here. It would be a classy thing to do. What do you say?"

She laughed at her own audacity for even thinking such things, much less e-mailing those thoughts to him.

As usual, Manning's response was terse. "I'll take your idea under advisement; however, until such time as you are embossed on the stationery and can singularly manage a takeover, perhaps you should be content to labor in the improved surroundings and not banish your benefactor to the broom closet just yet."

She laughed as she read the pithy words, particularly pleased that he obviously had run the spell check before he sent it. Funny for him to go the trouble to check the spelling when he was only writing to her. "Obviously the man is trying to impress me," she whispered, then laughed out loud at the idea.

She liked Mr. Manning more every day, particularly when her needling pricked him—drew blood but no threats. He had the clout to change her whole life with a snap of his fingers. And she knew Bixler, the vulture, sat ready to "throw the baggage out." In spite of her gentle needling, Manning never threatened her. She admired his restraint.

Manning liked Chelly Bennett. He liked her quick mind, her flashes of acerbic wit and her optimism. Particularly, he liked her being flippant, treating him like a person rather than an icon. He liked her nearly enough to forgive her for being a woman.

She seemed younger than her age, demonstrated the mixed confidence and insecurities of youth. She seldom behaved as he expected. Most beautiful women didn't bother to develop their minds or their personalities. And few he knew had the audacity to mock a rich, older man the way Chelly Bennett mocked him.

He liked thinking of her—clean and freshly scrubbed—and the fact she didn't wear enough make-up to conceal the freckles dusted over her nose. He smiled.

Driven by ambition, he had acquired wealth early. His experience of women had come early as well and he'd learned his lessons under fire. He no longer succumbed to feminine wiles. Sometimes he despised the inconvenience of his own irrepressible physical need for occasional female companionship. He considered that need a flaw in his character, a chink in his armor.

And this woman presented a particular threat, slipping under his shell disguised as an innocent. The damnable part of it was that on closer study, she was proving to be the genuine article.

He snorted a laugh. Had there ever been an innocent female?

Still, Bennett was a breath of fresh air wafting through his stuffy life; a haunting tune he couldn't seem to get out of his head.

He'd had her investigated. She had dropped into his world jilted by some pimply faced twerp in Dogtrot, U.S.A., a man not worthy to unlace her shoes, much less remove her clothes. Fool. How long before the oaf realized his error and came sniffing around trying to recover her?

Well, Manning would make sure the buffoon realized his loss too late. He considered it already too late. She was the nicest thing that had happened to him, maybe in his entire life. He wasn't going to let her get away now, not without a fight, and he was a seasoned gladiator with the battle scars to prove it.

He scowled and tapped an index finger on the table. His usual arsenal might not work with this one. And this campaign could prove more important than any courtroom battle where the winners only wound up owning corporations.

How was she going to feel about Texas Hansen's interest in Chastains, the twerp's family's company?

The situation could require delicate handling. If she harbored feelings for the fool, Hansen's threat might send her galloping back to young Chastain out of loyalty—even if the feelings she harbored were not l-o-v-e.

Manning smoothed the information sheets in front of him with both hands. "Damn!" It was easier to devise strategy when the results were measured in cold, hard cash.

His most trusted young gofer glanced at him. Manning must have disturbed the younger man by grumbling out loud, but that didn't deter him from adding, "Hansen needs a penny-ante outfit like Chastains like he needs another hundred-dollar-bill." The gofer turned his attention back to the file open in front of him.

Hansen was intrigued by Chastains, saw it as a sleepy little company with potential. He'd sent Manning, his pit bull, to fetch it.

Manning set his jaw. Hansen might have to get along without Chastains, if the acquisition meant losing the sweet, freckle-faced girl. She was quickly assuming unique value. But, of course, no one else needed to know that, even if a few suspected it.

Maybe Manning would perform Hansen's dirty little deed, but only after he secured Chelly first. Thinking of such a pleasant solution, he leaned back, propped his feet on his work table, and smiled. His grin broadened several times before his thoughts again became serious and he righted himself to focus on the file in front of him.

The matter of Chelly Bennett would require diplomacy. Manning hadn't had to be diplomatic in a long, long time.

Chapter Five

On her birthday, the Tuesday of her fourth week in Tennyson, Chelly received two surprising calls late in the evening. She had just gotten out of the bathtub and was wrapped in her frumpy terry cloth robe when the telephone rang the first time.

"Chel, it's me." Eric's voice sounded warm and familiar.

She smiled. It had been a month since the breakup. She'd missed him. "Hi."

"Happy birthday."

"Thanks."

He lowered his voice. "How are you?"

"I'm good. Really good."

"Your mom says you've got a job."

"That's right."

"That's good."

There was a brief silence. She felt obligated to say something. "I have a terrific roommate. Midgean Kitchens."

"Yeah. I've talked to Midge a couple of times." Another pause. "I asked her not to tell you I called."

"Oh."

"Chel," his voice took on a coaxing timbre, "I miss you."

She stared at the window. She missed him too and started to say so, but didn't. She wasn't ready to admit that just yet. She didn't want him to take it the wrong way. "I'm surprised to hear that, Eric. What happened to Rebecca, your true love?"

"Rosemary, Chelly. Her name was Rosemary."

"Okay. So what happened to Rosemary?"

"She wasn't the girl I thought she was."

Chelly struggled to subdue the laugh. Obviously Rosemary wasn't the girl Chelly thought she was either, since Chelly thought she was Rebecca something.

Eric continued. "I guess the big problem, Chel, was… Well, she wasn't you."

Chelly took a deep, knowing breath. "Your dad didn't like her, right?"

He hesitated a moment too long. "Right."

"And you dropped her on his say-so?"

"Well… "

"I'm sorry to hear that, Eric. I really hope someday you develop the spine to stand up to him. I mean that. I want you to be happy."

"Chel?" He said her name eagerly, as if he liked the way the conversation was going. "I'm coming to Tennyson tomorrow to pick up some equipment. Dad suggested I take you to lunch." He hesitated. "I want to, too."

"No, Eric, I don't want to see you tomorrow. I'm not ready yet." She might have come up with some excuse, but she was making an effort to be forthright these days. Anne and Midge, and even Manning, all were brusque. Blunt. Candid. She'd come to admire honesty, even the brutal kind. She wanted to be up front, like they were.

Besides, she didn't intend to be anyone's consolation prize.

Eric sounded contrite. "I understand. When can I see you?"

She gazed at a curtain fluttering over the living room window. Despite the fact the window was closed and locked, the brisk January air ruffled it. She pulled the neck of her robe higher around her throat. "I need more time."

"Okay. Say when."

"Let me call you."

"Will you?"

"Yes, I will. When I'm ready." She paused. "Eric, I've gotten used to my freedom. I say what I think now. I choose my own friends. Live my own agenda."

When he spoke, it was as if he hadn't heard her or as if her words had no effect. "You'll let me know when I should come?" He'd never had much regard for anyone else's preferences. "How long do you think it'll be?" He waited a moment. "Dad'll want to know."

She managed a little cough. "I'll call when I think it's time."

As they said good night and hung up, Chelly marveled at how quickly their positions had reversed. Also, she felt a little miffed that Eric hadn't bothered to ask if she were dating. He—and his dad of course—took it for granted that she wasn't. A little presumptuous of them. She smiled grudgingly.

Okay, granted, she didn't have a boyfriend, but she felt appreciated by a faceless commander who issued orders by e-mail, and she still daydreamed about the tall, nameless cowboy. The lanky one lurked in the back of her mind—a power suit in sunglasses and run-over cowboy boots.

Actually, when she thought about the cowboy, Chelly credited him with intimidating her into staying at DMD long enough to get the job.

He rambled through her dreams at night. She looked for him daily at the office, concluding, finally, that he was from another firm, someone who worked nearby or might be back. She scanned the food plaza, the elevators, the parking garage and the street. But after that one brief encounter, he seemed to have vanished, except for the glimpse she'd had of him at the theater.

She told herself she was simply curious to see if he was really as handsome as she remembered. She thought he might be worth a moratorium on her moratorium on dating. She grimaced at her own rationale.

Okay, she excused, so she'd gotten scorched. One burn didn't mean a person should give up cooking. And, certainly, her blister was healing. Eric's call helped.

A second ego-bolstering phone call came later that same evening—from Leonard Diet.

As he identified himself, Chelly couldn't imagine the junior partner knew who she was, nor could she fathom why he might be calling her.

"Would you have lunch in my office tomorrow?" he said. "I'd like to discuss something with you."

Chelly inhaled once, then again without exhaling. "With me? Mr. Diet, I'm only a clerk?"

His voice sounded waspish. "I know who you are. I wouldn't be calling, my dear, if I didn't know who you were. I would like your input on a little personnel situation at the office."

Chelly's eyes roved her modest apartment, again noting the rustling curtains. This was incredible. It took sheer force of will to control the stammer. "I'd be glad to help any way I can, Mr. Diet. I'll be in your office at noon."

The next morning, however, Anne Beed approached her with a quizzical expression. "Chelly, what's going on? Leonard called. Said to tell you he had to cancel on lunch. Said he'd call you later in the week. Gifts from Manning? Lunch with Leonard? Who are you, girl?"

Chelly stared, her baffled visage apparently more convincing than her denial. "I'm no one, Anne. Mr. Diet called me at home last night and asked me to have lunch in his office today. He wanted to discuss a personnel matter."

Anne bristled. "What personnel matter?"

"Heck if I know. I'm amazed he even knows who I am. I'm only a clerk."

"Actually you're making too much money for a clerk. You're on payroll as Manning's executive secretary."

"The label hasn't changed my job description."

Anne's eyes narrowed as she studied Chelly askance. "Come clean, woman. Who are you?"

Chelly returned the look with a blink, shaking her head before she began laughing. "Honestly, Anne, I haven't got a clue." Her renegade giggles eased the concern on her mentor's face.

"He called you at home and invited you to lunch in the inner sanctum?" Anne was incredulous as she repeated the account. "What did he want?"

Chelly, still sputtering, offered a placating shrug. "I don't know. And now he's canceled, so I guess I'm not going to find out."

Anne studied Chelly closely for several seconds more before the supervisor began snickering herself, sending Chelly into peals of laughter.

"Leonard often leaves people agog," Anne said, "but he's even got me stumped this time."

Chapter Six

"What's the holdup with Chastains?" Texas Hansen spoke over the phone in his normal modified roar.

Manning held the receiver away from his ear. "I'm working on it." That was true, as far as it went. He had the research. Chastains had been a solid little supply house until young Eric took over. The kid had no interest in hardware supply, other than income. He spent more time at the country club than in the office and the business was starting to fray around the edges. Obviously Harmon Chastain didn't realize Eric was paying himself in shares of stock, then immediately unloading them for cash.

A takeover would be necessary eventually to save the company. Then Hansen would have his new toy and no freckle-kissed wench could prevent it.

If he could just stall Texas a while longer, things might fall into place without upsetting Chelly. That was Manning's highest priority now—keeping Chelly happy. But he was getting restless. He wanted more. He wanted to see her antics in person. Hear her voice. Most of all, he would like to evaluate her response to him, face-to-face.

She'd seemed mildly interested—or maybe only curious—their first meeting. Of course he was eleven years her senior. But a woman as naive as Chelly needed a seasoned man. She had a lot of energy, a verve for living. Would he be able to seize and hold her interest?

He was damn well going to try. He felt like a yearling, high-strung, full of energy, eager to romp. He was normally a bold man. Why was he so reluctant to test himself against this new challenge? Was her opinion of him really that important?

He was afraid maybe it was.

Bored at the prospect of long winter evenings at home with her self-imposed restriction on dating, Chelly contacted Tennyson University's law school.

Classes for the spring semester would begin the last week of January. She glanced at the calendar. This was Wednesday before the last Monday. The registrar provided a laundry list of documents TU would require to accept the transfer of credits from State.

As an afterthought, Chelly inquired about the cost.

Law school tuition at State had been one hundred dollars a semester hour. The average semester class load was fifteen hours. Tennyson, however, was a private school. "Tuition here is four hundred dollars an hour."

Chelly slumped. No wonder they accepted transfer students.

After the call, she tallied up. She had the fifteen-hundred-dollar-refund from State and some savings, enough for the nine hours she could get in night classes. It would be tight but her resolve was back. She would spend judiciously, set aside part of each paycheck, accumulate enough for one term at a time.

On Thursday the registrar called to say the faxed transcripts had been received.

"When will I know if I'm accepted?"

"If everything checks out, we can have you processed by the time classes begin on Monday. Of course, you're going to be sectioning late and some of the classes you want may be closed. We'll do what we can."

There was good news and bad news on Friday. She was accepted. The bad news was: both tort sections were full. Only two classes she needed were open. Torts might be offered in the summer session. The anticipated nine credit hours were cut to six. Financially easier, it meant a delay in graduating.

Her advisor touted openings in other classes, ones Chelly had already taken or would not need. She wouldn't pay good money for frivolous classes.

Chelly fumed to Midge. "If I get lucky, I might be a lawyer by the time I'm thirty, but maybe that's just my optimism showing."

"So, take what you can get. What's the problem? You're in, aren't you?"

Since Chelly had not mentioned her law school credits or her scheme to continue to Anne or anyone at the office, she couldn't very well confide her disappointment, although she knew she could trust Anne's discretion. She shrugged it off. There was nothing to be done about it. She had constitutional law on Tuesday and Thursday evenings, five-thirty to eight-thirty, and oil and gas law on Saturday mornings.

It was just as well she hadn't found the cowboy. With Manning assigning her more and more work and the added pressure of law classes, she really didn't have time for a man. Men did seem to require care and feeding. Eric had taught her the price of neglect.

She hated thinking of Eric, hated the idea of swallowing her pride and making up with him. If he were her fate, she wanted to delay her destiny as long as possible.

That week Manning directed her to the federal statute books to research a tax question.

Because of her law school experience—particularly the required legal bibliography class her freshman year—Chelly was able to go directly to the information, then checked with Wayne Harned to make sure she had touched all the bases.

Harned insisted she come to him with pleadings she was drafting. One afternoon as they finished and she gathered papers into a file folder, stalling, Harned glanced up. "Was there something else?"

"Mr. Harned, are you and Mr. Manning friends?"

He smiled slowly. "Yes. Why do you ask?"

"Well, I can't help being curious. I've never even seen a picture of the man."

Harned swivelled his chair. "Here are a couple of pictures of him right here." He pointed toward a two-picture frame on the credenza behind him.

"I took those the day D.R. made partner. He had given the old man notice. Mr. Diet invited the two of us to his place to do some bird hunting and to figure out a way to keep Manning."

Chelly moved to the credenza, eager to see a picture of her mentor only to find her expectations dashed. The pictures were grainy and the figures at a distance. Obviously it had been raining. An old man stood tall in the background. In front of him another man hunkered over two black retrievers. Both men wore slouch hats and bulky rain suits.

"The one kneeling with the dogs is Manning," Harned said.

She swallowed her disappointment. The man's face was hidden in both shots. "Is the older Mr. Diet tall?"

"Oh, yes. Huge. Six-foot-five, easily three hundred pounds." Harned smiled. "I was brand new here then. Manning had issued an ultimatum. Either Diet was going to make him a partner, or Manning was going out on his own. God, he was a brilliant strategist, even then. Mr. Diet knew he had to sweeten the deal or lose him."

"You were just starting out?"

"With Mr. Diet. Yes."

"Then Leonard made partner when he came along later?"

Harned's pleasant expression dissolved. "Yes, well, the old man had to talk Manning into it, but finally wore him down."

She wanted to restore Harned's cheer. "And you were next?"

His smile brightened and he glanced at her as if he knew her motive for bringing the conversation back to something he would consider pleasant. "Yes."

She left the office smiling, but inside she felt deflated. Surely someday she would meet Mr. Manning, but she still wouldn't be able to recognize him. Not from Harned's pictures.

Chelly kept busy. Her days at the office were full, often extending into evenings. The assignments were a good excuse when men associates in the firm asked her out.

She didn't want to date and continued to skewer her hair into the bun on the back of her head, to wear the eyeglasses and alternate three dour, oversized business suits as her base wardrobe. All of it helped deter men's attention, particularly Tom Bixler, who had become suspiciously nice.

Midge kept prodding Chelly to date, or to at least "start putting out some signals."

Anne seemed the only person at DMD who noticed Chelly's nonexistent social life and the only one who mentioned Chelly's grim wardrobe—repeatedly.

In Chelly's fifth week on the job, after a particularly tedious, time-consuming project for Manning, Anne braced her.

"I'm worried about you." Chelly glanced from her computer screen to find Anne reading over her shoulder. "I think it's time I told you more about Manning. You seem preoccupied with the man." Chelly swivelled and gave Anne her full attention.

"He can be merciless, Chelly, if you stumble. And it doesn't take much to set him off." Chelly had heard the stories. "Has anyone mentioned Tina Bohreer?"

Chelly shook her head. Anne crossed her arms and eased onto the edge of a client's chair.

"Tina was older, closer to Manning's age. She worked like the devil to get his attention, both in and out of the office. It finally happened. She made a mistake. One glitch and she was right back into the icy waters of the secretarial pool."

"What did she do?"

"Nothing, really. Tina told everyone she was Manning's private secretary." Chelly started to say something but Anne held up a hand to prevent the interruption. "It wasn't like with you. He didn't choose her. She anointed herself. No one objected. Actually, we were relieved.

"Tina told people he had the hots for her." Anne winced significantly. "Not.

"Anyway, we had a brownout one afternoon. Tina forgot to check Manning's fax machine, which had turned itself off automatically. No one thought of it. There was no malice. It was an oversight. It wasn't a big catastrophe, only caused a minor delay."

"So, couldn't she just explain?"

"She tried. Manning had a fit, demanded to know why no one double checked her. Her supervisor tried to explain but Manning wasn't buying the 'no hands but her hands' explanation."

"Maybe it ruined a big deal or something."

Anne raised her eyebrows, shook her head and mouthed a significant, "No. It only meant that his majesty was inconvenienced one weekend. He hates time off. He took advantage of his leisure to fly back here and swab the decks with our butts, including Leonard's sizable derriere."

"You're kidding. Could he do that? To Leonard, too?"

"He can't, but he did."

"Did you know the girl's supervisor?"

"Intimately. She was me."

"Didn't you explain?"

"Yes, I did. That's why Tina got demoted instead of canned. He ranted that we'd let her assume too much authority for her mediocre skills. He thought she was being supervised. Tina was mortified. It turned out she'd made a bunch of errors which he'd been correcting. After she was out, he went over every file she'd managed. We had to tie a few loose ends, nothing major.

"Humiliated, Tina found another job, a better one, really. Once you've worked here—especially for Manning—you can go anywhere.

"Anyway, his temper is why I've kept a close eye on you. You're much younger than Tina, of course, and smarter. You've got good instincts for this stuff."

Chelly's curiosity was again piqued. "So, is he getting close to retirement age? Thinking of letting go?"

"Manning?" Anne laughed. "He won't ever retire. He'll go out with his boots on, having one of his fits, giving somebody hell, probably. My point is: Don't let him get too dependent on you. You're good and he's passed you a scepter. Nevertheless, keep other people up on what you're doing and where to find things.

"Like I said, you have a good feel for the work. You're good about asking for help when you need it. Harned's impressed and he has a calming effect on Manning. You also handle Manning real well yourself."

"Thanks for the warning. I'll be careful."

"You already are. That's why he made you his Girl Friday. Just let me know if you hit a snag. For sure, tell me before you tell him about it."

"Right."

Valentine's Day came and went in a whir of work and school and the scurry of life in the city. Eric sent roses. Chelly smiled at the card then tossed it, mumbling to Midge about needing to call him. That night, he called her.

"Chelly?" He sounded upset.

"Hi."

"How are you?"

"Good, Eric. And you?"

"Okay, I guess. Business is okay. Mom's got a cold. Other than that, everything's the same in Blackjack." He sounded tense. This wasn't just a social call. Something was up but she wouldn't ask. He'd get to the point in time. There was more small talk before he paused. Here it came. "Chel, have you actually met the cowboy face-to-face?"

What? How could Eric possibly know about her cowboy? She hadn't spoken to anyone but Midge about the man who starred in her dreams nightly. Surely Midge hadn't carried tales. "Who?"

"What'd you call him?"

"Cowboy. It's what everyone calls him. He wears boots and cowboy clothes. It's one of those corn ball image things. Dad says the guy's a showboat, has this huge inflated opinion of himself."

Chelly set her jaw, glad Eric couldn't see her. "Eric, the only contact I have with Mister Manning is by e-mail."

"He's got a big reputation, Chel, but Dad says he built it by walking all over little people, people who worked all their lives growing their businesses. Dad hates him, says he's a mean bastard and if you had any sense, you wouldn't be working for the S.O.B."

Chelly scarcely heard. Manning wasn't the only man in Tennyson who wore cowboy boots. A lot of young, trendy guys wore them too.

She only half listened to Eric's repeat of his dad's complaints. She might not know her boss by sight, but she knew his character. Eric's dad was way off base, but there was no use arguing. Eric thought his dad infallible. In Chelly's eyes, however, D.R. Manning was far more than an image. Anyone familiar with his track record knew it. As usual, the opinionated Harmon Chastain didn't know what he was talking about.

"Eric?" She interrupted his running diatribe, something she would never have done in the past. "Why all the yammering about Manning?"

"He's turned his evil eye on Chastains. Chelly, the man wants to take us over. He's out to ruin us."

Chapter Seven

Most windows in the fourteen-story Sheppard Building stared into the frozen February night like great onyx eyes by the time Chelly scurried through the lighted entry to the bank of silent elevators that blustery Thursday.

She slipped her key card into the slot, calling an elevator. The bell startled her, bonging eerily in the tomblike quiet as the doors slid open. Before stepping inside, Chelly patted the bun knotted tightly on the back of her head and slipped on her glasses. She wore tights and an oversized sweater that bagged nearly to her knees and concealed all her feminine attributes.

Her mind was on Eric. After Valentine's Day, he had called a dozen times. Chelly figured his dad was behind the flurry. Having forgiven Eric, she was enjoying herself too much to let him back into her life to burst her bubble… yet.

His dad was understandably concerned about Chastains being taken over. She didn't know what she could do about it. She didn't imagine she could influence Manning and had no idea how much sway he had over the client interested in Chastains. She had e-mailed her boss asking about the rumored takeover but, although they communicated several times a day, Manning hadn't provided any information about Chastains.

She stepped quickly into the elevator, pushed the "door close" button, slid her key card in the floor selector slot—required after hours—then looked up and fluttered her fingers in the general direction of the surveillance camera high in the corner. Mr. Dunn probably wasn't at his station in the basement security room. If he were there, she'd bet he was sleeping.

It was only seven-fifteen but the pale wintry sun had been down for hours. She had cut her con law class at the break.

She heard voices and the sounds of janitors sloshing mops on the marble entrance as the car raced by the eighth floor. The noise reminded her B.J. and

Doreen Rose would be on the eleventh floor, cleaning, keeping her company until ten or so.

Chelly didn't mind slipping back into dowdy character and returning to the office after hours when the janitors were there. She made it a point to leave before they left, or with them. She got a little spooked in the office alone at night, but she relished the quiet. She needed the extra, uninterrupted time. Besides, he needed her there.

She smiled to herself thinking of Manning, the old man she wouldn't recognize if he stepped into the elevator beside her.

Grudgingly, without having seen him or heard his voice, she had developed high regard for her boss. Certainly, she was not afraid of him, as coworkers hinted she should be.

The muted bell bonged and the elevator doors yawned exposing the DMD lobby, its newly bathed terrazzo entrance mute evidence of the Roses' reassuring proximity.

"Hellooo." She didn't want to startle them. She smelled furniture oil and heard the hum of a vacuum down a hallway to her left.

She noticed with pride the ornate brass nameplate marking the east hallway. "D.R. Manning."

Old Man Diet, as people referred to the original practitioner, John Diet, had been retired for ten years but his name still marked the north hallway. They said he'd been a great lawyer, nothing like Leonard who apparently inherited his mental prowess from his mother's side of the family, along with his weak chin. Leonard had asked her out four times.

Although he was engaging, Leonard was not blessed with gifts that appealed to Chelly. Besides, he was much too old for her. He probably thought of her as a daughter. For what he lacked in manly charms, Leonard made up for it with family money. Old money, which was not a consideration in Chelly's mind.

Wayne Harned's name led the list posted on the west hallway. Chelly liked Harned, the onsite *shop* manager, overseeing the eighteen or twenty associates—men and women lawyers occupying the cubbyhole offices—the people who, with paralegals, secretaries and clerks, actually cranked out the firm's grunge work.

Chelly tiptoed across damp terrazzo to carpeting then darted by the receptionist's desk and down the hallway to her office.

Her office? She smirked. During the day, East, the Manning corridor, like the other three, buzzed with telephones and young lawyers stuffed into their respective cubicles. Pacing clients mewled in well-manicured reception room pens waiting for their fifteen minutes allotted with the firm's two available named partners—Leonard Diet and Wayne Harned.

Nights, however, Mr. Manning's suite was hers. She alone had the keys, except, of course, for B.J. and Doreen and, she supposed, Mr. Manning himself.

Chelly told her parents that she hadn't met Manning, who was habitually away, schmoozing the corporate clients, making international *house calls*. Her mother disapproved of Manning, actually of any person or interest that kept Chelly away from her family, Blackjack, and the repentant Eric.

But Manning was Chelly's hero, the reason she came back evenings, to keep pace with his more and more difficult demands.

It wasn't fair to call them demands, she chided, as she walked quickly down the hallway past the conference room, the series of darkened cubicles and on to his suite. Manning had told her to ask for help if she needed it. He also said he would hold her personally accountable for flawless accuracy in the work assigned her, regardless of who did it.

He had become even more personable in their e-mail correspondence, and she liked their occasionally pithy exchanges.

"When is your birthday?" he wrote one afternoon while waiting a response from one of his harried corporate victims.

She was feeling flippant, her birthday having just past. *"Are you trying to ascertain my Zodiac sign or are we talking gifts?"*

"An idle question between friends."

"Friends at a singles bar or with my parents?"

"Never mind." When she did not reply, he tried again. *"Mine is March 15."*

"As in Beware the Ides of?"

"Correct."

She already had that information penciled in the important dates part of her address book. *"I'll try to remember."*

"Ms. Bennett, must I call Bixler for the information and set tongues wagging, or do I get an answer from you?"

"January twenty-second."

He didn't respond.

"So?"

"Mark that on my calendar and send me a photograph of you."

"An eight-by-ten or a mug shot?"

"Billfold size, preferably with your mouth closed."

She snickered after he signed off. Obviously, she'd been too impertinent. She might be getting overconfident. Landing on her feet after the debacle with Eric had made her brash. But in that instance, she had not only survived, she had thrived. And she would again, with or without Eric, or D.R. Manning, or any other man.

She daydreamed that after she completed law school, Wayne Harned would hire her as an associate. When Manning was curt with her, she imagined she would snub DMD for another firm, be a huge success and come back to thumb her nose at them. Not at Harned or at Anne, of course, but at Manning, for not appreciating her.

The direction of her daydreams was determined by Manning himself. Sometimes she hated his arrogant, self-absorbed soul for requiring so much, at the same time all but worshiping his acumen.

His favor had her proceeding handily up the corporate ladder, despite Anne's frequent reminders that others had soared only to plunge after one glitch—an oversight or a moment of self importance. Chelly wasn't going to suffer any setbacks, which was exactly why she was at the office tonight. She had to compile the Doff material for a merger Manning was orchestrating.

Vanessa Doff, a stunningly gorgeous heiress in her early forties, left daily messages for Manning. Chelly had been jealous at first, then comforted herself that she was in closer contact with him than the vivacious Vanessa. But the other woman was persistent and was obviously accustomed to having her own way.

Chelly riffled the file box that she had placed on Manning's desk before leaving at five. As she sorted busy work, which allowed her mind to wander, she pondered. Was Harmon Chastain right? Was Manning an evil man profiting from the life's work of others?

Even his most cynical opponents admitted Manning's genius and admired his brilliant strategies. He was particularly imaginative when a corporation targeted for takeover put up a fight. The man did love a good scrap. She had seen him in action and felt certain that if Manning had decided to take Chastains, Harmon Chastain didn't have a prayer.

But she would watch for the paperwork and do what she could when the time came.

She hadn't concerned herself with the morality of the takeovers until Eric brought it up. She followed orders, prepared and filed documents with the courts, the secretary of state, the securities and exchange commission, etc.

She did research, copied, collated and prepared pleadings, as she was doing tonight on the Doff file that she would send to Houston with the last courier Saturday.

Her mind drifted back to the business at hand. If she could finish Doff tonight, she would have a free Friday evening. She might take in a movie or something.

A loud thump in the hallway startled her.

.B.J. and Doreen were not usually clumsy or loud. There was another thud as something hit the outside wall. Chelly scurried into the suite's conference/reception room.

Tom Bixler reeled, staggering. She looked him over, wondering if he were injured. His eyes danced in their orbs and he flashed her a silly grin before he took a step forward, then hesitated, teetering. She sprang, grabbed his arm then blinked at the potent smell of bourbon.

Leering at her hands on his arm, Bixler's grin broadened. "Caught-cha." He slurred the words.

Chelly guided him to a chair and summarily shoved him backwards into it. Gazing drunkenly at her bust, he said, "How'd you know I'd be here?"

She snorted, a half laugh. "Don't be silly."

His face grew serious and his head wobbled. "You got wonderful shiny hair. Let me ast you somethin'."

"Okay."

"How d'ya keep your butt so tight, all the sittin' you do?"

Chelly shrank from him in disgust. The look on her face must have prompted the renewed grin. "Ahhh, I embarrassed you, right? Maybe you wouldn't be so self conscious if you got the surgery. The company's got a good health dealy. It'd probably pay for breast re-duck-shun, if you wanna cut down on the attention you get around here. Cut down. Get it?"

She tried to control her facial expression but obviously failed as Bixler hid his mouth behind his hands, spewing raucous laughter and inadvertently spraying moisture out his nose.

"I'd never tell you to do it. No, siree, not trim them melons of yours. No way." He wiped his dampened hands on the legs of his trousers. "No, ma'am.

Hooters can be a' asset to a gal. Help her get ahead." He snickered again, enjoying his own little pun. "You already know that, seeing as how you're doin' so good kissin' Manning's butt the way you do. I say his ain't the only ass you oughta be smoochin', doll."

Her temper spiked. "Bixler, what are you doing here drunk?"

"I'm a married man." He bowed his head. "Don't ever let anyone tell you third time's a charm. I can promise you here and now, they lie."

"You've been married three times?"

"Yep. Larry, Curly, and Moe. Dumb-an-Dumber, a whore, and a bitch. But findin' you waitin' here for me, late at night, well, you might say things are looking up. 'Course I figured you'd be here using them keys I gave you, snoopin', sniffin' out sum'um juicy, sum'um to help a big-busted gal move up in the world o' commerce. You'll need sum'um t'give you a' edge when the old man gives you the heave-ho."

"Bixler, you are a textbook example of sexual harassment in the work place." Chelly adjusted her eyeglasses and pursed her mouth, but Bixler offered another simpering smile.

"I'm gonna' tell ever' one that you met me up here t'night." His bushy eyebrows moved up and down over the wire-rimmed glasses and he picked a piece of what she hoped was lint from his overgrown mustache as he struggled to hoist his portly body to its feet. Arms open, he launched toward her.

Chelly dodged and considered the situation. Bixler obviously wasn't concerned with B.J. or Doreen working just down the hall. He probably could fire them. Suddenly she had a chilling thought. Bixler had told her several times he had full authority to fire her. He had reminded her again when he gave her the keys.

Retreating, she backed into Manning's private office. Bixler lurched, then pulled up short as Chelly skirted the desk, keeping the broad table between them.

He grinned again at her chest. Moisture glistened in the corners of his mouth. "People ignore a little office hanky panky, 'long as no one complains."

"I'll complain."

"And I'll fire you. And then we'll do that little whistle-blower two-step I do so well until you cave. Besides, you've got no corroboration?" He slurred the word. "You have to have a' disinterested witness. You can't get anywhere with a claim like that without corroboration. And me," he waved an arm,

"I've got this whole pack a' lawyers that'll work for me, free. You can't beat 'em."

It appeared Bixler had been that route before. He continued to leer. "Men talk, Chelly. We know you're a dyke, got no use for what a man's got to offer. You keep all covered up, tryin' to make yourself sexless, secretly wishin' you was a man. I heard it 'as 'cause a man dumped you." His voice dropped to a coaxing tone. "A real man could make it up to you. Make things right for you."

Chelly narrowed her eyes, watching him. "Bixler, what would anyone needing a *real man* do with a cretin like you?"

Sidling around the corner of the desk, Bixler exaggerated the sway of his hips as he slithered toward her. "Bennett, I'm about to show you a wonnerful use for a female's mouth as big as yours."

She shivered at the implication. After two more turns around the desk, she grabbed her purse, leaped toward the door and darted out, glaring back at Bixler, fairly daring him to chase or stop her.

She would never be that lonely, she consoled herself on the drive home. Even disguised, she attracted jerks like Tom Bixler. There were an abundance of leches like him. Where were the ones Bixler called the real men?

She hoped he wouldn't remember their encounter, wouldn't make after-hours visits to the office a habit. Now she'd blown her Thursday night. She would have to get Manning's project out Friday, probably work late into Friday night.

Of course, she didn't really have anything else to do—no life of her own. She could have a personal life. Go out with one of the guys in the office who asked, occasionally. One call and Eric would come running, of course. His dad would see to it.

She grimaced. In spite of Bixler's ranting, she wasn't desperate enough to go out with any of the guys in the office or call Eric. Not yet.

Why not? she puzzled.

The trouble was, she had trusted Eric. Trusting a man—any man—was a mistake she was not likely to make again. Yet, she didn't want to live her entire life alone.

Maybe Eric had learned his lesson.

Somehow she didn't think so. He didn't sound contrite or as if he thought he'd done anything wrong. Still, she considered him her safety net; there if she lost her footing on the high wire.

In the city, women outnumbered men. Chelly told her mother on the phone, she had tried to meet someone nice. She had hoped to distract her mother from Eric.

Chelly had gone to church, jogged in the park, had even visited a singles bar with Midge.

"Mom, the kind of man I'm looking for wasn't any of those places. Maybe there is no such animal."

"You'll find him, sweetheart," her mother assured her long distance. "And if you don't... well, Eric is awfully eager to get back together. But darling... "

"What is it, Mom?"

"Well, we have all hoped that since you didn't return his grandmother's ring, you might be planning to reconcile."

"What? What do you mean? I returned the ring—the night he dumped me. Who said I didn't?"

Her mother was quiet a long moment. "Doris did. Eric hasn't mentioned it and they just assumed you still had it."

"He put it in his pants pocket that night, Mom."

"Maybe he was hoping things would work out and he could give it back to you on the q.t., without having to involve his parents."

Chelly hummed, a sound she hoped her mother would interpret as agreement. Odd that Eric hadn't told them. His family had been terribly interested in that ring and its safety. She hadn't known it might be missing. She shrugged. The heirloom wasn't her concern. Still, she didn't want to be blamed for losing it. And it would be like Eric to dodge the responsibility. She hoped he hadn't given it to Rebecca.

She sighed. As a life mate, Eric probably was a dismal choice. Of course, there were always other types like Leonard Diet. She cringed. It was hard to imagine she'd saved herself for twenty-five years for Leonard. She examined the array of choices: Eric or Leonard... or Bixler's fourth. Ugh!

Shortly after lunch Friday, a thunderstorm raked the city, leaving the central business district without electricity. A decidedly holiday spirit assailed people abandoning DMD early, rejoicing in their good luck at getting a Friday afternoon jump on the weekend. The stairways echoed with enthusiastic evacuees, laughing, cracking jokes.

Chelly was the glaring exception.

Chelly had asked several times about Chastains. He had avoided a response but he was going to have to tell her something soon. Her concern for the floundering little company annoyed him. A woman like Chelly should not waste herself on a pampered fool like Eric Chastain. The dolt was not worthy of her. She was smart, ingenious, an accomplished companion for a mature man, not some wastrel. Her continuing devotion to Chastain didn't make sense.

It had been his experience, however, that love often defied reason, not that he knew from personal experience. He had never loved a woman. Possibly never would. His defenses had been established early.

Adopted and reared by an older couple, both alcoholics, he had learned to hide his emotions. As he grew to manhood, he vowed never to make himself vulnerable to anyone. He had successfully thwarted all comers... until now.

Chelly was different, unknowingly wheedling her way into his thoughts, his emotions, his heart. He could not seem to hold her at bay. She sauntered through his mind unexpectedly, prodding his imagination, stimulating his body, fascinating him. Against his will, a bond had formed between them. He needed to confront this... this woman/child... face to face. Soon.

He messaged her before he contacted the pilot. Harned had mentioned the power outage in town. He used that, assigned her more work, enough to assure she'd be in the office on Sunday. He would be there too, with a plan to squelch his blossoming infatuation.

He would arrive in town late Saturday. Staring at himself in the mirror, he winced. "D.R.'s going courting." It was a cruelty joke with which he chided himself. The confusing part was, while he was in Tennyson figuring out a strategy for purging Chelly from his mind, he also planned to destroy any residual feelings she had for Eric Chastain. Strange. He didn't usually work at cross purposes.

Frantic to get to the office on Saturday morning, Chelly barely slept Friday night. She would have to cut the oil and gas lecture entirely on Saturday.

Relieved to find power fully restored by the time she got onto the elevator at five a.m., her heart palpitated. She had to get the Doff material out.

She handed the box to the courier at four that afternoon only to find her e-mail included a terse new message. Manning wanted the Vance file shipped to arrive at the wholesale house in Atlanta by closing time Monday. To get it located, sorted, copied and faxed in time, she'd have to work Sunday, probably most of the day. She slumped into a chair. She had no choice. She'd have to be back there Sunday.

Chapter Eight

Sunday morning Chelly did the usual number on her hair, twisting and pinning it severely to the back of her head, grabbed her glasses and dashed out to seven-thirty mass, then on to the office.

The parking garage was closed. A small, black Porsche in front of the Sheppard Building was the only vehicle parked on the street. She pulled in behind. A late night reveler had probably abandoned it there on Saturday night. She frowned. The owner was some gambler to risk those high-dollar wheels on a downtown street overnight.

Because B.J. and Doreen would not be there on Sunday, Chelly made a mental note to finish and get out of the building before sundown. It was nearly eight-fifty. She had at least eight hours.

The DMD lobby smelled stale and was ominously silent as Chelly stepped from the elevator. She started down Hallway East but stopped. The door to Manning's suite stood ajar. She hesitated. It wasn't like the Roses to leave things out of place or doors that should be locked, standing open.

Stealthily she slipped down the corridor and peeked into the suite. A lamp burned on the sofa table in the conference area. She stood puzzling. There was no light in Manning's private office beyond.

Retracing her steps, Chelly heard a noise and cut across the lobby to Corridor North. "Hellooo." No answer. She called louder. "Yoo-hoo." Still, nothing.

A copier hummed in the supply room. Who was here? On Sunday? Some ambitious flunky maybe. She thought it unlikely a burglar would be making copies. Chelly continued walking, mincing her steps.

Could it be Bixler? She hesitated, then set her jaw. She had work to do. She wasn't going to let that jerk run her off. Not this time. She swelled to her full height, unbuttoned her coat, and realized she was comically dressed for intimidating, in tennis shoes and sweats—the white birthday Polo's her mom had sent for lounging in the drafty apartment on wintry evenings.

She stepped into an open cubicle, picked up a stapler and bounced it in her hand, testing its weight, getting a good grip. Prepared to brace Bixler, she flew around the doorjamb to the copy room, then froze.

There was something vaguely familiar about the stranger. Long, lean, muscular, mid thirties with chestnut colored hair. A gray T-shirt outlined his marvelous shoulders and chest. Faded blue jeans hugged narrow hips, muscular thighs and prominent calves. His worn boots looked like ostrich, probably expensive when they were new.

He was undoubtedly the best looking man she'd ever seen, except maybe for… Her eyes shot back to the boots. This man was not the exception. He was the rule. The cowboy. Her cowboy. The one who plundered her dreams. He was back. Finally.

On a Sunday?

His surprised expression mirrored hers for only a moment before it changed to a triumphant grin. Eying the stapler clutched tightly in her hand, his grin broadened.

Chelly's temper flared. That smirk negated his good looks. There was too much arrogance in his flagrant stare and she suddenly didn't want to give him the satisfaction of returning his smile; wanted, instead, to deflate the pomposity in his gaze.

"How did you get in here? Are you a courier? Who let you in? Who are you?" She expected him to say something about giving him a chance to explain, but he surprised her.

"Bennett? You are Chelly Bennett, right?" The rich tone soothed her in spite of the know-it-all grin.

Her breath turned hot in her throat. "And you are?"

"Don Richards."

Chelly pursed her mouth and folded her arms in front of her, stapler and all. "And?"

He nodded as his startling emerald eyes, enhanced by dark brows and lashes, impudently swept from her face to her toes and back as if verifying her height. "I'm here to pick up some papers for Manning."

His forthright inspection concluded, his eyes locked with hers. He lost the smile, obviously with some effort. "Mr. Rose gave me a key card. He said no one would be here, unless maybe you showed up."

She studied him, thinking frantically, trying to size him up. He knew the janitor's name, Mr. Rose. That gave him some credibility.

"Mr. Rose just handed you his key card and let you come in here without someone from security?"

The stranger's eyes narrowed and his generous lips broadened to a grim line. She had the impression he was attempting either to conceal annoyance or hide a smile. He nodded crisply. "That's right."

She stepped to the telephone on the supply room wall. "You won't mind if I call him then."

"He and Doreen went to K-Mart. You'll have to page him there. It's the one on Lakewood." He turned his attention back to the copier.

The guy sounded like he was for real. He looked—well—impressive; his green eyes, the broad shoulders and catlike grace as he moved, gathering and stacking the collated forms. Their conversation had not interrupted the steady flow of paper from the machine.

Chelly felt herself mellowing, at least enough to put the stapler on the work table, before a glance at the pages he was copying set her on edge again.

She snatched up a piece of the copied material. "The theory sheets in Muldrow? I don't think so. That's very sensitive stuff."

Again the guy seemed to be struggling not to smile, his look emphasizing the difference in their heights. He towered over her. "Look, Bennett, I'm here to get information out of this file. If you're uncomfortable about it, call Manning."

It sounded plausible. "If Mr. Manning wanted this material, why didn't he ask me to get it for him?" She had him there.

"I don't question his orders, sweetheart, I just do what he says. If you want to know why he went around you on this, you'll have to ask him."

His words were curt but his eyes had narrowed and grown sultry, shimmering with an intimacy that made her want to retreat. He was throwing her off balance. What was it, this peculiar effect he had on her?

Drawing a deep breath, Chelly made a decision and let her purse strap slide down her arm signaling a truce. "Okay. Do you need help?"

He flashed a grin. "You help by just being here."

She was annoyed before she thought about it. "I know what you mean. I get spooked up here by myself, too." She slipped off her coat and lapped it over her arm.

He removed a pile of finished copies and started a new stack of originals before he looked at her again. "You come up here by yourself a lot, do you?"

"I'm a workaholic and, like you, I work for one. The office here is my primary residence."

Still smiling, he pivoted all the way around to face her squarely. His long face and chiseled features fairly drew her to him. She couldn't seem to help being aware of his marvelous chest beneath the T-shirt, the two square plates of pectoral muscles swelling and falling with each breath. Obviously the guy worked out.

His mouth relaxed and he ran his tongue across his lower lip, a suggestive gesture, as he studied her soberly. "And you feel safer when someone else is around?"

She started to answer affirmatively, thought of Bixler and clouded up. "Mostly."

"Do you feel comfortable now? With me?" He spoke the words so softly Chelly wasn't sure she'd heard him correctly. "I'm a stranger. Didn't your mamma tell you little girls shouldn't talk to strangers?" His green eyes stared into hers a moment before he smiled, a gentle glow obviously intended to allay her concern. He was kidding her.

She pursed her lips again. "I'll be glad to help you, if you need a hand, otherwise, I have work to do."

He allowed a pregnant pause as he considered ways she might help. He needed her, all right, but not for collating. He hoped she didn't notice the growing physical evidence of that need. But she wouldn't. She didn't know to look. His teasing grin faded. "Go. Do whatever you've got to do. I'll be a while."

Chelly stood transfixed, gazing into his eyes. Black flecks invaded the green, which turned them the color of the deep forest. She murmured, "Right," but she remained where she stood, staring.

Slowly his insolent look was replaced by a predatory expression, which eased his broad mouth and arched his eyebrows. What was he thinking? Was he reading imagined meaning into her gape? And she was gaping. How rude.

Confused, Chelly pivoted and walked away. She moved briskly down the hall, her steps accelerating to a trot, then to a dead run. She shot into Mr. Manning's private suite, slammed the heavy mahogany door behind her, and flipped the privacy latch.

She felt foolish. Couldn't seem to catch her breath. Her legs were limp, her knee joints loose. Her hands felt icy, her face hot. She collapsed into a leather client's chair in the reception/conference room.

She had thought Tom Bixler was a threat. Next to this guy, Bixler was a pussycat.

She'd seen this man only twice before—here and at Les Miserables—and he'd had the same breathless effect on her both times. Who was he? What did he do? He was making copies for Manning. Of course, he was probably a flunky, a courier maybe, part of Manning's traveling entourage. That's why Monica had allowed him to pass unchallenged that first day.

Chelly leaned back in the chair to think of him, his broad chest and muscular arms, squared shoulders and narrow hips. The know-it-all grin.

And those eyes.

No wonder she hadn't recognized him immediately. When she had seen him close-up before, he was wearing sunglasses. She hadn't gotten close enough to him at the theater to see his remarkable eyes. Not at all the dark brown eyes, she had assumed. No, these eyes were an electric, hypnotic green. Confounding. His eyes were probably what made her so giddy.

She hugged herself. "It's awfully nice to have you back, Cowboy."

She might have sworn off men, but this spectacular specimen could make a girl forget all prior promises.

Chapter Nine

Cautiously Chelly opened the door, peered down the hall and listened. Running on tiptoe, she made two trips from Manning's suite to the file room to get both boxes of Vance.

She had a hard time staying focused on the project. It was sheer luck that she noticed an essential receipt missing. She scoured both boxes and found it finally, misfiled in correspondence.

An estate tax release was omitted from the transcript of probate proceedings for an inconsequential heir. She made a note to contact the court clerk in the morning, have them fax the release to Manning separately.

If this Don person were delivering papers to Manning, maybe she could send the Vance material with him. Where was he going? Where was the elusive Mr. Manning today? Maybe she could ask Don.

And what about the great man? This guy probably knew Manning personally. She wasn't sure she wanted a stranger's impressions of her boss, of the paragon she had created in her mind. Certainly she didn't want anyone to say unflattering things or provide snippets of damaging gossip about him.

One of Chelly's frequent daydreams took over as she made and collated the copies for Vance. It was her favorite mental exercise, daydreaming about Manning.

Sometimes she imagined him a morose, angry man whose hearing and eyesight were failing, embittered, tirelessly striving to prove himself. In that scenario, he only pretended to be tough. She was his right hand, cheering him in his dotage, boosting his sagging morale.

She had modified that image after he revealed the rakish sense of humor and showed himself to be sensitive to her needs, in spite of his cynical facade.

Don could probably tell her about the real Manning. If they had another chance to speak, she would ask the green-eyed gofer.

Just after noon, she heard the elevator bell and swallowed her disappointment. He had left without telling her good-bye. He had probably forgotten she was there.

Four hours and twenty minutes after she arrived at the office, Chelly wrapped packing tape over the top of the shipping box containing the Vance files.

Her stomach growled. She patted it and realized she hadn't eaten all day. Working as she had, however, doggedly, without a break and with no interruptions, the chore had taken less time than she had anticipated.

She felt vaguely depressed and remembered why. The cowboy had left.

What difference did it make? Obviously, none to him. What could a woman expect from a man? Hadn't she learned anything from her experience with Eric?

Still, she had hinted to Don that she was sometimes frightened in the office alone, a confidence she'd shared with no one else.

"Tough darts, farmer," she said, her voice loud in the silence. She didn't know if the remark referred to his loss or hers.

She turned off the copier in Manning's office and saw no need to check to see if the cowboy were still on the premises. She would drop Vance by the courier's box downstairs and call to leave a pickup message.

She opened the door, slipped on her coat and her purse shoulder strap, snapped off the table lamp in the reception/conference room, picked up the file box and turned to find the cowboy languidly leaning on the doorjamb, arms folded over his chest, one foot crossed over the other. A worn leather bomber jacket covered the T-shirt. His catlike eyes tracked her as if she were an unsuspecting mouse. A smirk twitched the corners of his mouth. "Ready?"

Startled and unexpectedly pleased, she cleared her throat, then looked down at the box occupying both her hands. "Yes."

She stepped forward to find him immediately blocking her way. She retreated a step as he reached for the box. "I'll take it."

"No." She clamped her fingers firmly in the cutout hand holds at either end of the box. "You have materials of your own."

"Already took them down. I've been waiting for you. I've been watching you on the monitor." She glanced at the security camera overhead, then back at him. The slow, taunting grin again took his face, creasing the long dimple-like slits on either side. He was marvelous looking. Embarrassed, thinking of the cameras, she tried to remember her movements as she worked alone.

"I particularly enjoyed the toe-dance sprints back and forth to the file room."

She clamped her lips just in time to keep her embarrassed laughter from bursting into the room. Despite her effort to thwart it, she felt a hard blush creep from the neckline of her sweatshirt up to splash heat over her cheeks.

Don grinned knowingly but he wasn't through yet. "You talk to yourself. Did you know?"

"I was probably singing."

He raised his exquisite eyebrows and rumbled with a rolling laugh. "I read lips some. 'Tough darts, farmer?'"

She winced.

"Not very musical." He gave her a playful frown. "You gave yourself some pretty harsh advice a time or two."

What had she said? Worse, what had he interpreted?

He stepped close and took the carton. "Get the doors."

She yielded the file box and motioned for him to move ahead of her while she secured the door to Manning's suite and snapped the outer lights. She trotted to catch up.

The elevator was already there. Don's foot propped the doors open. Chelly was thankful for no delay as they rode down, but she fidgeted under his steady gaze. She couldn't bear to look into those prying eyes for more than seconds at a time, eyes which had become azure, the color of the sea.

She focused instead on his hands, big, capable hands, experienced, she supposed, with women. She scolded herself for that kind of thinking. She was safe enough for the moment. The hands she had described to Midge were occupied. Dreading the time when they were not, she glanced at his face. He regarded her playfully, as if he were reading her thoughts. Heat shimmered up again in waves from her shirt collar.

"Lose the glasses."

The command startled her. "What?"

"I assume you wear them to fend off men, but those phony specs are not going to save you from me."

She again noticed the teasing in his voice and her expression apparently prompted more explanation.

"I stood behind you in the elevator that day. I looked through the lenses. Clear glass. I saw how you dressed. It was obvious you were hiding something. Why, I asked myself, would an attractive young woman go to so much trouble to look so bad?" He gave her a predatory grin. "Instead of putting me off, you intrigued me. Why the pretense?"

She flexed her jaw. When she spoke, it was like a teacher correcting a recalcitrant child. "I was here to apply for a job. I wanted to be hired for my abilities, not my looks. Also, I didn't want a bunch of guys hitting on me." She shot him an accusing glare.

"A lot of men come on with you, do they?"

"No."

He snorted a derisive laugh. "Oh, I think probably they do. I saw through the disguise. I imagine other guys do too, if they bother to look."

Chelly set her mouth primly. "Congratulations." Her smirk and haughty attitude seemed to squelch him, winning her a reprieve from his teasing, at least for the moment.

Exiting the elevator, they strode through the concourse of the silent Sheppard Building without a word. She opened both doors, which expelled them into the sunny chill of mid afternoon. There was little traffic on the downtown city streets.

"Car keys are in my pants pocket—right front." He stopped beside the Porsche that she had noticed earlier. Both his hands were occupied with the box. He flashed her a cocky grin that flustered her. Reach into his pants pocket? Not in this lifetime.

Her shoulder purse swung easily as she pushed it behind her and stepped toward him. "Give me the box."

"Nah, it's too heavy. Doors are your job."

He was enjoying this a little too much. "Put the files down, smart aleck. Get the keys yourself."

"Chelly?" His voice was low, seductive. She returned his frank look. "Don't be afraid of me. The boss has me on a tight leash. You're special, you know, a regular V-I-P at D-M-D." He laughed at his own rhyme.

Her smile wavered. "What?"

"Manning's crazy about you."

"No." He was teasing her again. "Mr. Manning is a businessman. To him I'm a machine at the other end of his computer. He types in orders. I carry them out."

"The man may be falling in love, Chelly. First time, the way I hear it."

"Not with me."

He nodded slowly as she stared.

Finally, she huffed, dismissing him. "Well, if that's true, Mr. Manning's even more eccentric than people say."

Don's knowing grin broadened. "Everyone knows. They talk about it— people who travel with him, his friends here in the shop, everyone. Surely someone's said something about it to you. It's the talk of the industry."

She tried to mimic his playful grin. "No, strangely enough, no one's said a word."

Don sobered. "I know him, Chelly. Maybe it's true."

She knew he was putting her on, making her the brunt of some acerbic joke. "Mr. Manning is too worldly and entirely too mature to think that way. It would be completely out of character."

Don leaned his backside against the car and laughed up at the wintry sky before the green eyes settled again on her face. His gaze was surprisingly tender. "You've never even met the man, Chelly. What could you possibly know about his character? You've created an image but, lady, if you think our boss is a saint, you're working for a figment of your imagination."

Chelly set her face in a defiant glower. "I happen to know Mr. Manning quite well."

"Oh, yeah? Describe him. I'll tell you how close you are."

He was baiting her but she had been looking for a way to see how accurate her image of Manning was. Maybe this was that opportunity.

Concentrating on her impressions, Chelly took the keys Don fished out of his pocket and opened the trunk. He stepped close enough for his seductive scent to wrap around her. Her breath caught and for a moment she lost her train of thought. She chided herself for the lapse. She needed to get a handle on these peculiar roller-coaster emotions. Needed to focus.

"First," she said, "he's fastidious, scrupulous, and terribly intuitive."

Listening with an amused smile, Don put the Vance box in a space he'd left for it beside the Muldrow files and closed the trunk as Chelly continued.

"He's a risk-taker, a high-stakes gambler, a daring negotiator." She flushed as she thought of Manning. "He presses an advantage, when he has one, but he hedges his bets by working hard, which often is the thing that gives him an edge. But all the while, he's unerringly fair."

Don beckoned her with his index finger and led her around to the passenger door of the Porsche without interrupting. She followed, continuing the description.

"I've studied his methods—old cases. Once, a long time ago, he was taking over this small, family-owned company for one of his gargantuan clients when the CEO of the target company died unexpectedly. Manning backed everybody off to give the family a chance to regroup."

Don opened the passenger door and motioned her inside. She looked at the leather seat and balked. "What do you think you're doing?"

"Taking you out to eat." He flashed the mischievous grin. "You're bound to be hungry. I know I am."

In spite of herself, she smiled ruefully. "Dutch?"

"Doesn't have to be." She hesitated and he shrugged. "Okay, we'll go Dutch."

She squatted onto the low seat and swung her long legs inside, securing her coat tail. He closed the door and trotted to the driver's side, slid in, started and revved the engine, and roared onto the boulevard. "You were describing our noble leader. It's very enlightening. Please continue."

Chelly frowned at her hands clasped in her lap. "He's a take-no-prisoners negotiator who plays hardball with the big boys and wins more than he loses." Her eyes leaped to his. "He's not devious. He forewarns his victims, lets them know he's coming. But he moves in like a saber-toothed tiger."

Don chuckled. "I'd say he's more alley cat. A tom."

Her eyes rounded and she stared out the window trying to dismiss thoughts the tomcat remark conjured in her mind.

"What's wrong?"

She tried to shrug off her disappointment. "I don't think of Mr. Manning as a regular person, you know, as a man with, well, with appetites." She felt reluctant to continue but Don's silence encouraged her. "Oh, I know he has women friends."

"What friends?"

"Vanessa the vamp, for one."

He grinned and she ducked her head. "Well, that's what I call her." Don started to say something but Chelly held up a hand and shook her head. "I really don't want details."

"What do you mean?"

"His women—like Vanessa—please don't describe them. I already know. They are stunning. Rich. Years younger than he is. Several obviously are interested in him, but Vanessa has the main track right now. Ladies call and send gifts to the office because they don't know where he is or how to reach him.

"Don't you see, that part of his life is none of my business. I don't know anything about older men like him, their ladies, or their lifestyles, or their tastes." She hesitated. "I know how aggressive he is in business. I figure he's the same way with women."

Don's face was thoughtful. "Are you wondering if he is sexually active? What's the matter? Can't you just say it?"

She frowned.

"He's a mature man, Chelly, with a mature man's predilections."

Was he apologizing for Manning?

"He has opportunities with attractive women."

She sat staring at her hands.

"Would you prefer I told you he was gay?"

She shot him a startled look.

He chuckled. "He's not." His laugh dwindled. "You were closer to right before. He's probably more tiger than tomcat. One thing's for sure, sweet innocent little girls like you... well, you shouldn't go waggling that sassy tush in his face."

She stiffened. "What the heck do you mean by that? I haven't done any waggling."

They rode in silence until Chelly mumbled, "You can probably tell, I try not to think of Manning as a flesh and blood person."

"So you imagine him too good to be true. What is this, hero worship?"

"Maybe." She thought a moment, then said archly, "Actually my relationship with Mr. Manning is none of your concern. Anyway, my original point was, you don't have to know a man's height and weight to know the man's character," she grimaced, "even if it turns out he has slept with lots of women."

"I believe you're jealous."

She didn't respond and ignored his subdued chuckle. Gazing at the road, Chelly's stare became a glower as she suddenly realized they were out of town. She looked back at the road. "Hey, where are we going?"

"I told you. To get something to eat."

"I thought you meant a burger. I'm not dressed well enough—and not carrying enough money—for any place fancy." She looked around, trying to determine their location. "Besides that, I have homework up to my eyeballs."

"Homework? What kind of homework?"

She continued scanning the scenery. She had made it a point to keep her law classes a secret. She had no idea why she had blurted that very private information to this guy. The only reason she could think of was because he was a stranger. Sometimes it was easier to confide in a stranger, someone a person didn't expect to see again. In addition to his great looks, there was something wonderfully trustworthy about this guy and she knew better than to trust her instincts for that. Still she said, "I'm a law student."

"Oh, yeah? How far along are you?"

"Second half of my second year." There was a prolonged silence, which she felt compelled to fill. "Eric, the guy I used to be engaged to, objected. He's in business with his dad. He didn't have to go to college to walk into a vice presidency. He resented my getting any degree at all, much less going for a jurist doctorate, which, I was afraid, was why I was doing it. Now I've decided it really is what I want. I love the law and I'm back at school."

"So how is Eric taking it?"

"When I went back to school last fall, he fell in love with someone else."

"His loss. What's this joker's name? Eric what?"

"Chastain."

"What kind of business is he in?"

"Hardware and plumbing supply."

"Hmm."

"Have you heard of Chastains?"

"Yes."

She stiffened. "Rumors?"

"Yeah."

She needed to pump him, find out what he knew. "Rumors about a takeover?"

His eyes narrowed and she guessed he wasn't going to answer. He smiled instead. "So are you and Eric Chastain quits, or what?"

Preoccupied, wondering how she could find out what he knew about the rumors, she mumbled, "I guess so."

"It sounds like you're not sure. Who broke it off?"

"He did." Chelly's thoughts reverted to the memory of Eric's stunning announcement Christmas night.

"You carrying a torch?"

She snorted a laugh. "No, but we've been friends all our lives. I still love him, of course, like a friend. He called me. Said he had made a mistake."

"I'll say he did." Don's sunny face looked like a squall had come through. "I guess you told him to stuff it."

"No. I told him I needed time. I said I'd call him."

"Naturally you can't go back to him. You know you'd never be able to trust him again."

How had he put his finger on the point so quickly? "Right. I know that."

"So, you want to make him crawl a little before you give him the final heave-ho?"

She flashed him an annoyed glance. "No. I don't think in terms of revenge."

"So, are you willing to give up Manning and maybe a law career, to patch it up? Is Eric-the-louse worth sacrificing everything else?"

This guy certainly seemed to have strong opinions about her personal business. "I wouldn't have to sacrifice anything. Practicing law is my dream, not his. I'll stay in school. It's what I want." She hesitated, wondering if that were true, if Harmon would let Eric allow her to continue her education if there should be a reconciliation. "After he dumped me, I came here—to get away from him and my parents. Everyone in Blackjack knew he had another girlfriend before I did. I didn't want to endure a lot of suffocating sympathy. Eric and I have lived next door to each other all our lives. Somewhere along the way his parents and mine decided it would be nice if we fell in love. They went from that to assuming we'd get married."

"Didn't anyone ask what you thought?"

"Not exactly. I thought Mom and Dad were crazy about him. It turns out, Dad was kind of putting up with him for my sake and I was planning to marry him for theirs."

"You mentioned his parents."

"Yes, well that's another little wrinkle. I'm really fond of his mother."

"How about his dad?"

She squirmed. What was making her bare her soul to this stranger? And why did he care? He was probably just making conversation. She shook her head.

Don laughed, a rippling sound from deep in his throat. "And you would be giving me the straight skinny about all this, of course?"

"Sure. Why not?"

He turned to regard her. "Chelly Bennett, I think I'm going to turn out to be your best friend."

Her laughter exploded unexpectedly. "What an ego. You are positively pompous, do you know that?" Her words sounded stern but she felt a peculiar joy as she saw the secretive smile slip back over his mouth. His profile, his hands on the wheel, everything about him spoke of strength and competence. He might be the most marvelous man she had ever met, entirely too sharp to be somebody's flunky, even Manning's.

He said, "The glasses?" He hadn't forgotten.

"Okay." She removed the horn rims and put them in the case in her purse. She had conceded a point. Now, it was his turn. "How long have you been Manning's gofer?"

The smile he turned on her was broad, revealing large, even, white teeth. His green eyes flashed. "Long enough. Why? What do you want to know about him?"

"Not about him. I just wondered if this was… well, is this the extent of your ambition? To be an errand boy?"

"I do considerably more than errands." His grin continued, but the emerald eyes narrowed, veiling something.

"You're more than his flunky?" She had a repulsive thought. A lot of handsome, sophisticated men experimented sexually these days and this guy was an Adonis. What did he mean, he did considerably more than errands?

Don grinned. "Are you questioning my sexual orientation?" He slowed the car and began checking out side roads.

What was he, a mind reader? His expression had turned almost sinister. "Let's find a private spot and I'll give you a live demonstration of my sexual preference."

Chelly smiled uncertainly. "Never mind. You don't have to prove anything to me. I'm no one." They drove on in silence until she risked a glance. "Are you making fun of me?"

"No, I'm not." He seemed suddenly serious. "Tell me about Chastains— the business."

The familiar warning bells rang inside her head. Still, maybe she could get a little information, if she primed the pump.

"It's a thriving supply business. Apparently they've heard the same rumors you have. They think someone's out to raid them."

"They think that, do they?"

"It's true, isn't it?"

"Maybe. Do you care?"

She raised and lowered her shoulders indicating indifference, then grimaced and nodded. "I don't want them to lose it."

"Because you're still in love with Eric?"

"No. I think it's mainly because I don't like his dad."

Don lightened his foot on the accelerator. "Does that make sense?"

"That business is practically Harmon Chastain's identity," she said. "If he lost it, he'd be a nonentity. Plus, he'd be humiliated. Eric humiliated me. It's pretty… awful. Besides, Eric doesn't have any other way to make a living."

"A takeover might make them rich."

"Not rich enough. Eric needs a lot of money coming in regularly."

Don stretched, relaxing back in the seat as he drove. "Okay."

"What do you mean?"

"I mean, okay, as in I understand."

"Is someone after them?"

"Someone was."

"But not anymore?"

"I'll check on it. Meanwhile, you've told me what you like about Manning. Now, tell me what you hate."

She recoiled at the question. "Nothing. There's nothing about Mr. Manning to hate. I admire and respect him." She regarded him seriously. "And I'm not kissing up hoping you'll replay this conversation for him."

She turned to look at the countryside, realizing the Porsche had gone a long way and she was with a man she scarcely knew. "I need to get home. Take me back, please."

"You're hungry. I'm hungry. I hate eating alone. I told you, we're going to get something to eat."

"What was wrong with Tennyson, with Dewey County? There are lots of burger joints there."

"I figure you needed a ride in the country. And I'm buying. No argument."

"Okay. But a burger's a burger. Why go so far?"

"It's too cold for a walk, and we've been cooped up all day. Enjoy the scenery. And the company, of course. What have you got to eat at home that beats a burger?"

Chelly gave him a pathetic little smile.

"What?" He prodded.

"Tuna. Tuna casserole. Tuna salad, tuna croquettes, tuna in mushroom soup over rice."

He laughed. "And the thought of beef is tempting?"

"Yes."

"I thought it was me... tempting you."

She thought of and discarded a crack about beefcake, didn't want to give him the satisfaction.

"You don't eat out alone?" he asked.

"I don't have enough confidence to eat out alone yet, even if I could afford to, but I get serious yearnings for beef."

"I recognize the symptoms," he said. "Overdosing on tuna. I've done that myself."

Smiling, Chelly gazed at him. He was definitely a charmer. At that same moment, he cut his eyes to her and smiled back, a warm, provocative smile.

She bet he left broken hearts strewn up and down roadsides everywhere he went. He was not only ruggedly handsome, he was fun, smart, stimulating and rich enough to buy her dinner. It didn't get much better than that. In fact, a free meal had never seemed so promising.

But what in the world was he doing here with her?

She lowered her eyes breaking the visual lock between them, then glanced up to find he was still looking at her and still grinning. "We're going to a place where they have the world's best chicken fried steak."

She pumped a fist triumphantly. "Yes!"

Laughing, he turned his eyes back to the road and Chelly became serious again. "Don, you like Manning, don't you?"

"Most of the time. He makes a ton of money. Even in places where he's not exactly admired, he gets respect."

"He isn't married, is he?"

"Why do you want to know?" He arched his eyebrows.

She knew he was teasing her again but she was serious. They stopped for a traffic light marking the intersection of two state highways. "He works and travels so much, I didn't think he had time for a family. But then, I hadn't thought about him chasing women, either, until you mentioned it. Is he married, or not?"

"No, he isn't."

"Has he been married?"

"No."

She lowered her voice. "Does he like women?"

Don laughed. "You're a little hung up on this sexual preference thing. Was Eric Chastain's new interest a guy?"

Chelly felt her mouth drop open in amazement. "No!" She thought it strange that he remembered Eric's name.

Chapter Ten

Don opened up the Porsche as they swept onto a four-lane highway. "Manning likes no-nonsense women. Flittering, fluttering females irritate him. He's a predator, which takes us back to your saber-toothed tiger comparison. That may be a more accurate description than I realized.

"He doesn't like females who give in too easily. He enjoys the hunt, likes his opponents tough in court and his women feisty in... " he shot her a startled look. "Well, feisty," he finished lamely. "Most of the women he knows," he gave her another hasty glance, "succumb too easily. Makes him suspicious. Makes him think it's his money they're after, even though most of them come from money." He hesitated, seemed to think a long minute before he continued, his words coming more slowly.

"Most of the ladies hot on his trail are debutantes. Trained huntresses. When he gives them the heave-ho, they don't take it well. What I'm saying is he's rich and eligible and he's got a history with some pretty savvy females."

Don paused and laughed lightly. "And then here you come, lollygagging right into his sights. You, Chelly Bennett, naive, unaffected, downtown in your jogging clothes on a Sunday afternoon, working on his projects, pleasing him yet willing to risk making him mad with your upstart suggestions."

He looked at her earnestly, as if startled by a new thought. "Manning gets impatient waiting for you to get online in the mornings. He had a fit when he found out where you lived, in that rundown... "

Chelly barked her interruption. "Wait just a darn minute. How does he know where I live?" She didn't give him time to answer and ignored his startled expression. "I live where I please. I like my apartment. I'm crazy about my roommate. I make my own choices now, whether they suit Eric Chastain or His Highness D.R. Manning or my parents or anyone else."

Don put the heels of both hands on the steering wheel and extended his fingers as if to ward off an attack from outside. "Okay. Okay." His green eyes danced as he pretended a startled look at her, before his rolling laugh made her noisy objection seem overblown and her self-effacing laughter chimed with his.

"Too defensive, huh?"

"Just a tad." He waited a minute, then continued as if giving the words extra thought. "Actually, Chelly, you make the man happier than I've ever seen him. You fascinate him. Intoxicate him. His whole staff is bewildered, watching you systematically disarm one of the most battle wary guys in the world."

Chelly screwed up her face and gazed out at the passing countryside. "You are so full of it. Is this some new game? If it is, it's way over my head." She brushed her hand over her hair, front to back, and shot him a questioning grin.

He chuckled. "I'm beginning to see why he likes you."

"He doesn't like *me*." She pivoted to face him. "He likes my work ethic. Business comes first with Manning. He appreciates that his business comes first with me too. It's not personal, believe me. We've never met, never spoken, even on the phone."

His eyes darkened to jade and his face became serious. "He watches you on the security tapes at the office, every damned day. You should see him. He hee-hawed after the Antenium deal when you went spinning and whooping down the hall. He laughed his head off the day you were kidding around with Anne Beed and the hat rack you said had asked you for a date."

She had told Anne she liked men who were tall, dark, and mysteriously silent.

"Manning likes watching you with that Tuggle person, too. Is she for real? Can any human being really be that ditsy?"

Chelly nodded. "It's a wonder she finds her way to work in the mornings."

Suddenly Don sobered. "There's a down side too. Manning saw a tape of you one night scrambling around his desk to dodge some unidentified bozo making a move on you there in his office after hours. That one burned his butt. Who was the guy?"

Bixler. Thursday night when he showed up drunk. She was tempted but didn't want to rat on a rat. Also she didn't want to jeopardize Don's job by drawing Bixler's attention to him. Bixler would probably fire a gofer like Don in a heartbeat.

Don's face darkened. "Manning didn't like you being cornered up there alone like that. He wants you safe, especially in his office. And you would have been, if you'd locked yourself in."

"He can't blame me."

"No, he doesn't. I didn't say it right." He lowered his voice. "Who was the guy?"

She stared at her hands folded in her lap. "I'd rather not say."

"Why not?"

"I don't want to get anyone in trouble." She looked at Don's profile. When he glanced from the highway to her, she tried to smile, but Don didn't intend to be put off.

"Manning hasn't got an I.D. on the guy yet, but when he finds out who it is, well, pity the poor slob." His eyes narrowed. "Who was it, Chelly?"

She bit her lips. "No one important."

"I'm going to find out."

"Okay."

Several moments ticked by as they drove in silence before Don spoke again. "He carries a picture of you in his billfold."

She spewed a laugh. "What?"

"Really. When people ask personal questions, Manning whips it out, tells them you're his Number One Girl."

Of course. It was the one he requested and she had sent. She eyed Don warily. "These people asking personal questions, are they huntresses?"

Don regarded her a moment, then arched one animated brow and began laughing quietly. "Yeah, some of them. And some are irascible old CEOs with debutante nieces." He looked at the road thoughtfully and laughed again. "And some of them are the fathers or brothers or male next-of-kin of huntresses. You are a very clever girl."

Grinning, she muttered to herself, shaking her head. "Our boss grows more inscrutable with every new thing I learn about him." She snorted another laugh. "Showing people my picture is ingenious, even if it's a little transparent. Using me to ward off unwanted entanglements. I wondered why he asked for my picture."

There was another lull in their conversation before Don again broke the silence. "You have an edge with Manning right now, Chelly. You could have anything you wanted."

"Don't be ridiculous."

"Press the advantage. Your favored-person standing might not last. You are in the driver's seat. You can squeeze him, one of the most influential men in the country. Right now, you say it, you've got it. If you don't believe me, ask him for something. Anything."

"I have everything I need." She ran the fingers of both hands together nervously. "He's already given me his office. I have my own keys, access to state-of-the-art equipment, the best law library I've ever seen." She stopped speaking abruptly.

Don glanced at her. "What?"

"Best of all, I have access to him, at least to the part of him that's most important to me."

"What do you mean?"

"The secrets of his success. He trusts me. He's made himself vulnerable to me, and to you, too. When I realized that, I knew it was no accident. He's too sharp not to know. His trusting me is the best gift of all. He gives me full access to his Achilles heel. And that alone commands my loyalty and my trust." She shot him a quick look. "That is, if I were going to trust any man. Let's just say he's restoring my faith—not in all men, of course. I never lost faith in my dad. Just regular joes, like Eric. Men who'll lie and betray you." She paused again. "Never mind." She puzzled a minute, thinking. "Maybe it's young men I don't trust." She gave Don a dark look. He remained silent, making no attempt to defend young men.

"Anyway," she continued ponderously, "I would never take advantage of Manning or sell him out, not to anyone for any price. I like thinking he might feel the same way about me."

Don looked deflated as he took an exit off the freeway to a truck stop. Chelly was surprised. She thought coming all this way meant they were going to some special restaurant.

He parked, cut the engine and turned to face her, his lustrous eyes serious. "I'm sure Manning does trust you, Chelly. And I know how much he appreciates loyalty. But don't get hung up on an icon. He's not perfect."

"Maybe not to everyone." She gave him a pointed glare. "But he suits me to a T."

Scowling out the windshield, Don's expression again darkened. "I'm trying to tell you, you've got an advantage right now. Ask for something—something exorbitant. I bet you'll get it."

"Like what?"

"Tell him you want an apartment closer to the office so you can walk or say you need to trade your car. See what he suggests."

She grimaced. "*Things* aren't important to me. I've already asked him for something that *is* important to me: information."

"And?"

"He ignored me." ·

Don drew a breath as he touched his index finger to her shoulder. "Maybe the information you wanted was privileged."

She regarded his finger thoughtfully. "Maybe." She flashed him an accusing look. "Is that where you got your Porsche? Did you manipulate poor old Mr. Manning into buying it for you?"

He blinked and his eyes issued a veiled warning before his expression softened. "Actually this is his car. And don't get confused, Chelly. Manning is not an object of pity."

Lazily, he ran his finger down her sleeve to her elbow and back to her shoulder. She tried to ignore the way her heart skipped at his touch.

"How old is he?" she asked, an effort to distract them both. "What does he look like? How does he treat people, face to face? Do you secretly admire him or are you just jealous? Does he gamble?" She spoke hurriedly, trying to ignore the chills pebbling up and down her arm behind his meandering finger, even beneath the layers of fabric. "Is he quick witted? Sometimes he snipes at me. Is he sarcastic in person? Does he like sports? I love sports and I like to think we have that in common. How about his taste in music?"

Don nodded, lazily watching his own finger trace up and down her arm. "He's got some mileage on him. He looks okay, I guess. He treats people pretty much like they treat him. If they're polite, he is. He has a temper."

"Which only indicates he is passionate."

Don's emerald eyes shimmered. "I guess you could say that. He cares about things and people."

"Passionately?"

"Yeah, okay, passionately, when he cares at all."

"How about his sense of humor? He has a good one, right?"

Don shook his head, looked like he was yielding, and smiled. "Yeah, I'd say he's got a fair sense of humor." He paused. "You bring that out in him. In fact, you seem to bring out the best of everything about him."

She ignored the inference. "Does he drink?"

"Yes."

Her disappointment must have shown.

"Not excessively."

She gave up a tremulous smile. "Don, you must be able to manipulate him, to be driving around in his car."

"I'm taking care of his business, Chelly. This is a fleet car. I don't own a vehicle."

"Are you trying to say you don't have a car or a life of your own?"

A boyish grin took his face. "I owe my soul to the company store." He regarded her boldly, his eyes a more temperate hue than before. "You're getting there yourself."

"Not me. I am devoutly my own person these days."

"And who is that, exactly? Describe Chelly Bennett to me."

"Right now?" She lowered her tone to a growl. "The Chelly Bennett you see before you could eat a hind quarter." She gave him a wicked smile. "You insisted on paying. Prepare to deplete your savings big time, big boy."

Don grinned as she opened her door. He leaped out of the car and sprinted but only got to the passenger side in time to close the door behind her as she hurried through the late afternoon chill.

Inside the café, he caught her shoulders from behind before she could sit. "Give me your coat."

Reaching from the back, he grasped the lapels then stopped. His arms slid and locked around her shoulders for a moment, molding the back of her to the front of him.

He exhaled slowly. When she squirmed, he eased her coat off, allowing his fingers to track along her collar bones and shoulders. She shivered as his warm breath caressed her neck before she broke from his hold and quickly slid into the booth.

He hung her coat and his jacket on a rack and returned to her side of the booth. When she didn't yield, he slid in and bumped her hip with his, obviously determined to sit beside her. Grudgingly, she allowed him space. He took that and more, squeezing in close.

Wedged between Don and the side of the booth, she breathed his invigorating cologne and the other seductive scents of the man. Feeling the heat emanating from his body, she shivered and inadvertently leaned into his warmth.

When the waitress came, Chelly ordered the chicken fried steak, fries and salad with ranch dressing. Grinning, Don ordered the same, and a beer; Chelly, hot tea with cream.

When the waitress had gone, Don put his arm on the back of the booth and the other elbow on the table, trapping Chelly in the confines of his body without actually touching her. "Come on now, woman, tell me your dreams. What do you want out of life?"

She felt nervous about his being so close and the effect it was having on her. Midge had warned her that when her cowboy returned, she'd need to hold on for dear life, but her roommate had not specified exactly how to do that.

"I'll keep my dreams to myself, thank you."

His hip touching hers, he pressed the warm length of his thigh against her thigh. Her breath came and went in short, quick bursts. He seemed pleased.

"There has to be something you need or want that you can't get for yourself."

What was he suggesting? She couldn't think clearly. He was sitting too close. "It's warm in here, don't you think?"

He studied the side of her face so closely that his breath tickled her ear when he laughed. "No. I don't find it overly warm." He seemed comfortable in his T-shirt and jeans.

Abruptly she turned toward him, put both hands on his ribcage and pushed. "Scoot over a little." She surprised herself with her audacity. It was awfully personal, touching him so intimately, his warm flesh covered only by the T-shirt.

He didn't budge and his voice so close to her ear was as hypnotic as his scent. "Am I too close, Chelly? Too close for what?" He pressed his thigh more firmly against hers and reached for her hand, which she immediately fisted with the other and folded on the table.

He wrapped one large, warm hand over both of hers. She shrugged away from him. He grinned before he retreated slightly. Removing the warmth of his thigh from hers, he allowed his knee to maintain contact as he coaxed one of her hands open and twined his fingers with hers. "Come on, Chelly." He lowered his voice, "tell me what you see in your future."

"Well... "

"What?" he prodded, studying her intently.

The air burned in her throat. "I'd like to get my law degree before I'm thirty."

"A cinch. You're in your second year already and you're what, twenty-four?"

"Twenty-five." She turned to look at him. His eyes on her mouth, he ran his tongue along his bottom lip. She averted her gaze, trying to concentrate.

"I could only get six hours this semester. I go Tuesday and Thursday nights and Saturday mornings. Some of the classes I needed were full." Her words came quickly. Her voice had a peculiar, breathless quality, which didn't sound familiar. "I don't really have time. Manning asks a lot." She shot a glance at his face. "I'm not complaining. He pays me terribly well and I love the work."

Don's gaze remained on her lips and he leaned closer. Chelly sat paralyzed. Then he appeared to have a new thought and retreated, frowning. "How the hell do you expect to get a degree going to school two nights a week?"

Chelly pulled her hands from his grasp, propped her elbows on the table and tapped her fingertips together as if she were thinking. She didn't suppose she was fooling him, but needed to avoid his persistent touching. "And Saturday mornings. I can do it, eventually. I just have a little over a year to go, but it may take longer than that to get the hours I need."

"Because Manning's overworking you?"

"No." She pretended an avid interest in her fingers, making a concerted effort not to look at his face, all the while appreciating the fact that he seemed to be shifting their conversation to safer ground. She needed to calm down.

"I enrolled for nine hours, Constitutional Law on Tuesday and Thursday nights, torts on Mondays and Fridays and Oil and Gas Law on Saturday mornings. Dean Labor is the only one teaching torts and his night section filled up before they approved my transfer." She suddenly realized he might not be familiar with the terms. "I'm sorry. A tort is a legal action for… "

His features hardened. "I speak legalese."

Flustered, Chelly lowered her folded hands to her lap. "I'm sorry."

"Quit apologizing." His harsh look softened as he put his warm hand on the back of her neck. "You're not the only one who's been to law school." He thumbed her earlobe. She tilted her head but didn't attempt to move away from him.

"You're in law school?"

"I was once, a long time ago."

"That's a shame."

"What is?"

"That you wound up being a flunky for Manning instead of having a career of your own."

She saw his jaw muscles flex before the emerald eyes regained their shimmer. His voice was quiet but carried an accusing tone. "Why didn't you tell Manning you were a law student?"

Chelly seared him with a look. "What if I flunk out? What if he thought it might make me double minded, distract me from doing his work?" She paused, considering, then dropped her voice. "How did you know I hadn't told him?"

He disregarded her question and instead posed another one of his own. "Since you started working at DMD, have you ever once put Manning's needs second?"

"I wouldn't do that."

"Why not?" He removed his hand from her neck.

"Like I said, he pays me really well. That buys him first claim on my time."

"On your life, you mean." There was an awkward pause before he continued. "So, it's the money?" He looked annoyed.

She slumped, surprised to be disappointed that he had stopped touching her. "No."

"Okay, Manning's fair with you. What else?"

"He's not just fair. I told you. He's generous. He not only pays me, he gives me much more than a salary." She saw the curious look and went on. "He compliments me. He gives me very imaginative bonuses rather than just cash. He encourages me to tell him things I notice, as if he values my opinion. My opinion! He doesn't mind when I mention something that might give the other side leverage. He thanks me many different ways for doing the job he's paying me so generously to do.

"It's gotten so, I can almost feel his pleasure through our e-mails." She smiled, pleased with another thought. "Sometimes, when I overstep or get too cocky, he scolds me, brings me down a peg or two, but he's usually funny about it. Not always, of course, but, well, sometimes he's funny. Sometimes he's sarcastic. Usually his comments make me laugh at myself." She regarded him oddly. "As you can see, it's only fair for him to like me. How could he help liking someone who's as crazy about him as I am."

Don chuckled politely but didn't seem to want to interrupt, so she babbled on, staring out the café window. "Truthfully, I'd be glad to work for him from now on, even if I never graduated from law school or never met him in person."

Don frowned and laughed at the same time. "Some people say he's ruthless and vicious and even corrupt."

She flashed him a threatening look. "So? What do you say? You know him better than they do. Do you think he's ruthless or vicious or corrupt?"

He sobered, his eyes vibrant as they captured her gaze. "Yes. When it's required, he can be all of those things, and worse."

"No." She didn't like that answer. "You know better."

"He can be hard, Chelly. The man thrives in a dog-eat-dog world. He's one of the biggest, baddest dogs you've ever seen. And he'll make you that way, if you let him."

Chelly felt an odd chill and lowered her voice. "Why do you think so? Is that what he's doing to you?"

Again he ignored her question, puckering his marvelous lips. It was his turn to survey the parking lot outside.

The waitress came with their salads and they ate in silence, both absorbed in their own thoughts as the noise of a new pot of coffee gurgled and hissed, dishes clattered and the cafe's furnace hummed to life somewhere in the back. They remained steeped in what Chelly considered a surprisingly companionable silence as the waitress returned with their meal.

God, he loved this woman. She was everything he had dreamed she would be, and much, much more. He felt a rush of fondness for that idiot Chastain, for preserving all this innocence intact, under the influence of one inept man instead of several men.

He liked the rapport developing between them. It probably didn't matter what name he used, but he doubted she would be as outspoken if she knew who he was.

He liked that she could be such a haughty know-it-all one minute and self-effacing the next.

Her blind devotion to Manning the icon troubled him.

His conscience nagged. At the moment, men were low on her trust scale and while he hadn't set out to mislead her, he had... and was continuing to do. But he didn't want to disturb the easy give and take between them. He had to exercise exemplary restraint when her thoughtless comments tweaked his resolve and sometimes his temper.

She seemed genuinely not to want favors from Manning. Of course, he would take care of the law school glitch immediately.

Would she resent his interference, if she found out? No. After all, she was partially to blame for the deception. Still, he would enjoy the subterfuge a little longer. What difference could it possibly make?

Chelly was first to break the silence between them. "Have you worked for him a long time?"

"Nearly all my life."

"Has he made you mean?" He stared at her without answering. "Weren't you suggesting I leave DMD before he makes me mean too?"

Don propped the elbow closest to her on the table, concealing his face behind his shoulder.

Chelly considered his well-formed biceps both a physical and an emotional barrier between them.

"No." He muttered the word without looking at her, the lower half of his face hidden.

"I could probably find another job, with another firm." She mumbled, speaking more to herself than to him. "Anne says once you've worked for Manning, you can go anywhere."

"Have you been approached by anyone else?"

"No. I was just thinking out loud. If I changed jobs, I'd want to stay downtown, so I could keep my apartment."

"What other firms do you know about?"

"Not much about any of them. Which one is second best?"

Don snorted an appreciative laugh. "Smoker's."

"Okay, then, I could apply at Weeden-Pricer and hope to work for Levi Smoker someday."

He peered at her over the shoulder that still separated them. "Don't do that."

She tried to read his expression but his eyes had become hooded and she still couldn't see his whole face.

"If you advised me to quit DMD," she said, "I'm not saying I would, but I might think about it." She grimaced at other thoughts interrupting her words. "Of course, Manning's paying me so much is part of the reason I can stay in school. My parents would pay for it, but I don't want them to do that. I'm twenty-five years old, for heaven's sake." She took another bite and chewed thoughtfully.

When he finished eating, Don removed his elbow from the table, again allowing her an unobstructed view of his face. He directed his veiled eyes to the beer glass under his hand. He didn't seem to want her reading his thoughts. No danger of that. She was not able to read his mind as easily as he seemed able to read hers.

He said, "Stick with Manning, for a while anyway, for the firm's sake, not for yours. Do you want dessert?"

"No, thanks. What do you mean, 'for the firm's sake?'"

Don stood, swigged the last of his beer, scooped up the check and walked to the counter. Chelly followed and ambled toward the door, lost in thought. Don whistled her back before she stepped outside. He was holding her coat.

After she slid her arms into her sleeves, he turned her around to button the coat and snug the collar around her neck. He grinned. She flushed.

Outside, he walked to the passenger side to unlock her car door. She turned her back to him but his body radiated heat that made her shiver from the inside out. She had the impression he was making a conscious effort not to touch her.

They drove back to town in silence.

Chelly considered how comfortable she felt with this man. He made her feel capable, but foolish; talented, but naive, important… and attractive. She knew she was all right looking, but his every glance made her feel prettier than she had ever felt before.

And he made her trust her own instincts again. She liked choosing her own friends and felt particularly confident about this new one.

She also felt relieved that this man did not make scenes.

Eric had thrown tantrums, particularly in public places. Because his behavior reflected on her, even when they were young, Chelly would do anything to avoid setting him off. She didn't challenge Eric when he handed her his grandmother's engagement ring at his dad's urging. Nor did she question why he only said "I love you" when one of their parents was within earshot.

At the University, exposed to other people and cultures, Chelly had changed. She hadn't wanted to return to Blackjack to live with the small town's narrow dictates the rest of her life. She had begged Eric to enroll, to get one year of college, one year away from his dad and Harmon Chastain's myopic view of life. When Eric finally agreed, she had discovered the genetic source of his tantrums. His dad threw the mother of all fits. Eric wasn't going anywhere that might take him out from under his dad's thumb.

It became obvious to Chelly then: figuratively, Harmon was going to be a third person in Eric's marriage bed.

Gazing out of the Porsche at the passing scenery, Chelly remembered the argument that peculiar insight spawned.

"I don't mind marrying you, Eric," Chelly told him one summer evening when she was twenty-two, "but I'm not marrying your dad."

Eric ruffled. "What do you mean by that crack?"

"I don't want him telling us what to do, where to live, how to act."

Eric stopped walking and stared at her in the moonlight. "He's my dad, Chelly. He'll always be my dad. A wife is an ornament. Dad gave me a vice presidency, a huge chunk of his business. He's how I'm going to make my living—our living."

She had hackled. "Meaning unless I come up independently wealthy, I can't compete with your old man?"

"Don't call him that."

"I'll call him anything I like."

"Not if you want to marry me, you won't."

"Fine."

"What does that mean?"

"If I can't reconcile myself to living with you and your dad, I won't marry you."

Eric's jaws and fists clenched and unclenched. She'd watched him carefully. If he'd thrown one of his tantrums then, she would have hurled that precious heirloom ring at his head and walked away.

But Eric had surprised her with his cold disdain. "It doesn't really matter to me if you marry me or not."

Before they got home, he apologized. "You like my dad, Chelly. I know you do. And he likes you. You're the girl he hand picked for me to marry. He chose you when we were still in grade school."

Somehow that explanation had left Chelly feeling more uneasy than ever.

Her thoughts brought her back and she took advantage of his concentration on the road to savor a long look at Don.

He seemed relaxed, comfortable with his masculinity. Eric had always been uptight, ever aware of trying to look and sound manly, which might help explain his sexual problem.

Although Eric had a certain appeal, she didn't think him sexy. Don, on the other hand, made her tingle in anatomical places she didn't think it polite to tingle. Certainly, she had never been as curious about a man's body as she had become while watching the lithe male beside her with his broad shoulders, his lean torso, the muscles following the curve of his haunches and corded in his long, powerful thighs.

Get a grip, girl, she chided herself and forced her attention back to the road.

When they parked in front of the Sheppard Building, Don stared straight ahead. It was dusk. The air outside hung still and silent as winter's cold settled over the city like a hen roosting over her nest.

Instead of getting out, Don swivelled, caught the lapels of Chelly's coat with one hand and tugged.

Chelly shrank back, grappling behind her for the door handle and said, "You don't have to get out."

He leaned ever so slightly, pulling the lapels and bringing her close.

She looked at his generous mouth and wondered fleetingly how he would taste. The renegade thought frightened her.

She fumbled with the door handle. He released the coat but before her legs were out of the car, he was standing in front of her, offering a hand up. At first, he didn't allow her space to stand. Finally, he shuffled back and she got out, giving him a tremulous smile. "Thanks, for the ride and the company and a great chicken fried steak. When you're in the mood for tuna, it's my treat."

He smiled politely but stood gazing into her face, again reminding her of a large, tawny, predatory cat.

She blushed, waiting for him to move aside and let her pass. "What is it? What do you want?"

His voice was husky. "You don't want to know what I want."

Slowly he traced her jaw with one finger, from an ear to the tip of her chin and back.

She stood there feeling paralyzed.

He reached behind her head to pluck away the banana clip securing her hair.

She shivered and swiped the wayward strands back as the long tangle tumbled to her shoulders. "What do you think you're doing?" She grabbed the profusion in both hands, fumbling, trying to pull the unruly mane back into some kind of order.

Her efforts were lost, however, when Don slipped his arms under hers and laced his fingers into the mass, gathering it in handfuls at her back.

He tugged her hair playfully, tilting her head from one side to the other studying her face. His grin broadened until he barked a quick, startling laugh.

As if suddenly aware of her annoyance, he sobered and released her, looking a little surprised, possibly at his own behavior.

He took a step back, turned to pace several long strides down the sidewalk, wheeled, and glowered at her. He was again the stalking predator studying a hapless victim.

Absently she fussed with her hair, trying to restore it to some acceptable form, and wondered what this man, practically a stranger, was thinking as he regarded her so intently.

Chapter Eleven

Pacing up and down the walk, Don tightened his range, drawing closer and closer until he was almost on top of her.

She straightened, attempting with body language to warn him back but he either didn't notice or chose to disregard the signal.

Arms at his sides, he squared himself in front of her, leaned and tilted his head until his broad mouth hovered scant inches from hers. She could feel his breath. He smelled like the crisp, cool air mixed with the masculine fragrances of aftershave and soap and leather.

Staring at the front of his T-shirt, visible under the jacket that hung open, Chelly's breathing became shallow. When she risked a look, he lifted his chin and spoke, his voice quiet.

"I'll make it easy, but you have to help. You don't have to want this as much as I do." His confidence seemed suspended as he studied her then added huskily, "I don't think you could."

A warm flush heated her earlobes. She wanted him to kiss her. Oh, yes, she did. She was embarrassed about how desperately she wanted it. She tilted her face, aligning it with his, a tiny invitation. It was enough.

His lips were soft and pliable at first, non threatening. Slowly, he unbuttoned her coat and his roaming hands found their way to her waist. His generous mouth coaxed hers. She yielded, quieting her conscience by telling herself she would make only small concessions.

His breath quickened and his mouth grew more aggressive, taunting, coaxing, beseeching at first, then gradually, demanding. His hands at her back, he drew their bodies closer.

Totally unprepared for the giddiness and the astounding hunger he aroused in her, and curious about how much more excitement he might produce, she yielded.

His hands roamed up the back of her sweatshirt and forward under her arms to cup her breasts.

Her mouth still sealed with his, she croaked a "no," but the intended objection sounded—even to her—more like a growl of pleasure.

The sequence had a dreamlike quality. She arched her back, thrusting herself forward, encouraging his hands. No man had ever fondled her so tenderly. She enjoyed feeling so lightheaded, enjoyed the butterflies swarming in the pit of her stomach, enjoyed the dizziness he elicited. She couldn't think clearly, could not fathom why she was behaving this way, much less on a downtown city street. Why was she allowing this relative stranger to handle her so intimately?

But her halfhearted effort at guilt was not enough. Like a curious student eager for the next step in some fascinating experiment, she sent her hands up his wonderful biceps and over his shoulders.

He lifted his mouth. Alarmed that she might somehow have signaled that she wanted him to stop, her eyes popped open.

He regarded her face for only a moment before he resumed the siege, slanted his mouth over hers, then opened as if he would devour her.

The fire inside her flamed, producing a pulsing, uncontrollable heat she had never generated before. She needed to stop him. Stop this. She needed to think. Instead she laced her fingers into the longish hair at the back of his head and lifted herself higher in an effort to get closer to him. She didn't know what possessed her to behave in such a wanton way. She rejoiced when his huge hand again cupped a breast. She swayed, encouraging him, enjoying the wildfires springing to life inside her. She had never known such consuming, delicious desire. This guy must be an expert, at least a black belt fondler. He rubbed a thumb over the sweatshirt stimulating the tip of her breast. She gasped, arched, inhaled once, then again without exhaling. He tongued her ear before his lips flittered down from her lobe and laved her neck. She rocked her head to one side and gave up a tiny sob.

Her mind again tried to assert itself. What was she doing? How could she allow him to behave this way, diabolically stimulating every nerve in her body? Because he could, her libido responded.

His mouth came up over hers again, inviting, encroaching, insisting, and she returned his kiss, meeting and matching his fire. She felt like some wild temptress enticing him and luring them both beyond control.

Her fingers massaged the muscles of his upper arms, which strained and flexed beneath the leather sleeves. She moaned. The sound seemed to heighten his burn. He pressed his length against her, crushing her between his hard body and the side of his car. His mouth again beguiling her ear, his mischievous hands slithered beneath the waistband of her sweatshirt. When he touched the bare skin of her midriff, she jumped, rudely jolted out of the hypnotic state. She planted both hands at his shoulders and pushed. "What are you doing?"

"Pay back for what you've been doing to me."

"What? Making you... "

He put his mouth against her ear, and whispered, "Hot."

She pushed him to arm's length as he continued a low croon. "I dream about you, Chelly. I hardly think of anything else. You haven't been off my mind since I followed you through that revolving door the day after Christmas." His voice mellowed. "You've got me climbing the walls, baby."

He had felt it too. She marveled. The connection the day she got the job at DMD, the day she first saw him and all but willed this... this debauchery.

Her legs quivered. She hoped he couldn't tell how shaky she was. He looked surprised when she shoved by him and wobbled to her car. It took a lot of unnecessary motion to put herself inside. She locked her doors and drew a long, steadying breath. Her fingers trembled as she put the key in the ignition. The engine hummed before she risked a look back.

He stood beside his car, exactly as she had left him.

She made a U-turn in the middle of the nearly deserted street and crammed the accelerator, lurching forward in a frantic race to her apartment. She was nearly there before she noticed the black Porsche in her rearview mirror.

Chelly parked in the lone remaining slot reserved for apartment four-twelve, relieved to see Midge's aged Dodge Dart in its usual place.

Don pulled into a vacant space beside her.

She scrambled out of her car juggling keys and purse. "This is assigned parking. You'll get towed."

Out of the Porsche, he prowled toward her. She imagined she could see his muscles rippling, like a great silky cat. She back-peddled toward the building, then turned and bolted.

The wintry bite in the air whipped her coat open. The cool felt good against the sweats that sheathed her overly warm body.

He allowed her to lengthen the distance between them, but he kept coming. "You can run, Chelly, but you can't hide. I like holding you. You like it too. Think how right you felt in my arms. How perfect. How safe."

She didn't want to think of how she felt in his arms. Safe definitely wasn't it.

Think? That was laughable. She had to get away from him to be able to think.

She darted into the building. Her hands shook and she couldn't get the key in the lock of the second door, the security door. Frantically, she jammed the buzzer.

"Midge, let me in," she called when her roommate opened the speaker. Chelly whirled for a quick look back. He was there, in the doorway, not five feet from her. Poised. Waiting. Watching.

Midge hit the buzzer and the lock clicked. Chelly flung the door wide and exploded through, but before it swung shut, Don caught it. He followed but stayed well back as she took the stairs two-at-a-time all the way to the fourth floor.

Again, she fumbled trying to fit the key to the door. Wide-eyed, breathless, she turned as Don reached from behind her to place one hand on the doorjamb. Chelly stepped to her left, only to have her escape blocked that way too.

Swiping at rebellious strands of her unbound hair, she turned to face him and they stood, a freeze frame, breathless from the climb—or exhilaration—studying one another.

What was he thinking? He knew her roommate was there, right behind that door. Would he try to force his way into their apartment?

No.

The greatest threat in him was the wildness he aroused in her. Staring at his face, Chelly realized her worst fear was of her own unplumbed passion. She was too unschooled to know her own appetite, much less a man's—particularly this man's.

Don put his hands on the wall on either side of her, waist high. He leaned close. His eyes took on a moss-like hue as they swept her face. His advance beyond that was again tentative and his uncertainty puzzled her. He was a god. Why did he hesitate?

The scent of him wafted, deliciously male. She thought her knees might buckle, but they held.

He seemed to be waiting. For what? Permission? His expression dared her, at the same time inquiring and compelling. Was it possible he didn't know the excitement his nearness stimulated. Hadn't he felt her desire that morning in the office, later as she stood beside him in the elevator, driving in his car, in the booth in the café when he pressed his thigh to hers.

As she tried to rein her thoughts into some kind of order, he remained poised, his eyes lazily caressing her face.

Don was annoyed with himself for behaving like some love-starved adolescent, nerves raw, ripped with sensations he had not experienced since puberty.

He had the bachelor's requisite little black book full of the names of sexy, lusty, willing women; women who could satisfy a man even if he were bored with the physical sameness of ordinary sex.

What was it about this woman that had him grinding his teeth, hard and hurting? He'd take her right here in the hall, if she'd let him. And she might. But he couldn't get a clear read on her signals. She had his usually reliable instincts spinning. She wanted something. What was it? More? Less? More? He found her stop-and-go indicators confounding.

Could she still be mourning what's-his-face? Eric?

She didn't behave like a woman who'd been engaged, had no finesse, no come hither moves. Yet he found himself completely captivated by her clumsy flurries, her spurts of fevered interest punctuated by occasional jabs of curiosity. She had a body built and ripe for loving.

Could she be a tease?

No, something about her was uncertain, as if she lacked experience.

Wrong. She had been engaged. It had to be grief. She was pining away for Eric the dolt. He grimaced with the thought. No, no, no. That lamebrain had missed his chance. He was history.

Don gazed into her flushed face. He would show her how real passion looked and felt. He would take it slow, make her forget every other man she had ever known. He would woo her with lavish gifts, more expensive, more imaginative plunder than Eric Chastain could buy her in a lifetime.

She shivered.

God, she was so responsive, yet, in almost the same breath, reluctant, also embarrassed, maybe intimidated.

The only certainty was, when he moved, she reacted—her mouth eager, the full breasts aroused. He had pushed and been surprised again and again by her fire, then her unexpected retreats. She, too, seemed surprised, maybe even alarmed, by her behavior.

He wanted another go at her, preferably some place where there was a bed.

Chelly was aware she mustn't raise her chin or give any indication she wanted him to kiss her again; therefore, her thrust surprised her almost as much as it seemed to please him.

He didn't give her time to change her mind. His mouth again took hers gently, stanching the power she could feel surging through his arms as he gathered her close. She felt him tremble, as if he were holding back. What more could he possibly want from her? He had it all, everything she had to give.

The apartment door popped as it broke the paint's sticky seal with the jamb. She heard Midge's embarrassed laugh before the door closed again.

For equilibrium, Chelly set her hands at Don's waist. The move seemed to ignite him and he nudged her. She eased back flat against the wall beside the apartment door.

He put his forearms at either side of her head and leaned, his thighs pressing her thighs, his stomach to hers, his chest... The hard male thrust of him prodded her abdomen.

Her mind ordered her to escape but her mutinous body ignored the command, melting into his, not just consenting, but inviting.

He ran his tongue along the seam between her lips and her mouth yielded, it too defying her mental directives. The invader caressed the cavern experimentally, then retreated. Her breathing ragged, she waited, her mouth relaxed, inviting his tongue to intrude again, but it didn't.

She became impatient, wanting the intimacy he'd withdrawn. Opening her mouth a little, she felt him grin. Was he teasing her? Maybe.

Timidly, Chelly let her tongue touch his teeth then retreat. Chills beaded up and down her arms at her own audacity.

She stood unmoving, aware of every swell and hollow along the length of his body. Her tongue ventured out again into this uncharted territory, surprising her. The timid thrust seemed to electrify him.

His tongue slid inside her mouth as his lips again devoured hers.

Disregarding mental commands, one arm twined around his neck and she pulled herself higher, more tightly into his heat while the rebellious fingers of her other hand laced themselves into his hair.

Before she realized what was happening his hands were under her arms, lifting. His knee pushed between her legs and she suddenly was astride his muscular thigh, which flexed, creating astonishing sensations. She grabbed his leather-clad shoulders for support, unable to speak or to breathe around his mouth, which seemed to be ravaging hers. Riding his leg, the erotic stirring stole all her ability to think, almost to breathe.

As she balanced on his thigh, his hands slithered beneath the band of her sweatshirt and over her bra. He kneaded both breasts through the fabric, fondling, tweaking their tips with his fingers until she writhed with mind-numbing desire.

His mouth on hers, his thigh flexing mercilessly, his hands at her breasts, she didn't know how to defend on so many fronts at once, couldn't decide how or where to begin a strategic withdrawal, then realized she didn't want him to stop the siege any of those places.

The seal on the apartment door popped again. Midge's voice floated through a haze. "You two had better come inside."

Don maintained the kiss but removed his knee from between Chelly's legs and slipped his hands out from beneath her sweatshirt.

Chelly slid down the wall. Her legs quivered as her feet touched the floor, yet she was the one providing the force that kept their mouths sealed.

Her roommate's hand on her upper arm pulled, coaxing her into the apartment. The vacuum between her mouth and Don's broke with a "smuck" and Chelly whined involuntarily at the loss.

"Hi." Midge's words lilted, fluttering around Chelly's head. "I'm Midgean Kitchens, Chelly's roommate."

Shuffling on her own two feet, Chelly gradually became aware that the three of them were inside the apartment.

Midge grinned broadly, her eyes gazing up into Don's face as she said, "Chelly, my Aunt Mazie called. I've gotta' run over to her place. Don't know how long I'll be gone." She cut her eyes to Chelly as if looking for a response. "I left the number by the phone. Call if you need me."

In Chelly's befuddlement she grabbed Midge's sleeve, her fingernails clawing at the fabric. "No." When she blurted the word, Midge and Don both looked at her oddly. She clamped her hands on Midge's arm. "No. You can't go. You have to stay here."

Midge looked bewildered. Don shifted his gaze from Chelly to Midge. "I'm Don. Do you have to leave?"

Midge nodded stiffly, looking from Don to Chelly and back. "I think probably so."

"You don't seem sure."

"Ah... well... Chelly looks feverish." Midge peered directly into her roommate's face. "Honey, are you sick?"

Chelly shook her head.

Don gave a half laugh, half snort and slipped his arm around Chelly's waist. "You go along, Midge. I'll take care of our girl, get her to bed as soon as I can." He flashed a roguish grin.

Chelly stammered. "I'll take you, Midge, to your aunt's or... " She risked a look at Don. "Or to the grocery store. I need to pick up some... thing."

Again Midge looked skeptically from one face to the other. "Okay." She said the word slowly, as if she were uncertain.

Don's teasing grin withered. He sighed and stood staring at the floor a long moment before he stepped back out into the hall.

Chelly's mouth twitched. Her chin dimpled and quivered. She didn't try to speak.

He reached back to place his open hand on her face. "It's okay, Chelly. Think about it. I'm at the Trenton, room twenty-eight-hundred. I've gotta' leave by six in the morning. If you want to talk, call me, or come by. I'm there when we're in town. You can leave messages for me at the desk." His expression softened. "Can you hear me? Do you understand what I'm saying?"

She nodded but shot him only a quick glance. Her throat burned and her eyes stung. She wanted to cry. She felt defeated and angry, not with him, but with herself. And disoriented. Completely disoriented. What was wrong with her? Her mind and body had always worked together, like a matched pair of horses pulling a carriage. Syncopated. In step.

Until today.

Today, her mind and her body defied one another, each pulling its own way, leaving her thoroughly confused.

Don turned. A dozen quick strides and he clattered down the stairs without another look back.

Midge nudged Chelly further into the apartment and closed the door.

"Was that who I think it was?" Midge asked. "Chelly Bennett, I promise if a man—any man—ever looks at me the way that man was looking at you, I am his."

Chelly stood absolutely still. Midge was right. How could she have sent him away? She could hear Midge prattling but it was hard to concentrate. Her mouth felt swollen.

"...you described, tall, built... bet women fall all over him. What's wrong? Is it that bozo back home? Speak up, woman. What's going on in that marvelous brain of yours?"

Chelly walked to the kitchen table and began sorting spiral notebooks full of school work. She stacked them neatly, then proceeded to stack and re-stack the half dozen textbooks. "Midge, you don't even have an Aunt Mazie."

"No, dopey, it's our signal. Remember? I saw his cowboy boots and I knew exactly who he was. I was clearing out to give you some privacy."

Chelly's eyes found Midge's face. "I must not be alone with him, Midge. Not ever. It's not safe. It wouldn't be smart or... or anything."

Midge snickered. "Passion finally reared its nappy head, did it? I knew it was there, laying behind a log." She tapped Chelly's forehead with her finger. "Looks like you got a healthy dose, too. Come on, tell me, what happened? Where'd he come from?"

"I don't know that it was passion exactly."

Midge grinned. "Well maybe I can help with the definition. Describe it."

Chelly barked an embarrassed laugh, happy that she seemed to be recovering. "I felt very... friendly."

Midge tried to conceal the smirk. "*Friendly*, huh? From what I saw, sweetie, that is a gross understatement."

"My body was like a runaway train. I couldn't find the brakes."

Midge laughed, rolling her eyes toward the ceiling. "Sounds like the animal's a little high spirited for you. You manipulated that yokel in Blackjack just fine, but a little time with a mature man with some hormonal hustle and you cave. You fooled me. I figured you could handle a little power under the hood. Obviously not. Where'd you find him? I'd like to browse there myself."

Chelly didn't answer.

"Chelly, he is your cowboy, right?"

Chelly nodded with a sense of wonder. "Yeah."

Midge shrugged. "What a waste. I might not be able to handle him any better than you did, but I'd darn sure like a try. God, Chel, you were right. He is gorgeous."

Chelly nodded as she continued systematically stacking and re-stacking notebooks and texts.

Because she couldn't concentrate, couldn't sit for more than three minutes at a time, Chelly decided to bathe. After that, she would force her mind to retake command, focus her mental and physical energy on homework.

Undressing, she mulled her theory of dating. Going out with almost anyone she had met in the city, even Leonard Diet, would have been better than Don.

As she showered, she decided Midge was right. She obviously was not ready for a mature man, one with... what had Midge called it? Hormonal hustle?

Oh, sure, Chelly was tooling herself at DMD to make it in the business world, but her social development was, to put it mildly, repressed.

Don was altogether too suave, too smart, too handsome, and, what was his word? Hot. She grinned as she turned off the spray and stepped out of the tub. Yes, he was definitely too hot.

"He was looking for a quickie," she whispered, staring at her reflection in the steam-clouded mirror. "And he picked you." Her uncertain smile wavered. "You were there. He was horny."

She clenched her teeth and bent to wrap her wet hair in a towel. She pulled on her panties and the oversized T-shirt/nightgown and exited the steaming bathroom, too humiliated by the memory of her behavior even to look at her own reflection again.

In her room, she towel-dried her hair and combed it, working the tangles out of the natural curl, and put on the terry cloth bathrobe before she returned to the kitchen table with new resolve.

The law. Now there was something reliable. Something a woman could sink her teeth into. She was good at it. It was an area in which she had some competence.

She worked three hours, disciplining her mind to the task, not once allowing renegade thoughts to interrupt. She finished by eleven, stood, stretched, and drifted into the living room to see what Midge was watching on TV. She found her roommate sprawled in the overstuffed chair and smiled.

"There probably aren't two women in the world who'd keep the TV low enough to let a girl study." Chelly plopped down on the sofa and propped her feet, sharing Midge's ottoman. "Thanks."

Her roommate laughed openly. "And there probably aren't many women who could even do homework after kissing a man like you were kissing that one."

Chelly allowed a heavy sigh. "Probably not. Most likely I was a convenience to him."

"And what was he to you?"

"I guess I'm not enough of a feminist to think that way."

"Take the plunge, woman. Get in the swim with the rest of us fish. Oh, and one more thing, staying with the fish analogy, if you throw this one back, please, please throw him my way."

But Chelly's thoughts were off on another tangent.

So she should have taken advantage of him? She sobered as she contemplated that.

Sure, she should have backed him into a corner and groped under his shirt and... She spewed laughter into the room.

Midge gawked at her. "What's so funny? I'm a darn good date."

It was Chelly's turn to gape, wondering what Midge was talking about.

As she lay in her bed that night, Chelly fantasized about how Don might have responded to her aggressive behavior, if she'd had... the balls.

"Ah ha," she whispered, giggling quietly into the darkness. "I think I've identified the problem."

She rolled onto her stomach, muffling her giggles with her pillow, then tried to get comfortable, to settle down on her right side, her left, all the while imagining scenarios in which she intimidated Don sexually. Each imagined performance was more daring and led to more astonishing results. She knew none of her fanciful endings would suit either of them but she enjoyed fantasizing and, after all, he would never suspect her of these nocturnal imaginings.

Then an eerie thought: what was he envisioning tonight?

Was he thinking of her? "No, no, brain, don't go there," she whispered in the darkness.

She glanced at the clock. Nearly two. She had to sleep. To do that, she had to stop thinking of him.

He'd probably taken his frustration directly to a woman who would satisfy him. Monica Lynch came to mind. Chelly recalled how the receptionist eyed him that first morning at DMD. Rolling onto her back, she squeezed her pillow up around both ears and groaned.

Midge was right. He was too big a fish for Chelly. She should start small and work up.

All right, she agreed with herself. Leonard Diet was old and probably far less bold. He had canceled the first date, lunch in his office, and the second. But Chelly had been the one dodging the subsequent invitations. If he asked her again, she was going.

Yes, the pudgy, younger Diet, probably twenty-five years her senior, would present none of the dangers inherent in Don Richards. Even if Diet should get all lathered up, he probably could be easily brought to heel.

It was a good plan. Chelly would begin her dissection of the sophisticated city male with him. She should have thought of it before.

The idea of going out with Leonard Diet lulled her quickly and she slept.

Chapter Twelve

The apartment buzzer sounded at seven-forty the next morning. Chelly was looking for her purse and Midge, switching off the coffee pot. Both were on their way to work.

"Delivery from Adrienna's," a young male voice cracked into the downstairs speaker.

"Be right down." Midge smiled sheepishly. "The kid's probably on his way to school. I hate to have him climb four flights when we're on our way out anyway."

Chelly nodded. She knew she'd been unusually quiet that morning and Midge had not interrupted her brooding.

In the hallway, Midge handed Chelly a box of clothing she was returning, and swung back to lock the dead bolt.

A skinny teenaged boy stood at the bottom of the stairs holding a bud vase containing a single red rose. "Ms. Kitchens?" His voice broke again.

"Here." Midge brightened as he attempted to hand the vase to her. "I'm pretty sure it's not for me, kid."

He glanced at the card and repeated. "Midge Kitchens?"

She nodded and looked perplexed but pleased as she again handed the box of returns to Chelly. Midge took the small vase, balanced it in the crook of her arm and fumbled as she opened the tiny envelope pinned to a ribbon around its neck.

A youthful hand had scrawled five words on the tiny card. "Thanks for your help. Don."

Chelly's roommate hesitated, puzzling, trying to think who Don might be, before she laughed lightly and handed the card to Chelly. "Heaven only knows what you might have gotten this morning if you'd been a little nicer to the incredible hunk."

The handwriting was not familiar. Chelly shot an intense look at the delivery boy. "Did he write this?"

108

"No, ma'am. It was a call-in."

Looking at the card, Chelly felt the warm blush crawl up her neck and face. "Midge, it's not from him."

"Not from your cowboy?"

"It must be someone else."

"No. It's him." Midge arched her eyebrows. "And he's after you, honey. You do lead a charmed life."

Chelly felt her blush warm to a burn. "I never have before."

Eying the delivery boy who stood patiently, Midge reclaimed her clothing box. "Give the boy a tip, Chelly. The item may be addressed to me, but this one's on you."

Chelly fished in her purse and turned up two quarters. "Is this enough?"

Midge nodded. The delivery boy grimaced, grabbed the change and took off, tossing back, "Thanks a lot."

Chelly eyed the vase. "I get the tip, you get the flowers?"

"Flower. Singular. Like you. All alone. Want my advice? Be nice. He'll make it worth your while—and we are not just talking floral tributes here."

Chelly walked to the parking area unable to stifle the smile. She got into her car biting back the grin before starting the engine. She was an ambitious woman. She had not known that about herself before.

Sure, she had gone to college over Eric's objections, but she thought at the time that was a power struggle between them. He wanted to show her he was boss. Chelly had never questioned her own motive for defying him. She had never wondered why she insisted on striving upward and onward, beginning with an undergraduate degree.

Now she was even more determined to finish law school. And she wanted a job with a big, prestigious firm, not some flunky's job, a mouse scurrying up the corporate ladder one cubicle at a time.

A mover and shaker would be foolish to saddle herself with an errand boy, even a big, strong, gorgeous one who said he'd been to law school, once upon a time.

And what about that? Assuming it was true, had he dropped out or flunked out?

Don implied he was Manning's right hand. That might or might not be true either. Maybe he was just trying to impress her. He had even jokingly referred to himself as Manning's secretary of state.

Bragging, exaggerating tales of their abilities and status was one of the idiosyncrasies she did not admire in the metropolitan male. The failing existed in epidemic proportions among the competitive young lawyers at DMD. They boasted and lied with impunity. She had endured all the mendacity she could stomach from Eric.

In a small town like Blackjack, liars were marked in grade school. A girl knew, early on, which classmates told little white lies and which told bald-face ones.

But here, among strangers, she read sincerity in most faces, trustworthy or not. How could she tell the liars from the truth tellers?

The answer was obvious. She needed to avoid getting too close, dodge suspect friendships and all romantic entanglements. If Don were intent on entangling, he could just get over it. She smiled at her own conceit and admitted, probably he already had.

She drew a deep breath. He was unusual. And he'd seen through her veneer. The horn-rimmed glasses were a good example. No one else had picked up on that little subterfuge. At least no one had mentioned it. With friends like Midge and Anne Beed and even Yarnell Tuggle, if they had noticed, they would have said something.

No, Don was different. If he were a deceiver, he was darn good at it. He was either a paragon of manhood or he was a con artist good at manipulating people. Either way, she couldn't afford to get involved. He could get in the way of her goals.

Then a niggling thought: was she more deceptive than Eric or Don, pretending to be something she was not? Hers was not an act. She didn't know exactly who she was, while Don was... well.

"He seems so... " She backed from her designated parking space without finishing the thought.

Then another question dawned. How could a man in moderate circumstances stay at the Trenton, the most expensive hotel in town? But was he? In moderate circumstances or staying at the Trenton? She didn't know if either were fact.

He said he was leaving early. Then, how did he manage to send the rose? She allowed a crooked smile. Sending a rose to Midge. Very cool. Was it meant to make her jealous? She felt her smile broaden.

"If it was, it worked." The smile became a grimace. "Very clever. Experimenting. Testing to see which buttons work what. Well, a twinge of jealousy won't do it, hot shot. I'm a little smarter than that."

Stopped at a traffic light, she glanced over to see a fellow commuter eying her. She hoped he thought she was singing with the radio to explain her smiles and her lips moving. He grinned and winked. The light changed. She rammed the accelerator and shot forward.

What was happening? Here she was talking to herself and apparently giving off come-hither signals, as Midge had suggested she should.

Don had her off balance. Midge seemed to have a good read on him. Chelly needed to hand him over to a woman who had lived in the city among sophisticated men, someone who knew the intricate steps to this little dance of romance.

Of course, Don wasn't exactly hers to give. If he were, would she?

All this conjecture was useless, just so much mental chewing gum.

After a routine week, at noon on Thursday Chelly received an urgent message from Manning. *"That dam Vernon Lee Merchison is still throwing wrenches."* She smiled, in spite of the tone of his missive. He had used the speller, but it had missed the "dam."

Manning had been angry all week about delays in the win/win merger, a friendly takeover he had brokered.

"Old man Buckley wants out and the Ginsburgs are eager to take over. This goofy kid keeps fowling (another obvious miss by the speller) things up. This is the third set of concessions he's asked for after the papers were drawn. The Ginsburgs have gone along, but they're getting testy. We may have to rework the contract. Cancel your weekend. Stay with me on this. The deal could unravel in the next twenty minutes, assuming I don't."

Chelly cringed. If they negotiated through Friday, the wheeler-dealers would sleep late Saturday while she had to toothpick her eyelids open for the oil and gas lecture. She had already missed once. She couldn't cut it again.

She shoved the cover off the first of the three file boxes containing Buckley materials, the one with historical data that obviously hadn't been opened in years.

Chuffing, sniffing and sneezing at the dust motes, Chelly thumbed through the first file. In 1954, the old man, Vernon Buckley, deeded his business, the real estate and the buildings, to himself and his then-ten-year-old-daughter, Priscilla, as joint tenants. That was unusual, but touching.

Papers slid around in the box. Carefully, Chelly lifted original documents stiffened by age and placed them on the table to one side as she sorted.

She paused at a marriage certificate—Priscilla Buckley wed Nathan Merchison—December, 1976. Doing the math, Chelly muttered aloud. "Thirty-two years old. Priss wasn't exactly a deb."

She found another deed regarding the Buckley property.

Maybe as a wedding gift, a show of confidence, Priscilla and her daddy cut the bridegroom in on the business property, re-deeding to the three of them jointly, survivor take all.

Chelly mumbled, "Nice gesture. Welcome to the family."

Deeper in the file she ran across a birth certificate. Vernon Lee Merchison, born December 2, 1984. Named for his grandfather.

"That makes him nineteen now and the Merchisons' definitely not a shotgun wedding."

She studied the birth certificate. "And they're letting Vernon Lee call the tune in this merger?" Her frown deepened. "Why? What gives the kid any say-so over Buckley's?"

She continued digging, glancing at the computer screen from time to time, awaiting Manning's communique.

When she got tired of bending over the box on the desk, she got on her knees in the chair and leaned, burrowing into the second box of old documents.

In 1985, Mr. and Mrs. Merchison created a trust and funded it with all their holdings. They named one another as co-trustees, each entitled to act in the absence of the other. Vernon Lee was successor trustee, heir to everything, eventually.

Chelly skimmed through the trust document, skipping the last three pages, the ones listing the couple's assets, at least all of those that had been deeded to the trust. She scanned a yellowed newspaper clipping that reported the death of Nathan Merchison, a scuba diving accident. His holdings all went to his widow.

Chelly turned up a death certificate for Mrs. Merchison issued a year later. Cause of death: Breast cancer.

"With all their money, she couldn't beat it." Chelly slumped. "I guess no one's rich enough."

As successor trustee, the boy, Vernon Lee, got everything, including his parents' interest in Buckley's. It gave him control. In spite of his grandfather's desire to sell, the kid apparently thought he could run the massive concern himself.

Chelly's thumbnail was uneven and she picked at it with her teeth. Warning bells were going off inside her head. Something about this deal wasn't right but she couldn't think what it was.

Rearranging, sitting down, she squared herself in the chair, pulled the stack of important papers into her lap and sorted back to the trust document. She scanned the three pages of assets while she systematically peeled her thumbnail down another level.

There it was. Buckleys, right there in black and white, on the list. What was bugging her? She stared at the paper as warning vibes prickled the back of her neck. "Think."

The old man had deeded his business to himself and his little girl as joint tenants. Then they had re-deeded it to themselves and Mr. Merchison, survivor take all.

Suddenly she realized what was wrong. There was no deed from any of them to the trust.

Chelly stiffened. In all those documents, the property was never mentioned again until it turned up in the trust. There had to be a deed from the three joint owners or a survivor to the trust for it to pass through the trust to Vernon Lee. She must have missed it.

Chelly went through the stack of documents again. There was no other deed.

Her stomach churned as she moved to sit on the floor, straddling the box, and dug through the files all over again, frantically sorting and resorting.

Everyone, including the usually infallible Manning, assumed the boy inherited his parents' interests in Buckleys through the trust. The trust itself said so.

"No," Chelly said aloud. "The deeds control. There has to be another deed, from the surviving owners or owner to the trust. The company—at least the buildings and land—belongs to the sole surviving joint tenant, the old man. Unless she had overlooked another deed.

She sat dumbstruck. There had to be one. Manning would never have made this kind of mistake.

"OUCH!" She yelped as her teeth ripped the corner of her thumbnail into the quick. She sucked on the injured appendage as she stared at the box of papers. The infallible Manning would have caught such a glaring omission. Wouldn't he have?

Yet, Buckleys was listed right there on the page of trust assets. Manning might not have linked the Merchisons' deaths—obscure as far as the company was concerned—with ownership of the real estate.

Old Mr. Buckley should have remembered the joint tenancy deed. Unless, in his grief, he hadn't thought about it.

What was more likely was she was mistaken.

Chelly called the county clerk's office in Springfield. "Will you run an ownership for me?" she asked the deputy clerk who answered the phone.

"If the legal description is involved, you can fax it to us."

"It's not. This won't take long." Chelly gave her the brief description. "I'll hold."

The woman was gone less than three minutes. "Joint tenancy deed in undivided interests from Vernon and Priscilla Buckley to Vernon Buckley and Priscilla Merchison and Nathan Merchison as joint tenants."

That deed was in the box. "Is that the last thing recorded?"

"Yes."

"Thanks."

Chelly strained her brain. Maybe a new deed had been signed but not recorded. She didn't think so and, if she were right, Vernon Lee Merchison, the contentious grandson, had no standing to influence the merger.

"Manning's got to know." She leafed through the papers again with the same result. She wrote out the message to Manning longhand. Too wordy. She edited.

Grinding her teeth as she typed, favoring the sore thumb, Chelly e-mailed her find, referencing the deeds, the deaths, and her conclusion that Buckleys buildings and grounds belonged to the old man outright, free and clear.

Then she waited.

She stared at the screen off and on for thirty-seven minutes before Manning responded. She used the time to ransack the other boxes looking for any document that might prove this the biggest mistake of her life. She needed to catch it quick, if it were.

When it came, his response was terse. *"Double check your data."*

She shot back, *"I find no subsequent transfers and the county clerk's office has nothing."*

"A new deed might not have been recorded."

"Everything else is. Could you ask Buckley?"

"How certain are you?"

"Pretty sure."

"I hate to raise Vernon Buckley's hopes on the basis of your being pretty sure."

114

Chelly nibbled at the cuticle on the side of her ravaged thumb, then typed, *"Unless you ask him, we're not going to know."*

His response was curt. *"Go home."*

It was after five. Buckleys was Manning's problem and maybe his mistake. She could still make it to class if she hurried. He didn't have to tell her twice.

On Friday morning the courier's pouch included a mailer for Chelly. Inside was a credit card issued in her name showing a five-thousand-dollar credit. There was also a note, handwritten in the bold scrawl she recognized.

"Your first merger is a success for everyone, except young Vernon Lee, who is in a funk. Enclosed is your bonus and my most sincere regards. Manning."

Chelly twirled around her office.

Passing in the hallway, Anne made a quick turn and came back. Chelly thrust the contents of the envelope into her hand and bounced up and down on her toes, knuckles at her chin, too happy to attempt an explanation.

Beed studied the contents, grinned and tossed the envelope on the desk while whooping a muted, "Wahoo!" She took both of Chelly's hands and joined her in victory twirls around the office, hopping, hooting, and laughing boisterously.

Late in the day, there was a new message from Manning: *"Thank you again, Chelly. Now that I no longer own your weekend, what are your plans?"*

"I love the bonus, boss. It is too much but I accept and promise to use it judiciously. Thanks. My roommate is a city girl who has never been on horseback. I had a horse when I was a kid and plan to provide Midge a brand new experience, if the weather holds. Does your influence extend to meteorological realms?"

"No, but I understand Sunday is to be mild," he wrote.

"Are you a horse enthusiast?"

"Yes."

When he didn't expand on his answer, she supposed he'd lost interest in the subject. She didn't want him to think she was dredging up that cowboy image thing Eric had mentioned. Then his message continued.

"Of three riding stables in your area, I recommend Hardaways. I have just reserved mounts for you and your friend there in appreciation of your recent efforts. Late morning or early afternoon would probably be best, weather-wise."

She chuckled as she typed. *"Your generous bonus more than paid for my effort. You didn't have to go to this trouble, however, I appreciate it. Late morning or early afternoon Sunday is perfect. Thank you."*

"Give Hardaway my regards. Manning."

Midge was up early Sunday making so much noise Chelly gave up trying to sleep and shuffled into the living room. Her roommate wore jeans and tennis shoes, obviously ready to ride. "I'm so excited, I couldn't stay in bed," Midge babbled.

"Shoes with heels work better in stirrups," Chelly said.

Midge's large eyes got bigger before she spun and darted back to her room.

Chelly swept her hair into a ponytail. She would dispense with the glasses for the day and ride unencumbered.

They arrived at Hardaway Stables at ten-thirty. The air was brisk but sunny and warming. Midge chattered nonstop, as excited as a child. She'd insisted they take her Dodge and her driving was erratic.

Hiram Hardaway was a spare, bowlegged little man in his seventies who hissed through his teeth when he laughed.

"So you little ladies want to ride the range, do you?"

The women glanced at each other, acknowledging the tenor of an outrageous flirt.

"Which of you is Midge?" he asked.

Midge shot a hand into the air. Hardaway's laugh sizzled between his teeth. "Thought so. We'll put you up on Smudger. He's an old man like me—still got some life left but he's not as fractious as he once was." He winked at her, his good-natured laugh spewing again. "He'll do you a job."

The horse was a huge black, intimidating, except for his ponderous walk.

Midge bounced on the balls of her feet. Hardaway handed her the reins and half of an apple.

"Open your hand out flat like this." He demonstrated. "Feed him a little apple and he'll be your friend for life."

Midge's eyes got wider, if that were possible. Chelly smiled at her roommate's obvious mental gymnastics as she forced herself to present the apple in her unprotected hand for Smudger's consideration.

The horse snuffled at the offering before his velvet lips nibbled over Midge's open palm and captured the chunk. Midge turned a wondering gaze on Chelly. Obviously, Smudger had a new devotee. Smudger snorted, Midge jumped, and laughter whistled though Hardaway's teeth.

"He's expectin' you to scratch his nose now." He raked the horse's muzzle with his fingertips. Midge watched for a beat before she pushed Hardaway's hand aside and scratched the horse's nose herself, crooning to him as she stroked. Chelly couldn't help laughing. Midge could now say she'd been in love nine times. Or was it ten?

Chelly's horse was a sorrel mare named Romance who had a spirited bouncing step. Chelly let Romance gallop ahead, circle and return several times when it became obvious Smudger believed in moderation. The big black apparently intended to cover the riding trail only once, in one direction and at one pace: slow.

The sun warmed their backs as the trail wound down to a picnic area, across a burbling creek, up a long narrow path, which looped a hill and continued over a dry high-water bridge. Midge chattered about Smudger's color, the scenery, Smudger, the equipment, Smudger, making Chelly laugh again and again at her friend's breathless excitement.

It took ninety minutes to finish the ride but Midge was not ready for it to end. "Please, Chelly, let's go around again. Just one more time. Please."

Several other people stood waiting for horses.

"We'll come back." Chelly's chuckle mingled with Hardaway's hiss. "You're going to be sore tomorrow. We want you able to get out of bed. Besides that, it's their turn."

When Midge's attention was directed to the waiting customers, she conceded. "But we can come again?"

"Sure."

"I mean next weekend, maybe."

Chelly's laughter effervesced. "Maybe."

Mr. Hardaway asked them to unsaddle the horses. "Strip the bridles but leave the halters on 'em," he said. "Set the gear in the shed. Turn 'em out in that lot yonder."

Chelly was surprised. "What about your other customers? Won't these horses be going out again?"

"Nah." Hardaway winked. "Other folks don't ride these. These belong to a fellow. He likes me to exercise 'em, but he don't want us to overdo. Like you said about your friend there, he don't want 'em miserable next day."

"And he won't mind that we rode them?"

"No, ma'am, he won't."

With Chelly's guidance, Midge wrestled the saddle off of Smudger and balanced it on the wooden fence, eying it suspiciously, willing it to stay put. She unbuckled and removed the bridle and hung it over the saddle horn. Clutching his halter, she led her new friend into the lot.

When Midge released him, Smudger ambled to the watering trough. She lingered a long time watching him drink as if she were hypnotized, absorbing the sunshine and the sight of her new love, smiling when his shoulder rippled to shoo a horsefly.

Content to watch her friend, only vaguely aware of people moving around her, Chelly stiffened as a familiar scent wafted close. She looked around to find Don standing beside her. Her heart leaped into her throat but her brain ordered her body to stay calm. "Hi." Her breathlessness made the word sound like a question.

"Howdy, ma'am." He touched a finger to the brim of his Stetson hat. She laughed at his affectation. He grinned, obviously pleased she caught his little joke. "You been out on the trail this mornin'?"

She liked the shimmer in his eyes. "Yep. Just rode into town, stranger. How about yourself?"

His expression sobered. "I'm no stranger to you, Chelly."

She ignored the butterflies in her stomach. "So, what are you doing here?"

"Meetin' someone." He glanced around and shrugged. "I guess she forgot."

Denim jeans strained over his muscular thighs and calves, all the way to the signature boots. He wore a long sleeved shirt with studs for buttons and doffed the hat, uncovering the dark hair that still hung a little long, curling behind his ears. Chelly doubted any woman ever forgot a date with him but, reluctant to feed his already adequate ego, she didn't say so. "Too bad."

"Yeah, and me with a nice picnic lunch." He gave her a questioning look. "'You hungry?"

"Maybe your date's just late."

"Don't think so. How about it?" He pointed to a picnic basket balanced on a fence post. "I'm buyin'."

"I can't. Not that I wouldn't love to, but I can't."

Midge emerged from the tack room frowning. "Chelly, I can't make that darn saddle stay on the sawhorse." She flashed Don an acknowledging glance. "Hello."

"How are you, Midge?"

"Fine, thanks." She glanced at Chelly then back at Don. "Thanks for the flower. It's still on my desk at work."

Without a word, Chelly walked to the tack shed. She would give them an opportunity to get acquainted.

She adjusted both saddles, rocked them to test their stability, and rehung the tack before returning to the sunlit afternoon. Don was there but Midge and her car were gone.

"Where's Midge?"

The emerald eyes widened, looking suspiciously innocent. "She said she'd forgotten an appointment. At the beauty shop, I think. She asked me to give you a ride home when you're ready."

Chelly's mouth gaped open and her legs felt weak. "A beauty shop appointment? On Sunday afternoon?"

Don shrugged, caught her arm and turned her toward the basket on the fence post. "Come on, let's eat before I take you home."

She pulled her arm free. "Not on your life, buster."

He grinned, all innocence. "What's the matter?"

"I'm not going anywhere with you—alone."

His grin faded and he lowered his voice. "Look, I'm sorry if I came on too strong. I didn't mean to spook you."

"You didn't spook me, I'm just smarter now and I don't intend to go trooping off to some remote place with you."

"Public picnic grounds. Lots of people. You probably saw it, near the dam where the stream cuts the bridle path."

Chelly felt herself thawing. She remembered the place, had noticed the picnic tables. She wasn't really afraid of him, especially now, in broad daylight, when he seemed so docile. After all, she needed a ride home and she was hungry. There were dozens of people close by. Also, there was his pride to consider. He'd been stood up and was probably stinging from the slight.

Chelly's glare softened and she exhaled.

Don touched her elbow tentatively, nudging her. He scooped up the basket as they passed the fence post and guided her toward an open Jeep. She took one look at the mud-spattered vehicle and relinquished a smile. "How the mighty have fallen."

"It's more terrain appropriate. Buckle up."

He started the engine, spun the vehicle in a tight circle and took off across country following a dirt trail that wound to the picnic site.

"Glad you lost the glasses. Your hair looks good." He reached over to brush his hand over the ponytail. "But I like it better all the way down."

She gave him a tolerant smile. It was hard not to be cheerful in the bright sunshine, the prospect of food to appease her galloping hunger, and a stimulating companion.

Don watched while Chelly spread a checkered tablecloth from the basket over graffiti and dried goo on the cement table. She anchored it against the persistent breeze with plastic bowls of potato salad, baked beans and cardboard salt and pepper shakers that toppled with each gust.

He started to sit on the fixed cement bench beside her before she flashed him a warning glare. He opted, instead, for the bench facing her.

"Do you come here often?" She didn't mind a little light conversation, if they kept to safe topics.

"Yes, Miss Kitty, I do."

She laughed again at the reference to the old *Gunsmoke* TV series.

They talked about horses—like Chelly, he had had one once—the riding stable; the weather; upcoming Olympic games; favorite foods, and Manning. Don seemed decidedly uninterested when she told him about their boss's oversight in the Buckley matter.

"So? Didn't you know Manning made mistakes? I told you, the guy's not God. He's a money mill. I imagine that's the kindest thing most people say about him."

The remark made her bristle and she got quiet.

Self-conscious, she didn't think she'd be able to eat much in front of him, but eating was better than conversation. When they finished, Don quickly began cleaning up, as if he'd made a decision about something. She helped. Neither of them spoke until he had put the basket in the Jeep, and said, "Let's walk."

Her eyes met his. It was a beautiful afternoon. Walking off all that fried chicken seemed harmless enough. "Okay."

He didn't attempt to touch her as they followed the creek bank, matching long strides. Without looking at her, he broke the mutual silence. "You surprised me the other night, running hot and cold the way you did. I couldn't read your signals. More. Less. More."

"I don't know what you're talking about."

"You've been engaged. I figured you knew the drill. I liked you." He gave her a sidelong smile. "You liked me."

Chelly felt the reliable blush, looked at the ground and continued striding purposefully.

"Which did you want, Chelly, more or less?" He caught her arm to pull her over beside him. She jerked away. He pointed to a green vine. "I figure you prefer me to poison ivy."

Carefully, he took her hand. She looked at their clasped hands and up at his face, silently seeking an explanation.

"My only intention is to provide a little guidance." His smile was innocent. "So you don't wander off and get into trouble."

Chills crawled up her arm from her hand enclosed in his. He steadied her as they negotiated rocks, caught her and kept her upright when she stumbled over a sinkhole. The casual contact gradually became an arm around her waist.

"Cut that out." She intended it as an admonishment. He grinned, obviously not intimidated. She paced ahead and bounced quickly across random rocks to ford the slow-running creek. She turned just as he flipped a handful of water at her head. Her movement brought her around so that the playful splash caught her full in the face.

Don stammered, trying to apologize, obviously making heroic efforts to keep a lid on his erupting laughter.

Exaggerating the gesture, Chelly scrubbed a hand over her face, swiping away water and spearing her assailant with what she pretended was a murderous glare.

His laugh exploded in a shout as he stepped out onto the rocks in the creek to cross and join her.

She retreated and tried to hide a mischievous thought as she studied his unsteady steps, hampered as he was by his continuing struggle to squelch his laughter. Toppling right and left, off balance, he proceeded over the treacherous footing.

Chelly pointed into the water at his feet and yelled, "Stop!"

He hesitated, sobering, balanced precariously on slippery stones midway across the stream.

Before he was able to find the fictitious threat, Chelly picked up a rock, one that required two hands to lift, and chunked it into the creek at his feet.

Water splattered his boots, his pant legs, his shirt and droplets even dampened his hair. As the splash trickled down the sides of his face, his emerald eyes glinted and narrowed. His startled expression became ominous as he arched his eyebrows.

Chelly wheeled and ran, giggling, darting from the footpath into the woods. She would keep well ahead of him and circle back to the Jeep.

Visualizing the startled look on his face, she was slowed by her own raucous laughter. Around and over underbrush and brambles, she ducked and dodged chortling, not listening for him, wondering how far back he was when, suddenly, he leaped from behind a broad Juniper.

Ambushed. She sidestepped but he was too quick, wrapped his arms around her and lifted. Her feet lost contact with the ground. Holding her high, he took wide strides to avoid her legs dangling in front of him.

Breathless, laughing at the justice her own orneriness had won, she struggled halfheartedly, offering only token resistance.

Summarily, Don dumped her onto a bed of crunchy brown moss at the creek's edge, dropped to his knees beside her, and pushed her down flat on her back. With an evil laugh, he stretched beside her, and threw an arm over her waist, pinning her.

She couldn't help the breathless giggling as she lay there, secretly pleased that he had outfoxed her. Looking into his eyes, which still shimmered good-naturedly, their gazes locked. The laughter dwindled to smiles, then casual regard. Their breathing slowed.

Chapter Thirteen

"Did you really have a date here?" she asked, breaking the hypnotic silence as he loomed over her prone body.

"Yep."

"And she didn't show?"

"Oh, she got here, all right. She just didn't exactly know we had a date."

"Where is she then?"

"Right here where she belongs." He shifted, placed his hands on the ground at either side of her and braced himself above her. She made a token attempt to shove him. He seemed to yield, but actually moved only enough to align his face with hers. He held himself away, poised, watching, as if waiting for a signal.

Chelly felt her lips quiver then pucker as she raised her chin, signaling surrender. He lowered his mouth to hers.

It was a spoils-to-the-victor kiss. She could feel him gloating, recognized his restrained arrogance as she relaxed into the easy contact. The sun was warm, the breeze cooling.

Her renegade body again wrested control from its cerebral restraints. Without waiting for instruction, her hand went to his face as he gave up the kiss.

He remained perfectly still, his gaze holding hers. Seeing that look in his eyes, Chelly's confidence soared. She put both hands on his face and tugged, again pulling his mouth to hers.

He lowered his upper body, the rest stretched to one side of her. Kissing her gently, his hand drifted to her face before fingertips slowly traced her profile and throat.

Chelly felt wanton, enticing this predatory male, inviting this intimacy in the open, in broad daylight, in front of God and any passing riders, even though they were well away from the riding trail.

They kissed again and again, long, breathless kisses. She could feel the strain in his shoulders and the burgeoning muscles in his arms. His whole body seemed taut.

Finally, he filled his lungs and looked up and around, reconnoitering. Again Chelly put her hands on either side of his face, but he groaned and pushed himself onto his hands and knees, creating a chilling space between them.

She felt rejected, foolish and completely confused. "I don't know what's gotten into me. I'm sorry. It's just that once I start kissing you, I... I just can't seem to get enough."

A rich laugh rumbled from his throat before he bent, again lowering his mouth to hers. When their teeth tapped, they both grinned, without breaking the seal between them.

"My mouth's too big." She intended it as an apology.

"Not as big as mine."

"Bigger."

He smiled ruefully. "Let's measure. Open your mouth as wide as you can."

She trilled an embarrassed little laugh, then complied by opening her mouth so wide she could barely see him.

"Good. But not good enough." His mouth resembled the entrance to a great cavern as it covered hers. She gasped at his approach and wound up giggling into the yawning expanse that engulfed her upper and lower lips.

Laughing, feeling ridiculous, she scarcely noticed his hands tugging playfully at her clothing, until he freed her shirttail.

Her mouth still captive, she made a halfhearted effort to interrupt the kiss before he pulled his knees under him. Bracing himself on his haunches, he slid both hands onto her bare midriff. In spite of her hands flapping at his, he pushed her shirt up under her arms.

Deftly dodging her flailing hands, he kissed her again and distracted her as he lifted her with one hand and reached under to unhook her bra in a single practiced motion.

She felt eager, curious, excited, and reluctant, all at the same time. Pretending to object, she actually moved closer encouraging him to touch her.

Freeing her breasts, he shoved the bra up, bunching it across her upper chest with her shirt.

Exposed, Chelly was surprised to be more curious than embarrassed. She stared at his face as he allowed himself an unobstructed view of her, practically nude from the waist up. He was the first man to see her matured body that way and she was eager to gauge his reaction.

"You are exquisite." His eyes darkened and glistened. His breath came in quick pulls. His smile faded. Suddenly, he swooped, hesitating only a moment before his mouth captured a breast.

She'd never imagined such sensations. Current traveled the length of her and prompted a peculiar reflex between her legs. No man had ever touched her naked breasts. She'd been curious, maybe even willing, but Eric had never fondled her.

As Don suckled, even token resistance to his actions seemed to melt. Her stomach fluttered. She couldn't catch her breath. Just as she thought she could not bear the pleasure one moment more, he caught one tip firmly between his lips and spiked her excitement up another notch.

She caught the back of his head with both hands and crushed him to her, arching her back, aware only of a flurry of fabulous agony. His hot hands moved to her waist and down until his fingers pried beneath the waistband of her jeans.

An alarm went off inside her. She had to make him stop. Had to get control of him. Of herself.

She grabbed for his hands, but he captured hers instead and pinned them at her sides before his lips relinquished the breast. His eyes were closed, his mouth wide as it settled over the second breast, suckling first, then capturing the tip between his lips.

In spite of the mental scolding, her body undulated and she gasped involuntarily. She freed her hands and wrapped her arms around him so tightly that her straining biceps spasmed.

Her brain chastised urgently as her legs ceased to resist his knee coaxing them apart. What if some rider veered off the bridle path and saw them?

She groaned and rocked her head from side to side. What if someone saw her? Half nude? Eager? Like this?

Don's body covered hers, effectively concealing her naked upper torso from nonexistent passersby. She pushed halfheartedly at his shoulders. Slowly his mouth gave up its ruthless siege, but when he lifted his chest, the movement pressed his lower body into hers.

Astonished, embarrassed, she felt his arousal, thick and hard against her thigh. Suddenly frantic, she planted both hands against his shoulders and shoved. "Stop." Her voice sounded remote. "Please. Please stop."

He responded with a dozen staccato kisses—at her waist, over her breasts, on her mouth, with finishing taps to her eyelids. Finally, he rocked back, his legs folded beneath him, pulling his body from hers but keeping a hand on her midriff.

She felt chilled. Goose bumps budded on every inch of her exposed flesh.

She put her hands over the hand that remained on her stomach. Her mouth burned and she had an uneasy feeling of need. "I don't know what keeps happening. I have never acted like this before."

On his knees, his eyes surveying, his hand maintaining physical contact, Don didn't offer an explanation.

Obviously, during her years with Eric, she had missed more than she realized. With some encouragement, it probably wouldn't take Don long to bring her to speed.

He gave her a withering smile. "You have a strange effect on me, too, Chelly Bennett." He gave no indication he wanted to move. His eyes raked her, feasting on her unencumbered breasts.

She shifted position. "Could I please get up?"

He snorted a laugh and lifted the hand from her stomach. She wriggled to a kneeling position, a mirror image of his, tugged and wiggled to re-affix her bra and straighten her shirt while avoiding his eyes.

"What are you worried about, Chelly?"

She kept her eyes averted and blushed.

"Come on. Tell me." When she remained mute, he continued. "I have to assume that young Chastain was not an accomplished lover."

Her eyes rounded as they met his, but her voice was only a murmur. "I guess not." She bowed her head, unable to look at him, and spoke so quietly her words were swallowed by the breeze. "I like kissing you. I like the way you touch me and how you make me feel. I've never done this kind of thing before."

The laugh began low in his chest and rumbled its way up before it emerged from his throat. They were both on their knees, face to face as he grabbed the back of her neck, rocked her toward him and planted another kiss on her compliant mouth. He took her hand, rolled back and up onto his feet in one smooth motion, pulling her to a standing position directly in front of him.

She blinked. "What are you doing?"

He tugged her hand, pulling her.

"Where are you taking me?"

"To the picnic table."

"But there are people over there."

"Exactly."

Clasping her hand firmly, he led her through the trees.

Since adolescence, Don had groped, fondled, explored, and experienced many women. He'd used some and schooled a few to satisfy his specific appetites. Six weeks was the longest any woman had ever held his interest.

Chelly would be a charming playmate, a fascinating toy, but she wasn't a woman to be enjoyed and tossed aside. She had already held his interest well over the usual six weeks. She represented a bold new concept for him: A keeper.

Although he hadn't been *with* her, his desire for her was barely controllable. He acknowledged the diminishing bulge still discernible within the confines of his denim jeans. He didn't look at her because simply looking might arouse him all over again. He sometimes got hard just thinking of her. The occurrences were annoying. He'd had more control when he was nineteen.

To complicate an already complex situation, he felt an answering passion in her, the way she became completely pliable in his arms. With his experience and her naiveté, he probably could take her anytime he wanted.

Okay, then, why wait? With very little finesse, he could coax her into the cheapo motor court down the road. They could spend the rest of the day and probably most of the night enjoying the intricate pleasures of the flesh. The appendage in his jeans stiffened again.

But the sensations were obviously new to her. He glanced at her. She was not perfect, but even her imperfections captivated him.

He felt her shiver and his conscience gave his libido a swift kick. All this speculating was ridiculous. He was a man who usually made hard, fast decisions that involved thousands of lives and millions of dollars. Why was he so conflicted about this one woman?

He ventured another look.

Because she was damned well a perfect match for him—intelligent, funny, beautiful in a provincial way, alluring, blatantly unsophisticated and sharing many of the same interests.

No, Chelly deserved better than a roll in the sack with some prowling tomcat. To enjoy the pleasures of this woman's body, a man needed to commit for the long haul. He had to be willing to marry her.

The silky smoothness of her full, ripe breasts was too fresh a memory. He would give his soul to be the man who could make and keep that commitment.

But, he wasn't. Couldn't be.

Or, could he?

He thought again of the first man she'd chosen, and he hated Eric Chastain. What a damnably poor match. She was too much woman for a Milquetoast like Chastain. She had integrity and ambition, humor and determination, not to mention that a body like hers should be enjoyed by a connoisseur, a man who could cultivate those untapped erogenous zones, provide her unimaginable pleasure.

He didn't actually have to be the one, but he felt a certain obligation, for he was a mature man who could plumb and appreciate her depths of passion as well as her other qualities.

Truthfully, he was the only man he knew who might actually be worthy of her.

Or was he over valuing himself?

He didn't think so. At least, he hoped not.

But marriage? No. Then he looked at her again and drew a deep, shuddering breath. He'd never seen a woman better suited for him or him for her.

He led her into the clearing, to the picnic table, and stopped. There was no one around. Good.

Chelly started to walk on to the Jeep, but he pulled her around, caught her waist with both hands and lifted to place her perfect bottom on the picnic table. He paced several steps back and turned to face her.

"I'm thirty-six years old, Chelly. I have steady employment, no outstanding debts, and no personal baggage—no ex wives or children, no communicable diseases." He hesitated. "I want you to marry me. Will you do it?" He spoke with no inflection or emotion, the only expression on his face, a scowl.

"Do what?"

"Will you marry me?"

She shook her head from side to side staring at him, obviously stunned to silence.

"Since the day you walked into DMD, I haven't been able to get you out of my mind for more than five minutes at a time." He regarded her closely. "When you're anywhere near me, I can't keep my hands off you. We are a perfect match. If you knew as much about us as I do, you'd agree." She started to say something, but he held up a hand to stop her.

"No, there's no use cluttering your head with a lot of extraneous information until you've made a decision about this. Trust me. Marrying me is the right thing for you to do. I promise you, it is."

She stared at him. Was he kidding or demented? Trust him? Trusting him or any other man was the last thing she was going to do.

As an afterthought, he added, "Marriage to me will be as confining or as liberating as you want. I will support you financially, give you everything you need and most of what you want.

"As for me, I'll insist only on my conjugal rights as your husband. You can come and go as you please. No strings."

Flustered, she looked at him doubting his emotional stability. "Don't be ridiculous. I'm not marrying anyone. Besides that, you sound more like you're negotiating a business contract than proposing marriage."

He thought a moment. "Maybe so, but then that is what marriage is, isn't it? A legal contract binding two individuals to agreed terms."

She felt injured by his cold assessment and wasn't sure why. "I have a plan for my life and a job I love. I want to finish school. I want to practice law." She dropped her voice. "How could I marry you. I don't love you. I don't even know you."

"You know me well enough. And I won't interfere with your plans. I'll even help you. I make plenty of money and you'll have access to everything you need. As for love, it'll happen," he eyed her skeptically, "assuming it hasn't already."

She bit her lips and stared at the ground.

He spoke quietly. "Chelly, I'll make it happen." As she looked up, he held up a hand to delay her interruption. "You can keep your job at DMD and stay in school. I won't make any demands on your time or your person, except the one. You'll be married to me. You will have to be faithful to me, of course, sleep only with me. Other than that, your life will be pretty much the same as it is now."

She looked embarrassed, glanced right and left and lowered her voice to an appeal. "You're halfway to getting me into bed without obligating yourself to any contracts." She hesitated and he remained silent as if waiting for her to finish the thought. "Why do you feel like you have to marry me?"

He laughed, a rolling sound, as he studied her through narrowed eyes. "Because you are who you are. I don't want you haunted by a lot of unnecessary guilt. I want you free to experiment with your passion—only with me, of course.

"You're a sweet, candid woman, Chelly, innocent, wise and transparent. I can practically read your mind most of the time. Your thoughts flicker across your face like a movie projected on a screen. Your empathy for people, pique when something annoys you, sorrow, excitement, joy... passion... all show in your face." He frowned. "I don't want to see shame or regret there. You're the kind of woman who has to marry the man."

He stared deep into her eyes. "I can give you a level playing field, Chelly, one where you can run with abandon, protected, provided for and indulged."

"What about children?"

He stiffened, obviously caught off guard. "That would be entirely up to you."

"Children would interfere with my career."

"Then we won't have them."

"But I want children."

"Your call, either way."

Her face twisted into a frown. "What about your other women? I'm sure you have girlfriends. Do you plan to continue seeing them after you marry?"

"I've had hot romances and pleasant acquaintances, Chelly. Some of those became friends. I've never before asked a woman to be my wife. I don't have a lot of regard for women generally. I do happen to be crazy about you. *My* fidelity won't be a problem. I will be a faithful husband to you just as I will expect you to be faithful to me."

Her throat ached so that she seemed to croak. "But why?"

He bowed his head rather than betray his own confusion, but his next words exposed his secret thoughts.

"Hell if I know. I'm quite a bit older than you are but you need someone mature, someone to watch over you. I am good at nearly everything I try. I think I can be a damn good husband to the right woman." He looked directly into her face. "You are the right woman. The one who has run from me in my dreams since I was old enough to know what dreams were. You're funny, uninhibited, optimistic, and frequently tactless. I have little regard for your taste in clothes or hairstyles, yet, I admire your indefatigable spirit, your courage, your resolve, and a hundred other things I know about you at this moment. I'll probably discover a thousand more in time. I'm asking you to give me that time. A lifetime. Chelly Bennett, will you be my wife?"

Sorrow came over her like a great dark cloud. "If I refuse, will... ?" She hesitated.

He frowned. "What? Finish your question."

She shot him a troubled look and held his gaze. "If I say no, will that mean we won't... well, will it mean... no more kissing?"

He arched one eyebrow and the intensity left his generous mouth, which curved up at the ends suggestively. He spoke slowly. "Not necessarily. Of course, in that event, you will understand if I continue to plead my case?"

"And keep trying to get me into bed?"

He thought a moment. "Maybe not. Maybe I'll hold that out as the carrot to entice you to sign *the contract*."

She smiled, suddenly feeling challenged. She'd been aware of his frequent arousal. His need seemed fierce at times. She did not want to think about her own need. It might be fun to take this challenge. She studied him a long moment. He was a magnificent, mature male. She didn't want to damage his ego or denigrate him in any way.

"I suppose we could keep playing games together," she said, "as long as you understand I don't intend to marry you."

He nodded but the slow-breaking Cheshire cat smile looked as if he thought he might already have won this contest.

Midge returned to the apartment at five o'clock to find Chelly and Don entwined on the sofa, clothing rumpled, hair disheveled, both flushed and breathless.

At their insistence, the trio fixed bacon and scrambled eggs for supper.

Don left before midnight. He would be out of town for two weeks, would call when he returned. In case of emergency, Chelly could contact him through Manning.

Chapter Fourteen

Leonard Diet slipped into Manning's private office mid morning on Monday where Anne and Chelly were discussing new employee e-mail policies. Diet stepped in front of Anne as if she were not there.

"How are you, Chelly?" His words were impersonal, but his small blue eyes glittered from his round, pink face. Looking at him, Chelly noticed the pods of fat that clung to his temples, melted over his cheekbones, and oozed down the sides of his face, pooling finally to form droopy jowls.

Diet was able to overcome the pods' effect somewhat with his smile, which drew the observer's eyes to his broad mouth and his short chin with its rippling aftershocks.

He seemed like a soft, good-hearted rich man who was genuinely fond of her. Chelly glanced at Anne who ignored them both, focusing on a typewritten sheet in her hands.

Chelly smiled. "I'm fine, Mr. Diet. How about you?"

"Dear girl, I've asked you to call me Len. Please. Mr. Diet makes me feel like an old man. Like my dad."

"Sorry, Len. I think it sounds disrespectful for me to call you by your first name here in the office, like we were buddies."

His smile waned and he regarded her earnestly. "I want us to be buddies, Chelly. To be honest, I want us to be more than buddies, don't you know?"

She smiled. "Mr… Len… I'm very flattered but I don't really have enough influence around here to… "

"Tsk, tsk. I figure you'll one day be a principal here yourself, not as an attorney, of course, but as someone who knows where all the bodies are buried. Scuttlebutt has it that Manning trusts you implicitly, don't you know?"

Chelly laughed at his repeated phrase and nodded to indicate she appreciated the compliment. He seemed to take encouragement from that.

"Would you consider having dinner with me?"

Anne's eyes shot to Chelly's face and the supervisor appeared to be about to say something but, instead, shifted her gaze back to the page in her hand.

Chelly again considered Diet's age-inappropriate crewcut and his beefy face. She had resolved to take him up on the next offer, but her determination flagged as she looked up into the pouches and chins that concealed any hint of a neck. She needed the practice handling city men, even more so now, in light of Don's challenge. And Len would probably be a piece of cake.

"What would people say about us together?" she asked.

"They'd marvel at how lucky I was to get such a great looking date."

She looked down at her frumpy, loose-fitting suit and smiled back at him. "No, they wouldn't. They'd wonder what new charity case you'd taken on."

"I would be honored if you would have dinner with me. It doesn't have to be tonight, although tonight would be fine. But on a Friday or Saturday night, I could really show you off, dinner and dancing, a stage show perhaps."

The color heightened in his round face and the chins' quiver became a quake. "I know just the ticket. The ballet. A week from Saturday. The Saturday night performance. We could put on the dog."

Chelly was surprised at his enthusiasm. "I've never been to the ballet. I wouldn't know what to wear. Wouldn't know how to behave."

Diet jittered two steps closer, gave her an alarmed look and teetered back to his original mark. "I'll call Mr. Woody's. You can go there sometime, during your lunch hour, or anytime, really. They'll fix you right up. A dress, jewelry, shoes, gloves, a wrap, anything you want. On me. They'll know just how you should dress for the ballet."

Glancing away from her, he paced to the door, wringing his hands. "I'll get us orchestra seats. No, no, better than that, I'll get us a box. You'll feel like a fairy princess. That's it, Princess Chelly, her royal highness for a night."

She marveled at his hand-wringing fervor. She didn't remember ever having excited a man this way. She smiled to herself. Well, maybe one.

Diet gyrated, his ponderous frame moving on tiny, tapping steps.

"All right, Len. I'd be delighted. But I'll get the clothes myself."

"Wouldn't hear of it. This is my treat, all the way, don't you know? I absolutely will not allow you to ruin your budget for me, no matter how willing you may be to do so.

"I'll pick you up at six-thirty that evening—that's Saturday week. We'll have a nice meal at... what do you like? Do you like steak? Lobster?" He snapped his fingers. "I know! The buffet at the Trenton. Picturesque, don't you know? We'll start there with drinks, take on the buffet, then off to the theater."

At the mention of the Trenton, Chelly became more alert.

Apparently taking heart at her interest, Len hurried on. "Afterward, we'll go dancing and then have an intimate little supper at my place. I'll handle the details." He shot a quick look at her breasts, startling her. Were those the details he was thinking of handling?

"Wait a minute, Mr. Diet... "

He flashed her a flirtatious, sidewise glance. "Len, Chelly. After the night I have planned, Len and Chelly will be an item. We'll be invited everywhere together."

"No, no, no." She tried to keep the panic out of her voice. "Len, I'm terribly flattered, but it's too much."

"I've overwhelmed you, haven't I?"

"I'm afraid so. Yes."

"I do that when I get enthused, don't you know? Didn't intend to frighten you. Let's back up. You were all right as far as Saturday night and the ballet, right?"

Chelly gave a slight nod but her voice wavered. "Well, yes."

"Dinner?"

"I would love to have dinner with you, and the buffet at the Trenton sounds great." The buffet in the Trenton's main ballroom on Saturday nights was famous. The crowd surely would help curb Len's exuberance. Niggling in the back of her mind was the other little thought. Don stayed at the Trenton. He might be back by then. They might run into him there.

"And about the clothes... ?" Diet interrupted her musing.

She offered a quieting smile. "I'll find something that'll work. I don't have anything appropriate for a box. Could we just sit in the regular audience?"

"Certainly. Certainly. That'll be just fine. And I'll wear a plain, dark suit, instead of my tux. Wouldn't want to outshine you. And six-thirty? Is that all right with you? And you understand, now, that's not this week. It's next Saturday."

"Yes, I understand, and thank you very much." She gave him a kindly smile. "I really do appreciate your inviting me. I'll try not to embarrass you in front of your friends."

He looked bewildered. "Surely you jest. It is they whom I fear might prove the embarrassment. We'll steer clear of the tiresome, stuffy types. In fact, I want to avoid everyone else Saturday night and just fill myself drinking in the essence of you."

Chelly smiled but inside she heard alarm bells.

Still flushing, Diet exited Manning's office.

Anne snorted, unsuccessfully trying to suppress the giggle that bubbled into the room. "Fill himself up drinking in the essence of you? I wonder how many gallons of essence that windbag can hold. Give me a break, Bennett. You and I both know what that old fart's got on his mind, don't you know?" She raised her eyebrows, mimicking his hackneyed expression. "Even you can't be that gullible."

Chelly smiled. "I'm sure we'll have a nice time."

"Sure you will, honey, but he'll bear watching. I saw where he was leering while he licked his chops just now. I'd be careful not to drink a snootful or that old coot'll be guzzling his fill of your essence from your bare body."

Chelly grimaced at Anne's crude suggestion.

Late that same Monday afternoon, Chelly had a personal call.

"Ms. Bennett, I'm so glad to have reached you. This is Edwin Streeter. Dr. Streeter, Dean of the Tennyson University School of Law."

Chelly straightened in her chair. What was wrong? She didn't ask, didn't say anything, encouraging the dean to continue.

"First let me say how pleased we are to have you as a student at the TU law school. I see by your records that you transferred to us from State. It isn't often we lure a student away from the University. We count that a feather in our caps."

Chelly shifted in her chair—Manning's chair. "Thank you." She waited.

Streeter cleared his throat. "Through a misunderstanding, we were not able to enroll you in Dr. Labor's torts class this term. I understand that may have worked a hardship and we want to make that up to you. We usually don't offer that class in the summer term, however, we've made some scheduling changes and will offer one section of torts beginning June fifth."

Chelly felt the small hairs bristle on the back of her neck and smiled. "Dr. Streeter, thank you. If there's any way, well, I need to be in the class." She thought she heard him sigh.

"Oh, Ms. Bennett, you—that is people like you, of course—are the very reason we are going to run this special section. I read over your transcript thoroughly this morning. You have only five required subjects left after this semester. And several electives, of course. We would like to work with you on the rest of your curriculum. Mrs. Delamater will meet with you at your convenience to review and perhaps enable you to graduate one year from this coming May, just as you would have, had you remained at State."

She would graduate on time, as if her law classes had not been interrupted at all. Chelly wanted to shout, turn cartwheels. Instead, she held herself in check.

·"Thank you, Dr. Streeter, but I work days. I'm only available for evening classes, which means I can only manage about nine credit hours a semester."

"Well, yes, but you only need a total of twenty-nine hours, required courses and electives, after this term. Mrs. Delamater is a genius at manipulating schedules, if we offer what you need when you need it, on Saturdays, for example. It may work out perfectly. And we are going to take a special interest in you. We had no idea when you enrolled that you worked at Diet, Manning, Diet, Harned and Associates. You should have told us."

Chelly felt her smile wilt. "Does that make a difference?"

"Ah." He hesitated. "Well, had we known... You see, we are indirectly affiliated with DMD." That was news to her. "The partners have been most generous and we try to reciprocate when we can. Now that we know your situation, we certainly want to help, within limits, of course."

"Of course." Chelly had no idea what Streeter was talking about, but she was getting an idea.

Leonard Diet had put pressure on TU.

No. It couldn't have been Leonard. He didn't know she was a law student. Then who?

Had Don mentioned it to Manning? She pursed her lips. Manning had clout. She just didn't know it extended into educational realms. She shrugged. If she'd known his influence could open these doors, would she have asked for his help?

Maybe.

Rethinking it, she hoped not.

Chapter Fifteen

Chelly thought of Don every waking moment: of his astonishing proposal, his laugh, his teasing, his catlike grace. She thought of the heat of his body hovering above her, his surprise when she splashed him in the creek, his mouth toying with those previously pristine parts of her body.

When she closed her eyes at night, he prowled through her dreams, a great tawny cat with flashing green eyes, stalking, beckoning, hypnotizing her with his antics, pressing himself against her cool skin—in dreams, always unclothed.

Several mornings she woke up halfway out of her sleep shirt, groaning as she grappled with the covers. But in her dreams, and during her days as well, he eluded her.

She had no word from him—not a phone call or a note.

The more she thought of Don, the more she dreaded the upcoming date with Leonard. What had made her agree to go?

Finally she asked and Midge reminded her. "He's your lab rat. Your research project. But, Chelly, this isn't gonna work. Studying Leonard Diet to learn how to handle Don is like studying a firecracker to learn to operate a Tomahawk Missile."

She would wear her blue dress, a swirling, midnight blue rayon number with a scalloped neckline that revealed just a hint of breasts for sexy, and long sleeves for demure. The color emphasized her dark hair and eyes. She'd pull her hair up on the sides and let it cascade down her back.

With a man Leonard's height, she could even wear the heels that made her over five feet ten. He would still have an inch or so on her.

"Should I wear the pearls?" Chelly emerged from her bedroom dangling the necklace she had received as a confirmation gift when she was fourteen.

From the kitchen, Midge turned, did a double take, and took several steps into the living room to stare close up. "Girl! Woman! You dazzle. Where'd you get the dress? Dress, heck, where'd you find that body? I've never seen you look so… damned sexy. Good grief!"

Chelly winced self consciously. "I've had the dress for three years. The body? Standard issue. You just haven't noticed."

Midge ignored the answer. "No wonder Don's ballistic. Obviously, he did. Notice, that is."

Chelly scowled. "I was in an oversized business suit or sweats when he got interested. He couldn't have seen my figure through all that fabric."

"Oh, yeah? Well, he could feel it, couldn't he? The way he was groping that night, he didn't have to see much to know what was underneath. God, I am such a dim bulb. And I'm your roommate."

"Big deal. Your noticing doesn't change anything, does it?"

"Chelly, I had plans to skulk around until you were finished with him, then nab Don for myself, especially if you developed a serious interest in Diet's money. I hear he's loaded. And you, my dear, obviously are in the hunt for fame and fortune. Diet has the wherewithal to back your ambition. Not many people do. Don Juan, however, can definitely provide what I crave. We needn't go into detail, need we?" She arched her eyebrows.

Chelly stifled a laugh. "No, we needn't. Now, how about the pearls?"

"Definitely not. No use overselling the goods. Dangle something from those delicious lobes. Are they pierced?"

Humming an affirmative, Chelly's mouth twisted as she studied her reflection in the mirror over the sideboard in the dining area. Midge was right. The necklace was too much. She didn't need to summon attention to her throat or cleavage. Long, delicate earrings would do the same thing, but more subtly. She returned to her room for the modification.

Midge answered the buzz and told Leonard Diet to, "Come on up."

Chelly darted out of her room. "He's coming up here?"

"Sure. I picked up. It looks presentable."

"Midge, he's a heft. The climb might kill him."

Before she finished, there were three soft raps at the door. Not only had he climbed all four flights, her date had apparently done so in record time.

Leonard Diet was leaning, one hand high on the doorjamb, sucking air. "Chelly," he huffed, "I need… a drink."

She saw a twinkle in his eye and knew he was kidding even though the gasps seemed genuine. Laughing, Chelly took his free arm and led him to the sofa while Midge ran to the kitchen for a glass of water.

He guzzled several swallows, then held the glass away from him and made an awful face. "Water? Yuck, phooey. Haven't you girls got anything else?"

"Kool-aid," Midge offered.

"Cooking sherry," Chelly said with an apologetic shrug.

"Never mind." He took several more sips as his breathing slowed. "I haven't had tap water in a while. No bouquet to speak of, which is probably a good thing, but it's not as bad as I remembered."

Chelly's smile broadened. "The trip down is much easier."

"And by the time we get back, we will have forgotten the torture of the climb, is that the way you see it?"

She laughed lightly.

His gaze swept her up and down. "I knew you were gorgeous under all that paraphernalia. Manning doesn't waste his attention on homely women." He paused but Chelly didn't want to endorse the crack about Manning with a response.

Diet continued. "I'm really pleased to see that you actually have some clothes that fit." He peered at her face. "I didn't realize you wore contact lenses."

"I don't, but I'm going without my glasses tonight."

"If you don't need them, why wear them?"

"I do need them, at the office." She gave Midge a sidelong glance.

He brightened. "Well, anyway, I'm glad you're not wearing them tonight." He paused, apparently remembering the climb because he said, "If we go out often, we may have to get you a place with an elevator, don't you know?" She must have looked startled because he winked. "Okay, if you're attached to this place, I'll have one installed here."

Chelly and Midge both laughed politely. Chelly hoped he was just being funny. Of course, with his mega bucks, he probably could have an elevator installed here, if he wanted.

As they descended the stairs, Leonard put a cool hand on her shoulder, then slid the hand to her neck, as if he were staking a claim. She tried not to make it obvious as she wrapped her velvet stole closer around her upper arms. He crooned, "You look delicious, positively good enough to eat. I'm salivating."

Chelly smiled and whispered a soft, "Thanks," but she had to concentrate on not shuddering.

A limo waited at the curb.

"I may have Hazelwood here call for you next time." Diet glanced at the elderly driver, calling Chelly's attention to the man who was older but trim and appeared to be in much better shape than Diet. She laughed as if he'd made a joke but she suspected Len was about half serious.

On the ride downtown, they talked shop. Leonard asked her opinion of several types and brands of computers, copiers, fax machines, and dictating equipment before he broached the subject of personnel.

His tone sounded casual. "Chelly, how well do you get along with Anne Beed?"

Anne had been at DMD for years, knew every employee by name and often spoke with them about their families and interests. Why would Leonard care about a newcomer's opinion of Anne?

"We get along very well. Anne's definite about what she wants and she's conscientious. If you do things to suit her and don't throw sand in the gears moving DMD, she's a pussycat."

"Have you crossed her?"

She thought he was teasing. "I wouldn't dare."

"You're saying she's never wrong then?"

She felt her good humor ebb. "Well, not that I would know of course, but occasionally she might make a bad call. She's quick to straighten it out though, as soon as she realizes there's a problem. Why do you ask?"

"Tom Bixler hates her."

While Chelly wondered idly why anyone would care what a Neanderthal like Bixler thought, Diet's expression fell to somber, and he said, "He always has, don't you know? Hated her. The animosity between those two reduces the efficiency of our whole operation. Tom's wanted Beed fired since right after he came on board."

"Oh? I didn't realize Anne had worked at DMD longer than Bixler had." Anne seemed officious with Bixler at times, but Chelly had never seen her rude or insubordinate, although Bixler certainly required straightening out... frequently.

"That's right."

"Len, I would think that over very carefully. Anne single-handedly runs the part of the office that deals with corporations. She knows her job and she has wonderful people skills. She keeps her crew happy in their work."

He glowered at the passing scenery. "I'm thinking of giving Bixler additional duties, moving him into Beed's job. You would be working directly under him. I understand most women prefer male supervisors."

Chelly's eyes rounded. "Me work for Bixler? Are you kidding?"

He turned his full attention on her. "No, I'm perfectly serious. Bixler tells me you have quite a good rapport with D.R."

Apparently the office wags were discussing her relationship with Manning more than she realized. And was Diet changing the subject or was he feeling her out about... what? She wasn't sure, but it sounded like he wanted her approval before replacing Beed with Bixler. Well, he wouldn't get it. The idea was absurd.

She squared around to face him. "First, I like Anne Beed very much. She is easy to work for. Secondly, Mr. Bixler and I do not get along. He is oppressive and chauvinistic. Often he neither knows nor cares what's going on. As an example, anyone who says I influence Mr. Manning does not know what he's talking about."

"A little defensive, aren't we?" Len's voice whined through his nasal passages.

Why did she always have to defend Manning or try to explain him? She didn't even know the man. "Len, Manning is nothing to me but a faceless entity on my computer."

"You haven't met him?"

"No. When would I have met him?"

"When he was here last week. I assumed... "

"Last week?" Her heart plummeted. "When last week?"

"One morning. He insists on breakfast meetings at the crack of dawn. It was Monday, I think. Yes, that's right, a week ago last Monday. I assumed you spoke with him then."

Manning, her mentor and hero, had been in the building, had been that close, and hadn't bothered to introduce himself to her. She felt completely deflated. "I may have seen him. Like I said, we haven't met. I wouldn't recognize him."

Chelly slouched into the seat and glared out at the darkened streets. It was silly to think Manning would care about meeting her. Anne said his last assistant got a schoolgirl crush on him. Maybe he was trying to avoid a repeat.

Diet sat forward on the seat. "He'll be back this weekend. Breakfast meeting, seven Monday. You can meet him then. You'll need to get in early, don't you know?"

Oh, sure, she could get to the office an hour early and crash a meeting of the upper echelon. She could just see that happening. Not. Her mood deteriorated.

When they swung into the Trenton's circular drive, several well-dressed patrons looked to see what celebrity might emerge from the limo. Chelly felt self conscious as Hazelwood opened the door, exposing her to the passersby.

One woman craned her neck, frowned, and took her companion's hand turning him toward the hotel. Chelly obviously had been found unworthy of celebrity status.

A handsome young man in evening clothes slowed and did a double take when he saw her, a gesture that bolstered her sagging morale. He smiled, straightened, then intercepted the doorman to hold the hotel door for her.

"I've got it." Len's voice sounded brusque, as if he were offended.

The young man's smile broadened and he motioned Len through ahead of him. "Come ahead, old man."

As Chelly smiled her thanks, Len caught her arm and abruptly swept her inside.

She and Midge had come to a Sunday brunch, but the hotel had a different, almost magical, ambiance at night. The lobby fairly glowed, lush in golds and reds with dramatic foliage wrapping colonnades and draping bannisters that outlined the dual sweeping staircases. Chelly took it all in as Len, firmly attached to her elbow, guided her toward the dining room.

She dawdled, realizing to her own chagrin that she was looking for Don. Just because he stayed there when he was in Tennyson didn't mean he would be there now or that they would meet, even if he were.

Why hadn't Don told her Manning would be in town?

Of course, to be fair, he might not have known.

She surveyed the crowd. As tall as he was, Don would be easy to see, if he were there.

What if she did see him? How should she react?

Then a dreadful thought: What if he had a date?

If she saw him, it probably would be better to pretend not to see him. So why, she badgered herself, did she keep looking?

The dining room was a theater in the round with tiers of tables that allowed diners, even those on the back rows, to see the dance floor. The lighting was dim but crystal goblets and sterling flatware glistening on linen cloths fairly shouted, "High dollar."

Len said hello to several people as they followed the maitre d' to their table, which was well located for seeing and being seen.

Just off center stage, a five-piece group played dinner music. As Chelly eased into the chair held by a waiter, she inhaled slowly, enjoying the wafting smells of meats and seasonings and yeast breads.

A giant of a man loomed at Len's side and glowered down at the top of her date's head, even though Diet was still standing.

The giant asked questions that Chelly, already seated, couldn't hear over the hum of conversations and music. The man was obviously complaining. Len raised his voice saying he would have to see the file to know the status of the man's legal work.

"I assure you I'm handling the matter personally." Len cast a helpless look at Chelly, but she could offer no assistance. He looked perplexed. "I just cannot recall off the top of my head where we stand." Another sidelong glance at Chelly. "When I'm able to get such a pretty girl on my arm, it's awfully hard to get my mind back on business." Len winked at Chelly. She gave him a smile.

Leonard habitually procrastinated, let time run on cases, missed court dates, trod treacherously close to malfeasance. She supposed he was using her as his excuse this time.

The giant frowned at Chelly and bellowed at Len. "I'm going to call first thing Monday. I expect to speak to you. I expect you to have answers or you and I are going to knock heads." He turned on his heel and strode back to his table.

Looking sheepish, Len shrugged. "I admire a man with great expectations, don't you?" She smiled as if they were conspirators. "Really, that was nothing. I can't go anywhere without somebody wanting to talk shop."

Chelly had eaten very little all day, saving calories for the splurge that night. When the bar waiter arrived, she asked Len to order for her, something light. He beamed at the request. "I know a very nice wine."

Chelly smiled gamely. "I don't care for wine, Len. Even good wines taste bitter to me. No palette. Could I have something fruity and frozen, or a Collins drink, maybe?"

He patted her arm affectionately. "Certainly. Your teeniest wish is my command, dear heart."

Chelly returned his smile but she felt embarrassed. "I think I'll powder my nose before our drinks come. Can you point me toward the ladies room?"

Len stood with her, stepped behind to put his mouth close to her ear and pointed, providing a lot of unnecessary detailed instructions. His posturing reminded her of Eric, posing for hoped-for spectators, always assuming other people had nothing better to do than watch him.

Don stepped off the elevator and looked right and left. He did a double take as he saw Chelly's long, lithe figure floating toward the ladies' room.

What was she doing at the Trenton? Was she looking for him? Though that might be flattering, he didn't like to think of her tracking him. Still, she was a quick study and she knew he stayed here.

He needed to avoid her here, where people knew him, called him by name. Besides, seeing her had an unsettling effect. His thinking got muddled when she wandered close—when he could smell her fragrance, see her move, feel her dark eyes on him.

He had work to do and no time for a woman, at least not this woman. He had made a serious mistake with her. "No personal commitments," was his mantra. His attitude toward women—use 'em and lose 'em—had proved perfectly successful in the past. Vanessa was a good example, insisting he meet her tonight, using the universal sexual blackmail to force his attention.

Chelly would complicate things. He would have to avoid her. If she realized, she might be offended. Who was he kidding? She would be offended. There was also the other. She wasn't going to like it when she discovered his identity. He needed to be the one to tell her, and then only in a private setting, one where she couldn't bolt and run until she understood the circumstances that had prompted his deception.

He glanced at the bar looking for Vanessa. The timing here might be tricky. He needed to maneuver quickly. He'd be glad when he finalized the Doss matter and could escape the tedious Vanessa Doss. The woman's smile did not signal joy, nor was it a window to her personality. She dressed well but Vanessa reminded him of meringue. She looked good but contained mostly air, a prime example of a spoiled woman eager to marry… again.

In the old days, a woman married and dropped out of circulation for good. Now women recycled, like used cars: on the lot, off the lot, back on the lot with a little more mileage but detailed so a man could hardly tell.

People in the shop didn't appreciate what his job required, forced to cultivate women like Vanessa to maintain billable hours.

He watched for Chelly. Who else did he know here?

There, in choice seating, he spotted Leonard Diet. Things were going from bad to worse. Leonard mustn't see him, greet him in that boisterous way of his.

He studied his law partner's son for a moment. Fat men shouldn't swagger. Obviously Len was trying to call attention to himself. He must have a hot date. Don rubbed a hand over his mouth as if he were covering a cough.

Chelly was probably with a date. He found that thought annoying. Which guy? He looked around trying to guess. Someone special to make her call off her moratorium on men. He hoped to hell it wasn't that wimp Chastain, but he didn't see anyone who matched his mental picture of Eric. Guys young enough to be with Chelly seemed to be sitting with women already. Hmmm.

He glanced back toward Diet to see Len pull a vial from his pocket, tap something into his hand, recap, and pocket the bottle. Len glanced around then dropped the something into what appeared to be his date's drink.

Poor girl.

Don slouched onto a bar stool and watched her reflection in the mirror as Chelly returned to the dining room. He smiled, enjoying her fluid movements, the most striking woman in the room, a woman a man could take anywhere.

Leonard stood and Don's pleasure turned to horror as he watched the man wrap a corpulent paw around Chelly's shoulders.

This wouldn't do. No, no. This wouldn't do at all. Standing idle while Leonard Diet slipped some bimbo a mickey was one thing. Letting him doctor Chelly's drink with something that might render her defenseless was quite another.

Don lowered his eyes and drummed the bar with his fingers. Vanessa Doss would have to fend for herself. Something important had just come up.

Chelly had primped in the powder room longer than necessary, had taken her time returning to their table. Len stood to seat her then moved his chair closer. Casually, he rested one beefy hand on her knee. She shifted position, moving the knee out of his reach. He seemed not to notice, his eyes locked on the musicians as if he were spellbound.

Chelly felt more relaxed after a sip of her drink. Len stood and said he'd be right back.

Studying the people clustered at nearby tables, Chelly inhaled a familiar scent at the same moment two large hands settled on her shoulders. Don's voice was brusque in her ear. "What're you doing here with him?"

Chapter Sixteen

Chelly's heart leaped, her pulse quickened, and a mysterious heat sluiced through her insides as she turned to look directly into Don's emerald eyes.

The man looked good in jeans and street clothes. In evening attire, he was stunning. The white dress shirt emphasized his tan, the black dinner jacket made his dark hair lustrous.

She squinted, allowing her eyes to play from his forehead to his waistband at eye level, then back to his face. "Hello."

He seemed to swallow his annoyance. "You look pretty. Way too pretty to be with him." He glanced in the direction taken by her absent companion. "How did this happen? I'm out of town for a few days and BLAM?"

Her own twinkling laugh surprised her. "Men actually do ask me out, you know. Not everyone depends on chance meetings."

"I understood you turned them down, those men who actually asked you out. You weren't holding out for him? No, no, Chelly. If you've been waiting for Leonard Diet, you need a keeper. You can do a whole lot better."

Chelly bristled. "Leonard Diet is a principal at DMD. He has influence. You know him, don't you?"

He nodded, glanced toward the bar, the direction in which Diet had disappeared, and picked up her purse. "Yes, I know him. That's why I happened to be watching when he stirred something into your drink while you were off powdering that exquisite nose."

"I hope you're kidding."

"No. It truly is exquisite. Come with me." Holding the back of her chair, he motioned her up with her purse.

As she stood and reached for her purse, he caught her arm, put her in front of him, clamped her bag under his elbow, fixed his hands on either side of her shoulders, and nudged her to and through a doorway into a smaller, empty ballroom. A waiter started to say something, but Don kept Chelly moving, not allowing any interference.

"When you're hungry, you tell me, and I'll see that you are fed."

"What?"

He ushered her into a service elevator near the kitchen and pressed a button. An older, uniformed maid with towels draped over one arm, ignored them.

"Where're we going?" Chelly kept her voice low.

"Supper."

"I didn't know there was a restaurant upstairs."

He smiled suggestively and slipped her purse into her hand. "Yeah, only they call it room service." He winked at the maid.

Chelly didn't want to appear alarmed, but her surprise must have shown. The maid cast her a sympathetic glance, tilted her head, gave Don a critical eye, apparently approved what she saw, raised her brows and sent Chelly a conspiratorial smile.

"What about Leonard?" Chelly asked.

"He'll get his just desserts in time."

She laughed lightly at the pun, but felt nervous, and a little feverish. She should not be going to a man's hotel room—particularly not this man's room. Still, as the elevator doors opened to expel the maid, Chelly allowed the opportunity for flight to pass, leaving her alone with Don.

He remained stoic as his hands slid down her sleeved arms all the way to her wrists and up again. She shivered. There was nothing sinister about him. He liked her. She felt certain of that. At least pretty sure. He had asked her to marry him.

"I've thought about you." His words sounded matter-of-fact, but his voice seemed charged with raw emotion. Chelly didn't know what to say. After a long pause, he spoke again. "Have you thought about me?"

She clamped her hands tightly over her purse and stared down at the toes peeking out of her toeless shoes. "No."

"Liar."

She turned to find him grinning. She tried not to smile, but the joy effervescing inside overtook her prim resolve and she spewed a giggle. "Okay, so maybe I thought of you. Once."

"But not every waking minute? I don't haunt your dreams at night either, do I?"

She felt the crawling heat of the blush. "A little smug, aren't we?"

"I prefer to think of it as self assured."

"Egotistical."

The elevator opened into what appeared to be the entrance to an expansive apartment. She stood unmoving. "Are we in the right place?"

"Yes."

"What is this?"

"The presidential suite."

"Is it Mr. Manning's?" She felt breathless and hopeful and wasn't sure who exactly was responsible for her escalating excitement. "Is he here?"

"May be up later." He snaked his arm around her waist. "For now, we're all alone."

Chelly rolled her eyes, miffed that he was teasing her again.

Directed by his broad hand at the small of her back, she allowed Don to usher her through the foyer into a well-appointed sitting room and across to a fireplace. He flipped a wall switch and flame leaped among the artificial logs. She glanced at him and he smiled wickedly.

"I can turn you on that quickly too. Want to see?"

He seemed to be carrying the self-assured thing too far. She sidled away from him, but he had something else in mind and went directly to the telephone on the small French desk.

"Do you like shrimp?"

"Yes," she said, "but I can't stay."

Pressing a finger to his lips, he shushed her. He spoke into the phone but she could see by his reflection in the wall of windows that the green eyes remained on her, following as she surveyed the lavish quarters.

"French onion soup for two, croutons and cheese. Salad with vinegar and oil." He listened a moment. "Baked, with butter, sour cream and chives. Yes, that's good. Rib eyes, medium rare, and the tail."

Her gaze drifted back to his. "I'm not staying."

He was straight and tall, all bronzed and silky, the line of his clothes impeccable. Chelly had a brassy taste in her mouth, her pulse raced, her heart thrummed. She shouldn't be here. Her own voice surprised her as she said, "No sour cream."

"What?"

She cleared her throat. "No sour cream on my potato, please." She needed to halt the warring inside herself, stop sabotaging herself here in the enemy camp.

He held the receiver away from his mouth and laughed softly. "They've got cheesecake, plain, or they drizzle chocolate, apricot, or raspberry sauce.

What'll it be?"

"Plain."

"That's what I love, a woman with definite opinions and simple tastes." She shivered.

He finished the order, hung up, then called the bar. Dinner seemed innocuous enough and, after all, she'd not eaten all day, anticipating. But what about Len?

Had he put something in her drink?

As far as she knew, Don had not lied to her before. What reason would he have to do so now? That thought made her feel more comfortable. She'd think that out later. For the moment she needed to concentrate on staying out of trouble here.

She wandered to an open door and peeked inside. In the muted light, a king-size bed dominated the far wall. She pivoted and marched back into the lighted sitting room. She didn't dare look at Don but she could feel him grinning.

Nonchalantly, she strode to the wall of windows. The view, a panorama of downtown, began below them with an industrial area and became residential beyond that.

She wasn't thinking about the view. Her thoughts kept returning to the bed in the next room, so prominently there.

Don's voice directed into the phone quieted her. "A strawberry margarita and a bourbon and branch." She looked at his reflection in the window, thinking to watch him without his knowing. His eyes worked their way lazily down her body, pausing occasionally, then back. When they met hers in the reflection, he winked.

He'd known she was watching him ogle her. The lascivious study was intentional. He was toying with her, as usual.

He continued speaking into the phone. "Bring a bucket of ice and make that bourbon a double." He paused. "Yes, the house bourbon's fine."

As he cradled the receiver, she turned to face him. Their gazes locked and her breath seemed to stop, moving neither in nor out. The man was altogether too gorgeous.

"I need to leave." She clamped her small purse under her arm and looked toward the door that led to the elevator. It seemed a long way off. "I can slip out through the kitchen and get a cab."

Her glamorous evening was over. She'd looked forward to it, particularly anticipating that she might see Don. Now, here he stood and all she could think of was escape.

Why had she allowed him to pirate her away, again? How did this keep happening?

She wished he could be credited with choreographing their incidental meetings, but it wasn't so. He simply followed his usual routine. She was the one who kept dropping into his life. He didn't call her for dates. He only capitalized on opportunities that any single male would consider strokes of luck. That pin prick in Chelly's fantasy balloon made her angry with herself.

Now, however, another consideration held her—the chance she might at last meet the elusive D.R. Manning.

Don smiled. "You have to eat. It might as well be here, with me."

He had ordered a lot of food. "Maybe Mr. Manning will show up in time to eat with you."

Don's smile dimmed. "I doubt it."

They stood facing one another like gunfighters in the old west, each waiting for the other to make his move. Don drew first.

His eyes riveted on her, he began drifting, removing his jacket. Slowly, hypnotically, he settled it around the back of a straight chair. There was something terribly intimate about seeing a man in shirt sleeves and suspenders in a hotel room. Watching his languid movements, Chelly thought again of her great cat analogy. This predator appeared to be sizing up his next victim.

He pulled the end of his tie, releasing the bow, unbuttoned the top two buttons of his shirt, unfastened his cuffs, and rolled up his shirt sleeves. She had the impression he was preparing for… something. Small hairs prickled at the back of her neck.

He kept his voice low. "Don't go out with sleazy guys, Chelly. Even rich sleazy." His eyes held hers. "You in that dress, your hair like that… you look too damned sweet. It does things to a man. You're having a serious effect on me right now. I promise, Leonard Diet had only one thing on his mind tonight. He's hungry for you, honey. But the man has no passion, Chelly. No soul."

She had heard that assessment before. They were the same words her sister had used to describe Eric. She allowed an uneasy laugh. "Unlike you."

He released a heavy breath. "Oh, no, you do those same things to me. I'm on fire, sweetheart. I get hard just looking at you."

Involuntarily, her glance dropped to the front of his trousers. Her face burned.

"The difference is, I admit it. To myself. To you. And you, standing there blushing, all innocent and demure, you're stoking the fire. Making me sweat." Using his open hand, he patted his fitted dress shirt, which emphasized his flat stomach, then scrubbed the hand from side to side, but he stopped walking toward her.

She didn't know whether to run or laugh, so she just stood there still and speechless.

After another lazy survey, Don again raised his eyes to her face, the green orbs so dark they were nearly black. "I can have sex anytime, Chelly. The physical act itself compares with a good foot rub." He shrugged. "Maybe a little better than that, but there are similarities.

"I can imagine getting more than foot-rub satisfaction with you. I'm afraid it's going to take me a long, long time to quench this thirst I've got for you. More than just one evening." He became quiet for a moment, stood absolutely still, studying her. "Am I making myself clear?"

Her face felt like it was flaming; her hands like ice, yet she had no desire to run. Instead, suddenly, she felt overwhelmingly curious. "Why?"

Her question seemed to break the sinister spell woven by his words and he chuckled softly.

"Really," she prodded. "I know something is going on between us, but I don't know what it is. Do you?"

Her question sounded academic, even to her, not like a desirable woman fishing for a compliment, but more like a researcher in a laboratory seeking evidence to verify a theory.

Don's light laugh rippled into the room and he shook his head, obviously bewildered. "I have no idea. Whatever it is defies definition. But you're right. There is definitely something going on between us."

Defies definition? Where had she heard that before?

Oh, yes, she had told Midge she couldn't describe her feelings for Eric because love defied definition.

The erratic emotions rumbling inside her were like bowling balls mowing down pins. All this commotion could not possibly be love. Maybe lust. She definitely needed to leave.

Her mind prodded but her body, stimulated by this astonishing man, held its ground, stalling.

As the warring factions inside her drew battle lines and the conflict heightened, Don prowled closer, his gaze gliding over her.

"I don't know if it's your innocence, Chelly, or your intelligence; your unmitigated honesty, or the physical thing we've got going on, but you have the power. I'm trying not to give in to it." He stopped pacing to stare into her face. "I'd love to bottle the irresistible something in you. I'd dose myself and pull you to me like a magnet draws shavings. It's potent and you don't have a clue about how to use it."

His breathing became labored. "I'm doing everything I know to resist it, but my willpower's hanging by a thread here."

He paused as if waiting for her to speak. What should she say? That she didn't want to have any power over him? It wasn't true. She liked how that made her feel. This whole unbelievable, tenuous situation pleased her.

Don balled his fists and his voice reverberated, almost a groan. "Whatever happens here tonight, sweetheart, depends on you. You set the boundaries. It'll be up to you to keep us playing by the rules." His breath came in quick, deep draughts. "I'll take everything you give. How much that is will be up to you. That was big talk the other day about my holding out. Smoke. I'm out of control. You have to be the strong one."

Surely his words were a come-on, a line of some kind. A pretty effective one. She quivered with anticipation.

Prowling again, he snapped off the overhead lights then doubled back to the sofa table to switch off the small lamp, leaving the room bathed only in the glow from the fireplace.

Behind the bar, he flipped a switch and music filtered into the room. He strolled to the sofa and settled his hard, muscular frame. Casually, he ran one arm along the cushioned back. His eyes narrowed as he drew her without a word or a touch.

She clutched her purse tightly. If she moved, her body language would expose her thoughts. In spite of his assurances, a step toward him might set in motion events she couldn't control. Her experience with men was limited to Eric's bland efforts. A hotel room with this virile force on the sofa did not look like a good place for beginners. Yet, shrinking from him might signal rejection and bear witness to a lie.

Don moved an index finger, beckoning. "You're trembling." His words were kind. "Are you cold, or frightened? Come here and I'll warm you while we talk about it."

Now that he seemed calm, what harm would it do to sit beside him on the sofa? The bellman should deliver their order soon. Manning might even show. They were alone but interruptions were on the way. What could happen?

She studied the man. He said he would allow her to dictate their level of

152

intimacy. Could she trust him? More the question, could she trust herself?

She had trusted Eric. He was a man—one she knew far better than she knew this one. Yet Eric had deceived her. What if it were her own judgment that was faulty? What if she were not competent to determine who could be trusted?

Another troubling thought: the numbing realization that Leonard Diet had put something in her drink. Or not.

Midge, Yarnell, Anne and the others might be right. Maybe all men should be approached with emotional whips and chairs. Chelly smiled. The jungle cat comparison again. With this tawny specimen, a real whip and chair might be better.

On his say-so, she had let him whisk her out of Leonard's clutches—and into his own. Still, she had come willingly.

Don's hooded eyes traced her face lazily, then meandered down. She must stay alert. She watched spellbound as the predator moistened his lips and waited. What exactly did he expect from her? Sex? But he said he could get that anywhere.

So strong. So handsome. She didn't doubt his boast. Don definitely wouldn't need to drug women into his bed. In fact, he probably had to drive them back with... with his own whip and chair. She allowed a half smile recalling Monica's obvious interest and Midge's remarks.

He beckoned again. The jaded eyes gleamed hungrily. His voice came again, quiet, hypnotic. "Come on over here. You know you want to." He smiled gently, all innocence.

She smiled back as she took that first step.

Once begun, she laid her purse on a side table and walked to him, one unhurried step at a time. He extended his hand without leaning. She stopped, inches from his grasp. He didn't move. Reaching, she slipped her hand into his. His fingers closed without drawing her forward. Again, he held his position, waiting.

When she took another step, however, he curled her captive hand over his own, took it to his lips, and kissed her fingers.

Her pulse raced. Her heart pounded. He tugged her onto his lap and leaned her back draping her over one solid arm as his face hovered above hers. His eyes twinkled mischievously, glazed as if they were newly kiln-fired. His voice thrummed. "Don't be afraid, Chelly. Not of me. Don't ever be afraid of me."

"I'm not exactly afraid." Her voice quaked and she gave him a sheepish smile. "Well, maybe a little."

"I don't think you're afraid of me at all." His admission disarmed her. "I think you're afraid of you." She wanted to argue, but he was right. "That's probably wise, Chelly. The voltage between us scares me, too. You may be naive, but you have good instincts. It's smart to keep away from an electrical charge this strong. This unpredictable."

She nodded and gulped, her throat too dry to speak.

The arm at her back steadied her while his other hand, at her knee, roved over her clothing, brushing lightly, skimming her hips, then up to cup her breasts. "Perfect fit," he said. He glanced at her face, obviously expecting an objection but she didn't want him to stop.

Chelly treasured the memory of her first actual intimacy with a man, on their picnic at Hardaway's. She liked having this man's hands on her. She wanted them inside her clothing again, fondling and touching intimate parts of her.

What would he think if he could read those wicked thoughts?

His hand continued its excursion. "You are high velocity, Chelly. You make me smolder. I want to please you. Excite you. Make you purr with pleasure."

She stared at him but didn't dare speak, afraid assent would bring a swift response. When she remained silent, his murmuring prompted her again. "I can feel you warming. The fragrance radiating from your body is like an aphrodisiac." He flattened his hand on her abdomen. "Is popcorn popping here in your tummy?"

She nodded.

His fingers skimmed lower. Startled, she grabbed the roving hand with both of hers and held on, afraid to speak, afraid to twitch for fear of losing the intensity. She could feel his desire building, as awesome as the blood in her own veins coursing faster and faster.

When she released his hand, he tapped the middle of her forehead with his index finger. "I'm going to kiss you right here... first."

She froze as the finger traced the bridge of her nose and down to tap her lower lip. "And here."

He drew the finger down, following the line of her chin, "and here." Tapping at the hollow of her throat, he whispered, "and here." He flattened his warm palm at the nape of her neck. "And then I'm going to camp out right here."

His eyes looked smoky. He sat her upright, still on his lap, placed his palms flat against her ears, tilted her face and pressed his lips to her forehead. He nibbled down her nose as she sat stiffly, scarcely able to breathe.

She'd never before known the feeling of raw power it gave a woman to incite a man, any man, much less a vibrant specimen like this one. She had seen it in movies, read about it in novels, but she thought it only fiction. This was more... She couldn't find an adequate word. More. It wasn't enough but *more* was close. Her mind seemed to let go. No, no. She needed to think to control the beast—not the one holding her, the one within.

His mouth found hers and he drew her into a long kiss, teasing her bottom lip with his tongue, asking permission to enter, but she wasn't ready. He pulled out the combs holding her hair and twined his fingers into it. She smiled, thinking of his words and tilted her head to allow him better access to her nape and throat.

He accommodated her, nibbling. Oh, she liked that.

Suddenly she wanted to touch him, with her hands and her lips. Eric would never have allowed it. Would Don?

She quivered as his fingers trailed the scallops of her neckline. She liked that too. Her breasts seemed to swell to meet his touch. How strange. Breaths she inhaled warmed her throat and turned hot in her chest. Her heart pounded.

When she didn't stop the wandering hand, Don moved his mouth to her collarbone. Chelly twisted, wanting to see his face.

His eyes were half closed, watching his own fingers lazily explore the soft swell beneath the neckline. Her breathing was erratic.

His eyes rose to her face and he smiled. "Don't worry. I'm not going to stop. Not until you want me to. If you're going to be my woman, Chelly, my wife, you must submit to inspection." He traced his fingers along the neckline, which scooped much lower—was more daring—than it had been in front of her mirror at home. "Next, I'm going to kiss you here." He plotted a course over the fabric between her breasts. "And here."

She held her breath. His fingers dipped to the fabric over her midsection. The fingers slowed as they inched below her waist and stalled at the hollow above her belly button. She'd been quiet, scarcely breathing until then, but suddenly she came alive, alert, alarmed as her torso, without permission, undulated to his hand.

What was he doing? What was she letting him do? She felt like a paid companion summoned to a man's hotel room. This... this man was practically a stranger.

But she was twenty-five years old. She wanted to have sex. She wanted to have it tonight. With him.

Still, she must be true to herself and her parents and her upbringing.

She grabbed the meandering fingers with both hands, bringing their travels to an abrupt halt. He captured both her wrists in one merciless grip. Again his eyes sought hers, but this time his look was ominous. She struggled to get away from him, to stand.

As she squirmed, his grip tightened. Feeling trapped, restrained against her will, she emitted an audible bleat. "No."

He blinked and released her, but before she could get to her feet, he slid off the sofa and onto the floor, his hands at either side of her knees, clutching the fullness of her dress.

"Everything's all right, Chelly. You're all right." His voice was a whisper. "We were just determining the playing field. Letting you set boundaries. Now we can begin."

Sitting stiffly, primly, both feet flat on the floor, Chelly realigned the shoulders of her dress.

Kneeling on the floor in front of her, Don eased her shoes off and wrapped his hands around her ankles. She wasn't sure if it was proper for a woman to let a man hold her ankles. She hadn't resolved that before those hands crept up her calves to the backs of her knees. She gasped, trembling. Was this part of innocent groping or should she stop him? He pushed her dress to her thighs and bent to kiss one knee. Oh, God, she definitely should not let him do that. Gently he nudged her knees apart to nuzzle the insides.

"Stop."

His eyes looked sleepy as he glanced at her face. His quizzical expression quieted her, then the mischievous grin returned, his expression playful.

She wanted to continue this bold, dangerous game. Their gazes locked for a heartbeat. He was teasing, testing her. Yes, she definitely wanted to play.

Chelly touched his face tentatively.

He continued kneeling at her feet, waiting. Her fingertips followed his hairline, detouring to trace the line of his ear. She rasped her fingernails against his closely shaved whiskers. Her tremulous smile triggered his but, except for the smile, he remained motionless.

Encouraged, she ran one finger down his flexing jaw line but stopped when he lifted his face, exposing his neck. Touching his throat seemed too intimate. Somehow its exposure made him too vulnerable. Yet, she wanted desperately to touch him there, and in other more intimate, more vulnerable places, ones that she had only imagined.

She saw the dark chest hair at the base of his throat, daunting as it scrabbled from beneath the open collar, daring her to touch him there.

Don's eyes looked as if they were closed, but she detected a glitter through those long dark lashes. His voice became a growl. "Go ahead."

"What?"

"Whatever it is you're thinking. Do it."

Hesitantly, Chelly put a finger on his chin, drew a deep breath and... jumped at the sound of the elevator chime. Don's expression darkened and he exhaled noisily.

Chelly swam through levels of reality returning to the real world. She had been lost anticipating her exploration of Don's anatomy, before the rude interruption of her erotic dream. She looked at the door. "Do you want me to get it?"

Obviously struggling to overcome anger or frustration or something, Don rocked his head from side to side. His voice was husky. "No. Stay put."

The bellman yipped as he wheeled the cart from the elevator into the foyer. "Room service."

Don pulled her dress up to cover her. She pushed his hands away, startled, devastated by his behavior. She didn't want it to be over. Not now. Still, she clutched at the dress as Don got to his feet and rearranged his clothes, smoothing and adjusting the front of his trousers with both hands.

As the attendant guided the cart from the entry into the sitting room, Don fumbled in his dinner jacket over the chair to produce a credit card. The server regarded him oddly. "We already charged it to the room, Mr... "

Before the man could finish, Don caught his arm and turned him back toward the elevator. The attendant must have spilled something for Don to have been so abrupt, but Chelly couldn't hear their verbal exchange, still partially mired in her dream.

Chapter Seventeen

The bellman was gone, at least for the moment. Don closed the double doors between the sitting room and the foyer, shutting off direct line-of-sight to and from the elevator.

Cool, almost distant, he handed her a drink, speaking with practiced courtesy, as if he were patronizing a stranger. He didn't look at her and his words sounded stilted. "The service and the food here are excellent."

He was right, of course. The service had been good when she and Midge had come for brunch. She said, "Yes."

Unexplainably thirsty, Chelly swigged half her drink before putting it on the side table, then continued taking occasional sips as she sat demurely silent, waiting.

He made small talk about the accommodations and she wondered how one man could run from so hot to so cold so quickly. Gone were the devouring looks, the intimate touches, the desire. This man was not the predator he had been mere moments before. And why wouldn't he meet her gaze?

Suddenly, he cut his eyes to her, his face marred by harsh, angry lines, green flame in his gaze. "What are you thinking right now? This minute?"

Mentally, she grappled for an acceptable answer.

The lines around his mouth and eyes deepened. "Please have the courtesy not to lie."

Who was this man? She floundered a moment before she answered. "I was wondering if there was blood in your veins or quick silver. How can you be so volatile, boiling one minute, ice the next?"

She sensed rather than saw him relax and his expression soften but his words were curt. "Are you being obscure on purpose?"

"Don't be ridiculous. You asked what I was thinking and you got it."

The hint of a smile played at his lips, those warm, generous lips that had nibbled so playfully.

She glared. "If you're one of those multiple personality people, I'd like the prior occupant back, please."

A suppressed grin commandeered his face as if he had lost his battle against it. "You liked him, did you?"

"Yes. Will you please get him back? Oh, and close the doors behind you on your way out."

A rolling chuckle rumbled from his throat as he strolled over to bolt the double doors between the sitting room and the foyer, then, studying her, he returned and lowered himself onto the sofa beside her. Slowly his mischievous fingers coaxed her dress off one shoulder. He pressed his lips to the goose flesh there and pulsed two singsong words against her skin. "He's ba-ack."

His smoky eyes captured hers but he had piqued her curiosity. "Why did you leave like that?" She peered at him, hoping he wouldn't laugh away her question. She sincerely wanted to know.

"It's a gimmick," he said. "A mood swing confuses people, keeps them off balance and at arm's length."

"You don't need tricks to push me away. If you want me gone, say so." She felt rather than saw him withdraw.

"You pry too deep, Chelly. You burrow into my core and set things spinning. You disturb the dark waters inside me."

She pressed her fingers against the biceps straining beneath his shirt sleeve. "Let's see if I understand. You want us to be physically intimate, but you don't want me to know what makes you tick?" She traced the muscle to his shoulder where she kneaded the tense joint.

"That's what makes you dangerous," he said, watching her solemnly, "that something that gives you access to my inner self. You pry straight to my weaknesses." He grinned at her puzzlement. "You are Kryptonite to my Superman."

"Oh. I make you weak?"

"Exactly." His grin broadened. "You make me weak… and strong, in all the wrong places, all at the same time." He glanced at his bulging biceps, then his eyes trailed provocatively to the front of his trousers. Chelly disregarded the suggestive glance.

"Why don't you want me to know what goes on inside your mind?" Preoccupied with her questions, she inadvertently slid her open hand over his shirt to his chest. He looked down. His eyes and hers, too, regarded her fingers tapping the exposed chest hair, but she persisted. "You don't want me to find out who you are in here?"

His breathing quickened and his face twisted as if her touch caused him pain. "It's the way you pry." He caught her wrist. "I can't keep you out." He flattened his hand over hers, pressing it firmly to his chest. She could feel his heartbeat. He gave her a detached smile. It should have been reassuring, she supposed, instead, it made her feverish. Her breathing again became erratic.

"Why keep me out?" The sound of her own voice, so calm, so controlled, comforted her as her own heart hammered against her ribcage. Beneath their hands, she felt his heart pitching and yawing in sync with hers.

He gave a half snort, half laugh, which seemed to interrupt their intimacy. "Maybe you guessed it before. Maybe I'm a split personality. But I'm not the only one here with hang-ups."

"What do you mean?"

"Why are you still here? I have frightened you twice now by being overly aggressive. Why did you stay?"

She sorted through a whole collection of runaway thoughts, seeking the most accurate answer.

Gazing intently, he added, "The truth, if you can."

She withdrew the fingers niggling at his partially open shirt. Timidly she touched the hair on the back of his hand and the relief she felt as the truth came to her made her smile.

"There is simply no place in the world I'd rather be right this minute than here, nothing in the world I'd rather be doing than talking to—and touching—you."

He smiled, then looked puzzled. "Touching me?"

She emitted an embarrassed little laugh. "I like touching your face. I like the sound of my fingernails rasping over your whiskers." She drew her fingers along his jaw to demonstrate.

His open hand followed hers, whispering over the five o'clock shadow. "I'll shave if you want me to. It'll just take a minute."

"No." The word snapped, surprising her. "I just wondered about how it might be to touch… "

"You don't have to wonder, Chelly. Touch me." He cocked an eyebrow. "Anywhere you want." He guided her open hand to his face. "Was Chastain's face smoother than mine?"

She ran the tips of her fingers down his chin, enjoying the sound, then stopped and regarded him curiously. He tilted his head, presenting more of his face, encouraging her.

She marveled as she stroked with the back of her hand across the stubble under his chin. "This part's rougher."

"More razor resistant."

"Hmm. Eric's a very private person." She hesitated again. "He doesn't like intimacy."

"Any kind of intimacy? Even with you?"

An embarrassed laugh caught in her throat. "Right."

"But he touched you."

She felt embarrassed talking about this to anyone, but it was something that had troubled her for a long time. Her body had not stimulated Eric to want her, sexually. "No, he didn't."

"You didn't pet?"

"Not... No."

Don's eyes narrowed. "How long were you engaged?"

"Five years."

"How long did you date before he asked you to marry him?"

"I guess, really, from the time we were toddlers. But he didn't actually ask me to marry him."

"He just handed you a ring?"

"It was his grandmother's."

Don's humor masked his obvious confusion. "His grandmother gave you an engagement ring?"

"No, Eric did. When his dad told him to. Eric couldn't think of anything to get me for Christmas that year and his dad suggested the ring since everybody knew we were getting married someday anyway."

"I see."

She withdrew her hand from his face. "Eric isn't like you. He's attractive, of course, but he doesn't exude... ah... what I mean is, he's not naturally sexy."

A slow grin stole over his mouth. "And I am? Naturally sexy?"

"Sure. Look at you." She patted his flexed arm again and suddenly frowned, remembering Rebecca. "At least with me he wasn't sexy."

Don rocked his head against the sofa's cushioned back, then rolled his face to stare at her. "It's hard to believe the guy wasn't all over you." He arched his eyebrows and grinned hungrily. "Did you keep him at arm's length?"

"No."

"How could he spend time with you and not want you?" He shook his head almost imperceptibly. "It takes all the willpower I've got not to rip off our clothes and ravage you every time I see you."

Not quite able to tell if he were kidding or just trying to make her feel better, she gave him an appreciative smile. "Nice talk."

He handed her the Margarita from the coffee table. While her hands were occupied, his index finger again roved to her scooping neckline. He was beginning again, the breathless ride. She fumbled as she put the drink on the side table at her elbow, placed her arms at her sides, and arched her back, making her body more accessible and signaling no resistance.

Don slipped his fingertips beneath the fabric, stroking, crossing back and forth, each time reaching further, tantalizing her.

She wasn't sure why the dress seemed to dip lower and lower until she realized his other hand, at her back, had coaxed the zipper down.

She needed to object.

She didn't want to.

Her breath came in irregular gasps, filling her, swelling her breasts as she swayed, joining in the dance, following where his fingers led.

He hooked his finger on the neckline between the swollen mounds and pulled, exposing the upper halves of both breasts. He pressed hot lips to the firm, bare swells, kissing, nuzzling, mouthing each in its turn.

She was afraid to move, didn't want to interrupt the jungle rhythm his movements generated, the excitement, the lightheaded feeling that the room was rotating.

She laced her fingers into his hair and smushed his face to her breasts as she clamped her lips between her teeth, and rolled her eyes to the ceiling, writhing with a newly discovered throbbing between her legs.

Arching her back, she helped him displace her clothing as his warm hands roamed places only his hands had ever touched her before.

He nuzzled lower, groaning as he pushed her dress to the small of her back and down, below her waist.

She scarcely breathed as his sorcerer's hands unhooked and removed her bra. When her dress and bra lay crumpled, Don drew back to look at her, panting as if he had been running. He gathered her naked breasts and held them firmly as he took them into his mouth in turn, hot and claiming.

Fully aware of what was happening, Chelly moaned. Eventually summoning his lips to hers, she yielded her mouth and inhaled, inviting his tongue, knowing she was probably signaling acceptance of the other as well. Her body grew feverish as her mind reeled out of control, pulsating with need and desire.

Rumbling, unknown words, vibrated into her mouth from his and distracted her from the systematic stripping. She squirmed and wriggled beneath his touch, feeling his hunger, offering herself to his feeding frenzy.

Eric's indifference had made her feel homely, too plain to arouse a man. She liked thinking she was driving this one, and herself, beyond reason. He suckled her, savoring, touching, kissing her in forbidden places. Salaciously, he mouthed her lower and faster, like a pirate claiming his spoils.

She hadn't expected to enjoy debauchery. In her pleasure, she tightened her stomach to entice his hot hands, urging them to the hollows at her waist. And, as she incited him, she launched an expedition of her own.

Her hands felt noticeably cold as they traveled over his feverish face and throat. Like her, he stretched to give her access, encouraging her to explore.

Boldly, she pushed the suspenders off his shoulders, unbuttoned his shirt and splayed both hands on his taut chest, riffling the thick, dark chest hair, tracing it down his stomach, shucking every piece of fabric in her path.

She ducked his kisses briefly to look, to memorize him. Her heart pounded and she wondered if it would fail, if she might die right there on the spot from the pleasure of looking at him.

But even under such gloriously excruciating stress, her heart continued pounding as she set fingertips raking his marvelous mane, this man, this lion of her dreams.

Her stroking seemed to please him, and his approval made her bolder. Still prone, she rolled onto her side, scrunched low, and strung kisses down his chest and stomach marking those parts of his anatomy as her own and aching to claim more.

Realizing the man had become very still, she glanced at his face. His eyes were nearly shut as he lay poised, studying her. His chest heaved in and out. A pained expression marred his handsome face. Gently, he took one of her hands and guided it to the front of his trousers. He shuddered as she touched his engorged length through the fabric, her fingers taking its measure in only a moment.

As quickly as she withdrew her hand, he recaptured and relocated it on the swollen member, which rose to meet her touch, throbbing with its need.

She trembled, wary, even frightened, but not ready to stop. Not until she had learned all there was to know of him. His arousal was enormous. Surely he must be spectacularly endowed. She had no reference, was only certain she hadn't enough experience to accommodate anything that size.

He didn't object as she withdrew her hand a second time, but immediately caught her up and resumed his assault, kissing and fondling, his movements decisive. She supposed his intensity signaled the end of preliminaries. Smoldering, she was ready to exchange all other reality for this. For him.

Surprising her, he shifted and rolled off the sofa to kneel beside her. He caught her legs and turned her. "Sit up," he said, his voice husky. When she did, he positioned himself between her legs and shoved her open dress to one side. She might have objected, except that he then resumed the debauching. Pain distorted his face as he raised his mouth to hers. Capturing it, she devoured him. His tongue kindled her desire, turning it up another notch until she wondered if she might spontaneously combust.

One hand at her waist, he set her away for a moment as he removed and tossed his shirt. Recklessly, she gathered him, hunger propelling as she scrubbed bare breasts against his shirtless chest. Every nerve felt raw, from her throat to her chest. Butterflies filled her abdomen and flew to her nether region, which began to pulse and yearn for something missing, sensations she had not known before.

She grappled to hold onto him when he stood and coaxed her to her feet. When she stood, her dress slipped down to pool at her feet. She didn't care.

As she raked her fingernails through his hair, he mouthed one nipple then the other while his mischievous thumbs eased her stockings and panties down her hips, clearing every remaining stitch in one artful sweep. He pushed her to arm's length and his Machiavellian green eyes shimmered, visually feasting on every inch of her as she stood unmoving, nude before him.

His eyes continued consuming her as he stripped off his own shoes and socks and trousers. Clad in black silk briefs, he straightened, allowing her time to consider and appreciate all of him. She stared, not the least bit self conscious.

He smiled sensuously. "What?"

The briefs provided scant concealment for the determined bulge throbbing beneath. Tentatively, she reached for the waistband, but he caught her hands in his.

"We can still stop, Chelly," he peered into her face, "if we stop now."

His eyes were veiled and she froze. The peculiar longing in the vortex between her legs continued to pulse. She wanted to have sex. She wanted to have it with him. And she wanted it now. Her physical craving overcame her inhibitions and her pride, demanding. Her voice caught as she whispered, "Please."

He removed his briefs and stood there as if he were posing, magnificently nude. She had never seen a grown man naked, much less one fully aroused.

He smiled a wicked little smile as he caught her wrists and tugged her close to wrap her arms around his waist. Cupping her bare bottom, he pressed her tightly to him.

Nudging her, sliding his feet, he guided her backward into the bedroom until the backs of her legs bumped the side of the king-sized bed. Abruptly she sat. Using their joined momentum, he pushed her down and buried his face in her abdomen.

She had never imagined the myriad erotic sensations he evoked after that, his tongue, his lips, even his breath setting her on fire as he touched and kissed and tasted where no one had ever touched or kissed or tasted. She clenched her fists and squeezed her eyes shut, afraid of the intensity of his occasional glance at her face as he explored the swells and hollows of her body until her arms and legs quivered.

"Who am I?" His voice was hoarse.

"A lion tasting me—getting ready to devour me."

Laughing lightly, he slid an arm under her back and lifted. Her head rocked back as he kissed her, feasting on her throat. He outlined her ear with his tongue. Pleasure percolated in her veins. His hands were hot and nimble and obviously practiced. She was about to learn the secrets every other woman her age knew—the pleasure of her own body, and his. His was such a marvelous man's body. She stole a glance, quivering to see the muscles rippling in his shoulders and arms. Touching his chest, her breath came and went in hot, pulsing gasps. Erotic stirrings bathed her beneath his silken touch. Without him, she might never have known such sensations. Little by little, one stroke at a time, he claimed her body... her mind... her soul.

His hands at her waist, he lifted and slid her across the bed. Emitting a low whine, she laced her fingers into the dark hair tracing the middle of his stomach, and drew them up through the mat covering his chest. She touched a nipple and he flinched. So, he was sensitive there, too. She smiled and leaned up to mouth the nipple. His eyes glowed. "Be careful."

"Could we turn off the lights?" Her voice sounded remote.

"Why? So you can pretend I'm Eric Chastain?"

She spewed a laugh before she realized he wasn't kidding. "Don't be ridiculous."

"I want to watch you. I want to see you see me. I want you to know it's me touching you. Inside you. Filling you."

She nodded, astonished by his green eyes, so watchful, so offended.

As he moved, prowling, she thought again of a great cat, muscles rippling as he shifted position to loom over her.

His hands continued their slow torment, gradually accelerating, stroking, probing, and fondling as she sent her fingers on safaris of their own.

When her hands skimmed down his body, guttural sounds signaled his pleasure. She pushed, he eased back to give her curious fingers free rein. She stroked and kissed and studied his reactions until his groans became a feral warning. Fitting his mouth to hers, he prodded hers open, then her arms and, finally, her legs, inducing her to yield access little by little to her most intimate places.

She writhed as his ministrations swept her up in pleasure.

Proceeding at a pace almost tortuously slow, he touched, caressed and kissed her until she thought she might have fallen into some erotic dream.

As he began a rhythmic movement between her legs, at the entrance to her, she murmured, gasping and wriggling. The swollen penis slithered just inside her. Don crooned softly, lulling her as he surged deeper and deeper.

The hypnotic spell ended abruptly as his arousal rammed nature's final restraint, the famous sacred membrane. Chelly jerked, the sudden discomfort sobering. Annoyed when he stopped, she peered into his shrouded catlike gaze. She couldn't interpret the look on his face. Surprise? Anger? Disgust? She didn't know. She wanted to avoid a recurrence of the pain, at the same time she wanted to hold him inside her.

Don stared into her eyes. "Chastain didn't… ?"

"I told you we hadn't."

"Why not?"

"We just didn't."

Don's biceps flexed as he prepared to lift himself away. She sank her fingers into his shoulders, desperate to continue the euphoria.

"Please." Tears seeped at the corners of her eyes punctuating some foreign emotion, perhaps humiliation.

His expression was a kaleidoscope of thought: amazement, anger, regret, followed by relief and, finally an uncertain stare.

"I want you," she rasped. "More than anything." She turned her eyes from the intensity of his stare as she whispered the one word again. "Please."

He pressed his lips to her forehead and her eyes, sampling the dampness of her abated tears. "Leaving you now will be the hardest—the noblest— thing I've ever done." His arms, bracing him over her, quivered. "And it isn't done yet. You have to help me do this honorable thing."

Instead of relenting, she arched her back and pulled herself up, lifting her breasts to his chest. He groaned, keeping his arms stiff, holding himself rigidly over her. His jaw clenched. He squeezed his eyes closed and took two or three breaths as he shifted, pushing himself further away from her without actually leaving the confines of her legs.

She clawed at his bulging shoulders and pulled herself tightly against him. No longer able to see his features, to read the expression on his face, she wrapped his lower legs with hers, securing him. They had come this far. She wanted to finish. It was her time. Her turn.

"I've waited long enough." Her arms locked in a death grip around his neck. She marveled that he could hold her weight and his own so easily.

He bent to put his lips against her ear. "I don't want just to be your first, Chelly."

"Okay." She answered. It didn't matter that she didn't know what he meant. At that moment, she would have agreed to anything. "I'll remember you any way you want." She released her hold and dropped back to the bed. "I'm not asking for a bunch of promises. I won't ask anything more from you. This is all I want." She couldn't look at him. "Please."

He was quiet for so long, she forced herself to glance at his face, so close above hers. She wondered at his incredulous smile.

"You don't understand." He hesitated, then eased himself lower. Her hands slid up his biceps. His lips brushed her forehead. "Chelly, I love you as I have never loved anyone else in my life. I don't want to only be your first. I also want to be your only lover ever—first and last."

Astonished and confused, she tried to think but found rational thought eluded her. He loved her? Most men in this situation probably employed those three little words to guarantee results. With her, surely he realized he didn't have to. But then, he wasn't like other men. Still, she had heard the words quite clearly. They made her feel tender and warm and welcoming. Maybe they didn't mean anything to him, as little as the act itself, barely better than a foot rub.

Her tiny sob escaped into his mouth as the campaign began again, this time his touching, his kissing, his tasting was, if possible, more thorough, more provocative than before.

She struggled not to move, not to writhe or make a sound as he continued the exquisite torment with his hands and his mouth and the other.

His tongue outlined her lips. "Remember," he sounded breathless and his words were slurred, "you were the one who… who insisted." He groaned.

The engorged member entered her again, touching, then thrusting. He strove carefully. When he reached the barrier, he gathered himself and drove straight into the innermost part of her. She felt the jolt as the membrane tore, but the discomfort was over quickly, leaving only a stinging sensation, like a paper cut.

His pace quickened as he pumped, thrusting and retreating, penetrating deeper with each effort.

She jumped as his fingers touched her, lingered, brushing here, pressing there. Her mind couldn't focus, couldn't keep up with his hands, his prowling mouth and the probe mining ever deeper in her nether regions. It was like a circus, too many rings to watch, too many on the trapeze overhead, too many cats in the cage below.

And then there was only the one, the velvet member, hard and hot and hammering. She breathed as she could, in quick, short gasps.

Then she exploded, swept up in a cosmic storm. She stopped breathing completely, raptured, soaring high beyond the heat and the dazzling sensations, beyond all knowing, surrendered and free. And she hung there a moment, beyond time and place, only a woman and a man. She, his guest or his victim, but surely his.

Too quickly the shower of celestial lights and colors subsided. Chelly expended all that remained of her strength to struggle against the plummet back into time and place and reality.

She felt a surge of tenderness for the sorcerer who wrought the magic, who had lifted her like a time traveler into another dimension.

Wordless, panting, he held himself just over her. She pulled, wanting to feel the weight of his body upon her, but he was too strong and she was again forced to lift her bare chest to his. He relented and dropped close without settling his full weight.

She lay quietly, listening for his breathing to become even. She sensed that he was waiting. Finally, gathering her courage, she asked, "How long before… ?"

"What?"

"Before we… can do that again?"

He grinned even though his eyes remained closed. "You want to do it again?" The green orbs opened to slits.

"I just wondered if… well, what I mean is… can it be exactly like that again?"

He laughed lightly and pushed himself high above her. "So, am I to understand you enjoyed making love? With me?"

She bit both her lips and nodded sheepishly, not sure if that was the correct answer, only certain that it was the honest one.

He laughed out loud. "Yes, darling, it will be that good again. Maybe even better. And I will make every effort to accommodate you as often as you like."

She gulped and smiled, rocking her head from side to side on the pillow. "You may not be able to."

He stepped over to stretch his length beside her, facing her. They were quiet a long time before he broke the silence. "Where do you want the wedding, Chelly?"

Her eyes popped wide. Of course. He had taken her virginity. He was an honorable man. He felt obligated.

"You don't have to marry me."

"I know I don't. I want to. We have already discussed that possibility. Remember? Now, where will it be?"

"We said no promises."

"I suppose you want to get married in Blackjack, make it a family/church event, right?"

"You are under no obligation."

He glowered. "What's the matter? Is it Chastain? Are you going to pine away now, wishing he had been the first?"

Suddenly she felt consumed with an unexplainable rage. "Damn it, maybe I don't want to get married. Not to you and most assuredly not to Eric Chastain. How can you even say his name here... at a time like this?" Her anger seemed to be spiraling. "Don't worry. No one is going to blame you for this. I'll take full responsibility."

He gave her a look of utter incredulity but when he spoke, his voice carried a threat. "Well, whether you want to marry me or not, you're going to." In spite of the harshness in his tone, she was glad that he pulled a sheet up to cover their nakedness. The room suddenly seemed cool.

She leaned up to brace herself on one elbow. "No way am I going to marry you. There. That ought to be plain enough for even a stubborn guy like you to understand."

He regarded her oddly before he seemed to make a decision and crooned, "Yes, I do understand your words. I also understand things you do not." His abrupt movements startled her, as he got up and left the bed, stealing his companionable warmth. He pulled on the black silk boxers before he looked at her, his face tense, his eyes shimmering. "We are going on a little trip, love. No questions."

"I don't want to go anywhere. You said we could... " She scarcely recognized the whine in her own voice. "I want to stay here. I want to have sex again. You said... " She suddenly felt like crying at the disappointment and was unable to find the words for what she wanted to say. She had told him she did not require promises, but it seemed such a little request. All she wanted was to stay in this room, cocooned in the warmth of his body, enjoying his full, undivided attention.

As he studied her solemnly, she sputtered. "I want to stay here. With you."

"Trust me. A little ride in the car, a short hop. This little excursion won't take long."

Her brain snagged on those treacherous words. *Trust me.* His face reflected a mix of questions, commands and pleas.

Maybe the sex, the drinks and no supper had addled her. He said he understood things she did not, but why did they need to leave? Was he afraid Manning might show up and walk in on them?

But why a trip? They could just get another room.

It would have to be a short trip. Don had a flight out Monday morning and she had to be at work. This was... what? Saturday night? Oh, yes, and she had a date for the ballet with Leonard Diet. But that was then. Things had changed.

What did he mean, trust him? Why should she have to trust him? The trouble was, she already did trust him. But she shouldn't.

"All right." Her response surprised her almost as much as it seemed to surprise him. It certainly defied her misgivings. Again, her mind had not ordered it and her own voice sounded foreign, not only willing but eager.

Getting out of bed she moved cautiously, afraid their earlier activity might have left her sore. But she seemed to be all right, a little messy, perhaps.

Clutching her clothing in handfuls, she located her purse and teetered precariously toward the bathroom.

She put herself back together, trying to ignore the continuing seep of moisture between her legs.

She had wanted to see him nude. She had wanted him to see her, to watch his face and read what he thought of her. And it had been a grand experience. So grand that she wanted more. Wasn't that what he wanted? For them to continue naked together?

Obviously not.

She redid her makeup and combed her hair, re-affixing the clips to direct the cascade of curls to the back of her head rather than tumbling around her face. When she walked out of the bathroom, Don was again impeccably dressed, again stunning, and talking on the telephone.

He smiled warmly but she felt shopworn, confident of only one thing: there was no way she could possibly look good enough to be seen with him.

On their way out of the hotel, he stopped the elevator on the second floor, insisting they transfer, take the luggage elevator to the basement parking garage.

From there, he put his arm around her and prodded her up a ramp to street level, emerging in the alley behind the hotel. She had a little trouble walking, starkly aware of a slight soreness in the muscles between her legs.

Don whistled down a cab, gave crisp instructions to the driver, then slid into the back seat beside her where he buried his face in her neck.

This virtual stranger was whisking her away to some unknown destination. Where was her good sense?

"Where are we going?" she asked.

Without answering, he nuzzled deeper, his groan soothing as he pulled her across his lap facing him. His mouth covered hers and she gave in to his warmth, comforted by the one controlling impulse. Of all the places in the world she might be at this moment, this was where she belonged, with him, no matter where he was.

Chapter Eighteen

They necked in the cab, hormones raging. From time to time, one or the other would withdraw, rest for a moment, then dive back into the fray. There was no conversation.

Chelly's lips and the soft flesh around her mouth burned. Her stomach roiled, pleading for either of the suppers offered then abandoned at the Trenton. Her arms ached from holding him. She had never felt such a delicious glow from so much discomfort and laughed at herself.

She was surprised when the cab turned into the winding drive to the airport.

"Where are we going? Is this trip for Manning?"

He ignored her questions. Instead, when the cab stopped at a well-lighted hangar, he took her hand and firmly drew her from the vehicle, through the hangar and out to a Lear jet, its engines revving.

"Where are we going?"

"To do the town."

She smiled uncertainly. "What town?"

"You'll see. Relax. Enjoy."

A small town girl is easily impressed, Chelly told herself as they boarded the jet. She knew a lot of urbane city women who would be impressed with this conveyance.

After they were airborne, Don fumbled in a kitchenette, produced a blender and mix and concocted yet another delectable strawberry margarita.

"How did they know I liked margaritas?" she said, feeling tired and washed out.

Looking smug, he cocked an eyebrow. "They didn't know, Chelly. I'm the one who knows what pleases you. I make it a point to study my objective. Some say I'm compulsive about it."

"I see." She hesitated. "Objective?"

He didn't speak, only smiled a mysterious smile.

Revived sipping her drink, Chelly found herself charmed and flattered to have been the subject of this man's study.

He refreshed her drink frequently, every sip or two and the sugar in it boosted her energy and her morale. After a while, however, her eyesight became fuzzy. She definitely was tipsy by the time they landed. "Where are we?"

"Las Vegas."

"What?" She stammered. "If I'd known, I would have... Well, this is great."

"You've never been here?"

"I'm here now. This is once, right? Yes, I've been here once."

He led her through the terminal. Through blurred vision, she noticed the slot machines lining the walls and became sullen. "I should have brought my quarters. You should have told me we were coming here."

"You don't want to play these machines."

"I don't?"

"No. We're going to the strip and when we get there, I'll give you all the quarters you want." He looped his arm around her and pulled her snugly against him as they emerged into the warm, desert night.

She laughed lightly. "The airplane flew us from winter to summer. That's good. It is still winter, right?"

Don got into the cab first, pulled her inside, wrapped her in his arms and held on tightly. "Yes, Chelly. I changed the seasons for you. I'll do more than that, if you'll let me." He kissed her throat.

"No, no. Summer's good. I love doing summer in February. What happens next?"

He leaned back and laughed at the ceiling of the cab. "I like a girl who goes with the flow."

A short ride carried them to the strip where the lights of the casinos gave the night the brightness of daylight. Chelly sighed. "It's summer in Las Vegas and daytime too? Maybe if we hurry, we can gamble before they close. What time is it?"

"They aren't going to close, Chelly. They heard you were coming and they're staying open round the clock just for you." Chuckling, he climbed over her and out of the cab, then gave her a hand. "Do you like to gamble?"

She shot him a sardonic smirk. "I am practically the champ of the annual Calcutta at the Blackjack Golf and Country Club. I've gone the last two years and cleaned up. I'm a pretty darn good crap shooter."

Don approved her with a scorching look. "I'm glad I'm here to see this: Bo Peep takes Vegas."

They went directly to a glitzy casino but Chelly didn't know which one. She couldn't focus well enough to read the marquis.

Don immediately and mysteriously produced a small bucket full of silver dollars. "Slots? Roulette? Craps?"

Chelly shook her head. "I don't know."

"Come on, we'll check out the slots. Get your feet wet. I'll get you situated then go get us a drink."

"No, no, Don. No more drinks. I'm pie-eyed already."

He sat her down at a machine, handed her the plastic container of dollars, left her, then returned almost immediately with a fresh margarita for her and a glass of brown liquid on the rocks for himself.

The room was warm and noisy. Chelly sipped the drink to quench her galloping thirst.

Don stood behind her, close enough to prop his free hand on her shoulder. She raised the shoulder and tilted her face to rub her cheek against his hand. He signaled a waiter to bring her another drink.

She leaned back, rubbing against him and he slid his hand to her throat. Nonchalantly, the hand moved until his fingers caressed the swells below her neckline. The area between her legs twitched. She breathed deeply, straightening, encouraging him to touch more of her as she set the machine spinning again and again, unconcerned with the results, aware only of the man's fingers creeping inside her dress, igniting her.

She started when his finger reached a nipple. Involuntarily, she arched her back, making the breast more accessible. She was scarcely able to breathe as his fingertip prowled lazily back and forth over the firmed tip. She couldn't control little gasps and whines vibrating from her throat, responses that sent tremors against his forearm.

Idle thoughts drifted lazily in and out of her head. Eric had yielded to the temptation of having someone "hot and all over him." Given the same temptations, she wasn't behaving any better. Inexplicably thirsty, she had another drink.

The pulse between her legs thrummed until it became nearly unbearable as she pumped the arm of the slot machine faster, scarcely able to think, her body alive with the desire those probing fingers generated.

The blast of bells and whistles startled her and she jumped at the noise as coins hammered from her machine into the metal tray in front of her. The machine regurgitated an endless stream of commotion, which prompted squeals of delight, groans and muffled booms of congratulations from bystanders. But Chelly felt devastated by the noise and attention that forced Don to withdraw his hand from inside the front of her dress.

Tears prickled and she scrubbed the palms of her hands into her eyes. Weeping for joy could be expected. No one would suspect she was crying because her companion had abandoned her again.

He behaved as if nothing had happened, as if the hand working that magic inside her clothing belonged to someone else. He harvested her winnings into a bigger bucket provided by a casino cashier.

"Come on, lucky lady, let's up the stakes."

Struggling to her feet, she wobbled as he guided her from the dollar machine to a five-dollar slot. She should have eaten something. In a haze, she giggled at the way the room and its contents rippled and swayed. If he wanted her to keep playing the machines, she would. She'd do anything he wanted if he would just keep touching her and maybe later do the other thing.

The higher dollar machine gave even more generously and Chelly soon had a bucket of five-dollar coins in addition to her earlier winnings. And she had another drink in an effort to quench the relentless thirst.

Don again stationed himself behind her. He seemed to be waiting for something.

In spite of her stupor, Chelly's attention was drawn to a woman playing the five-dollar machine next to her. The woman glittered, excessively large diamonds on her fingers. Similar baubles dangled from fleshy lobes and draped her crepey neck. Chelly's temper flared as the woman flirted with Don, either unaware or unconcerned that he was with someone.

When the flashy woman hit a small pot, she leaped to her feet squealing and threw her arms around Don. Already piqued, Chelly glowered. Did the old broad actually think anyone would believe that spontaneous celebration crap?

The woman obviously was too smitten with Don to notice Chelly's fury and said, "How about you let me buy you a drink, handsome? I'm suddenly even wealthier than I usually am and you make me feel re-al generous."

The woman was large, probably close to fifty years old and plain, but displayed the confidence of a person who was used to having her own way.

Chelly sneered and tried to stand, squinting at the intruder, barely able to focus. She was going to deck the old broad, just as soon as she could get on her feet. The woman's abundant frame swam before her eyes.

Don put a reassuring hand on Chelly's shoulder, applying enough pressure to keep her seated in front of her machine. He smiled at the woman but stepped to one side, allowing more space between them. "Thanks, maybe another time."

"Don't be like that, sweetums. You're too pretty to be ignored." She flashed Chelly an accusing glare, then snuggled close to Don. "Come on, baby, I can see you got the need. Let mamma help."

Chelly saw his tolerant smile give way to a less benevolent look as he pulled his arm from the woman's grasp. "I have a date."

The woman gave Chelly a dismissive glance. "She doesn't care about you, honey. She isn't even aware of your condition."

What was the old battle ax talking about? What condition? Chelly watched in dumb silence as the woman patted his stomach then slid her hand lower. Horrified by the woman's brazen stroke, which settled at his crotch, Chelly's head bobbled as she looked into his face.

He returned Chelly's gaze, staring intently as if hers were the hand caressing his trousers.

The woman's voice wheedled. "She's drunk, honey. Come on. I have a nice suite upstairs. Let me take care of this for you."

Chelly frowned from Don to the woman, then lowered her eyes again to the woman's hand touching him so intimately. Sudden, uncontrollable rage seized her. "Take your hand off him." She clenched her fists and flailed wildly as she again attempted to stand.

Smiling, Don kept the restraining hand on Chelly's shoulder maintaining enough pressure to keep her sitting. He turned toward the woman and his voice deepened. "We'll manage."

The woman removed her hand from his clothing, laughed loudly and rattled her plastic tub of coins. "You've got big trouble, honey. My money says she's ice. How about a threesome? After we let the pressure off, I can show you things with three that'll send us all into orbit."

Vaguely aware of what the woman was suggesting, Chelly felt strangely titillated and squinted at Don. His eyes narrowed as his shimmering gaze met Chelly's. "Not this trip." He started to say more but the woman held up her hand.

"I see how it is. Go ahead. Be her toady. Later, when you're not so gaga, look me up."

The woman swished as she walked away, swaying her ample hips in time to the music, which was barely audible over the noise of the machines.

How had he let things go this far? Watching Chelly play the slot machines, seeing how she trusted him, it was obvious he was taking altogether the wrong approach. He had started out fine, but she had him completely beguiled. It was her combination of sensuality, her astounding body and her total lack of sophistication. He had taken what she offered thinking to ease the pressure, but their activity at the hotel in Tennyson had only whetted his appetite.

She was so... perfect. She intrigued him and it wasn't just a physical thing. She challenged him. The more she gave, the more he wanted. He had been stupid to keep his identity a secret, but he had been afraid of intimidating her—of destroying the openness between them.

He had planned to tell her that first Sunday, there in the office, and later, in the car, when they drove out to the truck stop to eat.

If she hadn't talked about Chastain, about the idiot's betrayal. Eric the stupid had made her skittish, super sensitive to lies and liars. Now here he was mired in what was turning out to be the biggest lie of all.

It had been a bad tactical error, not telling her. His judgment was off with her. Probably the Kryptonite factor. She had charmed the pants off him, figuratively and literally. He couldn't risk losing her. Trying to think of a plausible excuse for why he hadn't told her who he was up front, he had waited.

What was even more stupid was letting her drink on an empty stomach. He'd been nursing straight cola since the flight, trying to figure a way out of this corner he'd painted himself into without upsetting her.

He hadn't done anything this shortsighted in years and Chelly was turning out to be the most important takeover of his life. Of course, he wasn't the only one to blame. How could he have anticipated the spell her dark eyes would cast or how responsive she would be or how she heat him from simmer to boil so quickly?

She had felt safe falling for Manning, a man she thought was old and perpetually absent. Don didn't know where she'd gotten the idea Manning was old, but her perception was well established by the time he realized it.

His greatest fear now was that someone might call him by name in front of her. He needed to be the one to tell her... and soon. But what if she wouldn't forgive the deception? What if he confessed and she ran?

After they made love at the Trenton and she refused to marry him, he had come up with this new plan. She might not admit it—might not even know it—but she was the kind of woman who has to marry the man. If his plan worked, by the time he told her the truth, she would be irrevocably committed. Of course, to seal this deal, he had to obligate himself... for a lifetime. Looking at her, he smiled at the prospect. His plan might be a little over the top, but she had left him little choice.

He had tried to be in love before, with goddesses. Time and exposure had canceled the mystique. But Chelly was different. Time and exposure to her only hooked him deeper.

If he could have kept his hands off her that Sunday, things would have been better. But, damn, his own body betrayed him. She had short-circuited his control.

Arranging the outing at Hardaway's Stable had been easy. She should have tumbled to his identity then, but she was damned gullible to be so smart. Of course, that naiveté was part of her charm.

She yawned a third time. The waiter was bringing new drinks to help her maintain the buzz, but she wasn't drinking them.

When she'd thrown the rock in the creek, soaked him and run into the woods, Don knew he had met his match. The devilish look on her face, his own physical response. He was in love and it was worse than he had ever thought possible. He couldn't claim she blind sided him. She nailed him fair and square.

Of course, after he enlisted Midge's help, without exposing his true identity, the maneuvering got easier. And he was glad to have an ally, someone who might side with him when he finally figured a way to tell Chelly the truth.

Of course, if this plan worked, he doubted Chelly would be able to leave. He was depending on her upbringing and that Bible belt morality to aid and abet. He would use that and any other ploy he could think of as leverage.

He hadn't appreciated interference from the old gal in the diamonds, not at first, not until he saw Chelly light up. He smiled. Oh, yeah, she had been jealous. Nice surprise. A very good sign. Surely she knew it wasn't the old lady that made him hard. The woman had only called Chelly's attention to his condition. He stayed perpetually aroused around Chelly, painfully so when she let him prowl inside her clothes. He loved her full breasts, her round, sensuous hips. Here it came again. He lowered one hand to his trousers, shifting the fabric to conceal what he could.

He had never actually considered marriage before. Maybe that revelation would help when she learned the truth.

His plan was a little rough around the edges, but things seemed to be falling into place. An impromptu wedding was a shoddy do for someone like Chelly. He watched her crank the arm on the slot. He'd told her it was easier to push the button, make the machine spin itself, but she preferred to do it manually, an old fashion girl. She was coming off her high and getting sleepy. Primed and ready. It was time.

Chelly staggered slightly when he coaxed her to her feet. He steadied her. Yes, it was definitely time.

"Let's take a little walk."

Chelly clung to Don's arm as they wound through the crowded casino. She waited while he cashed her coins and handed her a small satchel of winnings. They strolled along a boardwalk to a gaudy wedding chapel.

"What're we doing now?" Her words sounded like she was in a hole.

"We're getting married." Don's voice was playful.

She leaned forward and peered up, trying to see his face, but she couldn't focus. "You and me?"

"Yes."

"Now?"

"Have you got anything better to do?" Stepping behind, he slipped his arms around her and pressed his lips to her temple.

She trembled. "I'll do what you want to do now," she said, "if we can do something I want to do after."

"And what would that be?" He hoped he knew, but he was disappointed.

"A newspaper. I want to do the thing, you know, where we make up our own headlines."

"Okay."

"I love pretend."

"So, are you ready to get married?"

Don was being nice. She could be nice too. "Why not? We'll pretend what you want to do, then we'll pretend what I want to do."

The words seemed perfectly formed in her mind but they emerged slurred.

It was pretty corny, having a pretend wedding. She couldn't really get married, of course, ever. Men could not be trusted—except for her dad, and Manning, and men of their generations.

Don had asked her, at the picnic. And last night at the Trenton. She had said a firm no, both times. He acted like that wasn't the end of the discussion, but she knew it was just injured pride. Maybe this pretend ceremony would make him feel better. He could frame the marriage certificate, use it to fend off old ladies in diamonds who wanted to touch his… body. She groaned out loud.

·He took her hand. "Sign right here."

She couldn't see a line on the paper. "Where?"

"Start at the end of my finger. Sign your name."

She did.

They stood a long time. Chelly wanted to sit. Don made her stay on her feet in front of the phony preacher and his phony wife and the two other people she didn't know.

The long day, no food, the trip, and too many drinks finally caught up with her. Chelly stood until the preacher's drone stopped. The gold band Don gave her was too big. It fit only her index finger so she slipped it on there. Then he gave her a quick little peck of a kiss. That had been the only part of this charade she had looked forward to, and it definitely was not adequate. She followed quietly as he led her to a bench where he finally let her sit. Thank goodness.

She thought again of how nice he was. Beautiful, too, his hard face and even harder body.

She'd been eager at the Trenton, the only twenty-five-year-old virgin in Christendom, thanks to old what's-his-face. Eric. Eric the early. She covered her mouth with a hand to catch the naughty, spewing laugh. Then, suddenly, she felt like crying. She liked having sex or making love or whatever a person wanted to call it. She liked doing it with Don. She was old enough. She hadn't ever been interested in having sex with Eric, but she was thinking about sex quite a bit now. The bad thing was: Don was too damned busy. He couldn't even stay long enough to do it again at the Trenton. He had to make this trip. And she had come with him. She didn't know why he wanted her along, not in Las Vegas. When was he going to tend to his business and take her back to Tennyson? And would he take her back to the Trenton or back to her apartment?

She wasn't certain, but she might have said all that out loud when they were walking because he laughed as he nudged her onto an elevator at the casino.

Terribly tired, she didn't want to hurt his feelings. She didn't know what kind of machines they had upstairs and her arm felt limp. She might not be able to plug the slots much longer. But if he wanted her to, she would try.

He guided her out of the elevator, down a hallway and into a cool, dark room with a huge bed.

"Whose room is this? Do you think they'd let me use their bathtub?" She swooped across the room, arms out as if she were flying, trying to experience the whole thing in one sweep.

He caught her and aimed her in the direction of the bathroom. She balked. "I need to lie down a minute first."

"Okay." He sat her on the side of the bed and knelt to remove her shoes.

She squirmed, opening and closing her eyes trying to stop the dizziness. "The room's spinning and this dress is itchy." She clawed at her arms. She'd had the dress off and on too many times. "Close your eyes. I gotta' take this thing off. What's so darn funny?"

"Taking off your dress right now may not be a good idea." He stood, picked up the key card and started for the door. "I've made a mistake."

Staggering, Chelly vaulted across the room, whirled and flattened her back against the door, blocking his departure. "Don't go. Please don't. I've never stayed in a hotel room by myself. I'm afraid to stay here alone."

He smiled as if he thought she were kidding.

"I'm serious. Ever since 'Psycho.' Please don't leave me here by myself."

Don studied her a long moment, then nodded. "All right."

She teetered a little to her right then overcorrected left as she made her way back to the bed and collapsed. Squirming, twisting, she tried to reach the zipper at the back of her dress but couldn't seem to capture the tab.

The lines in Don's face were resolute as he strode across the room. He sat on the bed beside her, turned her to allow him access to the back of the dress and unzipped it.

She giggled. "You are keeping your eyes closed, right?"

"Right."

Standing, she wriggled out of the bodice. When she turned the top loose, the dress slithered to her feet. She glanced at Don. His gaze moved from the swell of her breasts above her bra, down her bare midriff. He drew a breath when he surveyed the transparent stockings and the outline of the lacy white panties underneath. He swallowed hard as his eyes followed the lines of her long, long legs.

She gave him a silly grin. "Kiss me?"

He tried to stand. "I don't think we should start anything."

She stepped in front of him, which kept him from rising all the way to his feet. "I don't want to start anything. I want you to kiss me."

His gaze again trailed from her face down her body and back. His tone was businesslike. "Chelly, this is not a good idea."

She tapped the upper part of one breast with her index finger. "Put your lips right here. Just once. Please."

"You've had too much to drink. It's my fault, but right now you don't know what you're doing."

She cast him a puzzled, unsteady glance. "What?"

"I'm not Eric Chastain."

"To tell you the truth, that's really the thing I like best about you." She blushed. "Well, maybe not the thing I like best, but it is certainly an item. What I really need to do is double check something. You have to help." Again she tapped her fingertips on the swell of her breast. "Right here."

His jaws tightened, his eyes narrowed, and he caught her waist with both hands to yank her close, positioning her between his legs. "Remember, you asked for it this time."

She giggled and drawled, "Yeah. Now, shut up and deliver."

Chapter Nineteen

She wasn't drunk, Chelly assured herself. The drinks had relaxed her inhibitions but she was fine. In the muted light of the room, her eyesight was fully restored and, except for the dizziness, she knew exactly what she was doing. She told him she wanted to have sex again and again and not stop until one of them died. He laughed before his expression darkened and became threatening. "Is this a challenge?"

She bobbed her head in comic agreement.

"We see who hollers uncle first?" he pressed, reiterating.

Clasping him tightly, his body sealed with hers, Chelly was overcome with an awful realization. From now on, she might be with other people, travel other places, but she would live—truly live—only in this man's arms. In those few spectacular moments at the Trenton the two of them had become one person, sealed, melded. He had become the center of her universe, the source of all she needed now or ever would need again.

Once again, they ravished each other, riding passion's wave to the pinnacle, then taking the rushing sweep to its end. As they finished, her fingernails raked his skin as she clutched and clawed and swallowed back tears, desperate to keep him inside her. She felt him smile as he allowed his body to remain sheathed. Momentarily content, she mourned knowing their oneness could not last.

To her amazement, the marvelous, still-captive penis stirred.

It was as if her appeal were private between her nether regions and his, disregarding the individual people they were, for the phallus swelled and pulsed as if it had a life independent of its host. And it roused her with its resuscitated urgency.

Again and again through the night they rode the wave, up and up to the crescendo where the surge rolled over and over itself in its spinning race to the shore.

His heavy breathing matched her own each time as she became aware of herself again.

It was nearly four o'clock in the morning when, embarrassed, she gave a little laugh, which rudely expelled him below. She whimpered, again feeling abandoned, shivered, and unexpectedly, began to cry.

Don shifted to stretch out beside her. She couldn't bring herself to look at him in the muted light, to see the accusations she knew must be written on his face. He splayed his warm hand on her trembling abdomen.

When she risked a glance, he was smiling, a gentle, adoring smile. The saber tooth was gone, replaced by a sleepy tom, content and finally sated.

He withdrew his hand from her stomach to pull up the bed covers, then gathered Chelly into his arms and pressed her firmly into the warmth of his body, chest to breast, torso to torso, thigh to thigh. Trembling, she gleaned more heat from his body than from the covers.

She couldn't find words. He had to know he was magnificent and what else was there? She would wait, let him be first to break the silence.

Unintentionally, she dozed in his arms, the raging fires quenched. Sex was turbulent, the aftermath calm. This had been like a night of storms followed by the quiet of rain-washed dawn.

Eventually, he roused and rose, wordlessly. He snapped off all the lights in the room, slipped into the bathroom and she heard the shower. Her mother's words pirouetted through her mind. "Nice girls don't. Boys don't respect easy girls. They certainly don't marry them."

Inside her mind, laughter and tears mingled. They had met her mother's criterion. They were married—even if it was only pretend. And this great, tawny brute surely could never be described as "a boy."

Then he was back, again restless, his desire scarcely concealed by the bath towel covering him from waist to knees.

Chelly's eyes met his for only one tick of the clock before she opened her arms. He tossed the towel on the floor and came obediently .

When he swept aside the covers, she trembled and wasn't sure whether it was the chill in the room or anticipation. She couldn't read his expression in the semidarkness, something between apology and need, as he again began kissing her nakedness. She pulled him tightly against her and he whispered. "I can't seem to get enough of you."

Chelly nodded, a non response. He probably felt he owed her some explanation. He didn't. The spiraling pleasure was all she needed. She ran her fingers into his dark, damp hair.

When their bodies were again electrified, then satisfied, the fires again subdued, and they had rested a while, he got up and offered her a hand. She was glad there was so little light.

Don's eyes again grew predatory as he studied her. Guiding her into the bathroom, he snapped on the overhead, exposing her completely to his gaze. When she tried to pry her hand from his, he pulled her into the oversized shower stall. She felt partially concealed in the spray.

Stroking her intimately, he pressed her against the wall, making her groan and twitch as he again exacted the now-familiar pleasure, this time using only his hands and his mouth. As she surged again, Chelly had an eerie thought. She never imagined she would be a woman who would have such a voracious appetite for love making.

Kneeling in front of her, Don laughed ruefully as he finished her. His huge hands clamped to her buttocks, he held her in place, his forehead pressed to her mound, a supplicant, as the shower pummeled his head and shoulders.

Later, so tired she was barely able to stand, much less resist, Chelly complied with each nudge as he soaped her. He turned her round and round to wash, then rinse, his hands gliding over her body as if claiming it as his own.

Holding her in the circle of one arm, he turned off the water and led her out. He grabbed a towel and proceeded to dry her surfaces and each sensitive crevice, ignoring droplets beaded on his own body. Chelly wondered why he didn't feel chilled as he dried her hair, wrapped her in a large, dry towel and sent her back into the bedroom.

She eased onto the side of the bed out of deference to tender parts.

"I need something to eat," he called, breaking the silence.

Chelly again became brutally aware of the realities of life: time, food, clothing—particularly the sudden, overwhelming hunger, and a wicked throbbing behind her eyes.

Was it morning? The heavy draperies gapped slightly at the center. She peered at that gap until satisfied it was still dark outside. The digital clock beside the bed read five-forty-two.

Could this have been only one night? However long a time it had been, her life was irrevocably changed. With him, she had disregarded moral rules she'd subscribed to all her life. She had gone from being a nice, small town girl to big city slut, probably in less time than it took to complete a work day.

Her throat was raw, her eyes ached, her head pounded. Her lips, her breasts and the area between her legs felt swollen, chafed, and invaded.

Miserable, she glanced up to find Don, partially dressed, standing in the bathroom doorway, the light behind him. Suspenders looped down either side of his pleated trousers, which hugged his narrow hips. Her eyes climbed to his bare, well-defined stomach and chest veiled by dark hair. Seeing him like that made it easy to remember what had induced her to such depravity.

He saw her staring at him and, misunderstanding, he grinned. "Don't look at me that way, vixen." The grin broadened. "Uncle. I am finished. Milked dry. You have taken everything I had. Maybe I can accommodate you again later in the day."

Chelly ducked her head. In three strides, he cupped her chin in one large hand, knelt in front of her and stared into her face, obviously alarmed at what he saw.

"Don't you dare regret this. What we have is magic, Chelly. It's love, sweetheart, the real thing." He lowered his voice. "I've said 'I love you' before. I thought I knew what the words meant. I had no clue. Not one. The words aren't adequate to express what I feel for you, Chelly, but they're all I know. I love you."

She shot him a quick look of appreciation, then averted her gaze, but he wasn't willing to let it go.

"I was your first for physical sex but, sweetheart, you were a first for me, too. It was the first time I have truly, literally made love. It's important to me for you to know that. Do you hear what I'm saying? Can you comprehend it at all?"

Chelly allowed her eyes to meet his. His glowed with chartreuse highlights. She nodded, hoping it was assurance enough.

He maintained a firm hold on her face, his eyes darting back and forth between hers. "Tell me what you're thinking, right this minute." He waited but she didn't speak. "Come on, Chelly, I want to know. Tell me all this somber soul-searching has nothing to do with Chastain."

She jerked her head to one side, but he maintained the hold on her chin. Where had that come from? The mention of anyone else's name in this room was ludicrous. Eric had no place in this marvelous world inhabited only by two. But Don refused to let it go.

"What's going on inside that quick little mind? What are you feeling?"

She twisted her chin from his grasp. "I feel naughty and cheap and completely inadequate."

Don tried to match her serious mood, but couldn't quite pull it off. "Chelly, you are naughty in the nicest way I've ever known. You are a class act, honey, and on a scale measuring sexuality, you send the needle spinning way beyond adequate, all the way to *perfection*."

He came to his feet, pulled her up and gathered her tightly, reaching around to cup her towel-draped bottom in both hands. She bumped her forehead against his chest, mortified to be warming to him again. He seemed to sense it and laughed. "I'll tell you a secret." He patted her backside. "This sassy tush has driven me crazy for weeks, in spite of the layers of woolly tweed."

Giggling involuntarily, Chelly shook her head. "It's a shame your memory's failing so early in life. The truth is, this tush was unknown to you until just a couple of weeks ago."

"Not true. I visualized this comely backside exactly as it is the first time I saw you, in the revolving door at the Sheppard Building the day after Christmas."

"You noticed me then?"

"Yes, I noticed you then. I told you that."

But she had stopped listening, plagued again by the memory of their recent activity. She had not known him long, knew pathetically little about him. She tried to push herself out of his arms. "What have I done?" She turned accusing eyes on him. "I've gone against every moral standard my parents ever taught."

He held on, tugged her close in spite of her squirming, and put his mouth to her ear. "Do you not remember the ceremony, love? You are married. Wives have a whole different set of rules in the bedroom."

"That wedding was a sham and you know it."

"No. I am your lawful husband. You are my wife, signed, sealed," he hesitated, "and delivered." He gave a wry smile. "The fantastic rituals of the bed mean we are not only married by law, we are joined in what you churchgoing folks call the bonds of holy wedlock. That's my ring on your finger. Granted, it's on the index finger of your right hand, which is not the norm, but it carries the same significance. Don't take it off."

"But what if it turns out I don't love you?" Her words were muffled against his shoulder.

She could almost hear him grinning. "Ah, but what if it turns out you do?"

"That would be worse."

"Worse? Why worse?"

The tension ebbed from her. Okay, so it wouldn't be so bad, being married... to someone you loved... especially if that someone were him. She liked being in his arms, yet she didn't want to let herself off so easily. What would her mother and dad say? Angela mustn't take this as an example, participating in a shabby little ceremony and hopping into bed with a man because he was so, so macho? In her misery, Chelly groaned out loud.

"Now, wait just a minute." Don sounded annoyed. "I think I resent your being so distressed about this. I've just enjoyed the best sex I've ever had and I've had a long," he hesitated, "well, maybe not so long as all that—history."

She blinked to clear her eyesight as he stammered to a stop. She tried to regard him objectively.

Unshaven, he looked a little sinister. His eyes had taken on a mystic hue. Maybe she could claim he was a wizard who put a spell on her and seduced her. She stared into his face, which again assumed the mischievous grin.

What must he think? She had practically begged him for this. What had he said? She vaguely recalled his words through the throbbing in her head. Something about remembering this is how she wanted it to be.

"You knew I'd regret it, didn't you? That we'd be sorry later?"

His rugged face lost the slash dimples as his expression fell again. "Yes and no. At that one crucial point, I was afraid you might regret having sex your first time with me. I thought it might offend your moral fiber. But understand this, Chelly, I have no regrets. I wanted you last night and I want you right now. And this need isn't only about sex or the intimacy of our physical bodies. I want to live with you. I want to make you laugh." He began swaying with her. "I want to comfort you when you're sad and nurse you when you're sick. What we have isn't going to go away." He hesitated, studying her face. "But in a way it is fragile. We probably could destroy it, if we don't nurture and protect and respect it."

The swaying stopped and his expression darkened. "Chelly, I need to tell you something. I haven't been altogether honest with you. You see, I'm not exactly… " He paused.

"Not what?" When he seemed reluctant to continue, she twisted and pulled away. She didn't want him to make declarations he obviously didn't want to make. She pushed by him, into the dressing area, scooped up the damp towel he had tossed on the chair and marched on through to the bathroom. "We can discuss it later. I need to put myself together."

Moving more quickly than she thought possible, he suddenly barred the bathroom door, the sensuous green back in his eyes. "You're just hungry and maybe a little hung over. We didn't have any supper last night."

Miffed, watchful, she retreated and spotted a banana in the hospitality basket. "Okay, I'll eat."

His eyes followed hers. "No, no, no." His voice sounded brusque and she shot him a look. "We'll order breakfast, piping hot."

"At five o'clock in the morning?"

"Kitchen's open all night. You want eggs, waffles, oatmeal?"

She glowered but her rebellious body chose that moment to betray her again. Her stomach growled audibly. He smiled and she wasn't able to subdue her own timid grin. "Yes."

He picked up the phone and ordered ham and eggs and sides, lots of food and juices.

"Coffee?"

"Yes."

After he hung up, he turned to look at her as if seeing her for the first time. She felt self-conscious, standing there wrapped in a towel being scrutinized by a half naked man. He gave her a tolerant smile. "You don't think coffee will keep you awake?"

"It's Sunday. I can nap at home this afternoon."

"Or here, with me, which reminds me, the Trenton is convenient to the office and comfortable but not exactly homey. Would you rather we got an apartment?"

Realizing what he meant, she felt a surge of panic. "No, no. I have to go home to Midge. That's where I have to live. There, in that apartment. She depends on me for half the rent and expenses. I can't move out."

He caught her up and pressed his lips to her ear. She wanted to resist but the scent of him, the memories of the night compelled her and she curled into his warmth as he murmured, "We can talk about where we'll live later also. Right now, I am spent. I want to rest for a while. Sleep with you in my arms."

Chelly didn't reply, tried not to react, certain that her heart gave her away with its noisy pounding. "I can't." The words sounded unconvincing even to her.

"We don't have to get dressed. We can stay like we are, at least until we've had something to eat."

Her eyes shot daggers. "You think that as long as I'm a fallen woman, you might as well get all the mileage out of me you can, is that it?"

"Right." His expression was closed, unreadable, as he pinched a corner of her towel. She jerked away from him, clutching wildly, ineffectively, as the towel unfurled.

Quick as a cat, he snatched it out of her hands, leaving her nude, trying to

SHARON ERVIN

cover her vital parts with her hands and arms. Without a word, he wrapped the towel around her lower half, tucking it in at her waist, leaving her breasts swinging free, and he smiled. "I like the native look. Fallen? As in fallen in love or fallen from grace?"

She clutched at the towel.

He gently cupped her breasts in his warm hands and bent to take them each in turn into his mouth while she pretended to be an impartial observer, struggling not to react.

Suckling, cradling them, he spoke to her breasts. "I love you," he said to one, "and you," to the other; "and you," back to the first; "and you," the second again.

Chelly's resistance melted and she bit her lips to control the silly laugh that bubbled out. Convulsively giggling out loud, she pulled away from him, turned her back, and readjusted the towel to cover her torso from under her arms to mid thigh.

She ran for the dressing room when the bellman delivered the breakfast tray but sneaked back, still wearing only the towel, when he was gone.

Don, still shirtless, popped a grape into his mouth. Chelly moved toward the tray of steaming food and grabbed a piece of toast.

They ate quickly.

Licking jelly off her fingers, Chelly said, "I can't go around like this." She raised her somber eyes to his playful ones. "I need to get dressed."

"Okay." He gave her a long, penetrating gaze, then took two strides and reached for the towel, his eyes darkening again.

She shrank from him, dodging out of his reach and turned her back to re-secure the towel. "Never mind. I'll stay like this, but you have to promise..."

Sauntering behind her, he slipped his arms around her waist and buried his face in her hair. "Last night you said you wouldn't demand any promises." He nuzzled, breathing warm, pulsing breaths. "At this moment I would give you anything. Ask for something—money, car, house, anything." He drew his head back to leer down at the crown of her head. "I'll give you anything I own, anything anyone else owns. Name it, I'll get it for you."

He slid his hands as he moved around to stand in front of her. She groaned with the pleasure of his lips on her bare shoulder, his hands skimming up under the towel to cup her bottom, his arousal again becoming pronounced.

"Please." She choked on the single word before she retreated a step.

He smiled down into her face and cocked one eyebrow. "That word got you into trouble before, you know."

She returned the smile, marveling. "Are you getting interested again?" She swallowed a nervous giggle.

His grin widened as he again caught a corner of the towel between his thumb and index finger. Tugging, he led her back to the bed.

He was inside her, pumping slowly as she began the ascent. A voice somewhere inside her head whispered, "We have ignition." She trembled as the last trusses fell away and groaned as the whispery voice in the distance said, "We have a launch."

And she soared again, up and up and up.

Eventually, sweating, shaken, she struggled against reentry, against her inevitable return to reality. She wanted to remain in that other place, weightless, guilt-free. What were the words of the old poem? "…slip the surly bonds of earth…"

The only consolation was, he was there to cushion her return, stroking, fondling, comforting. As he rolled to lie beside her, again sated, he smiled without opening his eyes. "Let's stay right here in this bed all day."

"Naked?"

The grin broadened but his eyes remained closed. "Certainly naked. I want to rest beside you—when I'm not inside you—get as close as two people can get. Who knows, wrapped up tightly, cocooned like this, we might change into butterflies and flutter away."

She attempted a feeble argument. "What if Mr. Manning needs one of us or…?"

"No problem." Don's words slurred as if he were already half asleep. He clasped her even more tightly against him.

Slowly she succumbed. Surrendered and supremely satisfied, she slept.

Chapter Twenty

The sun was high by the time Chelly heard sounds of traffic in the hallway and roused.

"Stay," Don murmured, his mouth against the side of her face. "Just a little longer."

"I'm just going to the bathroom."

He released her, rolled onto his back, smiling even though his eyes remained closed, and resumed the deep breathing of sleep. He was marvelously handsome in the half light of the room, only his upper body visible above the covers. Prodding herself, Chelly gathered her scattered clothing and the small purse that contained a comb and lipstick, and slipped into the dressing room.

She was embarrassed to look at herself in the mirror, to be reminded of the hours of wild, uninhibited sex. For someone who had never indulged before, she now felt thoroughly initiated and was scandalized at the idea of how she had enjoyed it. She mustn't think about it too much. There would be time for recriminations later.

Avoiding the mirror as much as possible, she dressed hurriedly in her evening clothes and emerged to find Don sitting on the side of the bed cradling the telephone between his shoulder and his chin. He wore the silky black boxer shorts. She couldn't look at him for more than seconds at a time. Even the morning after the debauchery, he looked entirely too sexy.

He hung up the phone and his voice was soft in the semi darkness. "Don't be embarrassed, love. Not with me."

She gave him a languid smile. He laughed, a warm, melodious sound, as he stood, stretched, twisted and flexed from side to side. She turned her head, fighting the desire to stare at him, to memorize his exceptional body, which could coax her out of herself and elicit unbelievable responses. His voice sounded hollow in the silent room. "You're a little overdressed."

She shot him a significant glance. "You're not." They both laughed. "I have to go. I have things to do."

"I know. I'm not suggesting anything other than perfectly civilized behavior. You'll find a clothes bag in the closet. Check it out."

Chelly opened the closet door, lifted the hem of the clothes bag hanging there and peered inside. Don walked up behind her. Inside the bag were midnight blue silk slacks and a matching knitted silk sweater with tiny dice and cards appliqued at the modest neckline. Chelly checked the tag.

"How did you know what size?"

"I guessed."

"When did you get these?"

"I saw the outfit in a shop downstairs last night. I had it sent up. It came a few minutes ago, while you were primping." He shifted his gaze to the dresser, indicating a shoe box. "Those will be more comfortable."

It seemed improper, somehow, his buying clothes for her, however, he was right, her evening attire was too dressy for a Sunday afternoon flight home. And, of course, she couldn't hold herself out as an authority on the proper etiquette between lovers the morning after. Maybe providing proper clothing was an equivalent to giving someone cab fare.

Thinking how much more comfortable she would be traveling in the new things, Chelly gathered them up. "Do you need a turn in the bathroom?"

"I'll wait."

She hurried, not wanting to keep him waiting longer than necessary.

She combed her hair and dabbed on more lipstick. The blue of the sweater heightened her dramatic coloring but she couldn't help noticing that she looked bedraggled. Had she gotten uglier overnight or was her evaluation tainted by the guilt she was struggling so hard to suppress?

She still didn't want to think about the raucous night. Not yet. She wouldn't be able to come to terms with herself about it until she was alone and had time to analyze things.

Chelly crept quietly out of the dressing area to find Don fully clothed in his tuxedo trousers and dress shirt open at the throat and his sleeves cuffed. How did he always look so perfectly turned out, dressed appropriately, regardless? She held those very private thoughts inside.

Several times as they prepared to leave, Don started a conversation only to have it die for want of response.

During the cab ride to the airport, he took her hand. She pulled it out of his grasp. "I love you, Chelly." His voice was businesslike. "You're mine now, just as I am yours. We claimed one another last night, physically, emotionally, mentally, spiritually and legally."

Anger sparked as she shot a look to challenge his. "I don't agree."

"Yes, you do." He emphasized the words by arching his eyebrows, speaking as if he would brook no argument. "Denials won't make it any less true. You are my wife and you are going to honor that commitment. We are going to live together, happily ever after, or not. Your choice." His tone softened. "In accordance with our picnic table agreement, I intend to exercise my conjugal rights any time the mood strikes."

She scowled but there was an annoying tremor in her voice as she said an uncertain, "No."

His eyes narrowed and his mouth set into a grim, determined line. "Shall I show you here and now how I intend to make you honor our vows?"

"Here?" She quickly surveyed the interior of their cab. "Now?" She felt the blush.

"Yes." He smiled, a glint in his eye. "I'll bet I can have you out of your pretty new outfit, voluntarily, in less than five minutes. Shall I demonstrate?" He glanced at his watch, obviously marking the time, then back at her.

She bowed her head, her hands limp in her lap as she muttered a less definite, "No."

He watched her for a long moment hesitating as if wanting to catch her eye but she was not going to give him the satisfaction of looking at him. His voice took on a coaxing tone when he spoke again.

"You may not admit it, Chelly, but your behavior the last twenty-two hours has convinced me of one thing. You care for me. You may not love me, not with the intensity I feel for you, but you are incubating something very like it."

She shook her head, blinking to thwart the tears. "It won't work."

"Oh, yes, sweetheart, it's going to work. I promise you it is. Had I known how amazing love could be, I would have waited, as you waited for me. Our marriage may not have been accomplished fair and square, but I caught you and I'm keeping you. We are man and wife."

"In the eyes of some charlatan posing as a preacher in a hokey chapel on the strip in Las Vegas maybe."

"No. The preacher was legitimate. I made sure of that. So is the license. You, my angel, are married, for better or worse, again your choice."

"Let me see the license."

He looked taken aback. "I… ah… I don't have it on me."

She set a hard stare on his face. Looking at him, it was difficult to maintain her pique. Even tired, out of sorts, in rumpled evening garb, he was striking. Virile. His physique thumbed its nose at her attempt to shun him. Where was her old self discipline? What was wrong with her? Had he negated all her reservations about men in one overnight adventure? She snorted, angry with herself. "I'm going back to my apartment."

His jaws tightened as he studied her a long moment. Then, ever so slightly, he nodded. "All right, but I'm not going to let you sulk long. I intend to spend my nights beside you."

On the flight, he left her to her silent preoccupation. The Lear was in its final approach when he moved into the seat next to her and caught her chin, forcing her eyes to his. She felt defiant, her strength of will returning, but her anger flagged at his words.

"I love you, Chelly. I am going to live with you. Accept that. I'm willing to give you some time, but not too long. Come to terms with it. Our situation doesn't have to be a problem. You can continue your days going about your normal activities, just pencil me into your nights. The one nonnegotiable point is: you are my wife."

She didn't say anything, didn't know anything to say. She wondered how close Don was to Manning. Their boss might be an ace up her sleeve. Maybe she was not totally defenseless against this man.

Chelly grimaced as she stepped out of a cab in front of the Epperly. Among the few words she had spoken on the ride into town, she had asked Don not to accompany her upstairs. His expression grew sullen but before he could respond, she whispered, "Please."

He appeared to reconsider what he was going to say, shrugged and grudgingly signaled agreement.

Despite what she believed was righteous anger with herself and with him, and some residual soreness, she scurried up the four flights. She wanted to be angry, to squelch the afterglow, but it kept washing through her, nullifying her effort to cultivate a bad mood. She didn't believe sinful behavior should be rewarded by euphoria, but she couldn't seem to get properly guilt-ridden, no matter how hard she tried.

She opened the apartment door ill prepared for the heady greeting.

Flowers exploded throughout the room in profusion, mushroom clouds of blossoms boiling from every water glass, dish and utensil she and Midge owned, along with dozens of flower shop vases. Containers covered every surface in the small apartment, spilling onto the floor where they lined the walls.

Midge sauntered in from the kitchen, grinning. Without a word, she opened both arms and turned back and forth, as if presenting the room for Chelly's approval.

Chelly giggled, clamping both hands over her mouth to muffle the uncontrolled laughter.

Midge smiled. "Actually, Chelly, this is not the way the Aunt Mazie code is designed, but, hey, whatever works, works." Her roommate's face became concerned as she studied Chelly for a long moment. Then her momentary apprehension broke and became a broad, beaming smile. "And I see it did work. My, my."

Chelly scurried to her room, Midge at her heels, babbling a happy report. "Mr. Diet called about nine-thirty last night, all a dither. He called every fifteen or twenty minutes until nearly midnight. That's when he finally told me about putting the stuff in your drink. The louse. He naturally assumed he had provided the sedation and someone else was reaping the benefits, don't you know?"

She grinned and waited for Chelly's smile, which broke on cue, token acknowledgment of Midge's little joke, before she continued. "He rattled on, absolving himself of liability should your luscious bod bob up somewhere down river.

"I couldn't decide whether to call the police or not. You're naive, but you're resourceful. I decided to give you until this morning to surface, so to speak.

"They delivered the first wave of flowers shortly after eight." She snickered. "When I saw they were from Don, I laughed. Floral deliveries on Sunday? The man definitely has panache."

Chelly listened, intrigued. At eight a.m., she'd been lying naked, sound asleep at his side.

Midge scoffed. "I went back to bed and snoozed like a baby, between deliveries.

"The delivery guy and I got a hoot out of it his first three runs. I met him halfway on the stairs after that. I'm glad you're home. You get the next batch."

She regarded Chelly out of the corner of her eye. "You must have performed brilliantly to merit all this. Will there be more?"

Chelly allowed a rolling, bubbling giggle. "I imagine the florist is probably out of stock, don't you think?"

"Yeah. He'll have to wholesale from us this week. You were with Don, right?"

"Yes."

Midge eyed her skeptically. "Are you in love?"

"I'm not exactly sure, but maybe."

Midge burst out laughing. "Give me the symptoms and I'll diagnose."

They moved in tandem back to the living room where Midge picked up the plastic clothes bag, which had slipped off the straight-back chair just inside the door, where Chelly had tossed it. It contained her evening dress and heels.

Chelly plopped on the sofa, slipped off her new shoes and inhaled the fragrance permeating the apartment. Her stockings were shredded. Midge's eyes followed hers to the telltale hosiery and they both laughed lightly.

Midge pretended to dictate into an imaginary microphone. "Subject arrived home in fine humor. There's a positive aura about her—pink, I'd say."

"I had chills and fever."

"All night?"

Chelly smiled. "Off and on."

Midge gazed at the ceiling. "Ah, flu symptoms. Yes, my dear, I'm afraid you're displaying all the usual suspects, er, that is, the usual signs, as we detectives like to say."

Chelly giggled. "I think that's 'roust all the usual suspects,' when there's been a crime."

"Precisely, Watson. I've always said you were a quick study."

The intercom buzzed. Midge flashed Chelly a wicked smile. "I believe that'll be for you. Give the kid a nice tip, will you? I'm broke."

"Flower delivery for Chelly Bennett," the adolescent voice cracked through the speaker.

Chapter Twenty-One

Chelly was alarmed at the office Monday morning when Monica buzzed to say "a Margaret Bennett is on the line."

Although Chelly had arrived early, at eight-forty, hoping to meet the elusive D.R. Manning on his way out of the breakfast meeting, he had already gone. She was doubly sorry when Anne told her Wayne Harned had commented on Manning's unusually relaxed mood, some of which Harned credited to Leonard Diet's absence.

"Mom, is everything all right? You? Dad? Angela?"

"Yes, honey, we're fine." Peggy Bennett hesitated. "How are you getting along?"

"Fine." Did her mother suspect something? That maternal instinct had been known to kick in at the most inconvenient times. Had her mother's intuition tattled on the daughter's Saturday night adventures?

"Chelly, honey, I'm calling because, well, Eric's mother is upset. It seems Eric's mooning around all morose and depressed. He can't eat or sleep and all he talks about is losing you. Honey, he is devastated."

"Mother," Chelly interrupted, annoyed at her mother's tone, "Eric didn't lose me. He dumped me. You do remember that, don't you?"

"Yes, but honey, you've always been the mature one. Your strength of character is what the Chastains love most about you. They want it to rub off on Eric."

Chelly chuffed, a response between a snort and a cough. Her strength of character. Now there was a laugh. Obviously her mother's intuition hadn't yet picked up on Saturday night.

Mrs. Bennett ignored the derisive sound. "Doris is worried about him, Chelly. She asked me to call you. She and Harmon thought if you were not completely happy, well, that you might be ready to come home." She hesitated to catch her breath without allowing her daughter to interrupt.

Chelly slumped back in her chair, crossing one leg over the other, acutely aware of stretched muscles in the region of her thighs, little mysterious aches in her calves. She couldn't suppress a secret smile at the sensations.

"We would all help," her mother continued. "We can put your life back together exactly the way it was. Eric's eager to get on with the wedding, if you're willing."

Chelly's eyes popped. She needed to control her voice, keep her mother from guessing correctly. "Mother, Eric fell in love with Rebecca while I was... "

"You see, that's part of what's tormenting him, Chelly. You didn't care enough about him to remember the girl's name. It was Rosemary, honey, not Rebecca."

Chelly's laugh escaped out her nostrils. "Listen to yourself, Mother. Eric is offended because I can't recall the name of the girlfriend he tossed me over for? You can't tell me that makes sense."

Her mother started to say something but it was Chelly's turn not to allow an interruption.

"And you're calling to tell me to do what? Apologize? Is that the solution you and Doris have cooked up? Fat chance! Give me credit for some of that character you mentioned. I'm not going to do it. I trusted Eric. I was going to marry him, have his children, cook his meals, subject myself to his tantrums for the rest of my life. He wants a simpering, Step-'n-Fetch-It whipping boy, not a wife. He belittled my ideas, ridiculed my friends, my dreams, made fun of who I was and who I wanted to be.

"No. I have no desire to go back to the way things used to be. Never. Tell his dad to buy him someone else, a nanny maybe, someone who'll like wiping his nose... and his butt."

"CHELLY BENNETT! Do not say things like that." There was a long silence on the line. "Honey, you're remembering the worst." Her mother hesitated. "Trust isn't everything."

Chelly chortled. "Easy for you to say. How would you have felt if Daddy had walked in from work one evening and told you he'd found someone else?"

Her mother cleared her throat. "Well, Chelly, our situation's a little different."

"Sure it is, because it would have happened to you instead of me. No, no, no. Thanks, but no thanks. I nearly made a catastrophic mistake. I escaped by the skin of my teeth. I wouldn't put myself back in Eric Chastain's clutches again for anything." As an afterthought she added, "And not for any money Mr. Chastain might offer."

"Chelly, how did you know?"

She wilted. "Because Eric is his dad's darling baby boy and if Eric wants something badly enough to whine about it, his dad's going to move heaven and earth to get it."

There was another long silence before her mother spoke again. "Eric is willing to change, Chelly. His father has assured us he will."

"Eric has been exactly like he is all his life, Mother. As my roommate mentioned only yesterday, I may be green, but I'm not stupid."

Her mother's voice became conciliatory. "Chelly, you're going to be twenty-six years old your next birthday." She hesitated and Chelly could almost hear the gears turning. "Are you dating anyone there in Tennyson? Do you have any marriage prospects there at all?"

Chelly took a sip of coffee to steady herself. "As a matter of fact, I do. And there is nothing about Don that reminds me of Eric."

"Are you getting serious about this boy?"

She bit her lips recalling an aroused Don. "He's not a boy, Mom. He's a fully mature man."

"Oh, honey, he's not old, is he?" As Chelly laughed, her mother's voice fell to an even quieter tone. "Do you think you love him?"

"Maybe. As Angela would say, he's way cool."

"But not very attractive physically, is that it? You know, Chelly, Eric's an unusually good looking boy."

"Good looking is a relative term, Mother. Don is not as pretty as Eric. He's more the rugged type."

"And has this man asked you to marry him, Chelly?"

It was ironic, how much her mother didn't know at that moment. This was neither the time nor the place for enlightenment. "Sort of."

"What does that mean?"

"It means yes, he wants to marry me."

"Chelly, Eric is willing."

"Mom, I am not."

"Eric may change his mind."

"I hope he does."

"But I hate for you not to have someone, Chelly."

"I have someone, Mom. I have me."

"You might wind up all alone, honey, if you turn Eric down and this Don

200

doesn't come through. Another thing you need to consider: Eric can make a very good living. A very, very good living. And now, since you've given up the idea of a law career... "

"Mom, first off, Eric isn't going to make a good living. He's going to run his dad's business into the ground, blow every dime his old man ever made."

Her mother sounded as if she were trying to be tolerant. "I'm sure his dad will guide him. I imagine Eric will be very successful in business."

"No." There was another pregnant pause as Chelly felt her mother gathering ammunition for a final thrust.

"What does this Don person do, Chelly, for a living?"

Selected words caught in her throat, so she evaded that question with one of her own. "And what makes you think I've given up my plan to practice law?"

"You haven't asked for tuition money. You said you were working full time. Isn't that so?"

"Yes."

"Well, we just made a natural assumption."

"I'm in classes nights and Saturdays. I am again following my rainbow."

"Chelly, I don't want to see you become a hard-bitten woman lawyer, growing old alone, without a home or a family of your own. It isn't right, baby, despite all the feminist literature you've read or the toughened women you've met there in the city."

Thinking of Midge, Chelly did not visualize the embittered spinster her mother assumed populated cities. Chelly drew a deep breath. She didn't want to try to defend the lifestyles of hypothetical single women.

"Mother, tell Doris that Eric made a decision last fall that he's going to have to live with—which is living without me. And if you see Eric, you tell him I'm sorry things fell through with Rebecca. Be sure you say Rebecca, not Rosemary. There are a lot of other Rebeccas in the world and I'm sure sooner or later Eric's daddy will buy him one. You can tell the Chastains they need to cross me off their list of potential Mrs. Eric Chastains."

Peggy Bennett didn't say anything for a long moment, then, "We love you, Chelly. We're on your side, baby, no matter what kind of mistakes you make."

Recalling Saturday night as being what her mother would definitely term *a mistake*, Chelly groaned. "Thanks, Mom, that's very sporting of you."

"When are you coming home—for a visit, I mean."

"I'm not sure. I work all week and have class on Saturdays." She wondered how she could possibly work Don into her schedule. "Maybe I can take off sometime soon, run down for an overnight. I'll let you know. Meanwhile, the highway goes both ways. You and Dad could come up here. I could show you some of the tourist traps and behind the scenes."

"Do you get out much? Does Don take you places?"

"Yes." If whirlwind trips to Las Vegas on private Lear jets counted, he did.

"You don't sound certain. Honey, you don't have to make up boyfriends to appease me." Chelly slumped back in the chair, chagrined. When she didn't argue, her mother added, "Well, I hope we get to meet this Don of yours sometime."

"Maybe you will. I love you, Mom. Tell Dad and Angela hi. Think about coming for a visit. Our apartment's not large, but we can accommodate the three of you."

She hung up, put her elbows on the desk and propped her forehead with both hands. What was she doing inviting her parents to meet Don? She groaned. "Perfect."

Chapter Twenty-Two

Leonard Diet slipped into Manning's office shortly before noon. "I think you owe me an explanation, young woman."

Looking up from her work, Chelly returned his glare. "Yes, I'd say we both have some explaining to do."

Diet ruffled. "It was humiliating to have my hot date vanish less than an hour into our evening. Do you know how that made me look?"

"Would it have looked better if I'd taken a nose dive into my plate after you doped my drink?"

He leveled a glare at her face. "Rohypnol doesn't work like that."

"You're an authority, I suppose?"

"I told your nosy roommate that trumped-up story to save face and to try to explain my extreme concern for your welfare. There was not a grain of truth to it."

Chelly returned his glower. "Someone saw you stir something into my drink."

Taken aback, Diet wrung his hands behind his back and paced to the door then turned. "I suppose this someone has proof to back up such an irresponsible accusation."

Chelly read his body language carefully. "No, but I imagine my roommate's story about your confession and some discreet inquiries among other ladies you've dated might provide corroboration."

Len cleared his throat. "Out of deference to our employer/employee relationship, Ms. Bennett, I am going to forget the entire incident and this conversation. If you take my advice, you'll do the same."

"Yes, sir, Mr. Diet." She noticed he no longer insisted she call him Len. "It probably won't come up, unless I hear your name bandied about in connection with some similar occurrence in the future. Then, of course, I'd feel obligated to step forward."

Nodding, he stared at her and, for a fleeting moment, she thought she saw a shadow of regret. "Good day, Ms. Bennett."

"Good day, Mr. Diet."

After a day of putting out procedural fires, Chelly went to Manning's office at four o'clock prepared for a long evening of catching up with the man's correspondence. She opened the computer to find e-mail.

"Chelly: I instructed Bixler to hire you an assistant. He thinks Laureen Fox is capable. Fox will arrive at four-thirty each afternoon to pick up your duties and finish by eight-thirty. Ideally, you will function like a relay team. You will brief her and hand off the baton."

Chelly fell back in the chair as if someone had jacked her jaw. Finally she typed a response. *"Are you angry with me?"*

His return came quickly. *"No. Your work is excellent. Mutual friends say I monopolize an inordinate amount of your time. They suggest I will be better served working you full time and another assistant half time."*

Still stunned, she typed: *"Yes, sir. I'll see that Ms. Fox is brought up to date each night before I go."*

Then, his message: *"I want you out of the office by five p.m. No overtime. Are we clear on this?"*

Gloom settled over her. She was on salary. The firm wasn't out overtime no matter how late she stayed. Was this the first step in replacing her? She felt an ominous shiver. She sent: *"Yes, sir. We're clear."*

She sat staring at the monitor, biting back tears. A snitch had thrown a wrench into the highlight of her career, her relationship with Manning. Who had done such a cruel thing?

Anne might have mentioned Chelly's long hours when she spoke to Manning. Or Bixler might have ratted her out incidentally as he bragged about being in the office himself, working after hours. The self-serving jerk.

Of course, there was an outside chance B.J. or Doreen might have said something, though it was not likely Manning had talked to the janitors.

The only other one—and the most likely candidate—was Don. He knew how much extra time she put in and how difficult it was for her to keep up with law school. Also, he was the one most likely to campaign for her to have a little leisure time. In addition, he had Manning's ear.

Okay, so if Don were the culprit, he probably had her best interests at heart. But, darn it, why did he have to butt in? She tried to nurture some resentment toward him, but she flushed thinking of him. She didn't want to think of him—get all hot and bothered.

She couldn't really be married to him, could she?

Of course not.

He had been pretty convincing. More likely, he'd perpetuated the lie to get her back into the sack. But why persist with the story after the goal was accomplished?

He hadn't said when they'd see each other again. She supposed not until he needed her. For solace, she rolled his ring round and round her index finger and smiled. No observer could guess the tender feelings that circlet recalled. And she didn't intend to share those feelings with anyone else until she had those vitriolic emotions under control.

"Conjugal rights, my eye," she said quietly, smiling without meaning to do so. The torment of not knowing if she had been duped or not added to her chagrin. Her shoulders slumped and she bowed her head. The smile wavered.

She heard voices in the reception room and straightened, bracing herself to welcome Laureen Fox. She was not, however, prepared for the I-told-you-so leer on Bixler's face as he escorted the long-legged beauty into Manning's suite.

Laureen Fox was aptly named, definitely what a man would term, *a fox.* Auburn hair tumbled around her shoulders, framing her exquisite face and long, white throat. Her lips were the color of moist bing cherries, the deep red emphasizing perfect white teeth as she flashed Chelly a smile.

Probably early thirties, Fox wore a stylish suit that hugged her boyish figure. Four-inch heels made her at least six feet tall. Worst of all, she focused all her attention on Bixler, hanging on every word as if wisdom flowed from his mouth.

Fatigued from the intense weekend and the long Monday, Chelly felt emotionally drained. As if sensing her weakness, Bixler yammered away.

"I told you, you wouldn't last, Bennett. This is Laureen Fox, your replacement, and I say it's high time. Yes, sir, a few more days and you'll be back swimming with the other guppies in the secretarial pool. After all this," his beady eyes swept Manning's plush office, "your poor widdle heart is pwobably going to bweak wide open." He grinned, obviously thinking his baby talk clever.

Bixler squired Ms. Fox around Manning's office, showing her the secreted wet bar and gallantly selecting a bottle of wine, which he opened on the spot. He poured two glasses, then regarded Chelly with feigned regret.

"Oops, five o'clock. You're out of here, Bennett. See you tomorrow—at the pool. Ha ha ha. Now, Ms. Fox, let's see how you look snuggled there in Mr. Manning's big leather chair." He glowered. "Bennett, move it or lose it."

For some reason, yielding the chair was the last straw. Chelly needed to evacuate the premises quickly.

"By the way, Bennett," Bixler called loudly as she hurried down the corridor, "you can keep your keys a few days, but I'd start packing if I were you. My money's on Thursday. Does that sound about right?"

Her chin quivered as she nodded without letting him see her face.

She got on the elevator in a stupor and consoled herself with the thought that things could hardly be worse.

Midge was not home when Chelly got to the apartment. Wilting flowers dropping petals did not help. To add to her gloom, there were no messages on the answering machine. She hadn't really expected Don to call. He had probably had his fill of her moods, at least for a while.

Chelly shook her head, annoyed with herself. "You're batting a thousand, kid. Some days a girl can't catch a break. What'd you expect? It's Monday." She eyed herself in the mirror over the sideboard and slumped. "You've always liked Mondays."

She took off her coat and looked at the telephone, almost willing it to ring. She'd like to hear a sympathetic voice. Her mother would be encouraged by these developments, if she understood what they meant. There actually was only one voice that could console her.

She hung her coat in the closet, strolled to the phone, fumbled in the phone book and called the Trenton's main number.

"I'd like to leave a message for Don Richards."

"We have no one here by that name."

"He's not an employee, he's a guest."

"We have no one by that name registered."

"He travels with Manning and stays in the presidential suite when he's in town."

"Mr. Manning occupies the presidential suite."

"Will you just leave a message in Mr. Manning's box, please."

"I can do that, miss, but I can guarantee the man will not receive it, unless Mr. Manning conveys it."

"It's only three words. 'Don, call Chelly.'"

"I'll put that message in Mr. Manning's box, miss, but... "

Too sapped to argue any longer, Chelly hung up.

By the time Midge got home, Chelly had the profusion of flowers and living room furniture in the center of the room.

"Circling the wagons?" Midge cackled at her own wit but regarded Chelly with a more serious look than her playful tone implied.

Without acknowledging, Chelly continued with her task. "I'm shampooing the rug."

Midge gave her a wary look. "And to what do we owe this servitude?"

"Nerves. When I get upset, I rearrange the furniture, clean, organize cupboards, work."

"Kinky. I think the standard cure for emotional upset is food. The more stress, the fatter we get. You really are a neophyte, aren't you. Cleaning, huh? Must be some kind of a rural remedy."

When Chelly aimed a stream of white foam on another spot, Midge scowled. "Are we expecting company?"

"No."

Midge's frown eased and slowly the light of understanding lifted her countenance. "Yippee yi yea! Is the cowboy coming to call?"

"No." Chelly bit her lips to conceal the irrepressible smile that came unbidden with even the mere reference to Don. Without looking up, she shrugged. "Maybe. If he's in town."

"I'd better make arrangements with Aunt Mazie."

"Don't you dare." Midge had finally gotten Chelly's full attention. "He's not staying over."

"Oh, yeah? Well my sophisticated lady, here's lesson Number Two. If they like it, they come back for more. And it's even harder to resist them after you've surrendered once, particularly if he thinks he has the legal and moral right. Wives are expected to cooperate. If you're not willing, I'm betting it won't take him long to get you there. Better quit scrubbing the floor and go change the sheets."

"Midge! I'm not like that."

"You didn't used to be like that."

"I wish I hadn't told you."

"You were busting to tell someone. Better me than good old mom or dad, don't you think?"

"Obviously that's what I thought. Maybe I should have kept it to myself."

"Yeah, right. Like that was going to happen."

Midge left to do some errands and stop by the grocery store. Chelly put the living room to rights but the smug look on Bixler's face haunted her. She stripped her bed, gathered her dirty clothes and crammed them into a pillow case. She was changing her sheets to fill out a load of whites, she told herself grudgingly. It had nothing to do with Midge's advice, or Don.

One stuffed pillow case threatened to split its seams, so she began loading a second.

The two were heavy. When she picked them up together, she staggered. Her coin purse and keys in her jeans pocket, she teetered into the hallway, closed the apartment door, regarded the stairwell thoughtfully and looked over. She could drop the two bundles to the basement four floors below but, eying the straining seams on the pillow cases, she reconsidered.

Quiet time alone in the dank basement calmed her. As she finished folding one batch of clothes and removed a final load from the dryer, she was humming. Part of her ease, she decided, came from forgiving herself.

Sleeping with Don had been inexcusable by her standards, but the sin had carried with it a measure of satisfaction that was more than just physical.

Although she might never have excited Eric Chastain, she had definitely stimulated Don, all the way to magnificent. She took a perverse kind of pride in that.

He'd spoken of their future, but she was sure that after serious reflection, he would reconsider. She felt good about not counting on statements made in the heat of passion. She considered the rituals of the bed Saturday night her initiation into the real world. And she had done okay. She smiled as she hand-washed pantyhose in the basin.

Someone had left a laundry basket on the floor in front of a dryer that had long since ceased tumbling. Chelly borrowed the basket for her folded clothes, stuffed socks and underwear in a clean pillow case and tossed them on top. She could barely see over her burden as she climbed the stairs.

She heard pounding before she reached the second floor landing. It sounded like someone beating down a door.

"Chelly. I know you're there. Open up. I want to talk to you."

The voice shouting for all the world to hear was Eric's.

She whistled first, then shouted. "I'm down here." She yelled again to be heard over the din he was making with his pounding. "Good grief, Eric. Give it a rest."

His face suddenly appeared over the bannister two floors above her. "I saw your car in the lot and I knew you were here. I thought you were avoiding me."

"I was in the basement doing laundry. For heaven's sake, you know I don't play games. If I were in the apartment, I would have opened the door. Who've you been hanging out with?"

He didn't offer to help with the overloaded basket. She set it on the floor by the apartment door and fished her keys out of her pocket. Her coin purse was missing. She must have left it in the basement. Darn.

"What are you doing here?" She opened the door and motioned him inside the flower-laden living room before she picked up the laundry basket and followed. She put the basket in her bedroom and pulled that door closed as she joined Eric.

He looked around, obviously ill-at-ease. "What's with all the flowers?"

She scanned the room, delighted all over again by the arrangements crowding every surface and much of the floor. "An admirer."

"Oh, yeah? Midge has a serious beau, huh? By the looks of this, you may be moving again soon." He shot her a triumphant smirk. She didn't respond, vexed that he automatically assumed the flowers were for Midge.

"Sit, if you want to," she said trying not to sound miffed. "I have lemonade in the fridge or I can make iced tea."

"Lemonade."

She went to the kitchen. "Make yourself comfortable. I'll be right back." But he was behind her.

"Your mom said you wanted to see me. Here I am."

"No, Eric. I did not tell my mother I wanted to see you. I told you I'd call you when I was ready."

"She said you wanted to apologize."

Chelly locked an unbelieving stare on him. Struggling to hold onto her temper, she intentionally put an icy edge in her tone. "What on earth for?" She allowed the awkward silence to hang between them, her eyes firmly affixed to his face. His ears reddened, a definite sign he was getting angry.

He stood there, pale, delicate, emaciated looking. She knew he was thinking about popping his knuckles to warn her of his displeasure. He was so transparent. What had she ever seen in him? Of course, he'd look better if she didn't keep comparing him with Don. Their bodies. Their minds. Their senses of humor. Their bodies.

Eric blinked first. "Okay. I forgive you anyway."

She blurted without thinking. "I don't want your forgiveness. I don't want anything from you."

He glowered at her a moment before his face softened, signaling a different tact. "Now, Chelly." His voice became conciliatory. "Our parents have counted on us getting married for a long time. You know… "

A quiet rap on the apartment door drew their attention.

"Who's that?" Eric's frown returned.

"My roommate? A neighbor? I'm not clairvoyant."

He caught her arm as she tried to step by him. "Let them knock. What I have to say is important."

"What you have to say is important to you, Eric, not necessarily important to me."

"Damn it, Chel, we're talking about your future too."

She slipped by him and hurried to the door. She didn't care who was there, as long as they interrupted this little scene. She opened without checking the peephole.

Don stood there tall, seductive, exuding an aura of sexy masculinity. He wore an olive colored three-piece suit that turned his eyes the same shade, an eggshell shirt that had a maroon pinstripe—the top button was open—and no necktie.

Chelly smiled and patted at her hair, which hung loose, hoping it was not as tangled as she thought, and tried to summon some kind of composure. "Hi."

Unsmiling, he studied her face a moment before his puzzled expression eased and he returned the smile and the greeting a little uncertainly. "Hi."

Her pulse raced and she felt herself swelling with excitement. "I'm glad to see you."

His eyes narrowed. "Good." He continued to regard her curiously. "I'm glad to see you, too." A mischievous grin erupted. "I've missed your face. It's been," he glanced at his watch, "nearly twenty-five hours."

Something caught his eye and he glanced behind her to see a glowering Eric poised in the middle of the living room. "Ah, I see you have other guests." He paused, appeared to assess the situation then leaned down to give her a light buss on the cheek, keeping one eye on Eric. She tilted her face to receive the kiss, then stepped aside. Concentrating his full attention on Eric, Don strode into the living room, offering his hand and a deprecating smile. "And you must be Eric Chastain."

Chelly puffed up another notch. Don noticeably took command of the room, his size, his demeanor dominant. "I'm glad to meet you. You have my condolences and my undying thanks. I look forward to meeting your friend Rebecca so I can thank her, too." He pretended to look around. "Is she not with you?"

Chelly bit the insides of her cheeks to stifle the smile. He had remembered Rebecca/Rosemary. He was too, too wonderful. The rims of Eric's ears turned scarlet. His eyes shot daggers at her before he turned his full wrath on Don. Chelly braced herself, but when she saw Don's playful expression, she relaxed. He seemed to know what he was doing.

Eric sneered. "What do you mean by undying thanks? Who the hell are you?"

Don allowed a Cheshire cat grin and feasted his eyes on Chelly as he prowled back toward her, the saber-tooth at his best. "I'm the guy who was waiting when this sweet thing slipped out of your clutches and dropped into my arms."

Don stole a proprietary hand around Chelly's waist and casually allowed it to settle on the swell of her hip. Eric's frown deepened as he monitored the move. Chelly was awaiting Eric's reaction when Don suddenly turned her and kissed her full on the mouth. The kiss set her reeling. She had to grab his arms to maintain her equilibrium.

"No, no," Eric protested. "Chelly's my girl. Since seventh grade. Before that, even." He jammed his hand into his trouser pocket to produce his grandmother's ring and waved it in their faces. Chelly thought he looked like some inept hero threatening Dracula with a cross. "She's supposed to be wearing this. We're working out our differences now."

Don arched his eyebrows, but held Eric's gaze and his face grew hard. He didn't give the younger man the satisfaction of looking to Chelly for confirmation. "Too little too late, Chastain. She's mine now."

Eric balled his fists and did a jitter step forward, eying Don belligerently, then hesitated, apparently reassessing the opposition.

Chelly steeled herself for whatever little scene Eric would orchestrate next. She doubted the tantrums of old would phase Don and wondered what new material Eric might add to his repertoire.

Her former fiancé lowered his voice. "Okay, fella', how much'll it take to make you disappear?"

Don's face eased with a wry smile. "Are you suggesting I sell you my woman?"

Chelly shivered and her jaw went slack. Eric's dad had deep pockets. She knew nothing about Don's circumstances.

Eric apparently saw her flinch and he smiled more confidently. "Name your price." He sounded to Chelly as if he were haggling over a piece of secondhand furniture.

"Don, don't say anything." Her unbelieving stare shifted quickly from Don's smug, unreadable face to Eric's grim one. "Eric, Don's not authorized to barter for my favors. These negotiations are over."

The two men stood glaring at one another. Slowly, Eric's eyes narrowed. "I know you." His words came slowly with his realization. "I know who you are."

Her mother must have told him about Chelly's new boyfriend.

Don's eyes became slits, as if he were warning the other man. "Good. That saves Chelly the trouble of introducing us."

"What're you doing here?"

"Protecting her interest."

"Why?"

"I don't believe that's any of your business."

Eric exhaled noisily, suddenly, seeming entranced by the floral pattern on the sofa. "Well, this is awkward. You see, I'm supposed to get Chelly back."

"Who says?"

"My dad. Don't think I can just haul my sweet ass home and tell him I gave her up. Not to you."

Chelly linked her arm through Don's and felt his muscles flex. His eyes sparked and his voice deepened to a growl. "Keep talking like that in front of the lady and you'll be hauling your sweet, beat up ass home and he won't have to ask for your excuse."

Men, Chelly pondered silently. The bottom line in negotiations: if you can't agree, put up your dukes. On a grand scale, that saber-rattling attitude had probably led to every war since the beginning of time. Her presence might be making things worse, if they were showing off.

"I'm leaving." She turned away but neither of the men moved. She stalked into her bedroom and slammed the door, then stopped just on the other side and pressed her ear against it.

She heard the outside door open and Midge call out a jovial, "Hello to the house."

Chelly's smile became a giggle in spite of herself and she clapped a hand over her mouth to stifle the sound. She would have been mortified to have blundered into a scene like the one being played out there. Knowing Midge, however, Chelly guessed her roommate would savor it, as soon as she figured out who the players were and the object of their contest.

It took both hands to muffle her giggles. Never in her wildest dreams could she have conjured such a scenario. Giggles escaped between her fingers.

Voices spoke but, while Chelly could identify the speakers, she could not distinguish the words, except for one now and then. The men spoke back and forth to each other, their voices low and impersonal.

Midge piped in. It sounded as if she were offering them something to drink.

Then the men's voices seemed to move away.

Finally, the apartment door opened and closed, followed almost immediately by a soft rap on her bedroom door and Don's voice, just loudly enough for her to hear. "Have you got the giggling under control?"

She flung open the door and leaped into his arms, laughing and planting staccato little kisses over his face and neck as he held her suspended several inches off the floor.

He gave Midge a lost puppy look. "I think it's her poise and sophistication that attracts me. Midge, you probably strive for her kind of control, right?"

Midge choked and sputtered between laughs. "Oh, Chelly, Eric is such a prick. That chubby Diet character was a barrel of monkeys compared to this twit."

Chelly exploded, giggling again, and looked helplessly at Don. "Name your price. My daddy'll buy her. Give me a break." With a climactic hug and a pat on his back, Chelly wiggled free of Don's arms. "Thank you, my hero. I'll never be able to thank you enough for those marvelous moments of vindication." She shook her fists and gritted her teeth. "It felt so good to watch him squirm. Did you see him size you up, then change his mind mid stride? What'd you say to him? Did you throw the bum out?"

He shook his head, watching her intently, and sobered.

Her crowing ebbed with her smile as she notice how solemn he had become. "So? How did you make him leave?"

Don shot a warning look at Midge, silencing her before she could speak. "I told him we were married."

Chelly flashed a startled look at Midge, then back at him. "No, you didn't." She stared at him horrified.

His green eyes darkened and grim lines again scored his handsome face. "Meaning you don't plan to honor your vows voluntarily?" There was something sinister in his terminology and in his glistening gaze.

Again looking from Don to Midge and back, Chelly tried to laugh. "You're joking, right?" She attempted a smile. "You put him down though. Whatever you said got rid of him. You proved you're definitely the better man. But you don't have to keep up the ruse. This is not one of Manning's takeovers."

"You might be surprised how similar it is."

"No!"

"No, as in you don't intend to acknowledge your marriage to me?" His jaw tightened.

Midge groaned.

Chelly bit her lower lip to keep it from quivering. "Yes," she snapped. "No. I mean, what you said is correct. I've thought it over. It's too big a sacrifice. For both of us."

"How do you mean?"

"You don't need a wife to be a millstone around your neck, and I have a career of my own to pursue. You'll hold me back. Neither of us needs this."

"You're wrong. You need me and I definitely need you."

She looked into his eyes. The playful mischief maker was gone, replaced by a bewildered suitor with more than a modicum of injured pride. She felt a knot form and shift from her chest to the pit of her stomach. It was nothing like the one she suffered when Eric dumped her. No, this was intense, unrivaled pain.

For the second time that evening, she turned on her heel and retired abruptly to her room.

How had she gotten into such a mess? She had come to the city to live away from the complications of her life in Blackjack. But things here had gotten a hundred times more complicated than they were there.

She could manage her life here, except for Don, who refused to be managed. He was the source of the inferno raging inside her. She shouldn't have gone with him to Las Vegas, shouldn't have had so much to drink, shouldn't have participated in the shabby little ceremony. Worst of all, she shouldn't have frolicked in the man's bed. Definitely should not have enjoyed it.

She groaned. Every other woman her age hopped in and out of beds like fleas on hounds. It was supposed to be easy. Obviously, she hadn't done it right.

City mores were too confusing for a country bumpkin who only thought she was ready for them. If she had any sense, she'd pack up and go home. Maybe she'd do that.

Subconsciously, she grappled for an excuse not to go. There was Midge, of course. Chelly definitely didn't want to leave her roommate in a lurch. Also, there was her job. And Anne Beed who depended on her at the office. And law classes. She was well into a semester with books purchased and tuition nonrefundable.

It would be hard enough to abandon Don, of course, but there was Manning, too.

Thoughts of her boss comforted her. He was so reliably stodgy. None of these emotional upheavals with him, not even one of his legendary, long-distance fits the whole time she'd worked for him. Anne said keep him happy and out of the office and Chelly had done just that, maybe to her own detriment.

Chapter Twenty-Three

Standing in front of her window, staring without seeing, Chelly roused from her thoughts when Midge slipped through her bedroom door.

"Is he gone?" She had mixed emotions anticipating Midge's answer.

"Yes. Now tell me what's going on?"

"What did he say?"

"Nothing. His eyes went positively Machiavellian. They got as black as the sea. In a storm. At night."

Chelly sank cross-legged onto the bed. Midge sat in the chair and wrung her hands. Chelly frowned. "He didn't say anything?"

"Yes. But he mumbled. All I could make out was, 'Junior, you're going down and taking your old man with you.'"

"What did he mean?"

"I don't know but I wouldn't take a million dollars to be in Eric Chastain's shorts right now. Don's mad at you and I think he's going to take it out on the twerp."

Chelly wondered. Chastains was a family business but they'd gone public after Eric became vice president, sold stock to boost the cash flow. Don worked for Manning, the master of the hostile takeover. "What else?"

"He mumbled something about 'serving him up Texas style,' or something like that.'"

Chelly stiffened. "Texas, the state, or was it a name? Texas Hansen?"

Midge looked startled. "He may have said the name Hansen."

"Lord." Chelly whispered. "Hansen's a client of Manning's. He's gobbled up a dozen small independent companies. Chastains may be ripe. A guy like Hansen could swallow Chastains and not even burp."

Midge looked confused. "And you do or don't want that to happen?"

"I don't want it to. I don't know if Don has enough juice with Manning to sic him on Chastains or not." She hesitated, clenching and unclenching her hands, thinking. "Maybe he'll get over being angry before he sees Manning. Or maybe Hansen won't go for the idea."

Midge looked perplexed. "Or maybe you can sway Manning your way. But why do you care about saving Chastains?"

Chelly took a deep breath. "Penance. I could have settled for Eric before and probably been content the rest of my life."

"Before?" Midge's face relaxed. "Before Don, you mean."

Chelly swallowed hard. "Maybe I can intercede. Maybe." She riveted her gaze on Midge, whose brown eyes rounded with obvious concern.

"You know people talk about jealousy being a green-eyed monster?" She hesitated, allowing Chelly a nod. "Well, now I personally have seen the monster and he has a name. Don Richards. Before he left, he started to knock on your bedroom door again but he didn't. Instead he paced a couple of rounds. By the time he noticed me, his face was calm. He even sort of smiled. He seemed to decide against talking to you and he left. As soon as I was sure he wasn't coming back, I came in here to report."

"What do you think he's going to do?"

"Honey, this is the stuff women dream. A big, smart, handsome man wants to build you a perfect world. What more could you ask?"

"But what should I do about Eric?"

"My advice: forget Eric. The guy's a loser."

"But we've been friends all our lives."

"Oh, yeah? Who's been whose friend? I can see you being loyal to him, including him when you got invited to things. He, on the other hand, seems to prefer his dad—at least his dad's influence or money or something. Don may have him by the short hairs."

Chelly sputtered a giggle at Midge's colorful description as her roommate continued. "Does Don actually know this Hansen guy or was he just blowing smoke?"

Chelly shrugged. "He'd know a name to throw around. I'll have to have a lot more information before I approach Mr. Manning myself."

Chapter Twenty-Four

Chelly ached. Her head throbbed, her stomach was in knots. She dreaded going to work Tuesday morning.

Bixler would try to humiliate her as much as possible when he demoted her or, worse, handed her the pink slip terminating her employment.

Anticipating this might possibly be the worst day of her life, Chelly toyed with the idea of not going to work at all. She could call in sick, save being mortified in front of the entire staff, or at least delay it.

But that would be the coward's way. Life's hardships could strengthen a person, if she had the character to face them. Since Saturday night's surrender, Chelly doubted she actually possessed the strength of character people had always credited her with having.

Her parents had bragged about her integrity since she was in grade school. But maybe they'd been wrong—too close to see her objectively.

Today she would test her mettle. She grimaced. She might be keeping the results of this test to herself.

When she got to the office at her usual eight-fifty, she heard the hum of voices before she exited the elevator.

"What's going on?" she asked, snagging Yarnell Tuggle, her mousy friend from the secretarial pool.

"Bad news. Bixler got promoted. They passed over Anne. Leonard Diet just announced it. Bixler's the new vice president for personnel. Lord help the girls in the pool. He'll have every one of us laid or fired before quarterly reports." The girl regarded Chelly oddly. "Look who I'm telling. We knew the story on you practically the minute it happened."

"What are you talking about?"

"Bixler brags about meeting you up here after hours. He says you come to... to accommodate him."

Chelly closed her eyes and exhaled. Denying it would only fan the flame.

She couldn't very well run around buttonholing everyone trying to convince them she hadn't slept with Bixler. The thought of her coworkers believing she had made her stomach roil harder.

Yarnell was peering at her oddly as Chelly opened her eyes. "That didn't happen, did it?"

"No."

"Why don't you say so?" Yarnell's voice was urgent. "Tell everybody."

"What's the old saying, 'You don't need to defend yourself to your friends and your enemies won't believe you anyway.'"

"Chelly, I'm going to tell everyone he lied about you. Maybe if we band together, we can appeal to someone."

"And say what?"

"That they shouldn't put the fox in charge of the hen house, for one thing."

Chelly gave a derisive snort. She needed to talk to Anne. One thing was for sure, she couldn't leave Anne and the women in the office defenseless. Anne had the guts and the brains to figure out how to fix things but she might need help.

She finally found Anne in the ladies' room, staring at her face in the mirror. Her eyes were swollen. Chelly walked close to her, shaking her head, but couldn't think of anything helpful to say.

Anne grimaced. "I could file a discrimination complaint. I could claim racism and chauvinism, but the papers would go straight into the dumper." She shrugged. "I guess I don't mind leaving. I don't have much use for Len, but I started here straight out of high school, got my paralegal on their dime. As lawyers go, old Mr. Diet was a sweetheart."

She drew a deep breath and shuddered. "It's Manning and Harned I'd miss. Not either of them personally, of course, but those guys are the reigning champs in this business, and I do like being ringside."

She suddenly looked at her protégé, a little startled. "I never wanted to mix it up in the ring myself, but I like rooting for contenders who know my name, if you know what I mean?"

Chelly nodded but remained pensive.

"So, what do you make of this?" Anne pulled tissue from a box on the vanity and wiped her eyes, working carefully around her mascara.

Chelly shrugged. "What I think doesn't matter. Bixler introduced me to my replacement yesterday. I think I'm about gone."

"He wouldn't dare." Anne gave Chelly a studied look. "Leonard tapped Bixler for the promotion. Manning doesn't interfere with in-shop maneuvering, but you're Manning's pick of the litter and Bixler damn well knows it."

"But he said…"

"I don't care what he said or who he told you Ms. Fox is, he's lying. The guy is his own worst enemy. You can probably put his butt in a sling with a word, but he's too stupid or too proud to admit it."

Chelly tried a scoffing laugh. "What are you talking about?"

Anne squared her shoulders and narrowed her eyes, regarding Chelly in the mirror. "You may be the one person who can set things right around here, Miz Bennett. Come on. Let's find us an online computer and a little privacy."

Chelly followed, wondering at Anne's new resolve. What was she thinking?

Anne led her to the last place anyone would look for them, Chelly's abandoned broom closet office in the north hallway. The aged computer sat silent in its usual place. Anne flipped it on, staring at the screen as the hard drive booted up. "E-mail the guy you date, Manning's gofer."

Chelly pulled back. "Anne, I don't want to get him fired too."

"That's not likely, if you don't identify him. Go on."

"And tell him what?"

"Tell him you got trouble."

Uncertain but determined to do what she could to help, Chelly sent a message to Don in care of Manning's laptop, hoping Don intercepted before Manning saw it. She typed: *"Don, I need help. Chelly."*

The message sent, they waited, hoping for an instantaneous response. Someone rapped on the door to Chelly's office and Yarnell Tuggle slipped in sniffling, twisting a tissue in both hands. Her eyes darted to Chelly in quick glimpses. "Bixler wants to see you, Chelly. He's mad. He's been looking for you everywhere."

Chelly nodded, cast an uncertain look at Anne who mimed a punch to the jaw. "Go get 'im, tiger, and don't take any crap off that old fart. A lot of law firms in this town will take you in a New York minute. Smoker's, for one. Don't make any bad deals or sacrifice any principles."

Chelly managed a token smile, straightened to her full height and walked out of Anne's office.

Bixler looked up as Chelly entered his lair. "Shut the door."

She closed it quietly and stood in front of his desk, waiting for him to say something. Instead, he continued rummaging through papers in a file folder open in front of him. Finally his eyes rose from the folder to Chelly's chest. "Did you hear the news?"

She regarded him somberly. "Yes. Congratulations."

"Thanks. Maybe now I can get some respect around here. Things are going to change. Attitudes. Got that?"

Chelly made a conscious effort to keep her eyes on him. Bixler, as usual, avoided eye contact. When he looked at her at all, his gaze rose only as high as her chest. "Office scuttlebutt is you have a boyfriend. One of Manning's muscle." His eyes met hers for only a moment. "Not good enough, Bennett."

She didn't follow his meaning. "What?"

"No clout. You need a man with a hammer to get you noticed around here."

"What are you saying?"

He stood, walked to the front of his desk and planted himself not three feet from Chelly.

"I'm not the only one who could be getting promoted."

"Oh." She wasn't sure what he meant, but she was beginning to suspect.

"They've created a new position—executive administrator. I can put you in it. But you've got to ask me nice." His eyes shot to her face for a second, then down.

"What's an executive administrator?"

His gaze again shifted from her chest to her face, then back. "How the hell do I know?"

Chelly shuddered at his vehemence but something about his demeanor boosted her confidence. "Bixler, you talk to me like I'm your least favorite huntin' dog."

His eyes met hers before he leered again at her torso, appraising her openly. He patted his trousers and rearranged his privates.

She flushed.

He snickered. "You're just now getting it, aren't you?"

She tried to look puzzled.

"The huntin' dog crack gave you away. You're familiar with the saying, 'This dog won't hunt?'"

She nodded.

"Well, you'll hunt now, missy, or you'll be sniffing for your paycheck somewhere else." He took a step forward and opened his arms.

She thought a long moment. Anne had told her not to compromise her principles. What Chelly was thinking was a leap of faith or a plunge into oblivion. But, when it came down to the nitty gritty, she trusted Anne more than she trusted Bixler. "Can't do it, chief."

He froze as he reached for her. "What?"

"If you're saying I have to fraternize with you to get promoted, the answer is no."

His fleshy jaw shook and his eyes rounded as they burned into hers. Slowly he turned, walked back around the desk to his chair and eased into it. "Pack your shit, Bennett. You're outta here."

She had asked for it. Had practically dared him. Still the words stung. Her eyes burned and a lump knotted in her throat as she spun and exited Bixler's office, leaving the door ajar.

She mumbled responses to coworkers who spoke as she trudged down the hall, uncertain of her destination.

She went to Manning's office first to pick up personal articles. The computer was on. Zombie like, she slid into the chair in front of the screen and typed. "Manning: I'm gone. I'll miss you. Chelly."

She pressed "Send," turned off the machine, picked up her box of belongings, plodded down the north hall to her broom closet office, and entered it for the last time, her chest aching. She hadn't been with DMD three months. She had spiraled to lofty heights—to a place where she had Manning's full confidence—before she crashed.

But she didn't cry until she considered her alternatives, the first, of course, was going home, back to Blackjack.

Her mother had been right all along. Chelly belonged there, contrite, with her family and Eric, if he'd have her. She would leave all this for one reason: to protect Don, to keep him from getting fired for associating with her. Obviously Eric was the best she was ever going to do.

Tears rolled down her cheeks as she thought of Don. She let herself give in to it, to wallow in total self pity for several minutes as she gathered hand lotion, a small framed family portrait, unopened packs of pantyhose and knee-highs, her Black's Law Dictionary and several reference books. She dumped new office supplies onto the surface of her desk and used the emptied box for her personal belongings.

The door to her office flew open and Anne strode in, swinging the door shut behind her. She held out a piece of note paper.

"Here's Faye Dell Bradley's name. She's been with Levi Smoker at Weeden-Pricer for years. I've told her about you. She's excited. Go straight from here. Now. I may be over in a day or two myself."

Chelly bit her lips and nodded but couldn't bring herself to look at her friend or to risk the emotional turmoil that might accompany her attempt to say "thank you."

Anne filled the gap. "I know how you feel. You don't have to say a word. We're simpatico, girl."

Chelly was afraid she would break down if Anne touched her but the other woman seemed to know. "How about we do lunch tomorrow? The Lunch Box. Noon okay with you?"

Clamping her lips even more tightly, Chelly nodded. Anne pivoted and marched back out the door, again closing it firmly behind her.

Chelly didn't want to go to Weeden-Pricer, DMD's most adamant competitor, but she made herself stop in the bathroom to freshen her makeup and practice her smile, then set her jaw resolutely.

Faye Dell Bradley was probably sixty years old with a dowager's hump and a dour look, which was immediately mitigated by her kindly voice and manner.

She welcomed Chelly with a firm handshake and led her to an airy office with a glass wall, which faced the Sheppard Building.

"You'll work here." Faye Dell snapped on both lamps, not to enhance the adequate lighting as much as to enrich the ambiance.

The desk was a slick glass and metal concoction, with matching credenza, return, and side tables. A computer occupied the return, and a laptop sat in its case on the floor underneath.

The room was carpeted in apricot cream and the walls were an off white. A small overstuffed sofa softened the room that also had two two-drawer lateral filing cabinets and a full wall of bookshelves. The motif of the place soothed Chelly as she looked around.

"I think you'll be comfortable here." Faye Dell gave her a questioning smile.

Chelly was overwhelmed. She had leaped into the unknown only to find she had apparently improved her lot. "Yes, I imagine anyone would be."

"We're starting you fifty dollars a week more than you were making at DMD, in case they try to steal you back. If they up the ante, let me know. We might do even better to keep you."

Both women started as the phone in the new office rang.

Faye Dell smiled. "I imagine it's for you. Anne anticipated you might be moving over here. That's why the office was ready and the switchboard alerted."

Chelly smiled, put her purse and box of personal belongings on the sofa, and hurried to answer the phone.

"This is Chelly Bennett."

Don's voice blasted her. "What the hell are you doing there?"

Chapter Twenty-Five

Chelly braced her backside against the desk and clutched the telephone with both hands. As she frequently did, she answered Don's question with a question. "Where are you?"

"Out of the country and I damn well want to know what's going on?"

"I've left DMD." His guttural groan rumbled over the line but she continued quickly. "There's nothing you can do. I made good friends at DMD but this is more money and I had to make a decision quickly."

He remained silent but she could hear him breathe deeply before his voice came again, this time calm. "Tell me exactly what happened."

"I've told you the important part. I want to be able to see your face before I say any more." She had a new, disturbing thought. "Does my changing jobs—law firms—will that make a difference to how you feel about... us? I don't want you to get in trouble for associating with me."

His caustic laugh warmed her. "I thought I had made my feelings about us perfectly clear."

She offered a nervous twitter. "We'd better keep us a secret for now if we want to come out of this still friends."

"We're a lot more than friends, Chelly, whether you admit it or not. A word of advice: Don't get to liking Levi Smoker too well. You won't be there that long."

"When do you get back?"

"In country, late Friday. I'll see you Saturday morning at your place, ten o'clock."

Chelly plodded through Wednesday, her first full day at Weeden-Pricer, in a daze, making notes as Faye Dell explained the routine, introduced her, and gave her three files to work for Ed Pricer for starters. Pricer reputedly was a laid-back old man who specialized in property law, wills and trusts.

"We'll line you up with a hard charger, maybe even Levi himself, after you take hold." Faye Dell's smile wavered only slightly as she spoke but Chelly could read the hidden meaning. They would hold the more sensitive cases in reserve until Chelly got her loyalties straight.

Lunch with Anne helped, as she soaked up the office updates. Things were not going well for DMD's newest V.P. and every calamity had boosted Anne's spirits.

Maybe things were not as grim as Chelly thought. She liked Mr. Pricer and Faye Dell, and the work was familiar as she eased into the computer programs, which proved to be only a little different than the ones at DMD.

Leaving promptly at five o'clock was a new experience. She had to concentrate NOT to glance at the Sheppard Building. She didn't want anyone reporting that she gazed longingly.

That week, Midge kept a running list of people who called for Chelly, most of them coworkers at DMD with words of encouragement and moral support. Midge allowed her to go through the motions of normalcy without a lot of questions.

At nine-thirty Thursday morning, as Chelly sat in her new office stirring cream into her coffee, a loud rap at the door brought her to her feet. She hurried across the room, flung the door wide and gaped to find Bixler standing on the other side, grinning affably.

"Chelly, girl." She detected a whine in his tone and her suspicion heightened as his eyes met hers. "Glad I found you. Honey, we need to talk, get some things cleared up."

She stood unmoving, stunned. He squirmed a step forward but she didn't invite him inside.

He lost the smile. "Okay, for starters, you misunderstood me the other day."

"What part of 'Pack your shit, you're outta here,' did I misunderstand?"

"I meant out of *my* office, not out of *the* office. I was real surprised when they told me you'd walked out like you did. Now grab your stuff and let's go home." He leaned to see around her, surveying her accommodations. "Tell me what's yours and I'll give you a hand."

She was too flabbergasted to speak or move.

Bixler, obviously reluctant to push by her, looked sheepish. "I may have flown off the handle for a minute the other day, Chelly. With the promotion and all, I was pretty high on myself. Apparently I need to clarify some things for you." He paused again, his eyes holding hers, pleading.

She stared, not giving an inch. She had no intention of making this easy. Obviously, Anne had gotten things back under control.

Chelly felt a surging warmth. She was pleased at having had the fortitude to withstand this roller coaster ride. For that, she could thank Eric. Getting dumped once was upsetting. The second bounce wasn't nearly as hard.

"All hell's broken loose over there." Bixler shifted his cumbersome weight from one foot to the other and his whine became even more nasal as his eyes dropped, as usual, to her chest. "It started ten minutes after you went out the door Tuesday and it's gone downhill ever since."

She shook her head, marveling. "Bixler, if you recall, your foot was planted firmly in my derriere as I exited. I'd say you have a very convenient memory?"

He stared at the floor. "Yes, well, like I said, I may have overstepped myself. The point is, we want you back."

Chelly glanced over her shoulder at her new office and smiled. "A misunderstanding is one thing, Bixler, but you lie. You told people we were having an affair. You've been the bane of my existence for three months. Do you expect me to forget all of your obnoxious behavior in exchange for some lame little apology?"

Bixler's shoulders slumped and he lowered his voice. "Bennett, I'm in trouble."

"And you expect sympathy from me? You wanted the partners to notice you. This sounds like justice to me, pal, like you finally got the attention you deserve. Who wised up?"

"Who?"

"Yeah." She was suddenly very interested. "Who?"

Bixler cut his eyes right and left, then back to the floor. "Harned."

"Wayne Harned? I thought he was immune to interoffice squabbling."

"Me, too." Bixler looked as surprised as Chelly felt. "He came roaring into my office at quitting time yesterday. It took him three minutes to say his piece. My door was open and he was yelling. Everyone in the office heard him."

A dozen questions shot through her mind. Why would Mr. Harned care that she was gone?

Anne! It had to be Anne.

The little minx. She'd had that partner's ear all along.

"Harned's an easy going guy, Bixler. You'll probably get a medal for making him raise his voice."

"Easy going? You wouldn't say that if you'd been there. He could have shattered crystal. Lucky there was none around. Bottom line: he wants you back and he put the onus on me to get you back."

Chelly half laughed, half coughed. She wished she could capture this moment, this feeling of triumph. But she had a sudden flash. "Bixler, you can assure Mr. Harned I would never talk about DMD business anywhere else."

"I thought of that. I told him I'd warned you not to carry tales out of school." He flashed her a quick look. "I know, I didn't really say that, but you're a smart girl. I knew you'd know better than to gossip about our business over here."

Laughter spurted again. This was too much. The man fired her, two days later he's asking for favors and paying her left-handed compliments. Unbelievable.

Still, she didn't move out of the doorway or invite him into her office. "Bixler, I don't want to work for you. Other people are ready to jump ship because of you. You could probably cause a wholesale walkout over there if you tried."

He jerked around to make sure no one in the hallway behind him had heard. "Don't even joke about something like that." He jutted his jaw and appeared to reconnoiter. "Chelly," he began again, in a subdued voice, "as you know, I am now vice president in charge of personnel, in sole charge of all hiring and firing."

"So, what's new?"

"In my official capacity, I'm offering you, not just amnesty for past sins, but a good promotion—to that executive administrator's job we spoke of. The new one."

"Why?"

When he raised his eyes, they were full of new regard. "It turns out the job was created for you."

"I see." Now that was a surprise. "You know, Bixler, I'm not much of a poker player. I can never remember what beats what." Bixler cleared his throat and waited for her point. "Does a vice president for personnel outrank an executive administrator?"

He scratched his chin. "I couldn't say for sure."

"Who'll make the most money, you or me?"

He rolled his shoulders. "That's another thing I probably need to research."

Passing in the hall, Faye Dell did a double take when she saw Bixler and came back.

Chelly introduced them before turning her full attention again on the man. "Is there anything else?"

He cleared his throat and glanced at Faye Dell. There was an awkward silence. He cleared his throat again. When he cleared it a third time, Faye Dell excused herself.

"Just one more thing." He lowered his voice and sneered as he spoke. "People say you're dating one of Manning's henchmen, that he's your contact. Honey, you don't have to sleep with the hired help. You've got looks, talent, ambition. I'll see you get a break. Be nice to me. Look how much I've helped you already?"

Chelly couldn't believe what she was hearing. "Are you telling me you got them to create the executive administrator's position, booted me out, then recommended they put me in the new job? How dumb do you think I am?"

He splayed his hands, palms up. "Who else do you know with that kind of clout?"

Chelly spewed a laugh, accidentally spritzing him. Apologizing, shaking her head, she noticed a reflected red light. Her e-mail indicator was blinking. "Excuse me, Bixler, this might be something important."

The man followed her into her office, to her desk, right to her side to view the screen, but Chelly waited, fingers poised to open the new missive. When Bixler didn't move, she turned. "Do you mind?"

He clenched his fists as he sidled toward the door. Chelly typed in her password and waited.

It was from Anne. *"Chelly: Bixler's head is on the block. He's coming to talk. Don't let him bully you. He's the one in deep poop. Rumor is, he gets you back or he's out of here. I myself have mixed emotions. Anne."*

Chelly smiled and closed the mailbox. Mixed emotions, indeed. Anne would finally be rid of Bixler, secure her job and others—including Don's—

and lose Chelly, or get Chelly back and continue being saddled with Bixler. Not a tough call.

Chelly shut down the machine, walked to her office door, beckoning Bixler to follow, then stepped aside to allow him to exit.

"Tom, I'm going to stay on here for now. It was good to see you." With that, she stepped back, shut the door in his face, flipped the security latch and dusted her hands together.

Late Thursday Chelly ironed her pinstriped suit, which had begun to hang even bigger on her shrinking frame, forced down cereal for supper and smiled as Midge recounted events and gossip from her workday. Both women went to bed early. Chelly lay fretting.

She wished she could cry, vent her pent-up emotions, but she couldn't make the tears come. Things simply weren't that bad.

She made several trips to the bathroom and her face in the mirror looked more haggard each time.

Sometime after two-thirty, sleep overtook her. That's why she was so slow to rouse to the pounding at three a.m.

Struggling up through layers of consciousness, Chelly groaned. Midge must be building something.

In the middle of the night?

Chelly sat straight up in bed. There was no light under her bedroom door, which meant the living room was dark. The hammering gained accompaniment as a loud voice bellowed her name.

She fumbled in the dark, feeling for her robe. Trembling, she shoved her arms into the sleeves and clenched her teeth when she recognized the voice. Bixler. The idiot. She ought to call the police. The neighbors probably would. It would serve him right if they already had.

"Bixler, go away," she hissed at the closed door.

The pounding got louder and his voice rose to a screech. "I have to talk to you."

Chelly kept the chain on the door as she eased it open but Bixler threw his massive body against it. The chain broke, the door gave and the man flew into the room landing flat on the floor with an "oof" at Chelly's feet, just as Midge shot out of her bedroom.

Struggling to get up, Bixler began ranting from the floor. "If you do this to me, Bennett, you're through in this town. I have friends. I have influence."

Chelly looked at Midge and, without a word, they each hoisted one of Bixler's beefy arms, lifting him to a sitting position. He scrambled to his feet and allowed them to escort him out the door, which Chelly slammed and locked with the dead bolt.

"I'm calling the police, Bixler." But she heard the whine of a siren on the street below. Bixler's protests stopped when he, too, heard the siren's wail.

From their window, the girls witnessed his lengthy conversation with the police before they gave him a ride—home, Chelly supposed, since they did not put him in handcuffs.

"Do you realize how many men grovel at your feet?" Midge said, shuffling back toward her room. Recognizing the tone, Chelly chuckled a non answer.

If she'd had the job at Weeden-Pricer first, Chelly could have been deliriously happy. She felt like a new woman, bolder, wiser, more vigilant without being cynical. She began to wear some of her better clothes, did her hair more softly, but kept the glasses.

She knew they treated her well because of the reputation she'd established at DMD. Unfortunately, her loyalty and thoughts remained there. She worked hard but looked forward to the weekend with even more excitement than usual.

Friday crawled by. Don didn't call. She'd hoped he might, if he got in early.

Saturday morning was crisp. The sun bristled, promising warmth. She dressed early, layering enough clothes to ward off the early spring chill.

Promptly at ten, he called for her to buzz him in. Her heart racing, Chelly pushed errant strands of hair back into the ponytail and darted to the door, listening as he mounted the stairs. She flung the door open before he knocked.

His marvelous form stood poised before her, his eyes shimmering. She held herself in check as she savored the first sight of him.

He was casual in wool slacks and a T-shirt under a V-neck sweater topped by a leather jacket and boots, which she looked at twice. "Lizard?"

"Snakeskin."

"You dress like a closet rich guy."

"Because that's what I am." He regarded her with a smug look that conveyed his approval and a sensual awareness of her.

Seeing the look, she backed away but he caught her chin and his eyes swept her face playfully before he kissed her. "I love you." His voice sounded husky. "My woman. My wife."

He kept his mouth close, nuzzling down her neck. She slipped out of his hold, grabbed her coat and darted by him and into the hallway, skittish about her accelerated pulse and palpitating heart.

Grinning, he closed the door behind them, caught up with her at the stairs and wrapped a proprietary arm around her waist, pulling her close to his side, stilling her for a moment before they began their silent descent.

He put her in the Porsche on the passenger side and was behind the wheel before he presented a solemn face. "For someone whose week got off to such a rocky start, it looks like you weathered it okay. You talk, I'll listen."

"I can talk better if you drive and don't look at me."

"Where to?"

"Anywhere."

"The Trenton?" He gave her a teasing grin.

"Absolutely not."

"How about Hardaways for a ride?"

She brightened. "Good idea."

"Okay, tell me everything, from the top." He started the engine and pulled into traffic.

"Like I said," she began, "I've made a lot of friends at DMD and an enemy or two. Tuesday morning, a promotion elevated an enemy into position to get rid of me. It's my own fault. I should have cooperated."

"Rid of you?" He stepped on the brake and turned a stormy look on her. "Someone fired you?"

"Yes."

The pleasant cadence was gone and his voice became a tenuous growl. "Who?"

"Tom Bixler."

"Bixler told Manning you and he were close."

"He's a liar. He also told people I sneaked back nights to have an affair with him." Don's jaw tightened and his hands clenched the steering wheel as

Chelly continued. "When they passed over Anne Beed to put him in charge, Don, he called me in, said I'd have to be nice to him. He patted the front of his pants, suggesting the kind of nice he expected. I smarted off."

"Why didn't you tell me this on the phone?"

"Bixler's vindictive. He said he knew I was dating one of Manning's gofers. He demanded that I give him your name. He was going to threaten to fire you in order to put the screws to me." She was startled by her own pun. "So to speak."

Don's eyes flashed green flame. She held up her hand. "Please don't get involved in this. There's no reason for you to risk getting canned by mixing into in-house politics. What's done is done. That's the reason I didn't tell you in the first place. I don't know how much influence Bixler has. He talks like he's got an inside track with Manning and Diet both, though I now suspect that Wayne Harned hates him. I don't want you to jeopardize your career defending me."

He stared at her with a look of stunned disbelief.

"Besides," she continued, "things have turned out great. I got fired from a job I loved and wound up with one that's probably better."

"How did he do it? Did he ask for your resignation or did you quit? Tell me his exact words."

She flashed him a searing look. "Don, no one could have made me quit voluntarily. You know how I feel about Manning. I'd never have left on my own."

Don waited.

She yielded. "His exact words were: 'Pack your shit, you're out of here.'"

Don nodded and turned his attention to the traffic light. He sat through a green. Other cars went around them. Don flexed and un-flexed his jaws. "Manning will survive losing his Girl Friday. Don't worry about his work at the office."

"Don, I am genuinely fond of Mr. Manning. I love working for him. We are on a same wave length."

She was surprised when he turned angry eyes on her. "He's not important. I'm the main man in your life, the only man who's ever... "

Her eyes rounded, cautioning him. He looked as if he were having second thoughts. "Me, Chelly. I'm important."

Unable to help adoring him, she gave him a gentle smile. "Yes, you are. That's why I can't let Bixler find out who you are. I'm hoping Manning is our ace in the hole; that he can save you and stabilize things at the office. I know he doesn't usually care how things go in the shop but, Don, I can't believe he'll tolerate this... this injustice. He'll make things right. I know he will."

Don diverted his gaze and Chelly had a sudden, chilling thought. "Now that he knows there is a problem." She looked at her companion and her voice deepened. "He did get my final e-mail, didn't he?" Don didn't answer. "Did you intercept my message?"

He gritted his teeth and barked a sharp. "What message? Was he supposed to get some hidden meaning out of: 'I'm gone. I'll miss you?' That message? Yes, I intercepted it. He doesn't have time to referee petty jealousies among unimportant people jockeying for insignificant positions."

Chelly slumped back in the seat and folded her arms over her midriff. Don offered only a placating shrug. "Ms. Fox will take care of Manning's work load. Like you said, as long as things are getting done at the business end of his computer, that's all he cares about."

"I don't think that any more."

"You don't know him."

"Are we arguing about this again?"

Don grimaced. "Appears we are, only this time you're claiming he's interested in what goes on in the office and I'm saying it ain't necessarily so."

Chelly peered out from under heavy brows. "Whose side are you on, anyway? One minute you're defending Manning, the next, you're criticizing him. Pick a side and stick to it."

Don looked chagrined. "Chelly, Manning's not all-knowing, all-seeing. He's not God."

She frowned. "Power is a relative thing. At DMD, Manning writes the commandments."

He drew a deep breath and lowered his voice. "I kept the message to myself because I wanted to hear your side."

She patted his arm. "It's old news now anyway. Today's a bright, beautiful day and... " She shot him an embarrassed shrug.

"What?"

A blush preceded her words. "I don't want to talk about ugly things. I want to look at you and laugh and enjoy just being together."

"That's good." He bit back a grin. "It's a start anyway. Will looking and laughing be enough for you?"

She chuckled. "Do I know how to distract you, or what?"

"You damn sure do." He reached over and tweaked her earlobe. "How about a nice motel some place?"

She shook her head. "I was jittery about seeing you. You change me from Dr. Jekyll to Ms. Hyde.

"What are you talking about now?"

"You know, as in Dr. Jekyll and Mr. Hyde?"

Don looked puzzled.

"Dr. Jekyll was a respected member of society but at night he became the demented Mr. Hyde."

Don grinned. "Are you trying to tell me you weren't yourself last Saturday night?"

"Ms. Hyde," she reiterated, returning his grin.

He arched one brow. "I kind of liked her, myself."

"Who?" She could feel herself blushing furiously with the memory.

He grinned. "The hot babe, with the moves. I'd like another date with her." He put two fingers on her shoulder and walked them to the tip of her breast where they circled as his playful grin turned wicked.

She pivoted out of his reach to face the passenger window, felt the flush deepen and heard his derisive laugh. "I really liked her—that feverish wench that milked everything I had. Then, after I was completely sapped, she slept in my arms. I've dreamed her into my bed every night since."

Chelly's breath caught as she saw hunger in his reflection in the passenger window. "I can't... "

"Sure you can. I've seen you *do it*. Felt you."

"That was then. Now is different. Then, we didn't have to worry about Bixler catching us together."

"Bixler's got absolutely nothing to do with us."

She whirled, alarmed that he didn't realize what a powerful threat Bixler was. "He fired me. He knows I'm dating one of Manning's assistants. He said if he found out who you were, you would be next." She gave him a pleading look. "Are you close enough to Manning to survive if Bixler comes after you?"

Don startled her when he threw back his head and laughed up at the ceiling. Still laughing, he took the next exit, which wound into a residential area of palatial homes. He pulled over, parked and pushed the steering wheel up.

"I'm the toughest, meanest guy you've ever known, Chelly. Bixler's a little fish, a perch. I'm an eagle. Do you know what happens to a perch who attracts the attention of an eagle? Hell, I had no idea you were worried about Bixler coming after me."

Chelly giggled, relieved, if not convinced.

"Now, get yourself over here, woman."

His big hands caught her at the waist and lifted her over the console to his lap. She felt giddy, unable to return his gaze, which blazed with a shimmer she had remembered over and over again through the whole, long week. And here it was, desire, rearing its head again. Her body responded almost against her will. She shivered as the tingling weakened her joints and released familiar butterflies into her stomach. Her breath burned in her chest as passion oozed from the dark depths of her, un-summoned.

He raised his voracious mouth from hers. "Are you physically involved?" His question startled her.

"Do you mean now?"

"No, this thing you have about Manning. Are you interested in him sexually?"

She snorted an unbelieving laugh. "You know better. An old guy like that? Besides, I wouldn't recognize him if I saw him on the street."

"Then what's all this loyalty? Is it his money? Has he bought your devotion?"

She felt her anger rising. "No."

"What then?"

"Maybe I idealize him some, but… "

"What?"

"He's funny, Don. Witty, brilliant, infinitely fair. He could force people to do his bidding, but he doesn't. He compliments people for extra effort, even though he pays—that is paid—us generously to make that effort. He forgives mistakes, even when they cost him money—and sometimes they do. He's gentle and caring but he works hard to conceal his tender side."

"Does he inspire this mindless dedication in everyone?"

"Not everyone." Her face darkened. "Some people fool him. I think that's strange."

"Like who?"

"Bixler's a perfect example."

"You haven't liked Bixler from that first day. Are you sure your prejudice isn't making you judge him too harshly, misinterpret his behavior?"

She sighed. "Bixler is DMD's Hitler. He is despotic and tyrannical, and about half nuts. He victimizes the employees. The lower they are in the DMD food chain, the worse he treats them."

Don's face tightened as he stared out the window behind her. "I see."

"I'm not saying anything I haven't said to Bixler's face. He's worse when he drinks. Boozing is probably the only way he can live with himself."

"Have you actually seen him drunk on the job?"

She thought a long moment. "Well, no."

"These are serious charges, Chelly. Are you only repeating office gossip?"

Her gaze followed his and she stared outside to keep from looking at Don.

"Tell me about Bixler, Chelly, things you yourself have actually observed."

Not wanting to make him angry, she spoke quietly, telling him Bixler was the unidentified man on the surveillance tape chasing her around Manning's office after hours, the man she'd refused to identify before. "He was drunk that night," she said, "but it wasn't during office hours."

Don nodded. "The one after-hours incident, is that it?"

"No." Feeling challenged, she flared. "I've seen him touch secretaries inappropriately, women who obviously did not welcome his attention. He terrifies Yarnell Tuggle when he catches her by herself." She took a deep breath. She didn't want to trigger an outburst. "He came to the apartment at three o'clock yesterday morning. My neighbors called the police.

Don's eyes hardened. "Your apartment? He showed up at your place?"

"Yes."

"What did he want?"

"He wanted me to endorse him for his new job."

"And you refused?"

She nodded.

"So what did he do?"

"He broke the chain and came stumbling in."

The knuckles on Don's hands on the wheel turned white and his eyes glittered as he fixed them on her. "And?"

"He'd been drinking. He knew I was dating someone. He demanded to know your name, implied he could protect your job and promote me at DMD, if I'd sleep with him." She paused. "He likes my body."

"Just what the hell does Bixler know about your body?"

"No more than anyone else around there does."

Don scoffed. "Speculating, like the rest of us, hoping what you were trying to hide turned out to be exactly what you are hiding." He shook his head and muttered. "Can't fault the man's taste."

Chelly rolled her eyes and looked pained. "He manipulates Leonard.

Kisses up. No one kisses up to Leonard. It simply isn't done."

"Oh, yeah?" He shot her a knowing look. "Did Bixler accompany Leonard to the Trenton, too?"

"I wasn't kissing up, Don. I had turned him down several times, and it was just for dinner and the ballet. Leonard was the one with illusions."

"Sounds to me like you inspire a lot of that."

"I don't flirt or try to get men to notice me." She pivoted and her eyes were drawn to Don's hands resting together at the top of the steering wheel. She admired his long fingers, the same fingers that had produced a kaleidoscope of... Startled by realizing the intimacy of those fingers, she blushed.

Don glanced at her, at his own hands on the wheel, and back. His quizzical expression changed to a knowing smile and he barked a quick little laugh. "I know. I've thought a thousand times of the places these fingers touched you Saturday night. I've relived those hours again and again." His expression became annoyed. "Hell, you're all I think about. People depend on me. This week I've had to kick start myself to concentrate and still you waltz through my mind, summoned by a laugh, a fragrance, anything—everything. I should have guessed you had the same effect on other men, too."

"But I've never... you know... with them." She smiled bravely, then sobered. Her voice was almost a whisper. "And you probably have the same effect on other women, too, right?" She hesitated. "Don, you're not married or anything, are you?"

Laughter spurted as he gave her a look of genuine disbelief. "Yes, as a matter of fact, I am." She felt the color drain from her face before he added, "To you, love. And I'm about tired of having to remind you of that. I'm legally, morally, permanently married to you."

She shook her head. "That all seems like a dream."

"Too good to be true?" One brow arched and he slanted her a look from the corner of his eye. "It was no con, Chelly. Sadie, Sadie, married lady, I want my connubial rights." His eyes were alive, shining, conveying a message she could scarcely believe. "Now, how about that motel?"

"No motel." She flushed and added, "Not yet."

His smile broke like sunshine on a dark day. "So, what do you want to do first? Let's hurry up and get it over with."

Chapter Twenty-Six

After a lively debate, Don drove to Hardaway Stables. Riding the bridle path together, their moods soared.

"You know, Don, sometimes you sound jealous of Mr. Manning."

He obviously recognized the taunt for what it was and his eyes shone. "He ain't all that much to look at."

"And you are?"

He laughed. "Yep."

"According to?"

"You."

She turned her face away to hide a smile and mumbled, "I genuinely like the man."

"Meaning?"

"I'm not using him. It's not like he's keeping me."

Don bristled, but the offense he took seemed phony. "Are you suggesting that I use him? That he is keeping me?"

Obviously she'd struck a nerve. "What do you want to do with your life, Don?"

"Why?"

"Well, you mentioned law school. I wondered why you hadn't finished."

"Who said I hadn't?"

Her eyes sought his face. "I thought you said… "

"I said I'd attended law school a long time ago."

"But, I thought… "

"You have a tendency to confuse what you think with what is."

She was not to be so easily deterred. "So you did finish?"

"Yes." The word was terse, as if he were through discussing it, but her curiosity was piqued.

"Have you practiced?"

"Yes." There was a warning in his expression. She made a mental note to get back to this later.

"Do you know Tom Bixler?"

He bit out another terse, "Yes." Obviously he didn't care for that subject either.

"I seem to be irritating you. Why don't you pick a topic, something you'd like to talk about."

Smiling at last, he settled a steady look on her. "Sex. Let's talk about sex."

Chelly ventured a look to see the green eyes ripen to a glistening verdant. "Not here. There are too many people."

He caught Romance's reins. "Then let's go find some place private."

The heat in his expression ignited a matching warmth inside her. Suddenly she longed to be alone with him. "Now?"

He had pulled both mounts to a stop and sat waiting, not seeming at all embarrassed by the thick silence as Chelly's mind raced to and fro, pro and con.

The arguments favoring the proposal—or proposition, as it were—overwhelmed the cautious, negative ones. She forced herself not to look at him in hopes her anatomy would not influence her mind. Her brain must rally and prevail. This had to be an intellectual decision and she knew what the responsible verdict should be.

At the end, it was not consideration for herself that governed her decision, for she had overlooked an important component to the mix—the risk to Don in being seen with her.

She rationalized. Don said Bixler was a small fish to his eagle, but Bixler was Leonard Diet's hand-picked perch and Diet was a named partner in the firm. If no one could identify Don to Bixler, Bixler couldn't fire him, nor could he use that information as leverage to force Chelly to give into him.

Just as she was about to explain all that, Don leaned close and brushed his lips over her cheek. She inhaled the scent of him and squirmed in the saddle, savagely aware of simmering desire shooting through her extremities, putting goose bumps up her legs, along her thighs, all the way to the vortex that had begun its throb.

Romance, the fractious mare, shivered, the saddle shifted. The combination of the unspoken promise of Don's body, his fragrance so close, and the movement between her legs, made Chelly gasp. "No." The word quivered from her throat. She must be strong, withstand the temptation.

His voice was hoarse, his warm breath tickled her ear as he gently tweaked her near breast between his thumb and index finger. "Please."

All her resolve melted at that one gesture. That single word. She kicked the horse.

They raced to the stables, handed the horses to Mr. Hardaway's hired hand, then drove to a nondescript motel a mile down the highway.

While Don checked in, Chelly thought of bolting but her flu symptoms flared. She fidgeted, rethinking, but it was too late. As Don returned from the motel office to the car, his face was set, his breathing harried.

The French call it the little death. Yes, Chelly thought dreamily, she could die this way a thousand times. If Don had his way, she might.

There was no clock in the room when she awoke, snug in his arms, his breathing slow and deep. It was too dark with the blinds closed to guess at the time by outside light. She needed to slip into the bathroom to look at her wristwatch on the vanity. She moved only slightly and he stirred.

"Where're you going?" He slurred the words.

Instead of answering, she relaxed, allowing him to spoon her into the curve of him. Minutes passed.

He spoke softly. "What are you worrying about?"

"We always wind up in out-of-the-way places, never where people we know might see us." Chelly hesitated but Don didn't argue. "We met at the office on a Sunday when no one else was around—not even the janitors. You took me out to eat. Way out. Not downtown or even in town."

"The food was good."

She scowled as she considered her own words, pushed herself up on an elbow, and twisted to turn a questioning gaze on him. "We came all the way out here to ride."

"It's where they keep the horses. In the country."

"That Saturday night at the Trenton, we rode the freight elevator. What was that about?"

"We were giving Leonard the slip, remember?"

"Yeah." She frowned. That was true. "We sneaked out through the parking garage and took a cab to the airport, instead of driving. Why did we do that, if you had access to Manning's motor pool? Wasn't there a car we could have used?" She waited for an answer.

"Yes. I guess I just didn't think of it."

Chelly blurted a caustic little laugh. "Didn't think of it? Give me a break. Your mind catches every tiniest little detail. You are a very thorough person."

"High praise. Lovemaking included, I assume."

She blinked slowly, not wanting him to see verification in her gaze.

He smiled, a lazy smile, his eyes only slits. "We were highly visible in Vegas, in very public places."

"Sure, in Las Vegas." She stared at him. "I don't know a soul there. How about you?"

"I didn't see anyone I knew."

"Then, today, you take me horseback riding and to this little out-of-the-way motel."

"We were in something of a hurry, as I recall."

She studied his expression, which he effectively concealed from her scrutiny.

"Don, did you get me tight that night on purpose?"

His expression was almost a dare, challenging her. "Yes."

"You did?" She had not expected that answer.

He reached for her hand but she jerked away, wrapped the sheet around her and swung her legs to sit on the side of the bed. "When are you going to take me out in public?"

"Any time you want to go."

"Where?"

"Name it."

Chelly slouched, realizing again that his future, his career, might depend on not being seen with her.

"Come on," he pressed, "where do you want to start?"

"I'd like to start at DMD, but I'm afraid."

"You don't have to be. DMD's closed today. No one's there."

"I know. We'd better just go back to my place."

"Not a very auspicious beginning for flaunting ourselves."

"No, not very."

Chapter Twenty-Seven

Midge jumped up and turned off the TV when Chelly and Don arrived at the apartment. "Aunt Mazie wants to see me."

Don looked at Midge so hard she twitched under the intensity of his stare. "Your Aunt Mazie again, huh?"

Midge glanced at Chelly, scooped her coat up off the sofa and darted out the door without answering.

Chelly made coffee and she and Don settled on the sofa. He buried his face in her neck and whispered. "Aunt Mazie certainly calls at opportune times."

Chelly's infectious laugh bubbled into the room. "That's code—to signal private time with certain friends."

He leaned back and gave her a hard look. "Is that how you happened to be alone with Chastain the other afternoon?"

She laughed again, a taunting sound. "Need you ask?"

Don's throaty chuckle vibrated against Chelly's highly sensitized nape as he resumed nibbling. "Does Midge have to abandon ship often?"

Chelly swayed to his mouth. "Nope."

He licked her earlobe before his tongue circled the outer rim of her ear. Her breath caught and she froze as he deftly unbuttoned her blouse, again.

The afternoon and evening evaporated in a cycle of lovemaking, recovery, food, and a repeat.

Don was showering alone at eleven that night, when someone pounded at the apartment door making it shiver with the ferocity of the blows.

"Bennett!" Bixler's voice reverberated in the closed hallway outside. "I'm here to settle with you once and for all. Open the damned door before I bust it down again."

How did he keep getting through the security door? She glanced toward the bathroom. The running water obviously covered Bixler's shouts. She had to get rid of him. To do that, she would promise him anything, but she would have to make it quick.

She unbolted the door and removed the new security chain before she opened.

He exploded into the room, his eyes bright with fury or lust or booze or a combination. "I have a guy keeping tabs on you. He lost you this morning but he caught up with your roommate this afternoon and called me. He says your boyfriend's here. You're busted, baby."

He looked her up and down making her flesh crawl beneath her bathrobe. He cocked an appreciative brow. "You look good, honey. Real good. Your hair's nice. Keep it that way." He lowered his voice, obviously trying to sound sexy. "Like I said, sweetheart, there's no need boffing the help, wasting the goods on an errand boy. Where's he at?"

The apartment's ancient plumbing rattled its objection as Don turned off the shower. She had to get rid of Bixler.

"Whatever you want, Bixler, you've got it, but only if you leave right this minute." She heard the alarm in her own voice and was certain Bixler picked up on it. His eyes narrowed as he turned them toward the bathroom.

"Bixler," she was beginning to panic, "he's bigger than you are, and younger, and in better shape. You need to go, now."

"Don't worry about me. I've got clout this gorilla's going to appreciate, if he has any hope of staying on at DMD. I'm a vice president now. I'm the man. After we get rid of him, you and I will negotiate him a new contract. I hope you like him, honey. I hope you like him a whole lot."

Chelly shivered when the doorknob turned and the bathroom door opened. She hurried to shield Don as he emerged behind her. One towel wrapped his hips, the other covered his head as he briskly rubbed his hair dry.

In spite of the dire circumstances, Chelly couldn't contain the satisfied smile as Bixler appraised his rival. Don's face was hidden but his muscular body obviously intimidated the new V.P. Bixler looked as if he were having a whole deluge of second thoughts.

Don's head emerged as he lowered the towel to his shoulders. Chelly remained protectively in front of him.

To her amazement, the stunned expression on the face of DMD's newest vice president ran a spectrum from smug to disbelief to outright terror. Chelly turned around. Don's physique was impressive but not alarmingly so. Then she saw his face.

The green eyes smoldered straight into Bixler's, glowing with a murderous glint. Don's fists wrung the ends of the towel he'd been using on his hair. Bixler retreated a step.

The men regarded each other without a word. Obviously they were acquainted. Chelly couldn't fathom the meaning of the expressions on their faces. She wanted to say something, but couldn't think of anything appropriate to the moment.

Bixler was first to break the silence, his pallor more ashen than usual. "What are you doing here?"

The lines deepened in Don's rugged face. The emerald eyes narrowed, his mouth hardened and his jaws clenched. Veins stood out in his forehead and his neck. He didn't seem to realize he had the ends of the towel in a death grip. "Bixler, don't say one word." Don's eyes glinted a steely warning. "The safest thing for you to do right now is to get as far away from me as you can."

Bixler started to speak.

"Not one word or, so help me, they'll find your body in a dumpster."

Bixler began backing. "I... I... I can explain."

Don took a menacing step and he seemed to swell to gargantuan proportions. "I said don't talk."

Bixler spun, ran for the door and yanked it open. It hit the toe of his shoe and ricocheted, slamming closed before he could get through. After another foiled attempt, Bixler rocketed out of the room, leaving the much-abused door vibrating in his wake.

Don walked over and closed the door, threw the dead bolt and reattached the chain, shuddering as he drew exaggeratedly slow breaths.

Chelly marveled that Don, barefooted and half naked, could command such obedience, even more astonished that he got unquestioning compliance from Bixler. While she reflected, Don turned his flashing eyes on her. "What was he doing here? What did he want? How the hell did he get in?"

She stared.

Don shook his head and adopted the docile mask that effectively veiled his thoughts. He lowered his voice. "I asked you what he wanted."

Righteous indignation oozed through her slowly, replacing astonishment. "He wanted me to have sex with him to save your job. Do you have any idea how much trouble you're in? There's no telling what he'll do next." She hesitated, squinting into his face. "What did happen just now?"

Don shrugged, his anger ebbing. "He left."

"I saw. But how did you do that?"

"I'm bigger than he is." He grinned oddly. "And a whole lot meaner."

She grimaced. "And for the satisfaction of that moment, you will probably get your pink slip Monday."

Don snorted a laugh. "I told you, Bixler's a perch."

"But he's Leonard's own private perch, Don. Can Manning protect you from Leonard? Leonard influences Harned and Harned runs the shop."

"Don't worry about it. Everything is going to be fine, now that I finally have all the players tagged."

"Have you got something on Manning? Is that how you finagle his car and his hotel suite, even his jet?"

"Extortion? Now you think I'm blackmailing your hero?" He laughed and ran a hand through his damp hair, smoothing it back. "You don't think much of me, do you?"

"Don, I don't want to be part of anything that compromises Manning."

Don's eyes caught hers and the laughter died. "You mean if it comes down to him or me, it's him?"

She bit her lips. That was it then? Competition. Don was contending for alpha male of her universe, even willing to risk his career. "You'd better get dressed," she said. "I'm getting really angry."

She didn't know if it was pride or indignation or anger on his face, but Don wheeled and stalked into her bedroom.

She stood unmoving, struggling to hold back an emotional blast that might detonate any minute. She would never have had sex with Bixler, even to save Don's job. But who did Don think he was, getting all incensed about Manning? She admired and respected her boss but surely Don knew how much more important he was to her than Manning. After all, Don had been her first—and last—lover, the man who had taken her innocence.

No, that wasn't fair. In the end, she had practically forced herself on him.

Tears stung behind her eyelids and she swallowed hard to stanch their flow. She stiffened when he came out of the bedroom, his face set, masking every emotion and thought. When he looked at her, his eyes shone hard with an intense resolve she could not read.

He strode to the outside door, opened it, then turned back. She braced herself, determined that he wouldn't see her flinch no matter how harsh his parting shot.

The rigidity of his face softened as he took a deep breath and expelled it. "I didn't know what this was, Chelly, this irritation that grinds like sand in a man's craw. I have never been jealous before." A grin transformed his face as he shook his head, obviously bewildered. "Forgive me. I love you. It turns out, loving you makes me crazy."

He was through the door and gone by the time the tender words registered. Reeling, Chelly walked to the sofa and sank.

What had just happened? What repercussions should she expect?

She did not have one clue.

Chapter Twenty-Eight

"It's love, pure and simple," Midge declared Sunday after listening to Chelly's account. "The guy's probably had easy women all his life. You're rare, Chelly. You've got his motor revved and running and he doesn't know which direction to go."

Chelly wondered if there might be some truth in Midge's speculation. "I thought it was all over when Don came out of the bathroom. I thought Bixler would fire him on the spot." She regarded Midge quizzically, remembering. "But Bixler shriveled like he was facing the wrath of God. They knew each other. They both understood what was going on. I was the only one who didn't."

Midge scowled. "And Don told Bixler to leave?"

"Yes. And ordered him not to say a word. I knew that wouldn't happen. Bixler talks more when he's got nothing to say."

"But he kept his mouth shut?"

"Yes." Chelly's face twisted as she pondered the mystery. "I take that back. He sputtered. He stared at Don and backpedaled. Next thing I knew he was duking it out with the door." She giggled at the memory. "He threw it open, but it hit his foot and slammed shut. He did the same thing again before he finally got out."

Midge seemed to picture the scenario and she blurted a bawdy laugh. "That man really has a hard on for our door." Laughing, the roommates regarded each other until Midge posed a question. "Don was angry, in spite of Bixler's comical exit?"

"Maybe it was because he thought I might have slept with Bixler to save his job."

"Would you have?"

Chelly grimaced. "Surely not. Don knows I haven't been with anyone else. Certainly he knows that... well, I don't think I could make myself have sex with Bixler if a life depended on it."

"Then why did he get so mad?"

Chelly shook her head slowly from side to side. "I don't know. I can't figure it out."

Faye Dell caught Chelly on the way into her office at Weeden-Pricer on Monday morning. "We've made a mistake, Chelly."

"Oh, Faye Dell, I've tried to be careful. I didn't think you had let me handle anything sensitive."

"No, honey, it's not your work. Your work is fine. Manning had a fit when he found out you had left DMD."

"He knew last week."

"Yes, but last week he thought it was your idea. That's changed."

"So, what are you saying?"

"Manning is in his office. He wants to see you. He called Levi this morning."

"About me?"

Faye Dell raised an eyebrow and regarded Chelly warily. "Yes, about you. Manning wants you there. Now."

Chelly felt her stomach lurch with dread and excitement. She had longed to meet her boss, face to face. But was he going to be angry—have one of his notorious fits?

Watching Chelly's face, Faye Dell added, "I'd think you would be flattered to have the two honchos discussing you."

"I thought Manning and Smoker were big competitors." Chelly unrolled the sleeves of her cotton shirt, trying to smooth the wrinkles and her nervousness as she re-buttoned the cuffs.

"They are. They are also friends. Two guys at the top of the game have locked horns so many times they have gotten close. Levi is seventy-five years old now and he's seen them all. He has a lot of regard for Manning."

"Most men the age of these guys are thinking of hanging it up by now." Chelly glanced up to find Faye Dell looking perplexed. "What? What'd I say?"

Faye Dell studied her, looking skeptical. "Chelly, how old do you think

Manning is?"

"I don't know. He's the partner older than Leonard and Leonard's forty-eight. He's younger than Mr. Diet, who is well over eighty. Why?" She paused watching Faye Dell, who was obviously fighting a grin. "How old is he?"

"Smoker and Manning are not contemporaries, Chelly." She shook her head. "It doesn't matter. You'll see for yourself."

"Why does Mr. Smoker want me go?"

"Professional courtesy. Manning wants you back. Levi agreed. Pack your duds, girl. You're going home."

"But... but... what if I don't want to go?" She stopped as Levi Smoker appeared, the usual cold cigar clamped between his teeth.

Faye Dell began to explain. "Levi, I was just telling Chelly... "

"That she had better get moving." He turned his most intense scowl on the younger woman. "I don't know what you've done, young lady, but you've got Manning on his ear. He's having a conniption fit over there." Suddenly he grinned. Obviously he thought there was something hilariously funny about his own statement.

Chelly didn't get it. "I don't know what his having a temper fit has to do with me."

Smoker's laughter diminished as his eyes narrowed. "You must have something he wants pretty bad."

"I don't even know him. Mr. Manning and I have never met."

Levi shook his wizened head, his gaze steady, scrutinizing her face. "Scuttlebutt says you're his main squeeze."

Chelly smiled. "That's what he tells people to keep the ladies at bay. I date a guy who works for Manning."

"What guy?" Smoker sobered.

"His name's Don Richards and he's Manning's... "

His eyes narrowed. "Manning's what?"

She gave him a sheepish smile. "He calls himself Manning's Secretary of State." Smoker's eyes twinkled, but he didn't say anything, so she babbled on. "Most likely he's just a flunky."

"What's this guy look like?" He shot Faye Dell a warning glance, then turned a benign expression on Chelly.

"He's six-foot-three, substantially built, has dark hair, and rather unusual eyes."

"Green?"

She was surprised at the accurate guess. "Yes. How did you know?"

Faye Dell took a breath and started to speak before Smoker silenced her with another look. He smiled and nodded again at Chelly. "Wait a minute, Chelly. I'll walk over there with you. I need to see Manning for a minute myself." A mischievous grin stole over his face. He stepped to an ash tray to pick up a book of matches teetering on its edge, and spoke to Faye Dell. "I've waited a long time for this."

He cackled quietly, nodding for Chelly to precede him to the elevators. "Young lady, you may have accomplished something I have wanted to see happen for years. I think I am about to see the biggest, baddest gunfighter I've ever known, blink." He chuckled again and the sound rippled around the room.

Faye Dell's trilling laugh followed them all the way down the hallway. Chelly hated inside jokes.

Apprehensive, she also felt at once vaguely flattered, annoyed, amused, and insulted. She felt like a human tennis ball being batted from court to court.

Smoker lit his cigar as they exited the building. Chelly didn't comment on it, muttering, more to herself than to her companion, as they crossed the street to the Sheppard Building. "I was afraid Manning would probably retire or his health would fail before I had a chance to meet him."

Her companion cackled again, removed the cigar and blew smoke rings straight up in the air, enjoying himself immensely. Maybe he was slipping into his dotage, too.

Remote voices sounded like a hive of bees as Chelly and Levi Smoker stepped off the elevator on the eleventh floor of the Sheppard Building. The lobby was deserted. Neither Monica Lynch nor a sub sat at the reception desk and the dozen phone lines were strangely silent. Chelly peered at the system on the way by. All the lines were blinking. Someone had put every one of them on hold.

Smoker stood patiently as Chelly slid her purse under the receptionist's station. He followed, grinning broadly, as she led him toward the hum coming from the east hallway.

Yarnell saw her first, pointed, and let out a little yelp. Standing next to Yarnell, Anne clamped a hand over the girl's mouth and said something that quieted her. Anne did a quick step to intercept others making a beeline toward Chelly. Smoker hung back, apparently enjoying his fly-on-the-wall status.

Grabbing Chelly's elbow, Anne guided her to an empty cubicle. "What have you done?"

"I don't know. What?"

"I've never seen Manning this bad and the man is famous for his tirades. First thing this morning, he summoned Bixler, took his keys, and fired him, on the spot. Told him to 'clear out his shit, he was gone.' Bixler made the mistake of trying to explain whatever it was, then puffed up and threatened to sue for wrongful termination.

"Peggy was listening at the door but couldn't hear Manning after the initial explosion. She said his voice was too low. She thought it was probably better she couldn't hear because Bixler came flying out of there like the devil had bitten his butt, all red-faced and shaking. He didn't say anything to anyone, just emptied his desk and left.

"Next, Manning summoned Leonard but he wasn't in yet. Probably a lucky thing for him, even if he is a name on the firm. You know Len. He usually ambles in sometime between ten and noon. He was early today. I felt sorry for the guy, facing Manning in the mood he was in, and I don't even like Leonard."

Chelly listened, awed. "So what's happening now?"

"Len's in there. Laureen Fox is directing traffic. No one knows what or who's up next. She's supposed to take you in, but I wanted to catch you first and warn you."

"Thanks."

"Laureen says Manning is livid about the way the shop's being run. He's going to stay a while, set us to rights. He's a bastard to work for, but he runs a great shop, as long as everyone does everything his way."

Chelly scoured her memory. "As far as I know, he shouldn't have any reason to be mad at me."

"Apparently he thought you had left DMD on your own bat."

"I didn't want to tattle or get anyone in trouble."

Anne's eyes rounded. "Well, we're all in it now."

"Anne, Leonard's one of the partners. How can Manning call him on the carpet?"

"I don't know, but Fox says Len is sweating profusely. Laureen wasn't with them at first, but Manning called her in later to take notes and to escort different people in and out, itemizing their areas of responsibility around here. Diet's still there on the hot seat. She's the one who told me Manning had called Smoker about you. In a real snit.

"All of us feel sorry he ordered you back to face him. You've got friends here, Chelly. No one wants to see you humiliated again."

If Manning had told Smoker to fire her, he would probably do the same with any law firm in the city. Manning had influence. Chelly set her mouth. No matter what, she would not give up the name Don Richards, even to Manning. She would return to Blackjack, cope with local sympathy, parental advice, Harmon Chastain, even Eric's I-told-you-so, but she would not betray Don.

Laureen Fox's perfectly coifed head popped around the doorway. "Chelly! Thank God I found you. Manning said to call in the full staff when you showed up. When I heard you were here, I did it. Everyone's in his office waiting. Come on."

Chelly could feel the heat creeping into her face. Her heart pounded, yet her hands were like ice. She needed a minute to organize her thoughts.

She wouldn't try to defend herself. She would listen to his questions and answer them directly, truthfully, with one exception. She would not utter Don's name.

When Manning finished with her, she would retrieve her purse from the receptionist's station and leave. She would stop by the apartment to tell Midge what had happened and ask her to hold onto her belongings until she could come back for them. Then she would go home, back to Blackjack, to her mom and dad and Angela. And Eric.

It wasn't much of a plan, but it was something to hold on to. She had learned valuable lessons. All she had to do was survive the next few minutes. Maybe she wasn't bad enough for the city. Her eyes stung. Or maybe the city wasn't good enough for her. Either way, she and it seemed to have irreconcilable differences.

Later, if Don wanted to risk it, he would know where to find her. By then she would probably be legitimately wed to someone else. To Eric?

She recalled Eric's meeting with Don at her apartment. No, she wasn't going to saddle herself with a loser like Eric. She would, by gosh, handle things on her own. But first, she needed to get her equilibrium back.

"Chelly?" Anne's voice interrupted her thinking, reminding her there was a lion yet to beard.

Chelly squared her shoulders.

The hum in the hallway had grown quieter with the forty or so attorneys and staff people in Manning's office.

Walking stiffly, Chelly looked but wasn't able to see the figure seated at the desk, hidden behind all the people.

Sitting to one side of the desk, Leonard Diet glanced at her, then quickly lowered his eyes. Yarnell twisted a tissue round and round one finger, refusing to give Chelly more than a passing glance. Leading her, Laureen Fox cleared a path.

Chelly bit her lips, mentally rehearsing and was surprised when she noticed Levi Smoker lurking in a corner watching, smiling with anticipation. He winked. What was he so damn jovial about?

She didn't have time to wonder long about Smoker's good humor. She would say hello to Manning, force herself to make eye contact, and offer to shake hands. She would say how glad she was to meet him after all this time. She would maintain her composure.

Then a final broad back shifted to one side and Chelly focused on the great man's desk. The form behind the desk stood. She didn't look up at him, but instead her eyes locked on the startlingly familiar hand he offered.

A hush fell over the room as Chelly lifted her gaze, stunned to silence.

His emerald eyes flashed and a slight smile played at his broad mouth, the mouth that had teased and coaxed and conquered her, not only her lips, but her body. Her soul.

"Chelly Bennett, this is D.R. Manning." Laureen glowed, obviously pleased to have the honor.

Instead of taking Chelly's offered hand, he grasped only her index finger, the one wearing his ring, and smiled into her eyes.

There were words she planned to say but those carefully chosen phrases rattled inside her head, unspoken. Instead she blurted, "What are *you* doing here?"

Don studied her carefully, not taking his eyes from her face, waiting, apparently giving her time to digest the revelation.

Staring at him, she remembered. They'd begun in the elevator that first day. He had blocked her retreat from DMD when she chickened out, probably had gotten her the clerk's job in the first place.

Manning had provided the tickets for "Les Miserables," a reward, and she had caught a glimpse of her cowboy for a second time, in the crowded lobby during the intermission.

He had maneuvered her into working the Sunday they met here in the office—when she braced him for making copies of sensitive material and he told her his name was Don Richards. *D.R.* Manning, of course. How could she not have known?

He had baited her about Manning, repeatedly, made her defend him... to him.

They had never gone anywhere they might be seen. Did he not want people to see him fraternizing with the help? Or did he not want someone to call him by name in front of her? If not, why not?

Fraternizing. A nice term for screwing the resplendent D.R. Manning.

She heard a low, familiar cackling behind her and recognized the sound of Levi Smoker's wheeze. Don glanced at Smoker, scowled, then set his gaze back on her face. Why was he just standing there? Why didn't he say something?

He could regale the gathering with stories of her stupidity, could tell Smoker how he had hustled and conquered her without revealing his identity. What a coup. A god besting a... a country bumpkin. Big deal.

And who was he to be so indignant about Bixler's sexually harassing the help when he had done the same thing himself?

Laureen Fox stirred, pushed a loose strand of hair from her perfect face. Fox was probably next in line for Don's attention, if she had not already been conquered. How many were there, right here in this room? A whole shop full of adoring, accommodating females, the occasional simpering debutante and who knew how many others? He had no doubt had them all.

Chelly clenched her fists, fighting the wave of humiliation. When she spoke, her voice echoed in the eerie silence.

"You insufferable ass."

The words escaped before she realized she had actually spoken that very private thought out loud.

The thick silence in the room was cut only by hushed voices whispering: "What'd she say?" and "Did you hear what she said?" and the sound of Levi Smoker's wheezing laughter.

Chapter Twenty-Nine

Manning's spartan face revealed nothing as his eyes surveyed Chelly indifferently. "Ms. Fox, thank you for your help." He raised his voice. "All of you, thank you for coming. I need a private word with Chelly who, I neglected to mention, also happens to be Mrs. D.R. Manning. My wife."

Laureen Fox's eyes bulged, but if she made a sound, it was lost in the chorus of inhaled breaths, a couple of muted cheers, groans, and hums of surprise, which followed the announcement. Then the hush reasserted itself over the room.

No voice disturbed the rustling movement of dozens of people abandoning the office. Levi Smoker leaned close to Chelly, patted her arm and said, "You have my very best wishes, Mrs. Manning. He's a great catch. Really. I love this guy."

Chelly couldn't think of a response.

Then Leonard Diet, obviously intimidated, ventured a step or two closer to be heard. "Look here, Manning, I don't quite know what's going on, but we need Chelly here in the office, no matter what she's done to you. She's tested my mettle, too, but I'm willing to keep her on. I'll let her be my personal assistant or something." He hesitated, his eyes pleading with Don, whose expression remained grim. "Hell, man, I'll pay her out of my own pocket."

There was a slight pause as Manning glanced into the junior partner's face. "No." The lone word was cold and dismissive.

"Manning?" Diet's pudgy countenance became stern. "You aren't going to… that is, even if she were actually your wife, well, I couldn't let you… "

Don's eyes narrowed to a cruel squint. "Leonard, don't be an ass. I wouldn't hurt her. You have no standing here. Get out."

Muttering a string of inaudible words, Diet bowed his head, turned on his heel, and marched from the office.

Chelly braced herself, knowing the door's slam would be Leonard's way of having the final word. He slammed the door, making it shudder.

Standing just beside the exit, his cigar again cold, Smoker tipped his head at Don. "Mr. Secretary of State." He arched his eyebrows and grinned broadly as he sidled to the closed door. "I believe you finally may have met your match." With that and biting back another rolling chuckle, he left, the last one out.

Her anger softened by inner turmoil, Chelly refused to meet Don's steady gaze. She did see his hand move, motioning her into a client's chair. She hesitated a moment, then lowered herself onto the chair's edge as Don reassumed his place across the desk.

"Look at me." His voice sounded patient but firm. She turned a sullen face to him. "Who am I, Chelly?"

"I have no idea."

"You know me. Better than anyone has ever known me. You carry my heart around in your pocket, kiddo." He waited, then whispered, "You own my soul, sweetheart. Oh, yeah, you know me."

Her temper suddenly flared. "Not as D.R. Manning, I don't. I thought Manning had a lion's heart and I thought Don Richards was a man of courage and character. Lies and deceit are a coward's way. Why didn't you tell me?"

He snorted a laugh. "My name is Donald Richard Manning. I told you the truth that Sunday, right here in the office."

It was her turn to snort her disdain. "A lawyer's truth. Just enough information to serve your purpose."

"Chelly, I'm thirty-six years old and high mileage, physically, mentally, emotionally. I came into practice with John Diet when he was already in his dotage. I've put up with Leonard out of deference to an absentee old man. I've worked hard, won a lot of lawsuits and in the process, I've made us all rich."

His expression softened as he spoke. Slowly she was beginning again to discern the tender, vulnerable spirit shining in his verdant eyes as he continued. "I have been totally immersed in the business, used any means available to beat some very able opponents. It has made me cynical. I never cared about the money or my reputation. All I cared about was the win, carving another notch on my gun. That motivation has been enough, has driven me all these years." He paused and smirked. "Winning was all I needed, until you came tiptoeing into this building and into my heart that brisk December morning.

"In the past, I was merciless to friends who carried on about love at first sight. I have ridiculed men who fell head over heels in a heartbeat. It was only fair—poetic justice, I suppose—that I should be toppled that way. What do you think Smoker is gloating about?

"I didn't know what was happening to me. I have jumped through hoops for you. It has been enough to make a grown man check his backside for Cupid's arrows."

Chelly bit back a smile and stared at her hands folded in her lap.

He continued. "I was slam dunked into love. I had built up emotional calluses dealing with rich, elegant, conniving women. It was great irony, really, for someone like me to fall for a badly dressed country girl with an old lady's hairdo and no sense of style." He laughed to himself. "Your whole getup gave me chills and fever. I went for the bait anyway."

"Do you know what set the hook?"

She looked up to find him watching her uncertainly.

"Those ridiculous glasses. How can a man even guess he needs to defend himself against a woman wearing phony horn-rimmed glasses?"

Chelly caught her bottom lip with her teeth fighting the smile. She didn't interrupt.

"I had to know your name, how to find you. You got off the elevator here, started boldly forward, then you withered right in front of my eyes."

Chelly clamped her teeth harder on the lip but couldn't contain the little laugh as she remembered the overwhelming feeling of inadequacy that nearly routed her. She raised her gaze to find Don's green eyes shimmering back at her. He arched his eyebrows.

"Maybe you were a client, I told myself. If you were, I wanted to do your work, no matter how trivial. Mid step, you turned around ready to run. Reading your body language, anticipating your retreat, I put myself in your line of flight."

Her eyes widened. "So that's how you happened to be right behind me."

"You weren't going anywhere until I knew who you were."

Mutely, she nodded, studying him, trying to reconcile the man who had romanced her so successfully with the one she revered by e-mail. How could they be one and the same?

She stiffened as he stood and walked around the desk. There was nothing threatening in his approach. On the contrary, she felt warmed as he closed. But there was the other, the deception. Another deception. How could two men who were nothing alike—Don and Eric—both have deceived her so thoroughly?

"I can't work here, now," she said, eying him. "I mean, how could I come back here? What would people say?"

He eased himself down to perch on the edge of the desk, directly in from of her. Splendid in his expensive suit, his tasteful shirt and tie, he splayed his huge, marvelous hands, palms down on the mahogany desk at either side of him and relinquished a tolerant smile as their eyes met and held.

"Chelly Bennett had to take orders from guys like Bixler," he said quietly. "On the other hand, Chelly Manning can do anything around here she damn well pleases. You call the tune, I'll see it's played. You can work or not, keep your own hours, name your own salary."

Her eyes narrowed. "As long as I masquerade as your lady, you mean, your own, high-dollar trollop, always on call?"

He fisted the hands at his sides and looked as if she had slapped him. With what appeared to be considerable effort, he overcame the initial response and his face relaxed. "Why do you insist on disregarding the ceremony in Las Vegas? You are my wife, not my girlfriend. We are married, Chelly, legally bound in holy wedlock."

Her scornful laugh caught in her throat. "You really do think I'm a hick, don't you?"

"It was real. You are bound to me, Chelly. You are lawfully and morally Mrs. D.R. Manning."

He leaned backward across the desk and reached into a drawer to produce a marriage certificate, which he presented to her. She recognized her own scrawled signature and read the print carefully.

"Why haven't you shown me this before?"

"It had to be filed. I just got it back in the mail from the clerk's office."

The certificate looked genuine and she could almost believe the fairy tale was true. She smiled wanly. "Is there a provision under civil law for entrapment?"

He laughed and she sucked in her cheeks trying to stifle her smile as he answered. "Chelly, try to see this objectively. Look at the up side. You can finish law school. You can continue working here in any capacity you choose. You have full access to my assets. You can have any home you want, leased, bought or built. If I don't already own a car you like, we'll get it. I might ask to exercise some prerogative in helping you choose your clothing, but you can have all the wardrobe you want. Anything. Name it."

"Name my price?" She felt her lifting spirits plummet. "You implied Eric's dad wasn't rich enough to buy him a wife."

"He was not rich enough to buy him *this* wife," he corrected.

"Well, maybe you aren't either, Don Richards or D.R. Manning, or whoever you are."

Confused and angry all over again, she got to her feet and started toward the door. He was there before she could turn the knob. He brushed a hand over her ear and put his thumb beneath her chin to tilt her gaze to his.

"I love your face." His eyes caressed from her forehead to her chin. "I love your many expressions—in costume or out, staunchly defending Manning; terrified, shielding me from Bixler's wrath—all of them. I want you in my office, in my bed, in my life."

She risked a look at him. The tawny cat, the long, lithe predator was back, his eyes the color of the deep forest, and he again looked hungry. She couldn't resist the desire smoldering in his ravenous gaze, not for long anyway. He followed her mouth with his. She turned her face away once, then again, more slowly with each pass. His lips caught hers on the third go-by and she knew she was finished, her will forfeit.

"Please stop," she whispered after yielding to a deep, breathless kiss. He went completely still, his lips not an inch from hers, waiting. She couldn't seem to make herself push him away. "This is too much to absorb all at once. I need time."

He exhaled a rueful laugh. "You've had long enough. I have never waited this long for anything, much less anything I wanted this badly." He continued holding her face with one hand, the other flattened in the small of her back pressing her to him as he regarded her solemnly.

"Your body is willing, is at this moment providing me consolation the rest of you may not intend. You are warming, darling. How long do you plan to punish us? How long will you deny a man whose only wish is to live with his own wife?"

She bowed her head. "I don't know. I didn't know I really was a wife, much less your wife. That is, D.R. Manning's wife."

"But you do know it now, don't you, Chelly?"

"Yes, I guess I do." She gave him a tremulous smile. "But I don't have a handle yet on the job description."

Laughing, he pressed her tightly against him with one hand as he removed her glasses and unclipped her hair with the other, lacing his fingers through the natural curl, tousling, thumbing wayward strands that had fallen into her face.

"Oh I think you do. You have a natural aptitude for it. You make a spectacular wife, every time you let yourself get into the part. I thank heaven every day that I'm the one who knows."

"Oh," she moaned and the utterance sounded like regret. "I was so bad insisting you... wanting... practically coercing you."

He put her a little away from him and smiled into her face, surprised. "I, too, have tantalizing memories of our lovemaking, sweetheart. You have an amazing depth of passion. You make love like an enchantress. You'll never burn like that with Eric or any other man. Not ever, Chelly. Don't even bother to try."

She was startled to hear Eric's name again dropped into the middle of such an intensely personal conversation.

Suddenly Don sobered. "You must never try to make our magic with anyone else."

She blushed furiously.

He again wrapped her tightly against him. "I didn't imagine your fidelity would be so important to me, Chelly. It makes me inexplicably happy that you never knew a man before me." His voice and the emotion in his face deepened. "We belong to each other, my angel, until death do us part. Isn't that what the preacher said?"

She nodded, enveloped by his scent, his warmth, him. She had no idea what the preacher had said.

When Don spoke, his breath whispered against her hair. "I love that you set no guard on your expressions. They reflect your thoughts—your guileless trust, your disapproval, your joy, pathos. Your emotions are displayed for all to see, but only I seem to be able to read them. Do you really mind that I know you so well and love you so much?"

She shook her head. "I don't mind anything when you're holding me. But you have to let me go. Give me time to... to tell my parents... to adjust."

Again he relaxed his grip and peered down into her face. "Let me come with you. We can go away for a couple of days, then we'll face your parents together."

She exhaled a doubtful laugh. "I don't think so. I need to think. Together we would spend all our time in bed and I know I couldn't map out strategy there. No."

"Don't leave." His voice took on a dark timbre.

"I'm going home."

"To your family? Or to Chastain?"

She shot a glance at his face that was curiously, bleakly intense. How could he even entertain such an outrageous thought? Then she had a ringing new insight. "Don't you dare say anything unkind about Eric. You and he are cut from the same cloth. You're both liars."

He winced but didn't try to argue.

"Better the devil I know than the devil I don't." She stared at him. Obviously he intended to dictate, not only advising her on her wardrobe, but her friends, her thoughts, her emotions and loyalties. That wasn't going to happen. She was not going be D.R. Manning's puppet any more than she planned to let Harmon Chastain or any other alpha male dictate her life.

She set her mouth with grim, new resolve. "I'm going and I will spend time with anyone I choose, with or without your permission."

His eyes glittered his displeasure, but Chelly met his glower with determination of her own. Slowly, his expression softened, although the concern remained. "You will come back?" He was yielding but his marvelous voice wavered. "When?"

"I'll let you know. I need time to decide... things."

"There's nothing to decide, Chelly. The decisions have already been made."

"Not by me and this is my life. I am not going to be manipulated by some self-proclaimed dictator."

He attempted a smile. "A benevolent dictator who loves you more than his own life."

She stared at her hands, gathering strength to fight the compelling eyes, his body, which was capable of taking her to heaven, his offer to make her every dream come true. But it was all the result of deceit and trickery. Wasn't it?

He studied her face a long moment, willing her to meet his gaze. Finally, she gave in and was surprised by the pain she saw in his expression. He was always so sure of himself, so in control. It was odd to see him uncertain.

"Chelly, tell me truthfully." She was puzzled at the tremor in his voice. "Do you still have feelings for Chastain?"

Why did he keep bringing Eric into the mix? Eric was the farthest thing from her mind.

"I need some time." She felt a twinge of regret as Don's broad shoulders rounded. "I'm just going home to think this through. You can understand that, can't you?"

He shrugged, lifting a defeated gaze to meet hers. "Yes, I'm afraid I do." He attempted a smile as if he were trying to put on a brave front. "That's not very flattering, you know. I offer you the world, my abject devotion, anything money can buy, and the only thing you ask is that I allow you to leave me."

He eased closer. She retreated with a wary glance. "Is that how you negotiate, intimidating people with your size, browbeating, guilt-tripping them into doing things your way?"

He snorted a laugh and his eyes narrowed as he minced another step, tracking her retreat. "No. But normally I negotiate from strength. I never admit a weakness in my position, not even to myself. However, in this instance, you hold the high ground. I want you any way you'll have me, darling. How will it be? Baked? Sautéed? Poached?"

They both laughed lightly.

"You see, Chelly, I'm knee-walking, groveling-in-the-dirt in love. Not at all an advantageous position for deal making."

She supposed she was dreaming and expected to wake up any minute in her own room. Was the stalking lion really making soft purring noises while laying his heart at her feet?

The dream persisted. She didn't wake up. "Don, all I need is a little time. And I don't want you to pressure me. No calls." She glanced around, suddenly aware of where they were. "I do have one other request."

The words seemed to give him heart. "Name it."

"No hanky pankying with Laureen Fox."

He hesitated before a broad grin spread over face and he asked with a teasing shrug: "Who is Laureen Fox?"

Her eyes narrowed to a squint. "An astute response, Mr. Manning. You appear to be as quick on your feet as they say."

They both laughed, although his joy seemed restrained.

Midge was not home when Chelly got to the apartment. Hurriedly, she packed enough for a couple of days.

Because she had not seen her former supervisor and friend in her flight from the office, Chelly telephoned Anne. "I'm going to be gone the rest of the week."

"Are you Manning's wife?"

"I think so."

"When will you know for sure?"

Chelly giggled. "Soon."

"But you are coming back?" Anne sounded relieved.

"I left my purse under Monica's desk. Will you put it in my old broom closet office for me? I have to come back for that, if nothing else. And, Anne, another thing, don't be filling my job while I'm gone."

"Which job?"

Lilting laugher bubbled over the line before Chelly cleared her throat. "How are things? What are people saying?"

"Nothing yet. We've been waiting for the other shoe to drop. No one has been brave enough yet to sound Manning's mood. His attitude sets the tone. When he's tyrannical, we dance like jumping beans. He hasn't come out of his office since you left and no one has dared to enter un-summoned. No one knows if it's Jekyll or Hyde in there." Chelly wondered if Anne's use of that comparison was just coincidence.

"I hope I haven't left you in too much of a lurch."

"I hope not, too." Anne laughed. "If I'd had any idea you had so much clout, I would have been nicer to you."

Chelly allowed an approving chuckle. "You were nice enough."

"Where are you going?"

"Home. Back to Blackjack to sort things out."

"How long do you think that will take?"

Chelly thought of Don—D.R. Manning—and she swallowed hard. "I need to sort through my options and come up with a plan for the rest of my life. How long could a little thing like that take?"

Chapter Thirty

She loaded the car, stalling. Chelly told herself she was waiting around for Midge but in her heart she knew she was hoping the telephone would ring. She wanted to hear his voice one more time. Of course, she had asked him not to call or pressure her.

It didn't ring.

Midge wheeled her aging Dodge Dart into its assigned space next to Chelly's Taurus as Chelly loaded a last laundry basket of clothing. Her roommate's face fell with concern as she got out of her car. "What are you doing home?"

Chelly tried to give her a reassuring smile but her mouth trembled. "I'm going to Blackjack for a day or two."

"Why?"

"To think."

"You can think here. I'll be as quiet as a mouse. I can even go over to Aunt Mazie's, if that would help."

Chelly took a deep breath. "Everything is haywire."

"Don't tell me you got fired again."

"Well, yeah, sort of, but that's not a problem. How did you know?"

"I called Weeden-Pricer. The operator referred me to DMD. I called there and, when I finally got through, the receptionist said you were in a meeting with Manning. Did you and he not hit it off, face to face?"

"Midge, Don Richards is D.R. Manning."

"What?" Midge's jaw dropped open. "I thought Manning was old." She rolled her eyes. "Oh, dear. This gives things a whole new perspective, doesn't it?"

Nodding, Chelly wrung her hands, wadding a tissue and struggling to hang onto her volatile emotions. "Weird, huh?"

"The guy who filled our apartment with flowers and can't keep his hands off you is the D.R. Manning?"

"Right."

Midge wrapped Chelly in an enthusiastic hug. "Yea, sister!" She stepped back, obviously confused by Chelly's dour expression. "I don't see the problem, girl. What's wrong? You are crazy about him, right?"

Chelly bit her lips and bobbed her head up and down.

"You're even married to him."

Another grimace and head bob.

"Why go any place, for heaven's sake?"

Chelly's eyes roamed the parking lot and she shuddered. "He lied to me. What is it about me that makes men deceitful? It's too... much."

"Too much? I see. The princess falls for the woodcutter who neglects to tell her he also happens to be the handsome prince. He pledges his troth and she runs home to the wolf for advice?" Midge winced. "That fairy tale ain't gonna fly."

Chelly didn't respond.

"You aren't going home for a second opinion? Not from the twit? Chelly, that's absurd!"

"I'm not going home to see Eric. That seems to be another widespread, wrong assumption. I want to see Mom and Dad and Angela, sleep in my own room, reconnect with me. I need to remember who I am and what I want in life, not what everyone else wants for me, not Eric's dad or Bixler or even..." her voice broke, "even Donald Richard Manning."

Midge lowered her arms from Chelly's shoulders. "I know it's only a minor consideration, but didn't you already marry the guy?"

"That was a Las Vegas wedding, Midge." Absently, she rolled the ring around her finger. "I don't... well I didn't... think it was the real thing." She was suddenly alarmed. "Please don't tell anyone about that."

"No one else knows?"

Chelly stopped fingering the ring. "Yes, well he announced it to everyone in the office today."

Midge shook her head sadly. "My roommate is married one of the most gorgeous, influential men in the country but we're keeping it secret so she can decide whether to keep him or throw him back." She skewered her face into a comical twist. "Another fairy tale bites the dust."

"I don't want my parents to hear about the marriage thing until I tell them. And I want to think it out before I tell them. Understand?"

"It looks to me like you are doing this bass-ackwards, Chelly. I don't think you're supposed to leap into the fire before you contemplate the eventualities."

Chelly mopped her nose with the frayed tissue and stared out across the parking lot. She wanted Midge's approval. The woman had common sense and had Chelly's best interest at heart. She needed confirmation that putting some distance between herself and the situation made sense, at least for the moment—if you could call being married to D.R. Manning a situation.

Midge pinched her bottom lip between two fingers before she relinquished a sympathetic smile. "You know, you're absolutely right. You do need to sort it out. I guess you're just too close to this particular tree to see the forest, or something."

Chelly smiled wanly before she gave in to a sputtering giggle. She was glad to have someone calm and marginally objective to talk to. Midge barked a laugh and the two women hugged each other. The laughing accelerated until tears trickled down their faces.

Chelly stayed at the apartment that night and drove the eighty-six miles to Blackjack on Tuesday morning, well below the seventy-mile-an-hour speed limit. She was halfway before she noticed little signs of early spring. Things were coming to life. It seemed appropriate that she should feel a kind of budding inside herself.

"Honey, I'm so glad to see you." Her mother hugged her hard as Chelly wrestled her suitcase and one laundry basket through the front door of the Bennett's home.

Things looked the same in the entry hall where the credenza with the silk flower arrangement never changed. Chelly smiled at her mother's enthusiasm, dropped the bag and basket and returned the hug.

"Baby, are you all right?"

"Absolutely."

"You've had a terrible time, getting fired one morning and getting such a wonderful new job the same day. My goodness, my goodness. No one could blame you for feeling overwrought."

Peggy Bennett took her older daughter's arm and guided her toward the kitchen. "Come in here. We'll get some carrot sticks and you can tell me about it."

Chelly laughed. Carrot sticks—her mother's answer to small crises, moral questions, and spiritual dilemmas.

"We'll crunch along together while you tell Mama all your troubles and she'll make them all better."

No, Chelly wouldn't be telling all this day. Some things were better sorted out alone. She told her mother about her crazy job situation up until yesterday's return to DMD and about Midge and the apartment. When her mother asked about her boyfriend, however, Chelly excused herself.

Peggy Bennett eyed her older daughter speculatively, but let her go, at least for the moment. Upstairs later, she peeked in to see Chelly sleeping, curled up under the old quilt that anchored the end of her bed. Mrs. Bennett smiled.

Angela ran in at four o'clock. Her pounding feet thundered up the stairway and she tossed Chelly a passing hello on her way down the hall as she ran by her sister's bedroom. Her hurried footsteps returned immediately as a horn honked in the driveway. Pulling a sweatshirt over her head, Angela called out. "Hey, Chell, how's it going?"

"Good."

Angela was out of earshot by the time Chelly drew a new breath. Definitely a non sympathizer. It was good to be home.

Chelly's dad got home in time for television news at five-thirty. He wrapped Chelly in a bear hug then sat to ask polite, impersonal questions— traffic conditions, weather, the perks of her new job and how Weeden-Pricer compared to DMD. She didn't mention being out at Weeden-Pricer. Getting canned twice in one week was overkill.

She noticed her dad's subtle glances at the clock but he made no move to turn on the television, so she did. "Dad, I'd really like to see what happened in the Middle East today."

He brightened. She watched the lead stories, then asked if he would like something to drink.

"I'll have a glass of white wine, if you're fixing."

She smiled at the predictability of life at home. The sameness made her feel secure, safe from the emotional highs and lows she had experienced recently in Tennyson.

She took her dad the wine and a little plate of cheese and crackers. He thanked her with a quick glance.

Back in her own room, Chelly unpacked, went downstairs to start a load of wash and help her mother with supper, patterning through the routine as if she'd never been away. Angela didn't return so the rest of the family, Chelly, Peggy, and Phil, ate without her.

"Marlo and Will got married two weeks ago," Mrs. Bennett began, triggering a barrage of accounts of events and gossip, most of it repeats of reports they'd given her in phone calls and e-mail notes.

After the supper dishes were done, Chelly joined them in the den and tried to concentrate on TV. Her mother polished the tea service and her dad tinkered inside a computer housing.

When the doorbell rang at eight-thirty and no one else stirred, Chelly eyed her mother suspiciously, then went to answer it.

Eric gave her his most practiced, charming smile, which she returned, genuinely glad to see him. In Blackjack, his appearance at her door seemed completely natural. "Hi. Come in."

"Thanks. My mom said you were home. Finally got a belly full of the fast track, huh?"

She led him into the living room where they could talk without disturbing her parents in the den. "No, I'm just here for a visit."

He looked smug. "On a work day? I am so sure."

"I had some comp time coming."

He shrugged, looked around, and settled on the couch, laying his arm casually along the back. He smiled. Obviously he expected her to sit under his arm. He would see that as a gallant gesture on his part. When she chose the wing back chair instead, he laughed as if it were an inside joke.

"Your mom told my mom you were keeping things bottled up. What's going on?"

Chelly planned to keep her own counsel but had not realized her mother would know, or that she would say anything to Doris Chastain. She shook her head trying for a convincingly bewildered look.

Eric pursued it. "My mom says you're miserable. What happened? Did Manning dump you?"

Chelly tried to hide her surprise. "You knew that was D.R. Manning? That night at my apartment?"

"Sure. Looks just like his pictures." He stared a moment before his face reflected sudden illumination. "You didn't know?" He grinned. "You poor, dumb schmuck. The way he kissed you… well, naturally I assumed you knew who he was."

Chelly shook her head, annoyed that Eric recognized Manning and even more chagrined that he now knew she hadn't known, at least not then.

"He is good, I'll give him that." Eric sounded as if he were gloating. "Using you to get to us. Good thing you didn't know anything about Chastains' inner workings. So, now, here you are, dumped, crawling back to me."

Chelly ruffled. "Did I come to you? Did I call you?"

"Shoot, you knew I'd see your car or your mom would tell my mom. You knew I would know soon enough."

Chelly did not want to dignify his assumption with a denial.

He filled the quiet. "I'll make it easy. Your mom said my deal with Rosemary knocked you for a loop. I owe you for that." He lowered his voice. "I'll take you back, 'cause that's the kind of guy I am, but no secrets. You tell me about Manning, and I'll forgive you, then I'll tell you about Rosemary, and you can forgive me. We'll start back right where we left off. No harm, no foul."

Chelly shook her head. "I can't go back, Eric."

"You can do anything you want to do, Chel. All you have to be is willing."

"It won't work."

Eric's face clouded. "It's worked just fine all our lives."

She raised her gaze to lock with his. "It's too late."

"What's the problem? Is it Manning? Chelly, my dad's a wheel. He can probably ruin Manning. If you want it done, say so and we'll make it happen."

Incredulous, Chelly wondered if she should tell Eric the truth about his dad's influence. Would it help him to know how vulnerable Chastains had been; how Manning—actually Don—had blocked the takeover, had kept them from being consumed? Then a new thought: had he done that for her? Maybe so.

Regardless, she couldn't divulge confidential client information. Hers was definitely a peculiar position.

When she spent so much time contemplating, Eric grew antsy and stood. "I'll let you get some rest. Talk to you tomorrow."

She stood with him. "Sure. Thanks for dropping by."

"The least I could do." He gave her cheek a peck before he turned, hurried through the entry and out the front door, not bothering to button his coat for the dash home.

Chapter Thirty-One

Three days passed. Don didn't call. On Saturday morning, three greeting cards arrived, each with a different postmark—Wednesday, Thursday and Friday.

She trembled as she opened the first.

A sorrowful male sheep was on the cover and the word, "Missing... " On the inside was a glamorous looking female sheep with long eyelashes and the word, "Ewe."

In the familiar bold scrawl he had written: "I never could spell," and signed it: "A not-so-secret admirer." She laughed lightly and her spirits soared. He was honoring her request. This wasn't a call. Plus, this was his own effort. No secretary had come up with this card.

The front of the second card showed a geometric design. The cover words were, "I can't say which I miss most." She opened it to read, "the hanky or the panky." It was unsigned. Chelly blurted a laugh.

The cover of the third card depicted a handsome man with a strong, chiseled jaw, and said, "In all sincerity, what is it you miss most about me?" On the inside, the character blushed brightly and the words were, "Oh, really?"

Her giggling burbled like water over rocks. She hugged the cards tightly to her chest. She needed to think, but could not seem to concentrate.

Saturday night, Chelly's mother invited Eric and his parents over for dinner.

As usual, the families meshed amiably, the older people discussing golf and pre-emergent lawn treatments while Chelly and Eric fixed drinks and prepared a snack tray in relative silence.

Also, as usual, Eric's dad told loud, entertaining stories, embellishing mundane happenings, lording it over his wife and frequently referring to Eric as his "son and heir."

"Chelly," Harmon Chastain blustered, calling loudly from the dining room, "Eric tells me he's ready to patch it up and get on with the wedding. What do you say?"

Dumbfounded, Chelly cast a dark look at Eric who stood facing the kitchen sink pretending he hadn't heard. She hated for this conversation to happen at all, much less shouted between rooms. She stepped to the doorway.

"I don't want to marry Eric, Mr. Chastain."

He laughed uproariously. "You want your pound of flesh, is that it? Look at him, Chelly. The man doesn't have an extra pound on him. He's prime. You don't seriously want to knife into a specimen like that, do you?" Peering into the kitchen, Harmon regarded his son with obvious pride. "No woman could turn down a man like that."

Chelly looked back at Eric. He was cute—a nice, tame house cat—but he was no saber-tooth. "I can."

A scowl creased the older man's face and his ears reddened. "Be careful, missy. I know you're exercising that Bennett humor, but let's don't sass our elders." He glanced at Chelly's dad, who appeared to be inordinately engrossed in stirring spaghetti noodles which were softening in boiling water.

"I didn't mean to be a smart ass, Mr. Chastain," Chelly offered, her voice conciliatory, despite the inflammatory choice of words. "I'm sure a lot of women find Eric attractive. I am no longer one of those."

Harmon again glanced at Phil Bennett, obviously expecting her dad to intervene, but it appeared he would have to look elsewhere for backup.

"I know you're not stupid, Chelly. Don't cut off your nose to spite your face."

Her heartbeat quickened. Her dad continued testing spaghetti. The two mothers stood mutely putting a great deal of concentration into their respective preparations of garlic bread and salad. Eric pivoted and leaned his backside against the counter, obviously willing to let his dad bully her. She knew Eric would never champion any cause but his dad's.

As she glanced from face to face, anger gurgled in her lower regions, a volcano rumbling warnings of an eruption, but no one else heeded the signs.

"Mr. Chastain," she bit into the words, "I wouldn't marry your son if he were the last man on earth. I have many reasons, the first of which is: you would think our marriage gave you license to browbeat me the way you do the rest of your family."

Harmon snarled. "I'll have you know…"

"No, no. I'm not taking orders or advice or money or anything else from you, ever. What's more…"

The doorbell rang, interrupting the combatants and spectators as surely as a bell suspends prize fighters in the ring.

As her dad hurried to answer the door, Chelly's anxiety spiked and she shivered. Once begun, she wanted to vent it all. She was on the verge of telling this windbag that Chastains was ripe for a takeover and she was married to the man who could make that happen.

She was not, of course, quite ready to reveal all that in this forum and felt immediately relieved that she had not violated privilege, no matter how good it might have felt.

She turned away feeling vindicated—as if they had split the decision on Round One.

Indistinct voices in the other room were cordial as her dad invited a man inside. Her dad returned immediately through the dining room. "Chelly. A friend of yours from Tennyson is in the living room." He shot warning looks at both Harmon and Eric.

Chelly elbowed her way by Eric to the sink, rinsed her hands, dried them on the T-towel draped over his shoulder and hurried to the living room.

Don's marvelous physique overpowered the room and commandeered her soul. As her husband turned to face her, Chelly froze at the French doors.

After a moment's surveillance, a slow smile eased his mouth, but it didn't neutralize the compelling power in the smoldering green eyes. "Hello."

"Hello." She felt at once spellbound and tongue-tied.

Apparently sensing her dilemma, he said, "I've missed you."

She smiled self consciously. "Thank you for the cards."

"Am I interrupting? Do you have time to talk?"

She nodded, couldn't seem to think of anything to say and didn't even have the presence of mind to offer him a chair.

He launched into what sounded like a prepared speech. "Before we can alter our situation, Chelly, there are basic truths we need to accept."

"Stipulations."

"Exactly."

She closed the French doors not wanting anyone to overhear.

He continued. "First: you are a married woman."

She had already conceded that point to herself.

"Your husband doesn't want to let you go."

She clasped and unclasped her hands.

"But, above all, he wants you to be happy."

She nodded to indicate she understood the meaning of what he had said. He drew a long breath. "I will do anything humanly possible, sweetheart, to make things right." His voice dropped. "I am fully prepared right here and now to give you Chastains, if you want it, and I will put no restrictions on what you do with it."

When she didn't speak, his broad shoulders rounded slightly before he whispered. "Hell, Chelly, I will even give you an annulment, if you tell me that's the only thing that will make you happy."

She felt stunned. Could this be her saber-tooth, the man whose will determined the careers and lifestyles of hundreds of people, maybe thousands? She didn't like seeing the powerful predator domesticated, as docile as any tabby. Had she broken him? Oh, Lord, no, she pleaded silently to herself.

His smile wavered. "I smell supper cooking. Have you eaten? Would you like to go out to eat somewhere? With me?"

She stared. He was like an apparition, haunting her with his suave good looks and his imposing physique, which dominated everything around him. How could she have run away from him? She shook her head almost imperceptibly. "What about Texas Hansen?" she asked.

His new smile was genuine. "He fired me."

"Over Chastains?"

"Yeah." He laughed lightly and shrugged. "He's fired me before. He'll probably get over it."

"What if he doesn't?"

"It won't matter. We'll get along fine without him. But, Chelly," he hesitated and the smile withered, "I don't think I can get along or be happy ever again without you. You are the one ingredient that makes everything else in my life worthwhile."

He had defied his most important client and protected Chastains, for her.

Chelly started when her mother rapped softly on the paned door behind her and opened it. Margaret Bennett directed her words at Don. "We're ready to eat. Will you join us? There's plenty."

Chelly stiffened. No, no. Harmon Chastain and D.R. Manning at the same table? What secrets might be exposed? What tempers? What would her parents think of him? What would he think of them? The imagined scenario set Chelly's already-frayed nerves jangling.

At that moment, the front door opened and Angela blew into the hallway, pulling her best friend Judith Schmidt along before she slammed the door against a brisk north wind. Angela did a double-take and stopped still, staring as her voice pierced the quiet. "You're Don, right?"

Chelly recognized his best smile. "I am." His voice had a husky quality, which caressed the teenagers as he obviously intended.

Angela and Judith looked at each other and giggled.

"I'm pleased to meet you." Mrs. Bennett's more mature, certainly more poised response oozed over Chelly, soothing her. "Don, I'm Margaret Bennett, Chelly's mother. Call me Peggy." She reached to shake his hand, suddenly displaying more feminine confidence than Chelly had known she possessed. The daughter felt comforted by this unexpected ally in the perturbing state of affairs.

"Mrs. Bennett, are you and Chelly often mistaken for sisters?"

A scoffing laugh emanated from Peggy Bennett as she looked directly into the emerald gaze, unscathed. Chelly smiled to herself. A formidable ally.

"Would you like to wash up first?" Mrs. Bennett asked. "Chelly, take Mr. Manning to your bathroom."

"Mom, how did you know he was Mr. Manning?"

Her mother dismissed the question with a mysterious smile. "Hurry up. We'll wait."

Don caught Chelly's hand and slipped a proprietary arm around her waist. She trembled. Putting his lips to her ear, he whispered, "I know you aren't shivering because you're cold." She snuggled against him. "You seem to be warming nicely. Do I detect an advantage my way?" She felt his bravado returning as he continued whispering. "Maybe I can help you with your dilemma. Is there a bed nearby?"

Hastily taking Don's hand, Chelly scurried by Angela and Judith and led him toward the bathroom, not wanting any awkward conversations to bloom. Things were complicated enough.

"We can go out and eat," she suggested when he emerged from the bathroom.

His knowing grin frightened her. "Fine with me." They stood a moment regarding one another before he put the palm of his hand to her throat. She froze. His hand slid up to her chin and he brushed his thumb over her lips.

Closing her eyes, she took the thumb between her teeth, then turned her face. "I wish you didn't always have this effect on me."

He grinned. "It's only fair. It works both ways you know, even long distance. Now, where can we go for some privacy?"

Chelly shivered again, trying to rein in her runaway emotions. "We need to stay, but there are other people here."

"Oh? Who?"

She gave him a apologetic glance. "Eric and his parents. His dad and I were just having an ugly little conversation. I was literally saved by the doorbell."

His smile wavered. "What were you discussing?"

"He was proposing."

"What?"

"For Eric."

"Again?"

"Yes." She twittered an awkward laugh.

"And where was Eric?"

"By the sink."

"Was he aware of your conversation with his father?"

"Yes. He didn't care to participate."

"Not participate in his dad's asking you to marry him?"

"Right. That's the way the Chastains do things—Harmon's way. Harmon is king of their castle."

"And, of course, you explained you were already blissfully wed?"

"No, we hadn't gotten to that part, but I'm afraid it was coming, despite my better judgment."

"Good." His eyes flashed with anticipation.

"No, no. I don't want to tell them about that."

His fervor faded, his jaw tightened, and his eyes narrowed, but his voice remained steady. "Why not?"

"I'm not sure yet."

"Chelly, did you come home to Blackjack to decide if you were still in love with Eric Chastain?"

Astonished, she didn't speak, only shook her head, but her expression must have verified the denial because tension melted from his face.

"Love, I have been preparing myself to give you up, temporarily; to agree to an annulment if you insisted. I had mapped a campaign to compete with Chastain and win; to convince you I was truly the better man. If you chose him over me, I had decided to give you Chastains as a wedding gift to show you the depth of my devotion. But the minute I saw you, I knew all that chivalrous posturing was crap. You're my wife, Chelly. It's a done deal."

"Then why am I here? Why did you let me come?"

"To give you the space you asked for, and enough proverbial rope to convince yourself. I thought with time, you would come to the only conclusion your conscience will accept." He regarded her closely. "And you have, haven't you?"

She struggled, her own internal arguments convincing. He was right. She had worked her way to the bottom line, the one he anticipated she would reach all along.

He opened his arms. She hesitated only a moment then stepped forward, drawing a deep breath. He gathered her close and kissed the side of her face. "We are meant for each other. Soul mates. I love you more than my life. You are my life. My woman. My wife."

A gasp turned Chelly's attention to the darkened doorway of Angela's bedroom. Her sister stood, mouth gaping, eyes wide. Angela's whispery voice cracked. "Chelly? You're married?"

"Shhh. We haven't told Mother and Daddy. I want to wait until the Chastains are gone."

"Sure." Angela stammered, eying her sister with new regard. "I won't say a word. Not even to Judith. By the way, we are both gaga over your... ah... your guy." She allowed a trilling giggle. Don grinned broadly.

"How are you, Eric?" Don nodded his acknowledgment of the younger man's presence as Chelly led him into the dining room to join the others, most of whom were already seated.

Eric didn't stand, only leaned to relinquish a limp handshake across the table.

Of course, Eric and Don had met already, at her apartment.

Angela and Judith twittered into the room, sliding into their chairs as Don was introduced to the others.

Phil Bennett and Harmon Chastain stood. Eric rose belatedly, at his dad's wordless prompting.

Don took Harmon's offered hand first. "Mr. Chastain, I'm D.R. Manning. I've been curious about you. Glad to have this opportunity to meet you in person." Without waiting for a response, he turned his full attention on Eric's mother. "And the charming Mrs. Chastain. How do you do." They shook hands and she appeared immediately smitten.

Chelly marveled at Don, at the way his manner soothed the antagonism of men and swept women off their feet. How could he seem so humble, flash that sexy, predatory gaze and confiscate the full attention of everyone in the room, all at the same time?

He worked his way around the table, shaking hands with the teens, and finally introducing himself to her father. "Mr. Bennett, I'm D.R. Manning, Chelly's boss at Diet, Manning, Diet and Harned."

Her dad looked puzzled. "You mean her former boss?"

"Technically. Actually, Chelly and I are much more than employer and employee. We... "

Eric leaped to his feet. "What's that supposed to mean?"

Don turned slowly, the saber-tooth tiger at his best—or worst. "I have developed a great and abiding affection for Chelly, Eric. She has integrity and what was known in the old west as grit." He leveled a sidelong glance, which fairly consumed her. "She has become very special to me, as I think you already know."

Eric slouched back down into his chair, suddenly sullen, the tips of his ears scarlet.

Dinner conversation seemed stilted. Eric shot Don evil looks throughout the meal, daggers that Don repelled with impertinent disregard.

The two matrons and the giggling girls made an effort to keep dialogue flowing and non controversial. Stymied, Chelly found their efforts heroic.

Phil Bennett was the attentive host, seeing to his guests' beverage needs without becoming embroiled in the sometimes terse exchanges between Harmon Chastain and anyone willing to pick up the gauntlet—except Manning.

"I understand you're quite the corporate lawyer, Manning." Mr. Chastain launched into his pecan pie and his commentary with the same gusto. "When you get a little further along in the business of business, you'll probably hear about Chastains. That's my outfit—mine and my boy's here."

Don nodded but his eyes were full of awe and directed at his hostess. "This crust is excellent, Mrs. Bennett. What's your secret?"

Chelly's mother flushed slightly. "Please call me Peggy. The crust is no secret, but I'm glad you're enjoying it."

"No, I mean it. What do you do to make it so light?"

Chelly noted her mother's sudden self-consciousness and came to her rescue.

"She neglects it," Chelly said. "She says you mustn't touch pie dough more than you absolutely have to. And it works."

"I'll say." Don's laugh almost drowned out Harmon Chastain's groan. "I beg your pardon?" Sobering, he turned his attention to the older man.

"I didn't know you were the kind of fellow who talked recipes and solicited baking tips from the ladies."

"Hmmm." Don restrained himself with a grace that Chelly found captivating and she wondered if the cat were toying with an unsuspecting mouse.

When they finished eating, Chelly's dad excused the teenagers who seemed reluctant to leave the tension-charged atmosphere.

"Better not go yet." Mr. Chastain grinned broadly, seeming better satisfied than he had been earlier. "I believe Eric and Chelly have an announcement." He winked at Chelly. "Am I right, daughter?"

Distressed, suddenly horrified, Chelly flashed a helpless look from Eric, who diverted his eyes, to Mrs. Chastain, who shrugged, to her own parents who appeared nonplused.

Exhaling all hope, Chelly began shaking her head but before she could speak, Don stood and directed his gaze at her father at the other end of the table.

"When we introduced ourselves earlier, Mr. Bennett, I didn't fully identify myself. I said I was Chelly's boss at DMD. What I neglected to mention is that I am also her husband."

Chapter Thirty-Two

There was a long moment of silence. Chelly's dad stared at Don as if he were stunned. "I don't think I heard you right."

"Chelly and I were married two weeks ago tonight, Mr. Bennett, in Las Vegas."

Chelly turned to her mother, her eyes stinging. "Mom, I'm sorry."

Assimilating the information, Mrs. Bennett studied her older daughter. There was no accusation in the look, no anger, just bewilderment.

In the doorway, Angela began bouncing on the balls of her feet, her hands fisted together. "I've finally got a brother." She arched her eyebrows. "And, sister, when you do a thing, you do it right!" She threw her gangling self into Don's arms. His surprise prompted a spurt of embarrassed laughter around the table.

Peggy Bennett stood and walked around to be closer to her husband who stood to provide a comforting squeeze. "I don't believe we quite understand." He looked from Don to Chelly and back.

Don's gaze captured Chelly's. "When we met, I didn't tell her who I was. I didn't want her influenced by what I considered nonessential information. She worked for Manning sight unseen, and liked him, in spite of his demands, but I didn't want to scare her off. I told her my name was Donald Richard, which it is. I just omitted the Manning.

"Before I knew what hit me, I went from smitten to head over heels. At my age and station in life, that was a shock. I had to play for time, let her get to know me, not D.R. Manning, but me.

"She realized we had common interests and values and goals. We laughed at the same things, admired the same qualities, both disliked tyrants and injustice." He paused but no one else seemed to want to speak.

"As you know, Chelly is a very moral person. I strive for that myself, although she may have to provide guidance from time to time. She has indicated a willingness to do that."

Mrs. Bennett smiled at Chelly, an exchange that seemed to encourage Don to continue.

"I have become somewhat vain. Chelly is leaching the vanity out of me, one pitiless drop at a time." He smiled at Chelly, the open, taunting smile she had come to love.

Love? She sobered. It was the first time she had labeled her feeling for him. Gingerly, she rolled the gold band round and round her index finger as Don continued, watching her.

"I wanted Chelly to be my wife but I didn't know how to go about convincing her she could trust her instincts in light of my subterfuge." He leveled a look at Eric. "Prior experience had made her wary about trusting men.

"Finally, desperately, I came up with a scheme. It was not forthright, but it would accomplish my objective.

"I created the opportunity and took advantage of a temporary incapacity." He flashed Chelly an apologetic smile. "I bamboozled her to the altar.

"Later, after validating her commitment, I had to figure a way to explain my deception to such a scrupulously honest person." He drew a deep breath. "She did not take it well.

"Nevertheless, we were and are and intend to remain married.

"Although we did not seek your approval beforehand," he gave her an apologetic glance, "Chelly wants your blessing, and it is my primary goal in life to provide everything Chelly needs or wants, an example of which is my presence here tonight." He seemed to be running down. "I came here to meet you, to let you meet me, to confess and, primarily," his eyes narrowed as he gave Chelly a heated glance, "to repossess my wife."

The grandfather's clock ticking in the hall was the only sound, barely audible over the thrum of her heartbeat.

"Well… " Eric's mother was first to break the silence as she looked from Chelly's parents, to Angela and Angela's guest, to Eric and finally her husband. "Harmon and I will host a reception for the bride and groom."

"The hell we will!" Chastain's voice pealed like thunder through the room. "Not for some little tart who went cavorting in the big city and… "

Don's eyes, soft as they savored his wife's glow, narrowed and his voice resonated as a low growl. "Be very careful what you say right now, Chastain."

Eric's dad turned on Don, his eyes venomous. "And why should I guard my words, Manning, around your little b… "

Don's eyes flashed as he took a warning step toward the older man. Harmon, and Eric too, shrank from the towering menace. "My wife, Chastain, has pled your case eloquently more than once. She alone has saved your business from being consumed by a hungry shark cruising your waters. Texas Hansen salivates every time your son there unloads his profit-sharing units.

"Hansen is a client of mine. I am all that has stood between you and him since January. I have done that solely because Chelly asked me to. Had she not interceded, Hansen would have had you as an appetizer before he gobbled up both Payne and Griswold. They have now been completely digested, as you probably know, and he's scanning again."

The elder Chastain blustered, putting together a string of inaudible words that emerged jumbled before he tried again to sort them out. "For your information, Manning, I met Hansen personally last fall."

"Right. In Houston. And your unrestrained boasting is what piqued his appetite in the first place. He probably knows as much about your annual reports now as you do.

"Chelly heard a rumor just before Hansen jumped and she asked me to stop him."

Chastain was incredulous. "And you put an end to it on her say-so?"

"No, I only stalled him so I could take a closer look. What I saw was a good, solid little business. You had run a tight ship until junior here came on board." Don puckered his mouth and raised his eyebrows. "If I were you, I wouldn't give the boy quite so much latitude." He glanced at Chelly. "And I damn sure wouldn't insult the one person standing between me and annihilation."

Chastain regarded Don with a jaundice eye. "Have you got Hansen stopped, or not?"

"No."

"Why not?"

"I wanted the leverage. I've been toying with the idea of giving Chastains to my wife as a wedding present."

Harmon looked from Eric to Chelly and back to Eric. The frown lines in his face deepened as he contemplated his son. "You've been selling your shares?"

Eric refused to answer or to meet his father's stare.

Harmon shifted his gaze to Don, shrewd enough to recognize the truth.

Don nodded. "Now that I have your attention, let me reiterate. I'm not going to tolerate any insult from you or your son. My wife is going to have the respect she deserves or, by Christmas, you are going to be working for her."

Eric's voice broke in, higher than usual. "You're doing this for her?"

Eric cowed beneath Don's glower before the bridegroom turned a thoughtful gaze on Mr. Chastain. "Do you see what I mean? Your son lacks judgment."

Harmon grumbled something that Chelly did not hear. He looked at her and his expression softened. "Manning, when Chelly was ten or eleven years old, she told me I'd better not let Eric run my business. She disapproved of the way he squandered his allowance. I thought it was kind of cute, back then."

Eric leaned on the table. "Dad, Chelly's a woman. She doesn't know anything about our business."

"As it turns out, my lack of confidence in you, son, has very little to do with Chelly and quite a bit to do with you. You've shown no regard for the business or for the customers I worked hard to curry back when they had no where else to go. Now they have options." Eric sputtered but Harmon didn't allow rebuttal. "Also, you have dipped deep and that does not include selling shares of stock."

"Perks, Dad. Why should I go around short of cash or have to buy my own car insurance and country club membership. I'm the key man now. And what's all this sudden devotion to Chelly?"

"I've always liked Chelly, Eric. Always knew she'd be good for you and good for Chastains. The girl's got a head on her shoulders. You didn't hear me cussing the law school idea. The more she knew, the better help she'd be to you and all of us."

"Well, then, you need to make her marry me, like you said."

Eric's dad cast a hasty glance at Manning, then regarded his son oddly. "Like I said, the girl has a head on her shoulders. When you made her choose between you and him, she took him. As much as I hate that, I'm afraid it pretty well proves my point."

Chelly smiled at Don across the room. He winked and beckoned her. When she walked over beside him, he caught her index finger, the one with the ring, and led her back to the privacy of the living room.

As he turned to face her, she leaped. He wrapped her in his arms but leaned away from her puckered lips. "My wife is very strict. She doesn't allow me to indulge in hanky panky with strange women."

Chelly smirked and waited for his point.

"What is your name, young woman?"

284

"Chelly."

"Chelly what?"

A mischievous smile spanned her face. "Chelly Bennett… Manning."

"Ahh." His smile mirrored hers. "Good. Chelly Manning has many pleasant surprises in store for her, but no one here seemed to recognize the name, including you."

She kissed him once. "She knows her name now, cowboy, and yours, too. I am definitely Mrs. Donald Richard Manning."

And Chelly Bennett Manning, secure in Don's arms, her feet suspended several inches above his aged, run-over cowboy boots, kissed and joyously forgave her genuine husband and his alter ego, her much-adored counterfeit cowboy.